XISLE

www.davidficklingbooks.co.uk

XISLE

STEVE AUGARDE

David Fickling Books

OXFORD · NEW YORK

31 Beaumont Street
Oxford OX1 2NP, UK

X ISLE
A DAVID FICKLING BOOK 978 0 385 61061 2

Published in Great Britain by David Fickling Books,
a division of Random House Children's Books
A Random House Group Company

This edition published 2009

1 3 5 7 9 10 8 6 4 2

Set in 12/15pt Baskerville by
Falcon Oast Graphic Art Ltd.

DAVID FICKLING BOOKS
31 Beaumont Street, Oxford, OX1 2NP

www.**kids**at**randomhouse**.co.uk
www.**rbooks**.co.uk

Addresses for companies within The Random House Group
Limited can be found at: www.randomhouse.co.uk/offices.htm

THE RANDOM HOUSE GROUP Limited Reg. No. 954009

A CIP catalogue record for this book is available from the
British Library.

Printed and bound in Great Britain by Clays Ltd, St Ives plc

CHAPTER ONE

The steady chug of the diesel engine drew closer, and eventually the salvage boat emerged from the mist, a blank grey shape steering a middle course between the ghostly lines of chimney stacks that rose from the water. It turned right and came sailing up John William Street.

There was a general scuffle of movement as the crowd edged a little further down the muddy bank. From where they stood, the two parallel rows of houses that had once been John William Street descended into the oily waters, so that the rooftops became a guiding channel for the approaching vessel, the steep pathway up to the bowling green acting as a kind of jetty.

Tense and expectant, the boys sat like jockeys astride the shoulders of the men – fathers, uncles, elder brothers – as though they were waiting for the start of a race. Many of the boys carried backpacks with extra clothes and belongings, in case they should be chosen. And on their foreheads, in paint or felt-tipped pen, many had scrawled the letter X, the symbol of their hoped-for destination.

'Get closer to the front, Dad – see if you can get to the front.' Baz put his hands on his father's damp mop of hair and tried to urge him forward.

'Doesn't matter where you stand, son.' The muffled voice was calm. 'It's what you've got that counts. It's all down to whether you've got something they want.'

And that was true. Already some of the boys were holding their offerings aloft – bags of sugar, bunches of runner beans, packs of cigarettes, whatever pitiful resources they had been able to muster in the hopes of buying their passage on the boat.

Idiots. It was stupid to show what you had. The gangs of thieves – Teefers – who circled the edge of the crowd would be taking note, getting ready to pounce once the trading was over. The Teefers would get much of it in the end, but there was no point in serving it up to them on a plate. Safer to keep your hands in your pockets until the last minute. Baz didn't even know what his father was carrying. Now some skinny boy over to the right had just lost his goods, judging by the brief scuffle that had broken out.

Skinny boys. Always skinny and always boys, for that's all that Isaac would take. No girls. They had to be boys, and they had to be small for their age. They were hoisted upon the shoulders of the men so that they could be seen for what they were – small and light. Some of them had taken off their shirts, lest there be any doubt, and their thin torsos glistened in the sticky heat.

The boat was drawing up to the tarmac pathway now, and its crew could clearly be seen: three burly men standing on the foredeck with machine guns slung over their shoulders. The Eck brothers. Isaac, Luke and Amos. Between them they controlled the coastline, the salvage trading, and the lives of all who stood before them. But it was Isaac, the eldest, who skippered the boat, and it was Isaac who would make the decisions. He was the one to watch. And with his long dark hair and beard you could pick him out easily enough. The younger brothers were both shaven-headed.

'Keep back!' Isaac's voice rang loud through the still air. 'Oi, you – get off the slipway!'

A boy had broken away from the crowd and taken a few steps down the strip of tarmac. He was waving what looked like a pack of cards.

'Get *back*, I said!' Isaac raised the automatic and fired off a short burst – *duh-duh-duh-duh* – a crashing echo that bounced around the half-submerged rooftops. The boy scuttled backwards into the crowd. The salvage boat rocked closer to the makeshift slip-way, its sign clearly visible now, painted in blue lettering on the bow: *Cormorant*. One of the brothers threw a loop of rope over the buckled gatepost that had once marked the entrance to the bowling green. He hauled on the rope and the boat swung diagonally towards the shore, until its nose bumped gently against the tarmac. The man held it there, kept it steady and then secured the rope to a cleat, repositioning his shot-gun with his free hand so that it swept upwards towards the crowd. The diesel motor was kept running on fast tickover, in case of trouble.

'Recruiting today!' Isaac's voice rose above the noise

of the diesel. 'We're looking for two new lads this trip. Orders from Preacher John.'

A murmur ran through the crowd. Two recruits! There was never usually more than one place on the boat, and often none at all.

Baz took a closer look at those around him, trying to judge the competition. Many of the boys looked quite a lot bigger than him. They'd have to have brought something pretty special to be in with a chance. A few were obviously too young to be of much use. There were maybe a dozen who seemed about right.

He noticed a lad with black hair away to his left, sitting upon the shoulders of a woman. Both were wearing the same yellow-coloured T-shirts. The woman looked oriental – Malaysian perhaps – the boy less so. It was unusual to see women here. Things could get rough, and a woman alone was easy prey for the Teefers. Whatever she had brought in that carrier bag was unlikely to leave with her.

The dark-haired boy was also scanning the crowd, weighing up his chances. He looked across at Baz, realized that he was being watched and turned away. Neither of them smiled. No sense in getting friendly with the competition.

'Right then!' The skipper jabbed a burly fist into the air, two thick fingers extended. 'We've just dropped a couple o' lads off a little way up the coast. They got too fat and lazy, as usual, and so it was back home to Mother for them. We mollycoddle 'em, that's our trouble. So now Preacher John wants me to pick two new ones. You know the rules by now. Free board and lodging for all boys we take, and you can trust us to look after 'em. We feed 'em well, and they're a dam' sight safer over there than they are here. Had no complaints so far. But they have to work, and those that aren't up to scratch'll soon find themselves sent back. So don't waste our time on buying a passage for useless layabouts. Let's see what you've got for me, then.'

This was the signal for the bidding to begin. All hands were raised aloft, and each was waving some hopeful offer – a packet of lentils, a bar of soap – a ticket out of here for those who were lucky on the day.

'Dad?' Baz was getting worried. His father had made no move as yet, but kept his hands jammed firmly in the pockets of his battered raincoat. Playing it close, as always.

'Let's just hold on a minute, son. No point in showing what you've got if you know you can't win. What do you see? Anything good?'

Baz looked around, ignoring the usual rubbish and trying to pick out the treasures. 'Um . . . packet of rice. A rabbit – no, two rabbits . . . cigarettes . . . soap powder . . . couple of big candles . . . more cigarettes . . . Blimey. Look at that. A box of cornflakes.'

Cornflakes! Now *there* was something you didn't see every day. It was the kid with the black hair, the one sitting on the shoulders of the woman. Where on earth had they managed to get cornflakes from?

'*Corn*flakes?'

'Yeah – just over there. See 'em?'

'Hm. Good shout. Could be an empty box of course.'

Isaac and his brothers were considering the goods

11

on offer. The three of them stood close together on the foredeck of the boat, craning their necks as they studied the crowd, occasionally drawing each other's attention to this object or that.

'You, there. Yeah, you – cornflakes. Full box?' Isaac had quickly picked out the dark-haired boy.

'Yes. New packet.'

'Come on down then, lad – let's have a look at you.'

The boy slid from his mother's shoulders, took a carrier bag from her and began to weave his way through the crush of people. He and his packet of cornflakes wouldn't have got two yards if it hadn't been for the protection of the Eck brothers.

Baz was beginning to lose heart. The cornflake kid was certain of a place on the boat, provided the box really was a full one, and the next likeliest candidate would be the owner of the white rabbits. But then his dad said, 'Anything better than the rabbits?'

'Don't think so . . .' Baz turned round and looked behind him, making sure.

'Try this then.' His dad took his left hand out of his pocket and passed a small square cardboard box up towards him. Baz reached down and nearly dropped the box, it was so heavy. ELEY it said on the side – red, white and blue lettering against a black background. There was a picture of some birds and another word, IMPERIAL.

'What's in there?'

'Shotgun cartridges. Twelve-gauge.'

'Wow. Where did you get them?' Baz felt the shrug of his father's shoulders beneath him.

'Poker game.'

Of course. Silly question really.

Baz lifted the carton into the air and waved it from side to side. He tried to catch Isaac's eye, but the skipper of the boat was reaching over the side for the cornflakes. Isaac shook the packet and then nodded at the black-haired lad. 'OK. Stay there.'

One of the younger brothers had noticed Baz. He muttered something to Isaac, and pointed. Isaac looked across, his dark-bearded mouth chewing casually.

'What've you got there, boy?'

'Shotgun cartridges!' Baz shouted back. He could feel his heart thumping. 'Twelve-gauge.'

'Full box? Twenty-five?'

'Yes.'

Baz was aware of the altering mood around him, the frustrated groans of those who now realized that they were out of the running. It was between the rabbits and the cartridges, and everybody knew it. A few people were already hiding their goods away, hoping to escape the notice of the Teefers.

Isaac was still considering. He nodded at the lad who was holding the rabbits – dangling them by their hind legs, one in each hand. Scrawny-looking things, they were, and not much on them, but meat was meat . . .

'Fresh?' Isaac asked the deciding question.

'Aye, killed this morning. You can check 'em.'

That would probably swing it then, thought Baz. He wiped his forearm across his brow and tried to fight back his disappointment. The game was as good as over.

But then his father's shoulders tilted slightly as he removed his other hand from his pocket. He was holding up a second box of cartridges. 'Better go for the full house, then, son.'

Baz snatched at the box and waved it high. 'Two boxes!' he shouted. 'Two!'

Isaac looked over at him; stopped chewing for a moment as he weighed up this new development. Then he said, 'OK.' He spat his piece of gum over the side of the boat. 'Boy with the cartridges, bring 'em down. Let's take a look.'

Baz slithered from his father's shoulders. 'Thanks, Dad.' He didn't know what else to say – or how he would say goodbye, if that was what it had now come to. 'I'll be . . . I mean . . . it'll be all right, won't it? And you'll be OK?'

'I'll be fine. You just worry about yourself, son, that's all. Look out for number one. That way you'll still be around when things get better. Take a tip from the old man, eh?'

'OK, Dad. I'll . . . well, I'll see you then.'

'You will, lad. Got all your gear? Good luck, then. Off you go.'

Baz began to shoulder his way past the people in front of him, clutching the heavy cartridge boxes to his chest, his small nylon backpack slung over one arm.

'Hey!'

Baz turned round to see what his dad wanted.

'Remember what I told you. You know you can always come back – any time you like. But try and hang on in there for a while at least. Just until things get better, son.'

'OK, Dad.'

Until things get better. When would that ever be?

Baz reached the front of the crowd with his boxes still intact, and hurried down the slipway towards the *Cormorant*. He had to wade out into the rubbish-strewn water before he could offer his cargo up to Isaac. The skipper reached over the side and took the boxes from him, tested the weight of them in his beefy red hands, and then placed them down beside him somewhere. He didn't bother to open the cartons.

'OK, they'll do. Give these kids a pull-up, Luke, and stick 'em in the wheelhouse,' he said.

One of the men then leaned over the gunwale. 'Come on, Cornflakes, don't hang about.' He grasped the dark-haired boy's wrist and swung him up into the boat as though he were no heavier than a kitten.

'Now you.'

Baz reached up and was also hoisted aboard, the huge fingers that closed around his upper arm feeling as powerful as a mechanical grab. He tumbled over the gunwale, found his feet, and was then hustled across the slippery deck and into the wheelhouse, along with the other boy. They had to duck beneath the makeshift winch that was used for loading and unloading.

'Shut the lid of that locker-box and sit there till we need to load it,' said the big shaven-headed man, Luke. 'Keep an eye on 'em, Moko. Not that they'll give you any trouble.' A sweaty Japanese man in a grubby white vest stood at the wheel of the boat. He looked briefly at the two boys but said nothing.

Baz did as he was told, reaching forward to lower

the lid of a big wooden locker-box that was built into the port side of the wheelhouse. He perched on the edge of the locker, next to the other boy, and tried to keep his breathing steady.

It had all happened so quickly that he still couldn't quite believe his luck. He was on the boat, actually on the boat, and getting out of here at last. For a while, anyway. He felt a burst of gratitude towards his dad, and he peeped round the wheelhouse doorway, searching the section of the crowd that was visible from where he was sitting. Yes, Dad was still there, standing on the banks of the bowling green, his thin raincoat folded over his arm now. He looked gaunt and scruffy, his face unshaven, his hair damp and straggly from the humidity. Not beaten, though. He didn't look beaten, like some men did. Dad was a survivor. As long as there was a pack of cards available, and men to play with, he'd survive. Best poker player around.

'What's the first rule of gambling, son?' his dad had once said.

'Er . . . dunno. Don't bet more than you can afford to lose?'

'No. Don't make the other guy bet more than *he* can afford to lose. That way he'll be round to try again. See, I make sure never to win too much, or too often. Maybe three games out of five, four out of seven. Just enough to get by – and that way we keep getting by.'

For nearly two years now, they'd been getting by. Ever since the floods came and washed the world away . . .

'Wheel 'em down, then!' Isaac was out on deck, organizing the Trolleymen. 'Let's get started.'

16

Baz could see the four laden supermarket trolleys being brought down the slipway, awkward things that needed the guidance and restraining hands of the dozen or so tough-looking men who accompanied them. Here was the scavenged wealth of the mainlanders, the pitiful odds and ends that had been raked from the ruins of the city, to be traded against the salvage goods that the Eck brothers had brought over from the island.

The Trolleymen began to unload their wares, spreading the separate lots about the tarmac slipway and along the muddy banks to either side.

'Six jerry cans o' diesel. Three hundred litres.'

Fuel was always the first commodity to be listed for trading. After that came the things that had been brought along for private sale – various small lots and possessions packed into carrier bags. All such goods had to be handed over to the Trolleymen, who would barter a price on the owner's behalf in return for a cut of the proceeds.

The men glanced into each bag, shouting out the contents as they went so that Isaac could chalk everything up, and begin figuring out how many tins of food or bottles of drink he would give for each lot.

'Small box of tea bags, four rolls kitchen towels.'

'Box o' firelighters. Bag o' flour, plain.'

'Stack of magazines – er, top shelf. Packet of barley, unopened. Box of household matches.'

'Er . . . cooking apples. Seven.'

Baz noticed the hesitation and surprise in the last caller's voice, and remembered that his dad had said something about managing to get hold of a bit of fruit. Seven cooking apples, though! Who else but Dad could have found such things? He ought to get quite a few tins for them, although the Trolleymen would take their usual heavy percentage of course. Being a Trolleyman was a dangerous occupation. They had to fight off the Teefers – most of whom had ambitions to become Trolleymen themselves – so it was only the toughest and most violent who held onto the job. You wouldn't argue with them.

'Bag o' dog biscuits.'

'Single duvet – still in its wrapper . . .'

On it went, and on it would go for the next quarter of an hour or more.

The Japanese man pushed himself away from the helm with a grunt, and stepped into the doorway of the wheelhouse. He leaned against the doorpost in order to watch the trading. Baz couldn't see what was going on any more. He sat on his hands and looked at the kid sitting next to him.

'What's your name?' he whispered.

The boy kept his head down, eyes fixed upon his feet as they swung to and fro, his muddy trainers kicking against a coil of rope that lay on the floor. He didn't seem particularly grateful to be here.

'Ray.' His voice had a husky note to it, as though it was about to break perhaps. Better for him if it didn't just yet.

'Mine's Baz,' said Baz, though the boy hadn't asked. 'Was that your mum who brought you down here?'

'Yeah.'

Baz guessed that there had been no man available.

'Lost your dad, then? I lost my mum. And my sister. They were away down south when it happened.' It was always good to try and talk about it, so his dad said. Better that way.

'Never had a dad,' said the boy, 'so it doesn't make much difference, does it?'

'Oh. Sorry.' Baz felt uncomfortable. 'Brilliant, though, with the cornflakes. How did your mum get hold of them?'

'How do you think?' Ray looked at him for the first time. His hair was cut very short at the back and sides, but long in the front, and his dark eyes were steady and defiant beneath the blue-black fringe.

'What?'

'I said, how do you think? Try using your loaf instead of asking dumb questions. How did your dad manage to get hold of the cartridges?'

'Um . . . gambling. Playing poker.'

'Yeah, well, lucky for him, then, if that's all he had to do.' Ray looked down at his feet once more, and kicked harder at the coil of rope.

Baz might have said more, but then the Japanese man, Moko, turned and scowled at them. It was a look of warning, and with it the man disappeared, apparently wanted out on deck to help with the unloading.

Isaac could be heard shouting out the rates he was prepared to offer for the goods that littered the slipway.

'Three hundred litres o' diesel – I'll give you five hundred tins. What? Don't come it with me, Goffer. We're trying to do an honest job here, and all you do is give us grief. OK, six hundred. But you'd better start cutting me a better deal on fuel, 'cos if we don't turn up here, you starve. Moko – load six hundred in the net! Tea bags and kitchen towels – I'll give you ten tins, mixed. Box o' firelighters, bag of flour – twelve tins, mixed. Bag of apples – forty tins, two packs of beer. What's next? Magazines . . .'

Baz did a calculation in his head over the apples. So if the Trolleymen had got forty tins for them, his dad might end up with twenty-five. Perhaps one of the packs of beer, if he was lucky. Twenty-five tins . . . maybe five of those would be stew or curry . . . two or three of fruit . . . the rest soup or beans. Dad could get by for over a week on that, and still have a little capital for poker stakes. Yeah, that wasn't bad for a few cooking apples.

'Listen up.' Isaac was bringing the trade to a close. 'We're doing an extra run next week – a Special. We got baby food – jars and tins – and we got wine. We need clean clothing, men's extra large. Boots, jackets, jumpers, shirts, trousers – whatever you've got. Boy's stuff we'll take, but you'll get nothing for it. If you've got a lad on the island with us and you want to send a parcel, then it's up to you. But we don't pay for it. OK, we're ready to offload – and let's have no funny business this time. Keep it civilized and there'll be no trouble.'

Moko yanked the winch motor into life, a cloud of blue smoke rising from its exhaust. The boat creaked and tilted as the heavy net with its cargo of bottles and food tins was swung out over the side of the boat and lowered onto the slipway.

'Keep back!' Isaac's voice yelled out, and Baz lurched sideways in fright at the sudden crash of the automatic – *duh-duh-duh-duh-duh!*

Maybe a few of the Teefers had edged too close, or maybe Isaac was simply taking no chances. With the boat halfway between unloading and loading, and nobody at the helm, this was always the moment when things could get dangerous.

'Sorry.' Baz had bumped against Ray when the gun went off. He sat up straight again.

'Jumpy, aren't you?' Ray said.

'Hey – they *shoot* people.'

'Good job. Some of them need shooting.'

Well, you're a tough guy, thought Baz, *for such a little squirt.*

Ray leaned forward and touched the helm, pressing his fingertips against the wheel until it moved slightly. He turned to look at Baz and said, 'Know anyone who's been there? To the island?'

'No.' Baz was feeling irritated. Or maybe he *was* just jumpy. 'Not really. A girl I know had a cousin who was there for a few months. I never met him, though.'

'What happened?'

'Same as always, I s'pose. He got too big. Got too expensive to feed and so they sent him back. Probably a Teefer now.'

'No, I mean what happened to him over there? What do they make you do?'

'Dunno. Work on the salvage, clean it up or whatever. It's gotta be better than here, or everybody wouldn't be trying to get on the boat.'

'Yeah. Wish I knew someone who'd been, though.'

21

Baz shrugged. Maybe this kid should have given his cornflakes to someone else if he was having second thoughts. He turned to gaze out of the porthole behind him, rubbing his bare elbow against the glass and staring into the blanket of steamy mist that hung upon the shoreline. On a clear day you could sometimes get a glimpse of the true horizon, miles and miles away, but clear days were few and far between now. Baz wiped the glass again, and peered closer. What was that? He thought he had seen something. Yes, a face – and there was another – pale faces coming through the gloom. Oil drums . . . a raft. A group of men crouching on a home-made raft . . .

What were they doing?

It was another long moment before Baz caught on. Oh my God . . .

'Down!' He grabbed at Ray's elbow as he threw himself to the floor. 'Get down!'

'What? Hey—!'

Ba-doom! The deep thud of a shotgun. Shouts. And then the answering fire of the automatics – *duh-duh-duh-duh-duh* . . .

More yelling and firing, the piercing clang of bullets against metal, and Moko came stumbling in through the doorway. Baz felt the heavy kick of a boot in his ribs as he tried to scrabble out of the way, heard the frantic rev of the diesel, then tumbled over onto his back. He squinted upwards, choking for breath, and was immediately blinded – *ugh* – something in his eye. All he could see was red. He squirmed into a corner beneath the bulkhead and desperately rubbed at his eyes. Blood – a long wet smear of it across the back of his wrist. It was the Japanese man, Moko, bleeding all over the place as he spun the wheel, heavy drips of bright red spattering the greasy floor of the cabin.

Ba-duh-duh-duh-duh . . . more shots and curses . . . the boat rocked wildly, engine going full throttle. Baz tried to sit up, but was knocked back down again as the vessel struck against something solid – a horrible grinding shudder.

'What're you playing at, Moko! Try going *around* the ruddy rooftops . . .' Isaac, yelling through the doorway.

Another few vicious bursts of gunfire, and then the motion of the boat gradually evened out. The shouting ceased, and the steady drub of the diesel was all that could be heard. Baz cautiously raised himself up, and saw that Ray was on the opposite side of the cabin, huddled beneath a bench seat. Had he been hit?

Isaac ducked into the wheelhouse, his broad bulk darkening the tiny space. He wrenched at the strap of his gun, pulling it furiously over his head. 'Right, that's it. I'm done with that lot. They can dam' well starve for all I— What the hell . . .? Look at all this! Moko? What's happened?'

'Nugh.' The big Japanese man grunted as he held up his dripping forearm, but kept his eyes on the window in front of him.

'Amos! In here, quick.' Isaac was already shouting to one of the men outside. 'Moko's been hit in the arm. Get him bandaged up. Oi, Luke, come and take the helm while I sort these kids out.'

Isaac bent down and yanked at one of Ray's ankles. 'Right, you little snot-nose – outside. Now! Yeah, you too – get up, and get out there on deck.'

As Baz staggered to his feet, Isaac gave him a shove, and he lurched into Ray. The two boys were catapulted through the doorway. Isaac followed and gave them both another push. 'Get down to the stern and out of the way. Amos, see what you can do to fix up Moko. Give him some brandy or something. Luke, we might as well head straight for home. No point in doing the rounds, now that we've got no flaming diesel.'

'OK, but the old man's gonna have a fit when he hears about this. What d'you wanna do with those kids?'

'What do I *want* to do?' Isaac's voice roared above the clatter of the engine. 'Feed them to the ruddy mermaids is what I want to do! But I'll find out what they know first. As for the old man – you leave him to me. *He* should try this caper some time.'

Baz and Ray stumbled through the maze of crates and boxes that littered the deck. The yawing movement of the boat kept them continually off balance, so that their progress was awkward and slow. When they reached the stern, they turned to find Isaac already bearing down on them, his bearded face set in an angry scowl. Fear instinctively drew the two boys closer together – but this simply made it easier for Isaac to collar them both at the same time. His huge hands shot out and grabbed at their throats, and Baz found himself standing on tiptoe, with Isaac's face thrust so close to his that he could smell his horrible black beard.

'Now then. Let's have some ruddy answers. How long had *that* little scheme been planned?' Isaac's breath stank of pickles and tinned fish.

'Don't know.' Baz could hardly get his voice to work. 'I don't know anything about it. Honest.'

Immediately he felt himself being shaken so violently that he thought his neck would break.

'Listen, you little toe-rag! That raft wasn't built without other people knowing about it. So who organized it – the Trolleymen? Who else was in on it? You?'

'No! I don't know anything. I just looked . . . looked through the window and there they were.'

'OK, then – what about you, Cornflakes? Come on! You're going overboard in any case, so start talking.'

But Ray seemed totally unable to speak. His mouth simply hung open.

Isaac looked from one to the other, as if making up his mind what to do with them.

'Gah!' He finally hurled the boys away from him, so that they both staggered against the bench plank at the stern of the boat. 'Over a thousand ruddy cans I've lost today! A thousand cans! And only you little snits to show for it. That's a hell of a lot of diving, a thousand cans. *And* I've got a man wounded, dammit!' Isaac snatched at the nearest thing to hand – an empty wine bottle – and flung it at them. The boys both ducked as the bottle whizzed over their heads and disappeared soundlessly in the wake of the boat. Isaac turned to go. 'I'll tell you one thing, though – we'll get our money's worth out of you two. You're going to find out what hard work is, boyos. And then I'll sling you to the mermaids personally. Dead or alive. Stay back there, and don't move till I come and get you.'

Isaac shambled off amongst the scattered cargo, his massive shoulders rolling from side to side as he walked, his hands dangling from his sides like the paws of a grizzly.

Baz let out a long, long breath as Isaac disappeared into the wheelhouse. He looked at Ray. 'You OK?'

Ray said, 'Yeah, why shouldn't I be?' But then he knelt upon the bench seat, leaned over the stern of the boat and threw up, all in one movement. It was very neat, almost graceful, the way he did it. Baz felt his own stomach tighten as he watched, and thought for a moment that he was going to come out in sympathy. But no, it wasn't going to happen. He reached across and put a hand on Ray's shoulder, feeling the sharp definition of the bones shivering through the baggy yellow T-shirt. God. He *was* skinny, this one.

'Don't worry,' he said. 'I'm scared too. You'll be all right.'

'I *am* all right.' Ray pulled himself back into the boat and wiped his mouth. His face was very white, and his eyes looked teary. 'I just get a bit seasick, that's all. Happens every' – he took a deep juddering breath – 'every time. I'm fine now. I'm fine.'

Why did he have to keep pretending he was such a hard nut? The last ten minutes had been terrifying enough to make anyone puke.

'Christ, I really thought he was going to sling us over, though,' said Baz. 'You wouldn't even know which way to try and swim. Can't see a thing.'

'Yeah, well. You can't blame him for being mad. He's just lost about a ton of gear.'

Baz rested his chin on his forearms and looked over the stern of the boat, staring down into the hypnotic swirl of the wake. After a while it seemed as though it was the boat that was standing still and the water that was moving, passing beneath them, foaming and snaking away into the surrounding smog. Awful to think that there was a whole city down there. Most of a city. Office blocks, supermarkets, shopping malls, streets and flyovers. And people. Thousands and thousands of people, all drowned. Baz thought of his mum then, and Lol, his sister – saw them leaving, smiling and waving from the car. Off to go and stay with Auntie Carol for a few days. A holiday. A little break. Back on Sunday. *Be good!*

But the car didn't come back on Sunday. It drove off down Maple Close, and by Sunday there was no Maple Close for it to ever drive back up again.

A terrible thought exploded inside Baz: maybe his dad had been caught up in the shooting. Accidentally. No – that couldn't happen. No . . . no . . . no. He *wouldn't* think that. Not his dad too. He wouldn't think it . . . wouldn't think it—

'Want some chocolate?'

Ray's pale hand was extended towards him, shaking. He was holding out a piece of chocolate. Three chunks.

'Wow. Where did you—?' Baz decided not to finish the question. He reached out for the chocolate, and saw that his own hands were shaking as badly as Ray's. 'Thanks.'

The chocolate was half melted and very old, but Baz couldn't remember when anything had tasted as good. He chewed the first piece quickly – a huge burst of joy that filled his entire being – but then let the second piece melt slowly in his mouth, trying to make it last as long as he could.

'Mum gave it me,' said Ray, munching on his own piece. 'In case the cornflakes weren't enough.'

It was miracle stuff, and it cheered them up.

'They must've been nuts, those guys on the raft.' Ray's eyes widened at the memory of it. 'What did they think they were gonna do? Pole-vault aboard?'

Baz laughed. 'Yeah. Pole-vaulting pirates.'

'You won't tell anyone, will you? About me . . . you know . . . being sick?'

'No. Course not.' Why would it matter? Ray was a funny kid. 'Tell you what, though, I reckon this smog's clearing a bit. Look.'

They could see wispy patches of blue above them, just here and there, and the circle of mist had widened, become less dense. The water was choppier now, and the boat bounced across it with a rhythmic smacking sound.

Baz turned to look back at the coastline they had left behind, clearer now that the mists had receded, and was amazed to see that the so-called mainland appeared to be no more than an island itself from this angle. A flat island with broken outcrops to either side. But perhaps beyond that long low ridge lay other ridges, land that stretched southwards for hundreds of miles. Had people survived there too? People who were better off, perhaps? People who still had cars and computers and mobiles . . . proper beds, proper food . . . people who would someday come and make every-thing right again . . .

No, you shouldn't think like that, his dad had said.

This was global. It had to be, or they would have heard otherwise by now. There were no phones, no planes, no helicopters. There was no electricity and no communication, and nobody was ever going to come to the rescue. Forget it.

Except that you couldn't forget it. It was like watching the same film over and over again – and maybe that was because it had all started with the TV. A big swirly spiral, white against blue, almost filling the screen. Smaller spirals, breaking away from the main one, dividing, subdividing. They were like slow-motion fireworks, huge Catherine wheels, hiding whatever country lay beneath them. India? His dad had been in the room, drying his mop of hair on a green towel as he stood in front of the TV. Baz had only been mildly interested. Terrible things always seemed to be happening in India, or China, or wherever it was. What could you do?

Words coming out of the TV, serious voices. A man and a woman taking it in turns to read: '. . . *originally known as Hurricane Delilah, continues to grow and to multiply . . . by far the highest readings ever recorded . . . now deep concerns over Mumbai and San Salvador . . . authorities are advising . . .*'

His father had stopped drying his hair. The green towel hung limply in one hand, a corner of it trailing onto the carpet.

'Dad? What's going on?'

'Don't know, but it doesn't look good. Not if you happen to be living in Asia, it doesn't. Or Central America . . .'

The TV pictures had changed. They weren't just

swirly patterns any more. Baz watched mobile homes tumbling end over end across a field, trees bending down to touch the ground . . . and waves – impossible waves engulfing row upon row of beachfront houses. People running, screaming, falling, being swept away. My God . . . where *was* this?

'Dad? That . . . that couldn't happen here, could it?'

'What?' His father didn't seem to be able to take his eyes off the screen. 'No. No, don't worry, son. We're about as far inland as you can get in this country, and a long way above sea level. Nothing like that's ever going to happen here. Not unless it happens everywhere else first. Come on. Time you were in bed. Go on up and do your teeth, then we'll phone Mum and say good night.'

'Wonder how long it takes.' Ray's voice broke in on Baz's thoughts.

'To get to the island? Dunno. Couple of hours maybe.'

Ray said, 'I still can't believe I'm actually on the boat. I just can't believe it . . .'

'I know. It's . . .' Baz leaned forward, arms across his chest, hugging himself. 'I mean, what d'you think it's gonna be *like* there?'

'Hard work, I reckon. But everybody says it's great, don't they? Getting fed every single day. Three times a day, I heard.'

'Hey – that's what this girl I know said! The one whose cousin was there. She said that Preacher John had built, like, a proper new factory with a canteen, and that you got three meals a day.'

'Well, I bet it's true. Must be.' Ray paused, and then

said, 'Why do they call him Preacher John? Did you ever see him?'

Baz nodded in the direction of the wheelhouse. 'No, but those guys are his sons. That's what my dad told me. Preacher John's the boss. It's his business – the factory and the salvage and all that. Dunno why they call him Preacher, though.'

'Oh. So the boat's his too?'

'S'pose so. Have you tried to get a place before?' said Baz. 'I have. Twice. First time we had eggs – half a dozen real chicken's eggs – but some kid had a big tub of cocoa, so that was enough. Second time we had American rice, but got beaten by a goat. A goat! Where do you get a goat from?'

'I never tried before,' said Ray. 'Mum said I was too small. She still thinks I'm too small.' He looked at Baz. 'I'm thirteen and a bit, though. Your face is a right mess. Blood all over it.'

Baz glanced around the deck area, wondering if there might be a bit of cloth or something that he could use to clean himself up. There was nothing handy that he could see – just empty plastic crates and a few remaining tins. The contents of the tins were written in black marker pen on the lids. B/BEANS. I/STEW. P/APPLE. That must be somebody's job in the factory. Marking up the tins. How hard could that be?

'It'll have to wait,' he said. 'Hey, look – is that it?'

The humid smog had faded away completely, and the boat was sailing on open water. There was a horizon now, and smack bang in the middle of that horizon they could see a dark shape, hazy grey, rising from the sea.

'Wow. Yeah, has to be.'

'Wow.'

The dark shape was a long way off, miles to go yet, but that was it all right. Their destination. X Isle.

CHAPTER TWO

The name was a kind of joke. The tiny island, once part of the posh Tab Hill district, was where Preacher John Eck based his salvage operation. So first it had become known as Eck's Island, and then X Isle.

Visibility from the mainland was usually poor – thick steamy mist followed by sudden tropical downpours – and the island was too far away to be seen in any case. The *Cormorant* was the only boat in the area, and no makeshift raft could cover such a distance. X Isle was a natural stronghold, safe from invasion.

In the hazy spells between smog and rain, the converted fishing boat would sometimes be spotted roaming the coastline or anchored far out to sea as the divers went about their business. All the underwater world was within the grasp of those four men, the treasure of the city theirs for the picking. The mainlanders could only look jealously on, and wait for whatever scraps might come their way. It was said that Preacher John and his sons had enough food stored on X Isle to see them through their lifetimes, and the thought of this drove the mainlanders to concoct ever more crazy and desperate schemes to get at it.

Hence today's attack. Baz breathed in deeply through his open mouth at the memory of those wild faces beyond the porthole, the sudden hammer of gunfire.

And he couldn't remember the last time he'd done this – properly filled his lungs. The surrounding water still looked grey and scummy, and the air still reeked of nameless decay, but it was far better than back on the mainland. There you learned to take short shallow breaths, preferably through your nostrils. You tried not to gag, and you hoped not to catch some terrible disease . . .

'Storm coming.' Ray was looking towards the dark confusion of cloud rising beyond the island. There was no outline to the cloud, no definition, just a blur of grey spanning the horizon. Such storms came and went nearly every day, sudden ferocious downpours that momentarily swamped the land, and then evaporated once more into a steamy haze.

'We might get there first,' said Baz, 'if we're lucky.'

The diesel motor drubbed on and on. Eventually the island was close enough for Baz and Ray to be able to pick out some of its features. They could see a large white building standing on a plateau. Lots of windows. Perhaps this was the factory – although it looked more like an office block or a school. Part of the structure, to the left, had collapsed. The remains of other buildings rose from the surrounding waters, their roofs shattered by the force of the earthquakes, timbers sticking up at crazy angles. And further out into the sea stood a great tangle of stone and iron girders – a square construction, like the battlements of a castle or a church tower. Yes, the top of a church tower, protruding above the choppy waves, all smashed in on one side where some huge metal thing had toppled into it. The metal thing was a crane, Baz realized. He could see the concrete counterweights and the operator's cabin, an open glass door dangling high above the water.

The boat headed directly for the church tower, keeping a steady line. As they drew close, the engine note changed, throttling back to a slow tickover. Two of the Eck brothers emerged from the cabin – Amos and Luke – to stand one on either side of the boat. They grabbed long wooden poles, obviously a practised manoeuvre, and made ready.

Where the twisted metal of the crane had collapsed against the tower, an archway had been formed. Baz and Ray looked upwards in wonder as the boat slowly began to nose its way beneath the rusting girders. The two men pushed with their poles against stone and metal, helping to guide the boat safely through the gap. It was a tight squeeze, and Baz wondered why they didn't just avoid the whole lot by going around it. Maybe there were other obstructions elsewhere, hidden dangers just below the surface of the water, and this was the quickest and safest way.

Baz leaned over the side of the boat, stretching his arm out horizontally as far as he could. He managed to briefly touch the tower as it passed by, the grey lichen-covered blocks of stone brushing warm against his fingertips. The scale of it all hit him anew. He was as high above the city as a hammerhead crane, as high as a church tower, and the world that he had known lay many metres below the swaying deck of the boat. It made him dizzy to think about it.

Isaac emerged from the cabin doorway, squinting upwards as he checked the sky. His beard looked darker than ever somehow, crow-black against the looming grey of the storm clouds. He glanced at the litter of empty crates and boxes, spat in disgust, and then lumbered round the outside of the cabin to make his way onto the foredeck. Baz and Ray could see the skipper's raised hand pointing this way and that as he helped guide the boat to shore.

They were almost there. The bulk of the island towered above the fishing boat now, a dark mass beneath the heavy sky, and Baz felt the first drop of rain spatter on the back of his wrist.

A steep tarmacked pathway ran down the hillside, and at the end of the pathway, extending out into the water, was a bank of rubble. On top of the rubble stood a small group of boys, three or four of them, watching the boat as it edged its way in. The boys were all dressed in T-shirts and khaki shorts, and they each had a wheelbarrow. Black wheelbarrows with red wheels. It looked as though the stone bank was a work in progress, the beginnings of a jetty. A row of old car tyres had been fixed at water level, wired into the stone blocks, and the boat bumped gently against these as it finally came to land.

'Steiner!' Isaac threw a rope to a big lanky youth who was ready and waiting to catch it, and the rope was made fast to an iron stanchion. Then three younger boys came scrambling down the slope carry-ing a makeshift gangway between them – a couple of builders' planks roped together. They laid this across the gunwales, and Isaac stepped ashore.

The big lad appeared confused. He looked at the empty crates that lay about the deck. 'Er . . . what's to unload, Skip?'

'Nothing.'

'What?'

'I said *nothing*, cloth-ears! Get out of my sight. Clear up the deck, and then go and find that lard-arse Cookie. Tell him we'll eat early tonight.'

As Isaac heaved himself up the slope, the skies broke in earnest. Down came the rain at last, an instant deluge that hammered on wood and stone and bare heads alike. The other three men were already ashore and hurrying up the tarmacked path behind Isaac, shoulders hunched against the storm, arms raised for protection.

'Pick up those crates!' yelled the big lad, Steiner. The younger ones were already hopping across the gangplank and down into the boat. They scrabbled about the streaming deck, gathering up the empty plastic crates, the bottles and the tins – whatever bits of rubbish came to hand.

Baz and Ray joined in, slithering and sliding on the greasy planking as the rain lashed at their bent backs. The job didn't take long. A last look around the deck and Steiner shouted, 'OK! Get it shifted! Come on, you bum-rags – I'm chuffin' soaked here.' His voice was almost lost in the roar and hiss of tumbling water.

Baz stuffed his backpack into one of the plastic crates, balanced two more crates on top of that, and stepped up onto the wobbly gangplank. He made it across OK, but then heard a scuffle and clatter behind him. Ray had slipped and tumbled – fallen from the gangplank down onto the rubble.

'You *stupid* little git! Now I've got to hang around waiting for you. Pick it all up – idiot!' Steiner stood on the planks, water pouring from his long ugly chin as Ray struggled to gather his crates and tins together below. Baz hesitated, wondering whether he should try and help.

'What are you looking at? Get after the others and quit gawping!' Steiner made a threatening move towards him.

Baz clambered up the rubble bank and onto the tarmac pathway. He began to climb the hill – not an easy exercise in such a torrent and with three big crates to carry. By the time he reached level ground his arms were aching, he was soaked to the skin and he felt that he'd gulped in almost as much water as he had air.

Before him stood the remains of a big modern building, the one they had seen from the boat. A broad flight of steps led up to a covered entranceway, a set of glass doors. Baz could see the knot of boys huddled in the entranceway, and he made his way towards them. TAB HILL HIGH SCHOOL. Red painted letters danced in and out of watery focus. They were carved into a big tablet of stone, a pale monolith that stood upright in the ground to one side of the overgrown driveway. Baz staggered past the sign and climbed the flight of steps. He dumped his crates on the top step, as the other boys had done, and scuttled for shelter.

Then he remembered his backpack, and had to run out into the rain again in order to retrieve it.

'Got any food in there?' One of the boys spoke as Baz ducked beneath the entranceway once more.

Baz pushed back his streaming wet hair and shook his head. 'Just clothes.'

'Maybe we should check, eh?' The same boy, a shaven-headed Asian lad, his expression cool, mouth unsmiling.

Baz wiped the water away from his face and stared back at the group. They hung close together, shoulder to shoulder, like a pack of bedraggled hyenas. None of them were any bigger than he was, but there were three of them – three sets of hungry eyes weighing him up, testing him. And they weren't just skinny. These boys were wiry, tough looking, their arms and bodies sharply detailed, as though layers of skin had been stripped away to leave just muscle and bone.

Baz let the dripping backpack slide gently to his feet. 'Go ahead, then.'

He kept his voice flat, no challenge, no aggression. But if they wanted the backpack they were going to have to come and take it from him. He looked from one to the other and waited. The rain bounced and splattered on the entranceway steps.

'Nah, it's OK.' The Asian boy again. 'We'll believe you. What's your name?'

'Baz.'

The trio relaxed into general movement, spread themselves out a little.

'Baz. All right. Well, this here's Robbie . . . and this other kid's Enoch. And I'm Amit. OK?'

'Yeah.' Baz let his shoulders drop. 'I can remember that . . .'

The attention of the three boys had already shifted away from him. Baz turned to see what they were looking at.

It was Ray. And the lanky older boy, Steiner.

Half hidden behind his stack of crates, Ray was making unsteady progress along the driveway towards the school building. From left to right he staggered, obviously exhausted. And Steiner was right beside him, bending down, bawling in his ear.

'That the best you can do? That it? You'll not last five minutes here, kid, if you can't even manage a few empty boxes. What's gonna happen when they're full o' tins? Come on, get those weedy little legs working properly! Gaaah! You're all over t' chuffin' place . . .'

Right to the very bottom of the steps Steiner kept goading Ray. 'What's your chuffin' problem? Got one leg shorter than t' other, is that it? Try walkin' bloody straight, then! Come on – keep moving. Pick 'em up! Pick 'em up!'

Ray got as far as the fourth step. Then he turned and with a final effort he heaved the crates towards Steiner. 'Pick 'em up yourself, dickhead.'

The crates bounced and clattered down the steps, empty plastic bottles, tins, bits of rubbish rolling everywhere. Steiner jumped as he tried to avoid the avalanche, but he missed his footing and tumbled towards the steps, arms outstretched. He landed heavily, his palms making a loud slap on the wet stone. With one knee forward and the other straight back, he looked for a moment like a sprinter about to come out of the starting blocks.

It took him a couple of seconds to recover, and

then he was up. 'Come 'ere, you little bleeder . . .'

As Steiner lunged towards him, Ray managed one kick at the older boy's shins, but it was a feeble effort and he was already off-balance. Steiner grabbed him by the hair, swung him violently to the ground, and immediately began punching him.

'I'll bloody kill you for that!'

Ray curled himself up into a ball and lay unresisting, abandoned to the kicks and blows that rained upon him. His utter defencelessness jolted Baz into action.

'Hey! Leave him alone!' Baz ran down the streaming steps, no thought in his head as to what he would do next, but knowing that he had to do something.

He threw himself half across the prostrate form of Ray, and did his best to keep Steiner away.

'Stop, OK?' Baz lifted an arm, half in defence, half in an attempt to push Steiner back. 'He's had enough!'

'Has he?' Steiner's mouth bubbled with spit. 'Then what about . . . *you* . . .'

Baz had a glimpse of Steiner's twisted red face, a raised fist, and then a jagged explosion went off in his head. *Wow-wow-wow-wow* . . . the world went scooting away . . .

Darkness. A confusion of sound. Angry voices. Baz was on his knees, and everything around him was being shaken. No, someone was shaking him. He was being hauled to his feet, effortlessly lifted up, as though by a crane. He blinked and saw a big black beard . . .

Everything wobbled back into focus, and there was Isaac. Shouting at Steiner.

'. . . you do as you're damn well told, *boy*, and keep your hands off 'em till I'm through.'

'But look what they did!' Steiner's voice honked and squeaked. 'They can't just attack me—'

Isaac's great arm lashed out, and Steiner fell back against the steps.

'Attack you? *I'll* dam' well attack you if I catch you damaging our goods again! Now get this mess cleared away, and then shut 'em in for the night. And send Cookie to me like I asked you to twenty minutes ago. You better sharpen up, Steiner. I can find plenty more in the same gutter you came from.'

Isaac splashed up the steps, heading for the entrance to the building. The three boys shrank to one side as he passed by.

Baz's jaw hurt, and his vision was still a bit blurry, but he was starting to get his bearings once more. Something had changed – something to do with his hearing – and it took him a moment to figure out what it was: the rain had stopped.

Ray was sitting on the puddled steps, not far from Steiner. His face was bruised and bleeding. He looked terrible.

'You OK?' said Baz.

Ray nodded. He got to his feet and stood there for a moment, as if making sure that he wasn't going to fall back down again.

'All right? Come on, then. I'll help you with this stuff.'

Slowly, painfully, Baz and Ray picked up the fallen crates. They gathered Ray's belongings together, retrieved the plastic bottles and tins, put them all back in the crates. Nobody came to help them. The other boys remained in the entranceway, looking down on them, just watching.

Steiner was watching them as well, still sitting on the steps, his cold blue eyes following their every move. He had pale, almost invisible lashes, and a face so massively freckled – freckles upon freckles – that it looked as though someone had drawn them in with a brown marker pen. There was an angry swelling on his cheek where Isaac had struck him, and both his bare gingery knees were grazed and bloodied.

'That the lot?' Baz and Ray stacked their crates and began to climb the steps once more. As they drew level with Steiner, he stood up.

'You're dead.' His voice was low and quiet for once, a husky whisper. 'Hear me? You're both chuffin' dead.'

The two boys kept on going. But Steiner was at their heels, chanting in time with each step they took, 'Dead . . . dead . . . dead . . . dead . . .'

CHAPTER THREE

A mit and the other two boys had picked up their crates again. They waited for a few moments, perhaps for some signal from Steiner, then began to shuffle into the school building. Baz and Ray followed.

A long dim corridor straight ahead. Keep walking? No, the group came to a halt almost immediately, lining themselves up beside a fire door on the left. Steiner walked to the head of the line and grabbed the door handle.

'Take 'em in and empty 'em out.' Steiner swung the heavy door towards him and stood holding it open as the boys filed past.

Baz was the last one through. He instinctively flinched away from Steiner, expecting a kick or a blow of some sort. But nothing happened.

The room they entered was large, and at first sight chaotic: scattered crates and pallets, bits of machinery, bicycles, furniture, pots and pans ... and there were more boys working here – another three or four maybe.

Baz looked around in wonder, but was then jolted forward, his crates tumbling to the floor. Steiner had shoved him in the back.

'Don't just stand there gawping, you little twerp. Get this stuff sorted. Tins back into their right crates – rubbish in t' big wheelie bins over in the corner. Hutch! We're knocking off early.'

As Baz began to scramble about for the fallen tins, another lad appeared – a big solidly built boy of about Steiner's age, dark hair on his upper lip, quite spotty. He wore a grubby white lab coat and carried a clipboard.

'Knockin' off? Why?' He stopped. 'Hey – what happened to your face?'

'Huh. I'll tell you later,' Steiner muttered. 'But I'll tell you summat right now – there'll be payback.'

Baz did as those around him were doing, sorting tins into plastic crates according to how they were marked – BB, T/SOUP, G/PEAS – then hefting the crates onto wooden pallets. It was only a few minutes' work, but it gave him a chance to try and make sense of what was going on.

The room seemed to be both packing area and workshop, a place where salvage was brought and made ready for trading. The corner nearest the door was piled high with plastic containers, a tumbling mountain of soap and shampoo dispensers, medicines, bottled water, soft drinks – all covered in the smeary grey film that was X Isle's trademark. These were goods that had been dredged up from the devastated world below, and it was a world that clung to them still. The sickly odour of rot and decay hung in the air.

At the far end of the room stood a long workbench stretching from wall to wall, and as the boys finished what they were doing, they began to gather in this area. Baz joined them, seeking out a space next to Ray. An upside-down bicycle stood on the oily bench, its rear wheel missing. And there were other bits of machinery: part of an engine, a woodburner stove, several paraffin lamps, all apparently in the process of being dismantled or restored. Beneath the bench lay a nameless jumble of scrap metal.

'OK, Steiner – we're done!' The bigger boy, Hutch, approached the workbench, making notes on his clipboard. The base of his neck was so thick that his head seemed to taper upwards. On top of his otherwise shaven scalp was a flattened-down patch of greasy hair. It looked like a bit of wet seaweed clinging to a rock. In fact Hutch could almost have been made of rock. When he turned towards Steiner, his head and shoulders moved as though locked together.

'Check this,' he said.

'Give it here, then.' Steiner took the clipboard, glanced at it and handed it back. 'OK. We're heavy on the usual then. Beans and spaghetti. Oi, you – Jubo.' Steiner gave one of the boys a shove, a broad-shouldered kid with dreadlocks. West Indian maybe. His naked torso was streaked with grey dried-on mud. 'Hook out nine tins from the pallets and put 'em on t' floor. I want to see three meat, two beans, two spaghetti, two tomatoes.'

'*Tomatoes?*' The boy sounded surprised.

'You heard.'

Jubo went over to the stacked pallets and began to rummage around. He shifted the plastic crates this way and that in order to get at what was required, picked out an armful of tins, then ferried them over to the workbench area and placed them on the floor.

Baz looked at the tins. The lids were all marked in the familiar black pen: I/STEW, B/CUR, C/CUR, B/BEANS, TOMS, SPAG. And now he could feel tension around him, the circle of boys edging closer to the tins. What was going on?

'OK, Gene,' said Steiner, 'pick out your tin. Rest of you stand up straight, arms at your sides.'

An olive-skinned boy, Mediterranean looking, maybe a bit older than the rest, stooped casually and chose one of the tins. He stepped back from the group. Baz saw that one of the meat tins had gone – B/CUR.

Steiner spoke again. 'Right then, Hutch. Who's your top dog?'

Hutch waved his clipboard towards a tall boy with very long blond hair. 'Dyson,' he said. 'Yours?'

'Amit.'

A few sighs and groans from the group.

'Top-dogs-ready-go!'

Steiner's words came out as one, with no warning, and Baz's jump of surprise was a delayed reaction. Amit and the blond boy had immediately dived forward, sliding on their knees towards the tins. A quick scuffle, a snatch of hands, and they were back on their feet. Baz blinked. The whole thing had taken no more than three seconds. Amit and Dyson moved to one side, clutching their prizes – a tin of food apiece.

Baz scanned the jumble of words on the remaining lids and saw that I/STEW and C/CUR had now gone. Two tins of beans left, two spaghetti, two tomatoes. So if—

'Rest-of-you-ready-go!'

Baz had been caught out again. He lunged forward,

47

throwing himself into the scrabble of bodies, but by the time he hit the floor he already knew what he was going to end up with.

He'd been slow off the mark, and Ray, crashing to the ground beside him, had been slower still. Ray's hand snaked out, desperately grabbing for whatever it could find . . . but the race was already over. Only one tin remained on the floor, and nobody else wanted it in any case. Ray's small brown fingers hesitated a moment longer, then slowly closed over the last word: TOMS.

'Ha!' Steiner was clearly delighted with the way things had worked out. 'Just a bit too slow there, girls. Better luck next time, eh?' The grin disappeared from his long freckled face. ''Cos there's gonna be a next time, don't you worry. I'll teach you little tarts to come it with me! Yeah.' He prodded Ray in the chest. 'And especially you. Go on – back to the slob room, the lot of you. Line up there and wait for one of us to let you in. OK, Hutch, let's lock up.'

Baz and Ray picked up their belongings and followed the rest of the group out of the sorting room. They turned left down the corridor. Again they didn't go very far. At the next door along the boys stopped and formed a queue.

A little light fell on them from the row of filthy windows opposite, and Baz looked around at the once-familiar signs of school life – the notice boards with their torn and fading posters, the line of grubby marks all along the lower walls where many feet had scuffed the paintwork. The far end of the corridor was lost in gloom, a square tunnel into which parallel rows of overhead strip lights disappeared, their covers smashed or missing, bare wires hanging down.

'So where's the factory?' Baz asked the question of his neighbour, Jubo, the black kid who had doled out the tins.

Jubo blinked in apparent surprise, but then just muttered, 'We don' talk here, guy.' He nodded his head towards the dark end of the corridor, as if this was explanation enough.

The boys stood silently waiting, each holding a tin of food. Baz looked along the queue and counted nine of them including him and Ray. How many of their names could he remember? There was Jubo, standing next to him. Amit, the Asian lad, who had been given first choice of the tins, along with Dyson, the tall kid with the long blond hair. Gene, the older boy who had been allowed to choose his own tin of food. And . . . and a couple more that he hadn't got yet.

Someone was coming down the corridor jangling a bunch of keys. Hutch. Baz was glad to see that it wasn't Steiner. He'd had enough of Steiner for one day. But Hutch didn't look too friendly either. He walked down the line and stopped in front of Baz.

'I got my eye on you,' he said. His voice was quieter than Steiner's, but menacing nevertheless, and the grubby lab coat seemed to give him extra authority – permission to do what he wanted. God, he looked unhealthy, though. Hutch's pockmarked skin had a kind of sticky glaze to it, and his eyes were almost invisible, hidden away in the dark slits between the puffy lids. He smelled funny too. Like someone had spilled beer over him. 'And you.' The glistening face turned towards Ray. 'Yeah, that's right. I've been hearing all about it, and if I get any of your crap I'll stomp on your skull. Got it?' Hutch flicked a finger against Ray's bruised cheek. 'I said, *got it?*'

'Ow!' Ray flinched away. 'Yes. Hutch.' He put his hand up to his cheek.

'Hutch? *Hutch?* It's Hutchinson to you, kid. And keep your voice down. That's summat else you'd better learn fast. And you'd *better* learn fast. Dyson!' Hutchinson walked to the head of the queue. 'You and Amit get these two newbies shaped up. Kit 'em out, and make sure they're ready and knowing what's what by morning – names, work duties, the lot. You know the deal by now. I have to tell 'em anything more than once, and it'll be your fault. Yeah?'

'Yes, Hutchinson.'

'Yes, Hutchinson.'

Amit and Dyson murmured in unison, heads lowered.

'Right. We're slobbing down early. Half eight start tomorrow. Usual split, workshop and jetty. Amit, you're on the jetty. You take one newbie, don't care which. Dyson, you take the other.'

Hutchinson rattled the keys in the lock, but then paused. Steiner was running down the corridor towards them.

'Hutch,' he gasped. 'I forgot! Cookie's in there! Come on, open t' chuffin' door.'

'What?' Hutchinson unlocked the door, and Steiner pushed past him.

'Cookie!' Steiner was in the room, his voice audible to those still out in the corridor. 'Shift your fat tush.

Get down to t' kitchen now! They're eating early tonight.'

Hutchinson put out a hand, preventing the gaggle of boys from entering the room.

'Come on, lardo! Move it!' Steiner was still shouting at someone in there.

A big red-faced boy came stumbling through the doorway, one arm through the sleeve of a dirty white jacket. His torso was naked, and his belly jiggled from side to side as he searched frantically for the other sleeve.

'Don't worry about yer friggin' coat – just keep moving! Go-go-go!' Steiner hustled the fat boy all the way down the corridor. They disappeared round a corner, the boy still struggling to get his jacket on properly.

'OK. In there, the rest of you. I'll be back to put the light out in' – Hutchinson looked at his watch – 'an hour and forty minutes.'

The boys filed into the room, and the door closed behind them. There was a collective whoosh of escaping breath, and then everyone was talking at once.

'Sheesh! What's been happening? What's going on?'

'It's those new kids – they went for Steiner! Kicked him, that one did! Or tried to . . .'

'. . . and the boat came back empty. Dunno why . . .'

'. . . chucked his crates at Steiner, and then Steiner beat them both up . . .'

'. . . lucky he didn't kill 'em. Prob'ly would've done, but then Isaac turned up and whacked Steiner . . .'

'Whaaat?'

Baz was half listening and at the same time looking

51

around the room. Mattresses lying on the floor, side by side . . . a few tatty chairs that might have once been in a staffroom . . . jumbled blankets and clothing . . . more clothing strung out on washing lines.

The air smelled damp and fetid. Cabbagey. Like old farts. Baz stared up at the ceiling. A light bulb! An actual working electric light bulb . . .

'Huh?' he said. Someone was talking to him. Amit. A muddle of other faces gathering round.

'I said, why was the boat empty?'

'Oh, that,' said Baz. 'It was attacked when they were unloading. Some men on a raft tried to – you know – attack it. With shotguns. Tried to get hold of it. But then Isaac and the rest, they started shooting back and they got away. But all the stuff was left behind.'

'Yeah? Oh well – less work for us. Anyway' – Amit tossed his tin into the air and skipped backwards a couple of paces – 'snap's up. Come on, I'm starving.' He caught the tin as though he were a rugby player, turned and ran with it.

The boys charged after him, pushing and jostling one another as they crowded towards a corner at the far end of the room. Here there was a cheap sink unit – not that there would be any running water of course – and a few pots and pans on a shelf. The draining board was half hidden beneath a pile of kitchen rubbish. A drawer was yanked open, and everyone tried to get a hand in there at once, in competition for eating utensils, as it turned out. The more successful bagged themselves metal spoons and forks, the rest had to make do with plastic. By the time Baz and Ray got to the drawer there were just two plastic teaspoons left, and one of them was broken. Baz took the broken one.

'Hey, you newbies.' It was Dyson, the boy who had won first pick of the food along with Amit. He'd already opened his can and was carefully stirring bits of meat and potato around with a metal fork. 'Those mattresses over there, by the curtain – they'll be yours from now on. Eat first, and then we'll tell you how things work round here. Are those tins ring-pull? Yeah? Well, there's an opener hanging by the sink for when they're not.' He turned his back on them and walked away.

Next to the sink area was a curtained-off doorway, and beside that lay the two mattresses that Dyson had indicated.

'Which one do you want?' said Baz.

Ray shrugged his shoulders. 'Doesn't matter, does it?'

Baz chose the one furthest from the doorway, dropping his backpack beside it in order to stake his claim. He'd already taken the broken spoon, so he thought it only fair that he got the mattress least likely to be disturbed by any passing traffic.

The mattresses themselves were stained and tired looking, their cheap nylon coverings fuzzy with wear. No sheets, no pillows, just a rolled-up grey blanket apiece. Baz sat on his bed with his blanket propped up behind him and leaned against the wall. His hair and clothes were still damp from the rain, but he was too exhausted to bother about it. He couldn't even summon up the energy to eat, at least not straight away.

Instead he let his eyes wander where they would. He counted four beds on one side of the room, and three on the other. With his and Ray's that made nine. The sink was down at their end, in the corner closest to the curtained doorway. Up at the other end was the door where they had come in, and to the right of that a seating area with a scattering of chairs and a low table. There was one more bed, he realized, all by itself, to the left of the main doorway. So ten altogether. Vertical blinds, very grey and dusty looking, covered two windows, and there were various notice boards fixed to the walls. The floor was carpet-tiled. Baz would have bet anything that this had once been a staffroom. It was certainly no factory. And ten boys didn't seem like much of a workforce, either. Surely there must be more somewhere?

One or two of the boys sat as he and Ray did, on their mattresses. Others occupied the chairs in the seating area. Was that a privilege? Baz tipped his head back and let it rest against the wall. The single bare light bulb glared down at him. It was draped over an existing fitting, a loop of cable hanging down from a hole in one of the ceiling tiles. Electricity, though. How could they possibly have electricity? The light was sort of fizzy . . . vibrating . . .

'Are you gonna eat that or not?'

'What? Oh yeah.'

Ray had already finished his tin of tomatoes. He tossed the plastic spoon across to Baz.

'Use this if you like.'

Baz forced himself upright. His jaw ached from where Steiner had punched it, and he still didn't feel like eating, but he reached over for his tin of tomatoes and picked at the ring-pull.

'Blimey. Do you reckon this is it?' Ray was running his finger around the inside of his empty tin. 'We better get something more than bleedin' tomatoes for breakfast, that's all I can say.'

'Yeah? Or what?' Baz couldn't help needling him. 'You're gonna start another fight? Take on a few more this time?' He dipped his spoon into the tin and tried to break up one of the tomatoes. The thing kept slipping away from him.

'I might,' said Ray. 'He doesn't scare me, that Steiner. He's a pig. You let pigs like that walk all over you and then that's it. They . . . well, they walk all over you.'

'Yeah, I noticed.' Baz gave up trying to cut through the tomato and brought it out whole instead, carefully balancing it on the feeble plastic spoon and leaning forward to suck at the juice. God, he was hungry. At the first taste of it his stomach seemed to wake up properly, and start grumbling out loud for something solid. Baz managed to bite a piece off the end of the tomato and swallow it. Then he got the rest of it in his mouth in one go. That was the way to do it. He fished around for the next candidate.

'Doesn't seem that great to me, either,' he said. 'Bit of a dump, actually. And I hate that Steiner already. If I wanted to get my head kicked in I could've stayed on the mainland. Reckon you'll stick it?'

Ray answered him immediately. 'What? Yeah, course.' He nodded in the direction of the other boys. 'If that lot can stick it, then I can.' But after another few moments he said, 'Anyway, got no choice.'

Baz thought about that. 'Well, you could always go back if you wanted to. See, the divers get paid every time they take someone on. So if you wanted to go back, they'd just take on some other kid and get paid again. Another packet of cornflakes, another box of cartridges. What difference would it make to them?'

'Hey – I've only just got here, OK?' Ray was on the defensive again. 'What's all this "if you wanted to go back" stuff? What makes you think I can't hack it like anyone else?'

'Well, I didn't mean *you*. I was just saying like if *anyone* wanted to . . .'

Dyson was coming towards them, and Baz was relieved not to have to get into an argument. He put down his half-finished tin of tomatoes.

'You better come and talk,' said Dyson. 'There's stuff to get through. Come on down the other end.'

'OK.'

Baz and Ray got up and followed Dyson to the seating area. The chairs were all occupied, but some of the boys were sprawled about on the floor, so Baz and Ray found space between them and sat down. The boys who had been lying on their beds wandered across to join them.

'OK, we better start with names,' said Dyson. 'So what are yours?'

'I'm Ray,' said Ray. 'And this is Baz.'

'Right. Well, I'm Dyson. This is Amit, you already met, and Robbie and Enoch, yeah? And then there's Jubo and Gene, and this last little guy, Taps. Got it? I'll go through it again in a minute. See, you have to remember in case you're asked. Like, if Steiner or Hutchinson says, "Go and get Gene for me," then you better know who Gene is. 'Cos they don't expect to have to ask you twice. Not for *anything*. You screw up and we get blamed for it. So you better get it right.'

'How it works is like this.' Amit spoke – the Asian boy – and his tone was less aggressive. 'You're just trying to stay here as long as you can, 'cos it's better than being back on the mainland. That's all you're trying to do. This place is crap, but it's still better'n being back there. So you wanna stay – we all do. But they'll send you back for any excuse, 'cos they just get paid again every time they take on a newbie.'

'Yeah, we worked that out,' said Ray. 'So why don't they just get new kids every week then? If they get paid every time . . .'

'Prob'ly would if they could,' said Amit, 'but they gotta have kids here who know what they're doing. If it was all newbies, nothing'd get done right. So it's only every month or so someone gets knocked off. You just gotta try and make sure it's not you. So here's what you guys need to know.' He splayed his fingers as if to begin counting on them. 'Work. You'll either be on the jetty crew or in the sort room. Most days we swap about – 'cept for Gene. He only works on the bench. Gene's the mechanic round here. Gene the Genius.' Amit glanced sideways. Maybe this had been a dig of some sort. 'If you're on the jetty crew,' he said, 'you're barrowing stone. It's hard graft, but you don't have to think. Just do what everyone else does and you'll be OK.' He scratched his cropped head and looked doubtfully at Ray. 'You're not so big. Reckon you can push a barrow full of rubble?'

'I can if you can.'

'Well, you better. OK, working in the sort room. We bring the stuff off the boat, clean it up and label it. For the tins you have to learn a list of codes so you can label 'em. Then everything gets stacked on pallets and locked in the storeroom. We don't go in there. That's about it.'

Dyson took over. 'But there's rules,' he said. He was sitting cross-legged, a curtain of long blond hair hanging forward over his face. His chin was in his hands, so that his head jiggled up and down as he spoke. 'Rule number one, you don't mess with the Eck brothers. You don't speak to them, you don't go anywhere near them. You just stay out of their way. We're scum to them. They don't know our names even.'

'But you better know theirs, man,' Jubo muttered.

'That's right. So, there's the brothers – Isaac, Amos and Luke, yeah? Amos and Luke do all the diving. Isaac stays on the boat with Moko. Moko's the Japanese guy. He works the winch. We'll show you who's who tomorrow, but learn the names tonight.'

'Yeah, I already—' Baz started to say something, but Dyson kept right on going.

'Rule number two, you don't cross Steiner or Hutchinson.' Dyson rolled his eyes as he looked at Ray. 'I can't believe you're still here, mate. Not after what you did. And rule number three – no swearing.'

No swearing? It seemed to Baz that people had been cursing at him all day. 'What?' he said.

'No swearing.' Dyson glanced at the door and

lowered his voice. 'Preacher John's orders. He ever hears you use a proper cuss-word, you're straight back on the boat.'

'So what about this Preacher John?' Baz asked the question he'd been wanting to ask all along. 'What's he like?'

Dyson threw back his hair and puffed out his cheeks. It was a moment or two before he replied.

'Well, I s'pose that's really rule number one,' he said. 'You don't even *look* at Preacher John. He's hardly ever around anyway – 'cept on Sundays. Just stays in his room. But if you ever see him coming, you better keep your head down.'

'He's not a real preacher.' Gene spoke for the first time. He was definitely a little older, this boy – loose dark curls, Italian looking. 'Not like a legal one – a priest, or a vicar, or whatever. But he's religious mad.'

'Or him just mad,' Jubo muttered. 'All this' – he waved a mud-streaked arm around – 'all wh' happen, man – the eart'quakes and the floods and all – him say it God's will. Him act like him Noah or somet'ing. But scary, man. Him ever look at you . . . you gonna know it.'

'He even scares Isaac,' said Amit. 'That's how scary he is.'

'Wait till Sunday,' Dyson went on. 'You'll see him then. We get Sundays off, 'cos Preacher John says it's wrong to work on the Sabbath. All it really means is we get Sunday afternoons off – 'cos on Sunday mornings we have to go to chapel.'

'*Chapel?* What, you mean, like, church?' Baz was overloaded with information, struggling to take it all in.

'Yeah. Hymns, psalms, prayers – the lot. And Preacher John gives a sermon. Then you'll see what we're talking about.'

Baz let out a deep breath. 'Jesus . . .'

'Yeah, and you better watch how you use that word as well,' said Amit.

'Taking the Lord's name in vain, it's called,' said Dyson. 'So try not to. OK. Any questions?'

'What about food?' Ray seemed to have this at the top of his list.

'Tin a day,' said Dyson. 'What you've just had – that's it till tomorrow night.'

'Whaaaat?'

'Get used to it. At least you're not likely to grow much while you're here, and that's good, 'cos if you did grow, then you wouldn't *be* here. Big kids get shipped back – they cost too much to feed and they're more likely to cause trouble.' Dyson nodded at Jubo. 'There's a couple of us here now a bit bigger than we should be. Like me and Jubo. We gotta watch out. Keep our noses extra clean.'

Baz looked at Jubo's nose, all smeared in mud, but said nothing.

Amit said, 'It's not usually tomatoes. Steiner just did that to get back at you. It's nearly always beans – maybe a coupla tins of stew thrown in to give us something to work for. You saw what happened tonight – top dogs get first choice, after the Genius. And sometimes you get lucky – maybe manage to smuggle something out of the sort room. Sardines are easiest 'cos the tins are small. But then you have to watch your breath, 'cos it'll stink of fish. And you have to get rid of the tin. And if you get caught you're done for.'

Dyson stood up and stretched himself, eyes closed, fists clenched above his head. Despite his shoulder-length girlish hair he was a tough-looking kid, tall and wiry. Too tall to get a place on the boat, Baz would have judged, if he was to try now.

'One of you take 'em down and show them the jakes.' Dyson yawned. 'Then we'll go through the names again, and that'll have to be it. Go on, Robbie. You do it. I'm knackered.'

Knackered. Was that not a cuss word, then? There was obviously a fine line between what was acceptable and what was not. Baz got to his feet, along with Ray, and they both followed the ginger-haired boy called Robbie.

CHAPTER FOUR

What Dyson had called the 'jakes' turned out to be the washroom. This was behind the curtained-off doorway at the other end of the room. There were two lavatory cubicles, a sink and a shower – quite impressive at first sight, if not especially clean.

Robbie pointed up at the window. 'We got running water,' he said. 'Sort of.'

A length of hosepipe led in through an open quarterlight. It was looped over the shower rail and fitted with some kind of garden hose attachment. An oval tin bath stood in the shower tray. The bath was full of water.

'You just turn on the hose,' said Robbie, 'if you want a wash. Or stand in the tub if you want a shower. But if you want to wash your bum, you fill that red bucket with water from the tub and use that. Tip it down the pan. We got soap over there on the windowsill, and toothpaste. We share that. Spit down the pan. You want to wash your clothes, you do it in the tub. Hang 'em on one of the lines to dry, back in the slob room. Got it?'

Baz looked round at the red bucket. 'Yeah.'

'Try not to waste water. We got enough of it, but it all has to be carried. See that scaffolding outside the window? There's a big water butt up there. We have to carry water down from the rain butts up at the sports centre and cart it up a ladder to fill the shower butt. The divers have got one as well, and the capos too. It's hard work. You'll be on water duty soon enough. You'll find out.'

'Who are the capos?'

'Steiner and Hutchinson.'

'Oh. And the water – you can drink it?'

'Yeah, it's just rainwater. It's OK. A lot better than back on the mainland. Get yourself a plastic bottle and fill it from the shower hose. It's fine.'

'What about the sink?' said Ray.

'Don't use it.'

Baz studied the plumbing arrangements for a little longer. 'It's really good,' he said.

'Yeah, it was all Gene's idea. He rigged it up. Course, then he had to do the same thing for the divers and the capos, so it ended up being a load more work for us. Worth it though.'

Robbie seemed a friendly guy – helpful, happy to talk. His skin was unusually dark for a red-head, his nose flat and broad, as if whoever had put him together had got the bits muddled up. He wore khaki shorts, as all the boys did, and battered trainers. No shirt, no socks. But then in this heat that was all you really needed.

'You wanna try it out?' he said. 'You're both pretty bloody.'

Baz had forgotten that he'd got covered in blood on

the boat, though he would have thought the rain would have washed most of it off. 'Yeah, OK.'

'Yeah.' Ray stood on tiptoe and turned on the shower hose. The water poured steadily out.

'So, Amit and Dyson . . .' said Baz. 'Are they like in charge or something?'

'Nah. They're often top dogs though. Top dogs get picked at the end of the shift – whoever the capos reckon have worked the hardest. They get first go at the tins, after Gene.' Robbie stepped into one of the cubicles for a pee, and his voice echoed around the washroom.

'Top dogs get to choose their crew for the next day. We usually keep to the same teams though.'

'So what about that guy Gene?' Baz remembered the boy who had been allowed first pick of the food. 'Is he like a top dog all the time?'

'Kind of. Gene's clever. They wouldn't get rid of him in a hurry.'

Baz decided that he might as well pee while he was waiting for Ray to finish washing his face. He went into the cubicle that Robbie was now coming out of. There was no seat on the toilet bowl, and it didn't look too clean down there, but it was better than things had been in the house where he and his dad lived.

When he came out, Ray was shaking the water off his hands, and Robbie was standing watching him.

'You need to go?' Robbie said to Ray, nodding towards the cubicles.

'Nah. I'm all right.'

'OK. You get washed up then, Baz.'

Baz scooped water from the trickling shower hose

and remained with his hands pressed against his face for a few moments. It felt good.

'OK. Let's go.'

But as they ducked through the curtain, Ray said, 'Maybe I need to pee after all.'

'Sheesh,' said Robbie. 'Make up your mind.'

It was a lot to remember, but Baz was pretty sure he'd got it straight. He sat leaning against the wall, finishing off the last of his tomatoes and putting names to faces. All the boys were getting ready for bed now, and Baz let his gaze travel up one side of the room and down the other.

The boy they called Taps was in the bed closest to his. A nervous-looking kid, small and pale. The most striking thing about him was his dark wavy hair, quite short at the back and sides, but piled up in such a great mass on top that it made his head seem too big for his body. Taps sat staring into space with his knees drawn up. His hands patted gently against his ankles, first one then the other, and his mouth was moving silently, as though he were counting.

Enoch was in the next bed along. What sort of a name was Enoch? It sounded old fashioned, like something from the Bible. And Enoch looked kind of ancient somehow, with his wizened little face and hooked nose. After that came Robbie, and then Amit at the very end of the row.

Starting from the top on the other side was Gene. The genius. Then Dyson and Jubo. And that was it.

Baz still couldn't understand why there weren't more, but he was pleased that he could remember those that were here. Steiner and Hutchinson he wasn't likely to forget – nor Isaac. When it came to the other two brothers, Amos and Luke, he wasn't quite sure which was which. But he'd be able to figure it out.

'Wanna test me?' he said to Ray.

'Huh?' Ray was flicking something up into the air with his thumb and catching it again. A pasta quill.

Baz hadn't thought to ask about that. Was dried pasta still currency here on the island, then? He'd brought forty-four pieces, wrapped in a polythene bag. Forty pasta would buy you a tin of curry in the mainland markets . . .

'Test me on the names,' he said.

'What?' Ray continued to flick his pasta piece into the air.

But then Dyson suddenly appeared, ducking his head beneath the nearest line of washing.

'Lock-up's supposed to be at ten,' he said. 'That's whenever Hutchinson can be bothered to turn up, so let's have a run-through on names. Ray – go ahead. See how many you can remember.'

Ray sighed. 'OK. There's Taps, Enoch, Robbie, Amit, Cookie, Gene and Jubo. The divers are Isaac, Luke, Amos, Moko. Capos – Steiner and Hutchinson. And you. Dyson.'

'Friggin' hell,' said Dyson. '*You're* good.' He turned to Baz. 'Reckon you've got it too?'

'Yeah,' said Baz. 'No problem.' But he was annoyed. He'd forgotten about the absent Cookie. 'I got a couple more questions, though. What about pasta?'

'No good,' said Dyson. 'You can't buy anything with pasta here.'

'Oh. OK. One more thing – how come you've got electricity?'

Dyson looked up at the light bulb. 'Genny,' he said. 'A generator. They don't keep it going all the time, just in the evenings. Runs on diesel, and it powers the lights and everything. Cheaper than burning candles or tilley lamps. They use it for the compressor too.'

'What's the compressor?'

'Compressed air. To fill the divers' air tanks. Don't know how it works exactly, but Gene'd tell you. If Preacher John ever ran out of diesel, though, he'd be stuffed. I know that much.'

Dyson's words faded away as he turned his head round further. The door had opened and someone was coming in. Baz leaned sideways to get a better view.

It was the fat boy in the white jacket, Cookie, followed by Hutchinson.

'OK, all of you – slob-down!' Hutchinson remained in the doorway, his hand on the light switch. 'Dyson and Amit to pick crews in the morning. Four on the jetty, four in the sort room. One newbie apiece. Cookie, stop fannying about and get yourself sorted.'

'But I need to go to the washroom.' Cookie's voice was a whine of complaint. He was down on all fours, looking through his belongings.

'Do it in the dark then, ya big lump.' The light went out and the door closed.

There was silence for a few moments, and then a low mocking chorus of voices began.

'Coo-kie . . . Coo-kie . . .'

'Yo! Sir Plus!'

'Cook-cook-cookeeee . . .'

Baz propped himself up on one elbow. The darkness wasn't quite total, and he could see movement, the shadowy bulk of a figure stumbling closer. Cookie was making his way blindly down through the room, ducking to avoid the lines of washing. Baz heard the flat thump of bare feet on the carpet tiles, and wheezy laboured breathing. The washroom curtain was drawn aside, and Cookie disappeared.

The mocking voices dissolved into general chatter.

'Amit – get out of Enoch's bed. I know you're in there.'

'Yeah, leave her alone, you homo.'

'But she likes it!'

'Ha, ha!'

'Naff off.'

Baz wasn't yet familiar enough with the voices to know exactly who was speaking. He peered into the darkness and listened.

'God, my hands are killing me from hauling that rubble about.'

'Get Amit to kiss 'em better.'

'Yeah, yeah. Very funny.'

'Hey – did any of you see that packet of cornflakes that came in today? I couldn't believe it.'

'Yeah. Came in with the newbies. Oi – newbies! Whose were the cornflakes?'

Baz waited for Ray to reply, but there was no sound from the next bed and so he said, 'They were Ray's. He brought them.'

'Can't he speak for himself, then? What – he asleep already?'

But then the curtain was drawn aside and Cookie

reappeared, the sound of his breathing heavy and asthmatic. He ran the gauntlet of jeers and hoots once again as he headed back towards his bed.

'Hey, Sir Plus, mind where you're going.'

'*God*, yeah. Please don't fall on us, Cookie! We're too young to die!'

Cookie made no reply that Baz could hear. Eventually he must have got to his bed. At any rate the voices died away, and all became silent again.

Baz lay back and stared up into the darkness. He was tired, but there was too much going on in his head for him to be able to sleep just yet.

X Isle. This had been his goal for the last year, and yet he hadn't imagined that it would be anything like this. He'd thought that it would be a refuge. A safe haven. And he'd expected there to be a lot more than just ten boys here. He must have seen at least ten or twelve get on the boat from his area of the mainland alone. How could that be? And what would his dad do, or say, or think, if he could see this place? *Dad. I miss you already* . . .

'Uh-oh!'

'*Uh*-oh!'

'Blue angel alert!'

'Look out, lads, she's flying tonight!'

'*Uh*-oh!'

Baz sat up again. What was going on now? He heard the faint click of a cigarette lighter from about halfway down the room . . . saw flickering shapes in sudden illumination . . . a confusion of shadows, hard to make out. A body? Yes, but strangely contorted, legs pointing up towards the ceiling . . .

It was Robbie, lying upside down in nothing but his shorts, his backside raised into the air, knees up around his ears. Baz caught a glimpse of bare ankles waving about before the lighter flame was abruptly extinguished and the room went black.

'Ohh . . .' Groans of disappointment. But then the lighter wheel sparked up again, throwing bright asterisks into the darkness, and *whoomff* . . .

A burgeoning sheet of blue flame appeared from Robbie's bum, springing forth like an unbottled genie, a fiery will o' the wisp that leaped and danced in brief abandon before swallowing itself, disappearing into its own vacuum. There and gone.

'Yay! Good one, Robbie!'

'The blue angel!'

'How come I can never do 'em as good as that?'

Baz remained leaning on one elbow, staring into the shadows in amazement. Lighting your own farts! He'd heard of such a thing, but had never actually seen it done before. Wow.

'Hey! I got one! It's coming . . . it's coming . . .'

'Uh-oh.'

'*Uh*-oh.'

Another lighter sparked up – from the far side of the room this time. Someone else was having a go. Jubo. He too had propped himself into an upside-down bicycling position, buttocks in the air, and as the lighter flame steadied, he said, 'Ey! Here we go . . . here we go . . .'

Jubo's effort was even more spectacular than Robbie's had been – a flaring jet of blue and yellow that roared out of him like a bunsen burner, a blowtorch, a fire-eater's incandescent belch. *Whurrffff* . . . the flame launched itself into the darkness and disappeared. Absolutely amazing. And amazing that Jubo hadn't blown his insides apart in the process, thought Baz. Wasn't it supposed to be really dangerous?

'Christ, Jubo! Were those *curried* beans you got tonight?'

'Ha! Blue angel or *what*, man? Respec' to the champ!'

'Yeah, yeah. I got one brewing make that look like a fairy fart.'

'Ey – newbies! See what it does to your guts living here? Got anything for us yet? You soon will.'

Baz considered the state of his own inner workings, but decided that any rumbles he felt down there were merely hunger. He peered towards Ray's bed.

'Ray – you awake?'

There was a pause before Ray replied. 'What do you think?'

'You been watching this?'

'Yeah, sure. Like I'd be interested. Go to sleep.'

Baz bit his tongue for what seemed like the umpteenth time today. There was just no talking to the guy sometimes.

'Uh-oh!'

'*Uh*-oh!'

Another lighter flared into life . . . and then another . . .

And now it seemed that they were all at it. Demon shadows chased each other up the walls and across the ceiling as boy after boy attempted to ignite his own body gas. It was like some weird firework display or

Halloween thing – the rasping flick of lighter wheels, the twisted shapes and shadows of the boys, and the occasional ballooning bursts of flame.

Some efforts were more successful than others, and there were accompanying hoots of mockery or approval.

'Hey – good one, Dyse! Woo-ee!'

'Yah! You call that a fart, guy? Me little sister do better than that.'

'Hey – watch this! I'm going for the rocket!'

'The rocket! The rocket! Come on, Amit. Countdown! Ten! Nine . . .'

'Eight . . . seven . . .' Other voices chimed in.

Amit was upright, standing on one leg and bouncing gently up and down on his mattress in time to the loud chanting around him. With his other leg hugged close to his chest and his cigarette lighter waving around his backside, he looked more like a demented stork than a rocket.

'. . . four . . . three . . . two . . . one . . .'

'Lift-off!'

Frrrr-rrr-rrrt. The high-pitched sound of escaping rocket fuel was audible enough, but Amit had got his timing wrong somehow. The lighter simply went out and Amit could be heard collapsing onto his mattress with a thump, cursing in the darkness.

'Damn! No way!'

'Ha, ha! Amit blew it!'

'Blew it out, you mean! Amit, you're friggin' useless!'

'Er . . . Houston, we have a problem . . .'

'Ha, ha . . . yeah—'

The chatter came to a sudden halt. A pause – a rapid shuffle of bedclothes – and then silence. Instant breathless silence. Some signal, some squeak of the door handle perhaps, must have given the boys warning, for the light that came streaming in from the far corridor fell upon rows of bodies that now lay stiff and still as those in a morgue.

Baz was still sitting up – hadn't had time to react. A huge swaying bulk filled the doorway, throwing a shadow down the centre of the room, so long that it reached the foot of his bed.

Isaac.

There was a glint of light on glass – a bottle in the skipper's fist – and as Baz shrank down onto his mattress, he saw the bottle being lifted high. It seemed to him that he was the focus of Isaac's fearful glare.

A pause, and then Isaac flung the bottle towards the middle of the room. Baz automatically ducked. He heard the roar of Isaac's voice above the sound of breaking glass as the missile smashed onto the floor, its broken shards bouncing and skittering along the carpet tiles.

'Graaagh! Now belt up, the lot of you – I can hear you down t'bottom end o' t' corridor! You're here to *work*, not to sod about! Or maybe you don't have enough to do? Is that it? Well, I'll soon change that. You can all start an hour early in t' morning. Aye, and you'll stay in your ruddy beds till then – unless you fancy picking bits o' glass out o' your feet!'

The door slammed shut and Isaac was gone. From the carpet arose a strong smell of whisky, heady fumes that filled the darkness.

It was a long while before anyone moved. Eventually there were a few creaks and shuffles, the sounds of bodies turning over on their mattresses, bedclothes being rearranged . . . deep sighs . . . and then silence.

Baz let out his breath and curled up into a ball, his blanket wrapped protectively around his bare shoulders. But the heat was too stifling for this, and anyway the blanket reeked. It stank of mildew and old sweat, and it was unbearably itchy, the texture of it prickling against his skin. Baz scratched his neck two or three times, then his ear. God, it was driving him crazy – almost as if—

Ugh! Now he understood. The blanket was crawling with *lice*. He threw the thing off him in disgust and scratched furiously at his head, his arms, his legs. There wasn't a part of him that didn't require attention. Finally he lay down again, on his back this time, spreading himself into a star shape in order to try and cool off. He must get some sleep.

But the thoughts and images that came jangling through his head were too frightening to allow him any peace. This place was dangerous. Not a factory, but a madhouse. Once again he heard Steiner's voice, chanting at his heels: *Dead . . . dead . . . dead.* Steiner might have carried out his threat already if Isaac hadn't been there to stop him. And who would stop Isaac? Who was going to pull Isaac off – a man who used whatever weapons came to hand, guns and whisky bottles alike?

He should quit now. Try and get back to the mainland while he was still in one piece. But the thought of what it had cost his dad to get him here, and what it might cost to get him back again, made him feel bad. He knew how hard it was on his dad, continually trying to find enough food for the two of them. No, running away after less than twenty-four hours would be weak and stupid. He'd have to stick it out, for a while at least. Try to.

Some tiny sound caught his attention. Baz turned his head towards Ray's bed, listening. There it was again, a brief shiver of movement, almost lost among the snores and grunts of the other sleepers. Bad dream, probably. That was some hammering Ray had taken today, poor kid. He was a tough one, though. No way was he going to give up, and you had to admire him for that . . .

A sniff. He'd definitely heard a sniff. Baz rolled over onto his side.

'Ray?' He kept his voice to a whisper. 'You OK?' There was no reply, and after a few moments of hesitation Baz reached out in the darkness. His fingertips found the rough texture of Ray's blanket, and for a moment he was sure he'd felt it quivering. But then there was a startled jerk of movement. Baz pulled back his hand.

'What the hell are you doing?' Ray's voice sounded angry, suspicious. But not weepy.

'Nothing. Nothing . . . I just wondered if you were all right. I thought you were—'

'What? Course I'm all right. What's the matter with you?'

'Nothing. Sorry. It sounded as if you were—'

'Well, just keep your hands off me, OK?'

'Sorry . . .'

Baz shrank back onto his mattress. He wished he hadn't said anything – wished he could wipe out the last few moments and start again. In fact he wished he could wipe out the whole day and start again. Not get on the boat. Not meet Ray. Not come here at all. Since saying goodbye to his dad he'd been shot at, half strangled, punched, given death threats . . .

And what had he done wrong? He'd tried to be friendly, tried to look out for Ray, someone smaller and weaker than himself. But he'd just ended up being slapped down and made to look stupid. Right now he could be sitting with his dad, the two of them together in their room, playing cards, sharing a bit of food, whatever his dad had managed to win . . .

Except that he couldn't. There wasn't enough food for two, and that was why he was here – alone and friendless in the dark – the smell of whisky in his nostrils and the hot sting of tears in the corners of his eyes.

CHAPTER FIVE

The urgent clamour of an alarm bell brought him from the depths of sleep, dragging him upwards amid a swirl of images: Mum walking into his bedroom with a cup of tea . . . cereal packets on the kitchen table . . . lunchbox . . . uniform . . .

School! It was time to go to school.

Baz opened his eyes and jerked upright just as the alarm clock stopped ringing. Was he late?

But of course there was no school. He'd forgotten. No school, no Mum, no anything. There was only this. A roomful of strangers, an empty feeling in his belly, and the stale smell of alcohol.

He had reason to be grateful for the whisky fumes at least. They reminded him that there was broken glass on the floor. As Baz fumbled around in the semi-darkness for his shorts and trainers, he glanced towards the huddled-up bundle on the mattress next to him – Ray.

'Watch out for the glass,' he mumbled. The back of his mouth was dry and sore, and it tasted of metal.

No reply came from the next bed, and Baz realized that Ray wasn't there. Could he have run away in the night? No. Even as the thought occurred to him, Ray appeared, ducking beneath the makeshift curtain as he came out of the jakes – already washed and dressed, apparently.

'Christ. You're up early.' Baz pulled trainers onto his bare feet.

'Yeah, I always am. Makes no difference what time I go to bed, I always wake up at stupid-o'clock. It drives me nuts. You snore like a pig, by the way.'

Baz didn't say anything to this. He stood up and peered around the room. The rest of the boys were only now beginning to stir – grumbling and muttering as blankets were thrown aside. He saw that Taps was awake and sitting up, a forlorn and tousled little figure in the dingy light.

'Hey, Taps,' said Baz. 'What happens now?'

'Pardon?' Taps rubbed his eyes. 'What did you say?'

'I said what happens now?'

'We have fifteen minutes to be outside the sort room.' There was something slightly odd in the way Taps spoke. Quite careful and precise, as though he were reading from a piece of paper.

'OK.' Baz nodded and made his way into the jakes.

Steiner and Hutchinson appeared as the boys were congregating in the corridor outside the door to the sort room. The capos looked bleary-eyed, and more sour-faced than ever.

'Right then, thanks to you lot we've all got to start an hour early,' snarled Steiner. 'And Hutch and me get a rollocking for not keeping you in line – too soft on you, Isaac says. We'll soon see about that. Amit, you're on t' jetty. Dyson in t' sort room. Dyson, take first pick.'

'Jubo.' Dyson spoke without hesitation. This was obviously a well-worn routine.

'Robbie,' said Amit.

'Enoch.'

'Taps.'

'Er . . .' Dyson looked from Baz to Ray – the only two now remaining. 'Er . . . I'll take Ray.'

'OK. Baz,' said Amit, 'you're with me.'

Baz had been surprised not to have been chosen first. He was sure he must be stronger than Ray. Why would Dyson have picked the weakest?

'OK.' Steiner looked straight at Ray. 'So today you got lucky. You're in t' sort room. But tomorrow you'll be with me. On t' jetty.'

It sounded as if the jetty was the tougher option. Maybe that was why Dyson had picked Ray.

Hutchinson unlocked the door to the sort room. 'Dyson, get your lot in there,' he said. 'The rest of you go on up to the sports centre.'

'Yeah,' said Steiner. 'And I want to see you back down on t' jetty with t' first load o' blocks in ten minutes.'

So Baz was one of four climbing the steep asphalt path that apparently led up to the sports centre. Amit, Robbie, Taps and himself.

'What's at the sports centre?' he asked.

'Stone and rubble and stuff,' said Amit. 'They were building a new science block when it all happened.'

'So that's where the stone for the jetty comes from? We have to carry it down?'

'Yeah.'

'What, in wheelbarrows?'

'Yeah, listen, mate. Don't talk so much, OK? It's too early in the morning, and we've got a hell of a long day ahead of us.'

'Sorry.' Baz took a swig from his water bottle. It was still only about seven-thirty, and the island was hung in mist, but already he was sweating from the humidity.

At the top of the hill was an area of flat open ground. There were tennis nets and rusty goalposts rising amongst the tangle of overgrown grass and nettles. This must have once been the school playing field. A big modern building with a curved corrugated roof stood at the far end of the field, and next to that the beginnings of another construction – tall iron stanchions set into concrete. Baz could see a couple of diggers and a cement-mixer truck, grey shapes in the mist, and beyond them a group of trees. A small wood, perhaps, or a copse.

And that was the extent of the island. From up here the sea was visible whichever way you looked, an endless circular horizon. Closer to the shores were the half-submerged ruins of buildings that had once dotted the slopes of Tab Hill. The only structure that had survived was the school itself, standing just that bit higher up the hill than its neighbours.

A flash of white caught Baz's eye – something popping up from among the tall grass, out towards the middle of the overgrown playing field.

'What . . . what's that thing?' said Baz. But even as he asked, he saw that it was an animal of some kind. A sheep? No, a white goat.

'Oh, it's only Old Bill,' said Amit. He laughed. 'That was some kid called Yusuf's ticket here. His old man was a butcher or something.'

'What happened to him?'

'Who, Yusuf? Couldn't hack it. Sent back at the end of his first week.'

'Oh. So the goat – it just lives in the field?' said Baz.

'Yeah. Surprised Preacher John hasn't eaten it yet. Mind you, Cookie'd have to catch it first. I can just see Cookie chasing round after Old Bill with a meat cleaver. Ha.'

They followed the pathway round the perimeter of the field, and the full extent of the construction site came into view: mountains of rubble and chippings, massive stacks of building blocks, timber, scaffolding poles.

'See the roof of that place – the sports centre?' said Amit. 'We get most of our water from that. Gene rigged it so that all the rain that comes off the roof goes into those blue barrels 'stead of down the drains.'

Baz looked at where Amit was pointing. He could see six plastic barrels, arranged in pairs along the side of the building with the huge corrugated roof. The barrels were mounted on stacks of concrete blocks, and had downpipes leading into them.

'There's more on the other side,' said Amit. 'We got a couple outside the main building too, but they don't work as good, so we have to cart water from here to fill the shower butts. It's a pig.'

'Yeah. Robbie told me.'

'Right. Well, water duty's three times a week – Monday, Thursday, Saturday. Takes four of us to do it.

You get one week on, one week off. You'll be on next week – if you last that long. Come on.'

'So what's in the sports centre?'

'Swimming pool and stuff. It's all locked up though. You can't get in there.'

Robbie and Taps were already pulling wheel-barrows from a stack that leaned against a pallet of concrete blocks.

'What are we on today, Amit?' said Robbie. 'Blocks or rubble?'

'Er . . . blocks, I guess. OK, Baz. Grab a barrow and just do like we do. Four blocks at a time. I'll show you.'

After the third journey Baz was beginning to get the knack of it. He copied the other boys, stacking the concrete blocks into the front of the barrow so that most of the weight was over the front wheel. This made the load easier to lift, although if the blocks were too far forward, the whole thing became unstable and likely to tip over. The barrow then had to be pushed around the playing fields and down the steep path to the jetty. Keeping it upright on the descent was the hardest bit, and Baz's arms and shoulders were already aching from the effort.

The jetty extended about thirty metres out into the foggy sea – the same long mound of stone and rubble that Baz had seen the night before, topped with its flattened pathway of pinkish-coloured chippings.

Here stood Steiner, directing operations. The boys brought their barrows to the edge of the pathway and tipped their contents down the bank of rubble towards the scummy water. It wasn't easy to raise the handles with enough force to shoot the load of blocks any distance, and Baz, teetering on the brink, was wary lest Steiner decide to trip him or give him a push at the last second. But Steiner seemed content to do no more than yell at him.

'*Tip* it, you little turd, don't just lift it!'

The process was long and slow and laborious, each circuit taking between ten and fifteen minutes and each load of four blocks making only the slightest difference to the overall construction. By mid morning Baz was dizzy with fatigue and lack of food. He didn't see how he was going to keep this up until evening.

'Don't we get a break?' He was third in the chain of boys, staggering down the hill with a loaded barrow for the umpteenth time. Taps was ahead of him, and Robbie brought up the rear. Taps was muttering to himself as he walked, a constant low and rhythmic drone. With his massive head of hair wobbling about above his skinny white body, he looked like a tadpole.

'Yeah.' Baz heard Robbie's panting voice behind him. 'Gotta be time for a rest. Hey, Taps – how many loads do you make it?'

'Thirteen. Two hundred and eight blocks. Seven-six-two . . . seven-six-three . . .' Taps's voice faded back to a mutter once more. What was he doing?

'Christ.' Robbie drew level with Baz as the path broadened. 'We usually get a break about every ten loads. Wouldn't get that 'cept that Steiner wants to sneak off and look at his porno mags. So he's got it in for us all right – gonna make us work all friggin' day, looks like.'

But this time, as Baz tipped his load of blocks over

the edge of the jetty, he heard Steiner say to Amit, 'OK, break it up. Back here in half an hour with the next load.'

'See?' muttered Robbie as the gang made their way back up the hill. 'He had to crack in the end. Look out, Miss July.'

'Ha. Yeah, right.'

Baz didn't understand this last exchange, but for the moment he was too tired to ask questions.

They threw themselves into the long grass and lay flat out, staring up at the white featureless sky. Nobody spoke. After a while Baz rolled onto his side and examined the state of his hands. His palms were red, though not yet blistered, and the skin on his fingertips was becoming rough and sore from continually lifting the breeze blocks.

'Bad?' Amit had turned sideways to look at him.

Baz nodded. 'Could be worse, though.'

'Yeah, well, it'll get worse. There's a medicine box in the slob room with plasters and stuff – under the sink. You can fix yourself up later. But that's another rule: you don't get sick. If you can't work, they just send you back.'

The sound of a diesel engine drifted up from far below – *dub-dub-dubdub* . . .

'Is that the boat?' said Baz.

'Yeah. Diving day today. They dive Monday, Wednesday, Friday. Trade Tuesday, Thursday, Saturday. They're usually late back, diving days, so it'll be tomorrow morning before we have to unload whatever they bring back tonight. Clean it and sort it. And the other crew'll be on the barrows.'

'Right.' Baz tried to imagine how Ray was going to cope with this. But if weedy Taps could manage it, then maybe anyone could. He drank the last of his water and said, 'Can I go and fill this up from one of the water butts?'

'Sure,' said Amit. 'You can do mine as well while you're about it. Make it quick, though. We gotta start again in a few minutes. Three shifts to go. Next break we'll try for a few blackberries over in the copse.'

As Baz stood up to go, Robbie said, 'Hey, Baz . . ' He raised an empty Coke bottle. 'Do mine, willya?'

'OK. Er . . . what about you, Taps? You want some water?'

Taps sat up and looked around. 'Beg pardon?' The kid seemed like he was in a permanent daze.

'I'm gonna get some water,' said Baz. 'You want some?'

'Oh. Um, no thank you. It isn't time for my water yet.'

Baz glanced down at Taps's empty water bottle lying beside him on the grass. He might have said something more, but then he caught a look from Robbie – a pursing of the lips, a tiny shake of the head.

'OK.' Baz collected the offered bottles and made his way over towards the nearest of the water butts.

At the next break Baz was too dizzy and exhausted to even think. He collapsed with the others onto the patch of flattened grass, his head throbbing, forearm thrown across his eyes . . . and immediately saw an angel . . .

The angel was blue, transparent, a ghostly figure sailing horizontally above a darkened landscape. Huge storm clouds were coming over the skyline, rolling and boiling like smoke from a million burning tyres. The angel floated past him from left to right, and at the last moment before disappearing she turned her head and spoke to him. Baz could see the angel's lips moving but couldn't catch the words, because now the storm was crashing towards him – just like before – and this time it got him. He was flung this way and that, caught up in the huge waves, helpless, choking, drowning . . .

'For Christ's sake, Robbie. Over his forehead, not up his soddin' nose.'

Baz sat up, spluttering, half blinded. Robbie was kneeling beside him with a water bottle poised in mid air.

'What the hell are you doing?' Baz coughed and wiped his streaming face.

'Trying to wake you up, that's what. You've been asleep nearly half an hour.'

'Jesus. I thought I was drowning . . .'

'Eat some of these. The sugar will help give you energy.'

Someone was standing over him, offering him something in cupped hands. But the hands were so strangely coloured: inky blues and deep magentas. Baz brought his waterlogged vision into focus. It was Taps, reaching out towards him, his palms full of blackberries.

Load . . . walk . . . tip . . . walk . . . load . . .

Round and round the cycle continued, the hours

passing in a tingling haze, his body locked into continual movement and almost numbed by it. Follow the person in front of you, stay ahead of the one behind. That was all you had to do: keep moving.

The final break was the worst. Stretched out on the grass, motionless, Baz felt as though he had collapsed in the middle of a desert. The pain that had circled him while he was still walking now descended upon him like a vulture, tearing at his palms and fingertips, at his neck and shoulders and legs, rending him apart tendon by tendon, shred by shred. He was a bloodied carcass, flayed to the bone, helpless . . .

'Come on, Baz. Last shift.'

Up again somehow, and now the wheelbarrow handles felt as though they were poker-hot, burning into his raw palms, the weight of the breeze blocks threatening to pull his arms from their sockets. But still he kept going. And going.

In the late afternoon the skies opened and the steep tarmacked pathway became a treacherous torrent of water. Baz found it impossible to grip the slippery handles of the wheelbarrow, and he continually stumbled and fell, watching his load slide down the hill time and again. It broke him. The rain struck the top of his unprotected head with such force that it felt as though iron rods were bouncing off his skull, and he knew that he could do no more. Baz teetered and wobbled along the chipping pathway of the jetty, ready to throw himself into the sea along with his load of blocks rather than ever climb that hill again.

But perhaps the rain that finally bludgeoned him into submission also saved his life – because it didn't fall on him alone. It fell on all around him, Steiner included.

'OK, that's enough!' the capo's hoarse voice yelled above the roar of the deluge. 'Pack it in! Take the barrows back up top, and then get to the sort room.' Steiner hurried away towards the school building, one arm over his head for protection.

So the torture was at an end. The hill still had to be negotiated one more time, but knowing that it would be the last time gave Baz the will to find strength from somewhere. He tipped his blocks down into the sea. The power of the falling rain made the surface of the water look as though it were boiling, covered in a blanket of steam. Baz stood gazing at it for a few moments, then turned round.

OK, then. One last effort.

They stacked their wheelbarrows against a pallet of breeze blocks and staggered back down the hill, a wordless gang of scarecrows. Flip flop, flip flop. Baz was concentrating wholly on keeping his knees from buckling. The pain was another issue, something to be put aside and dealt with later. All his thinking was in his knee-joints. Don't let them bend too far. Just stay upright.

Here are the steps to the school. One-two, one-two. Here's the shelter of the entranceway, and there goes the hammering rain, behind them now.

The door to the sort room was open. Amit paused there for a moment, perhaps waiting for some un-spoken permission to enter, then led the way in.

They congregated by the workbench, intermingling

with the other boys, heads down, water still streaming from them. Baz stared at the pool forming at his feet, watched it grow and break away, trickling in zigzags across the dusty floor to join another pool at the feet of the boy standing nearest to him: Taps.

'What d'you think then, Steiner?' Hutchinson said. 'Reckon this lot'll give us any more trouble? Reckon they'll be up for more fun and games tonight? Another early start tomorrow?'

Steiner said, 'Couldn't give a stuff. It's up to them. Yeah, OK, Taps, you can get the tins. I want t' same as last night – three meat, two spaghetti, two beans, two tomatoes.'

Baz raised his head. So here it was again – the food game. A moment of panic ran through him. If he was going to survive, then it was going to have to be on something more substantial than tomatoes. No way could he get through another day without food. And tomatoes didn't count as food. Think, then.

Taps collected tins from various crates, counting them as he went, his mouth moving in silent whispers. He was slow, and it gave Baz a chance to study the faces around him, weigh up the competition. The other boys were watching Taps too. Only Ray met his eye, with an expression of – what? Sympathy? Worry? Baz turned away, trying to clear the wooziness in his head, to concentrate on the matter in hand. It was crucial that he figure out the odds, find some kind of strategy . . .

The tins were on the floor. Taps took up his former place, shuffling into the circle next to Baz.

'OK, Gene,' said Steiner. 'You first.'

Gene stepped forward, same as he had yesterday, and took one of the three tins of meat. B/STEW. Baz studied the pattern and positions of the remaining tins. He inched a little closer to Taps.

'Who's your top dog, Steiner?' Hutchinson shifted his clipboard from one arm to the other. Baz was alive to every twitch of movement in the room. He'd already made his decision – and his plan. He would go for the spag, the tin that was positioned between the two toms. Instinct and reasoning told him that it was least likely to be anyone else's first choice. So concentrate on that and forget the rest.

'Got no top dog,' said Steiner.

What? This was a deviation from yesterday's pattern. Baz tensed himself.

''Cos they're a total bunch of crap, the lot of 'em. All-of-you-ready-go!'

Baz was straight off the mark. He crashed into Taps, a deliberate and vicious shoulder-barge that sent the smaller boy spinning, and threw himself into a dive across the floor. His hand was on the tin of spaghetti so quickly, and so far ahead of the other flailing bodies, that it was almost a disappointment. He could have probably gone for the meat after all. As it was he still had time to knock a tin of beans away from Enoch and roll it towards Ray's scrabbling fingers.

'Hey!' Enoch's aggrieved voice was muffled in the general struggle. Baz untangled himself from the melee and stood up. But then one of his knees suddenly sagged and he wondered if he actually *could* stand up. He took an unsteady pace backwards, fell against the workbench, and remained there, using the bench for support. By now the others were back on their feet, each clutching whatever tin they had managed to get. Baz was aware of the looks that were directed towards him, the bewilderment of Taps, the outrage of Enoch, the gratitude of Ray, the scowling disappointment of Steiner. But he ignored them all.

He felt his breathing begin to relax into normality, and was amazed at himself. Shocked. He had entered this room barely able to stay upright, was struggling even now, and yet when it came to pure survival he had found some reserve of animal energy deep within him. And an animal he had momentarily become.

'OK,' said Hutchinson. 'Back to the slob room.'

Baz pushed himself away from the workbench. He held his tin of spaghetti close, and focused on the open doorway ahead of him, taking it one step at a time.

Deep down he cared only about himself. Lying on his bed, unable to move, this was what he was starting to realize. He would do whatever was necessary to save his own skin, and if anybody got in his way, then tough. His assault on Taps was proof of that. A boy who had done him no harm, a boy who had collected blackberries for him out of sympathy. But what shocked him more than anything was how calculating he could be. Even in the act of helping Ray he had known that he was actually thinking of his own well-being. Because if Ray had proper food – something other than tomatoes – then there would be no question of feeling obliged to share his own food with him. And he had understood this in the moment that he had flicked the tin of beans away from Enoch.

Baz allowed his eyelids to droop. Had he always been this selfish? And was everybody else just as bad?

'Look after number one,' his dad had said. But could that be right? Baz was too tired to think about it any more. Or to care.

His head spun away into the darkness, rolling over and over across the heavens, and he left the low murmuring voices of the other boys far behind him. But after what only seemed like a few moments he was tense and alert again. He'd felt something touching his hands, his fingers being gently prised apart. Someone was after his food!

'Gerroff me . . . you friggin' thief!' Baz lashed out against his molester, opened his eyes, tried to sit up . . .

The bare light bulb danced above his head, scribbling wild patterns across his vision.

'Whoa – it's OK. I'm just . . . just trying to . . .'

It was Ray, kneeling beside him. 'Look – I've got some plasters and stuff.'

'What?'

'Plasters. There were some under the sink. You're all bloody.'

Baz lay back down again and let out a long breath.

'For Chrissake, Ray. I was asleep. Ow – what are you playing at?' Baz felt sudden renewed pain in his hands. Ray had pressed a damp cloth, a T-shirt maybe, against one of his palms. The cloth smelled of disinfectant, and it stung like crazy.

'You gotta eat. Come on. Let me try and fix you up a bit.'

Baz was embarrassed, but could find no energy or will to resist. And anyway, it made sense. He allowed Ray to dab his hands with the wet cloth, juddering and wincing at each fresh wave of pain. It was hard to keep back the tears.

Dyson walked past on his way to the washroom. 'What's this – doctors and nurses?' he said. But then he paused and said, 'Is it bad?'

'Take a look,' said Ray.

Dyson leaned over. 'Ouch. Yeah, that's bad. Your skin hardens up after a week or two, though. You'll be OK.' He walked on.

'Might be better to leave it open tonight,' Ray said. 'Let it all dry out a bit, and put the plasters on tomorrow.' He was holding one of Baz's hands in his own, frowning as he studied the wounds, his eyes lowered in concentration beneath long dark lashes. Baz watched him.

'I found some Dettol,' murmured Ray. 'It should help keep out the germs at least.' He looked up. 'My mum used to be a nurse,' he said. 'Before all this.'

'Yeah?' Baz felt vaguely uncomfortable. Here was a side to Ray that he'd never expected to see. He pulled his hand away, but then wondered if this action would seem ungrateful.

'Thanks,' he said.

Ray shrugged. 'You're probably going to have to do the same for me tomorrow. And anyway' – he lowered his voice – 'you got me the beans. Saved my life, that did. Want me to open your spaghetti for you?'

Baz struggled to sit up. 'No. I can do it.' But every

movement he made was agony, and he decided that he could use whatever help was on offer. 'Yeah, go on, then. Thanks.'

CHAPTER SIX

The deck of the *Cormorant* looked like a breaker's yard. It was piled high with bits of rusty metal, a mountainous jumble of scrap, all of it smeared in stinking grey ooze.

Baz followed Amit across the gangplank, his limbs weak and unsteady, his eyesight bleary. He was exhausted before the day had even begun.

The heap of junk turned out to be tools – handsaws, planes, pliers and screwdrivers, hammers, bags of screws and nails, nuts and bolts, half a dozen fold-up workbenches. Yesterday's dive must have been to some kind of DIY store.

'Isaac gets a good price for this kind of stuff,' said Amit, 'when it's cleaned up. Everybody wants tools on the mainland.'

Baz worked in the same team as before, although this time it was Hutchinson who was in charge. Amit and Robbie surreptitiously tried to give Baz the easier things to carry, and he was grateful for that, because he was struggling desperately to cope. Every bit of him ached. His plastered-up hands were quickly covered in muck, and apart from the stinging pain he was also worried about getting infection in there. It took a good couple of hours to unload the boat.

They brought the heavy crates to a patch of gravel outside the back door of the sort room. Here were two large plastic bathtubs, both filled with water, and it was here that the clean-up operation apparently began. The goods were tipped out of the crates into a great oozing heap on the gravel, ready to be immersed in water and scrubbed down.

'You get the worst of it off in the first tub,' said Amit, 'and use the other one to give it a final rinse, yeah?'

The water in the first bath was already disgustingly filthy, and Baz could see long strands of hair floating on the surface. He swallowed and tried to keep from retching.

'Two to a tub, then,' said Amit. 'We better get started.'

Baz took a deep breath and sank to his knees beside the first bathtub, opposite Taps. He felt his stomach heave, and thought he was going to throw up over the side of it.

But then the back doors to the sort room were opened, and Hutchinson appeared.

'You – newbie,' he said to Baz. 'Get up. Come on – on your feet. You've got more important things to learn yet. Leave that, and go and work next to Gene. He'll show you the codes.'

Baz pushed himself upright, relieved to be able to turn his back on that reeking grey soup. He followed Hutchinson into the heat of the sort room.

'Gene – get this kid shaped up,' Hutchinson called

across the cluttered space. 'Show him the codes. I'm off for a crap.'

'Well, that's great to hear,' murmured Gene as Baz approached the workbench. 'Tell us all about it, why don't you?'

He turned to Baz and glanced down at his hands. 'Take a minute to get washed up,' he said. 'There's a bucket in the corner. Clean plasters in that Tupperware box over there.'

Baz was so grateful that he felt tears spring to his eyes. 'Thanks,' he said.

As well as an assortment of plasters, the Tupperware box contained a pack of multi-coloured balloons. Big ones with PARTY TIME! printed on the side. Some party, thought Baz.

But this was so much better than yesterday. Baz stood next to Gene, an array of tins before him on the bench, and a thick black marker pen in his hand. There was a sheet of paper stuck to the back wall with masking tape, and on the paper were handwritten codes, groups of numbers and letters.

'Every tin has a code printed on it' – Gene looked up from what he was doing – pulling a cigarette lighter apart with a pair of pliers, or so it seemed – 'and you can tell what's in there from that. Once you've learned the codes you can mark 'em up. You start with own brands. That's the supermarket's own stuff, not Heinz or anything. That comes later. Look – grab that tin just there . . . yeah, that one. That's Somerby's. They're dead easy 'cos they just have a little box with three letters. CCS, or whatever. What does that one say?'

'Er . . .' Baz found the three printed letters on the upended tin. 'LBS. Is that it?'

'Yeah. Lentil and bacon soup. So write LB SOUP on it. You can pretty much guess Somerby's without even learning them. But Patterson's, they use just numbers and so they're trickier. And then there's ones with letters that don't make any sense – like V for beans. That's Costcut. It looks a mess to start with, but there's only three warehouses that the divers can get to, Somerby's, Costcut and Patterson's. You soon get used to which is which. Gotcha.' The cigarette lighter came apart in Gene's hands.

'OK.' Baz picked up a tin, looked at the code, and then searched the list on the wall for something that matched. It took him a while.

'So this is . . . Patterson's,' he said. 'New potatoes.'

'Mark it up, then.'

N/POTS. God, he could eat some n/pots right now . . .

'So . . . what's to stop anyone, you know, pinching this stuff?'

Gene laughed. 'Yeah, I wondered when you'd get to that. Well . . .' He glanced over his shoulder, and then leaned a bit closer. 'It's not easy, 'cos every tin has to be accounted for. The divers have a pretty good idea of how many they've brought back, and Hutchinson tallies 'em up on his clipboard as they come into the sort room from the washtubs. Then he counts 'em again once they're marked up to go to the storeroom. So he knows exactly what's come in here, and the same amount has to go out. He tries to count 'em off the boat too, before they go into the washtubs, but everything's in such a state that he can't be too sure of the

98

numbers. So that's when one or two tins can get lost –
between the boat and here. Know what I mean?'

'Um . . .'

'Let's put it this way. It's easy for a couple of tins to
accidentally get left in the tubs, and Hutchinson ain't
likely to go sticking his arms in there to check.'

'Oh. Right. Got it.'

'We usually manage to store a few extras up for
Sunday,' said Gene. 'You'll see tomorrow, with a bit of
luck. Damn. Lost a screw.'

'What are you doing, anyway?' said Baz. Gene was
making something out of a piece of wood – a square
offcut of planking. Fixed to the centre of the
square was a shallow plastic cap that might once have
been the lid of some small container, with a couple of
thin electrical wires protruding up through it. The dismantled cigarette lighter lay in bits around the
working area.

'Little experiment. I'm *supposed* to be trying to fix
that Seagull motor, but Hutchinson's so thick I could
tell him anything and he'd believe it. As long as I come
up with the goods every once in a while, he's
happy . . .'

And then, at that moment, the door opened at the
far end of the room and Hutchinson walked back in.
Gene casually pushed the piece of wood to one side,
along with the bits of cigarette lighter. He picked up a
solid-looking brass flywheel, held it up to the light and
squinted at it. Then he began fitting the wheel into the
heavy workbench vice.

Baz concentrated on looking at the codes on the
wall. He heard Hutchinson's footsteps behind him,

pausing for a moment before passing by. Hutchinson disappeared through the half-opened back doors, and his voice could be heard growling something to the clean-up team.

'He'll be gone again in a minute.' Gene retrieved the bit of wood with the cap screwed to it. 'He doesn't hang around here any more than he needs to – but he'll expect you to know those codes, so keep at it.'

'OK.'

By midday Baz had learned the most common codes off by heart. He would have progressed even quicker if he hadn't been so intrigued by whatever it was that Gene was building. The click-button from the cigarette lighter was now mounted onto the wooden base, and there was a piece of metal – like a miniature two-pronged fork – sticking up through the centre of the plastic cap. Gene pressed the lighter button and a tiny spark appeared between the prongs of the fork.

'Go on,' said Baz. 'Tell me what it is.'

'Wait till we get a break. Then I'll show you. Might not even work.'

Hutchinson reappeared briefly a few minutes later. 'Got those codes yet?' he said to Baz.

'Um, I can do a lot of the—'

'I don't want a lot of them. I want all of them.' Hutchinson walked over to the back doors and shouted to the clean-up team. 'Haven't you finished yet? You should be on the wire wool by now. Everything polished and oiled by tonight, or you'll stay here till it is. Right. Take twenty minutes.'

'Yeah, yeah. See you in an hour,' Gene muttered

under his breath as Hutchinson left the room. He waited a few more moments, then said to Baz, 'Go and get the others. Tell 'em to come in here and take a look at this.'

Baz stuck his head out of the back doors. Amit and Robbie were standing up and stretching themselves. Taps still had his arms in the tub. He was swirling them to and fro, gazing down at the grey water. All three boys were filthy, streaked in muck, their clothes soaking wet. Baz felt guilty looking at them. He'd had an easy morning by comparison.

'Er . . . Gene says to come inside,' he said. 'Got something to show you.'

'Huh? What is it?' Amit and Robbie wiped their hands on the backs of their shorts and moved towards the couple of steps that led into the building. 'Hey, come on, Taps! Give it a break.'

'God, you lot stink,' said Gene.

'Yeah, well, we can't all be privileged professors. What do you want?' Amit sounded irritated.

'Got a new toy,' said Gene. 'In fact it was you that gave me the idea – reminded me of it anyhow.' He picked up the little wooden construction he'd made and placed it on an upside-down crate in the middle of the room. 'Who's got a cigarette lighter they can lend me?'

The boys gathered round the crate, but nobody offered a lighter.

'Come on. I had to break mine up to make this.'

'Well, what's it supposed to be?' said Amit.

'It's a rocket base.'

'Yeah, right.' Amit didn't sound convinced, but

he handed Gene a lighter. 'I want it back though.'

Gene squatted down beside the crate and produced a small black plastic container from his pocket.

'What's that?' said Robbie.

'Film canister. What they used to keep camera films in.' Gene held the canister close to the grey plastic lid that was fixed to the piece of wood. Then he put the top of the cigarette lighter into the mouth of the little canister and gently pressed the button, allowing lighter gas to escape into the canister. He kept his thumb on the button for a few moments longer, before quickly pushing the canister down onto its plastic lid. So now the film canister was a sealed unit, full of gas, with an electrical element inside it. Baz had watched Gene testing the spark earlier on, and thought he could guess where this experiment was going.

'OK. Stand back, guys.' Gene leaned away so that he was at arm's length, and clicked the lighter button that was mounted on the piece of wood . . .

Bang! It was a surprisingly loud explosion and everyone jumped back a mile. The film canister shot into the air, hit the ceiling and bounded away across the room, finally coming to rest on the workbench once more.

'Woo-ee! Friggin' amazing!'

'Jesus! Did you see that thing go?'

Baz and Robbie were delighted, and Taps – just arrived – put both fingers in his ears and stared up at the ceiling. 'Oh! Oh!'

'And that, gentlemen,' said Gene, 'is what we call rocket science.'

Even Amit must have been impressed, although he

didn't really show it. 'What – did you invent that or something?'

'Nah. I saw it on the internet, years ago. First time I ever tried to make one, though.'

'So how come it was me that reminded you of it?'

'When you were doing your rocket act the other night, in the slob room.'

'Do it again, Gene,' said Robbie. 'Go on.'

'OK. Just once more, then. But somebody better keep an eye out for Hutchinson, case he hears it.'

'Yeah, but make it someone else's lighter this time,' said Amit. 'You're using up all my bleedin' gas.'

Something he'd seen on the internet, Gene had said. The internet. Websites and Facebook, blogs and music downloads. How far away it all seemed now . . .

Baz sat on the back steps of the sort room with the others, rubbing down the blade of a handsaw with a pad of wire wool. Hutchinson had decided that it was time he grafted a bit. He had plasters on each of his fingers, but they didn't do much to ease the pain. The saw blade was rusty, and the wire wool kept getting caught on the serrated edge.

'Still don't know why they make us do this,' said Robbie. He'd tied a broad piece of rag around his fore-head, white with purple stars on it. Corkscrews of red hair spilled out over the top of the material. He looked like a firework. 'Waste of time, if you ask me.'

'Isaac gets a better price for the stuff if it's all clean and working, I s'pose.' Amit was struggling with a fold-ing metal workbench, trying to free the seized hinges with an oilcan.

'Nah. They'd have to pay the price anyway, back on the mainland. Where else are they gonna get tools from?'

Baz looked at Robbie's erupting hair and thought about the rocket toy. 'How old's Gene?' he said.

'Fifteen,' Amit grunted. 'I think. You wouldn't know it.'

'God, he's brilliant though, isn't he?'

'Huh. Gene has it easy. He just mucks around all day, pretending to work, while the rest of us have to do crap like this. Gets the pick of the food every night . . . doesn't have to fight for it like we do . . .' Amit yanked viciously at the legs of the folding workbench. 'He's just out for himself, is our Gene.'

Baz remembered his own desperate tactics to get food the previous evening. 'Well . . . I suppose you sort of have to be, don't you? Out for yourself, I mean?'

Amit stopped what he was doing. 'Well, that's pretty good, coming from a newbie. No, actually, you don't. You try and look out for your mates, is what you do – that's if you want any mates. Like we tried to look out for you this morning, yeah? Tried to make it so's you didn't have carry any of the really heavy stuff.' Amit stared at him for a moment longer, then returned his attention to the workbench.

'*And* that was after what you did last night,' he muttered. 'To Enoch. And to Taps. Don't think we didn't notice.'

Baz rubbed at the saw, moving his hand back and forth mechanically, not really concentrating. 'I know,' he said, aware of the disapproval surrounding him. 'And I've been feeling bad about it.' He looked across at the kneeling figure of Taps, who was busy sorting through a rusty tin of nuts and bolts.

'Sorry, Taps. I shouldn't have shoved you like that.'

'Beg pardon?' Taps glanced up at the mention of his name and looked around the group. But his eyes were quickly drawn back to the nuts and bolts. 'Yes, it's a shame, isn't it?' He shuffled sideways, as if to cut himself off from further interruption, and delved once more into his tin of secrets.

'Well, it's not all your fault, I suppose,' said Amit. 'You'd had nothing to eat 'cept tomatoes, and nor had Ray. So we decided to lay off you. But the real reason we decided to lay off you is 'cos you were just trying to look out for your mate, yeah? For Ray.'

'Er . . . yeah.'

'But now Enoch's gotta to do a day on the jetty with only tomatoes inside him. And Taps must be starving too.' Amit stopped work again as he thought about this. 'God. What'll we do if Steiner decides to keep pulling the same trick? Maybe every night from now on?'

'Nah, he wouldn't do that,' said Robbie. 'Baz and Ray are gonna get quicker. It wouldn't be them that'd end up with the tomatoes all the time. And anyway, there's always Sundays for getting their own back. I mean . . . you know . . .'

Robbie's voice faltered, and Baz stopped rubbing at the rusty blade. He caught Robbie's sideways glance at Amit, a look that was almost apologetic. Something had been hinted at, some communication had passed between the two boys that he wasn't in on.

Amit sighed. 'OK. He might as well know. Listen,

Baz, newbies usually have to find this out the hard way – 'cos it gives the rest of us a break. But you're not a bad guy. You do your whack and you don't moan about it. And that kid Ray's got some guts too. So we're going to do you both a favour and warn you. OK?'

Baz had the sense of something horrible in the air. Something sinister, from the way that Amit and Robbie were looking at him. 'What?' he said. 'What is it?'

CHAPTER SEVEN

'We already told you about Sundays, yeah?' Amit put down the oilcan he was holding.

'You mean Preacher John and the chapel thing?' said Baz. 'Going to church?'

'Yeah. Well, after chapel we get the rest of the day off. It ought to be the best day of the week, but often it's the worst – 'cos it's the capos' day off too. And what they do, every Sunday, is they get legless. From midday on they're drinking . . .' Amit blew out his cheeks. 'And it can get pretty scary. If anyone's given them trouble during the week, then Sundays is when they'll cop it. And this week it's you and Ray that's given them trouble. Know what I'm saying?'

Baz felt his stomach begin to tighten. 'What, you mean . . . like . . . they beat you up or something?'

'It's worse than that. You get sent down the hole. See, there's this one little job they save up for Sundays—'

'Hang on. I thought you said nobody worked Sundays?'

'Yeah, well, you wouldn't call it work exactly,' said Amit. 'And it doesn't happen every Sunday. But there's this drain – a sewage drain – just round the other side of the building. That's what they call the hole. Every newbie gets sent down there. There's a kind of handle thing, and you have to turn the handle before they let you back up again.'

Baz didn't like the sound of this, but it seemed as though it might be preferable to a beating. 'What does the handle do? What is it?'

'Doesn't matter about the handle. Gene reckons it doesn't really do much anyway. What matters is you get put down the drain.'

'Oh. And that's . . . bad, is it?'

Amit gave a short laugh. 'Bad? It's bad if they don't let you back up again, yeah. It's bad if they decide to put the drain cover back on and leave you trapped down there in the pitch dark, up to your armpits in sewage. Forget all about you for a few hours, maybe, while they go off and get bladdered. Yeah. *Then* it's bad.'

'All the newbies have to go through it.' Robbie spoke, and Baz turned his horrified attention to him. 'And usually you're just down there a couple of minutes. It stinks, and it's scary, but most people can stand it as long as the lid doesn't go back on. It's just to show you who's boss, see. After that, you don't give any trouble. But if the capos have really got it in for you – then look out. 'Cos that's how they get rid of you.'

'What do you mean "get rid of you"?' Baz had visions of being locked in a drain for ever, drowning in sewage . . .

'If they give you the real treatment, a few hours of it, then you'll do anything not to go down there again,' said Robbie. 'Anything. So if the capos wanna get rid of you, they tell you it's gonna be the same next Sunday, and the Sunday after that. If you don't want that to happen, your only chance is to get out of here – back to the mainland. Quickest way to do that is you refuse to work. So you refuse to work, and you're on the next boat back. And I'll tell you what – you'd need some guts to tell Isaac you're not gonna work. But that's how bad it is down the hole.'

'Christ. Do the divers know what goes on? Does Preacher John?'

'Preacher John knows everything. And yeah, Isaac knows for sure. He's only got two capos. How're two capos gonna keep eight kids working flat out? By scaring the crap out of 'em, that's how. See, they can't beat us up too badly, 'cos we belong to Preacher John. You saw what happened to Steiner on the day you got here. But if you know the hole's there waiting for you on Sunday, then you don't give 'em any trouble during the week.'

'So . . . you reckon that's gonna happen to me and Ray?'

'Happens to everyone, mate. But for you it could be worse than normal, 'cos you went for Steiner. That's why we're warning you. Last Sunday it was these other new kids, Danny and Simon—' Robbie stopped talking and looked at Amit. Once again Baz got the impression that too much had been said. But then Amit picked up the story.

'Yeah. Danny and Simon. Gobby kids – gave the capos some lip. And we didn't like them much either.' Amit looked uncomfortable. 'So on Sunday they both got shoved down the hole. Came up yelling and puking, and next thing you know they're gone. Back to the mainland. Didn't you see them get off the boat?'

'No, they'd already been dropped off, somewhere up the coast. But did you warn them too?' Baz wanted to know. 'About what was gonna happen?'

Silence.

'No? So that's what you call looking out for your mates?' Baz couldn't help making the dig. He felt that it was justified.

'Yeah.' Amit sighed. 'I know. Those of us that've been here a while, we . . . we've kind of got used to just looking out for each other, I s'pose. Newbies come over on the boat, they take their chances. If they get the treatment and they can't stand it, well, tough. They get sent back. And at least that means it wasn't one of us. Some other newbie turns up, and then *he* gets sent down the hole and . . . that's how it goes.' He rubbed his forehead. 'But you're right. This place is such a screw-up. Something's gotta change.'

Baz picked up the saw again, and his wad of wire wool. Simply for something to hold onto. 'Couldn't we just hide and keep out of their way? Like in the main building? It's big enough.'

Amit laughed at that. 'No. There's nowhere to hide. You can't get up to the next floor. There's only two staircases. One of 'em's collapsed, and the other's down in the divers' bit. You could probably stay out of the way if you kept moving, but then somebody else'd cop it for not telling where you were. We can't all hide every Sunday. Not till night time, we couldn't. And you know – I gotta say this, Baz – I think Ray might

110

get it worse than you, anyhow. He'll probably be first.'

'Oh, great. That's all right then.'

'Yeah, but I'm serious. See, that Ray . . .' Amit shook his head. 'Steiner's got it in for him already. And he'll get him one way or another, so you better warn him.'

Baz began rubbing down the saw again and didn't say anything for a while. He thought about Steiner's ugly face, rain dripping from his long freckled chin . . . bare gingery knees . . .

And he thought about Ray, out there now, pushing his barrow up and down the hill. No idea of what was going on, or what might happen to him. That seemed almost worse for some reason. God.

'Anything else we should know?' he said. 'What about that guy Cookie? What's with him?'

'Cookie?' Amit shrugged his shoulders. 'He's just a fat slob. We hardly see him. He's gone in the morning before the rest of us, and he's down there in the kitchen till night time. Doesn't usually come back till after dark. Sometimes they lock him in the slob room during the afternoon for a couple of hours if there's nothing for him to do. He cooks for the divers – cleans up, I s'pose. Don't know what else he does, but it's seven days a week. We don't have anything to do with him.'

'He can't help being overweight, can he?'

''Tisn't just that. He spends more time with the divers than he does with us, so we can't trust him. Gotta watch what you say around Cookie, case it gets passed on, so it's best to say nothing.'

'And what about the divers? Are they dangerous as

well?' Baz wanted to get as much information now as he could.

'Yeah. They'd dump you in the sea for a bottle of vodka – kill you soon as look at you – but it's easy enough to keep out of their way. Drinking and Ladies' Day, that's all they care about.'

'Huh?'

'Ladies' Day. That's what they call it. 'Bout once a month they pick up a bunch of women from some-where on the mainland – trade 'em, you know, pay 'em. They bring 'em over on a Friday night, take 'em back Saturday morning. The girls come here all dressed up, make-up and stuff, but they don't look so hot next day. Gets a bit rough, I reckon. Preacher John knows about it. He doesn't join in, though.'

Baz carried on working. He'd learned a lot in the last fifteen minutes – more than enough to be going on with – and he'd have to give it all some thought. But the first thing he needed to do was warn Ray of what was about to happen.

'This saw's about as good as it's ever gonna be,' he said. 'What do you want me to do next?'

Come supper time the tools were all cleaned, oiled, stacked and logged onto Hutchinson's clipboard.

'You got those codes, newbie?' Hutchinson said as he walked past Baz. 'Yeah? Gimme tomato soup – Somerby's and Patterson's.'

'Er, Somerby's is just CTS. Patterson's is oh-oh-oh-four, er, stroke thirty-two.' Baz was looking at the broad figure of Hutchinson with new eyes. Trying to imagine being shoved down a sewer by him . . . and then trying *not* to imagine . . .

'OK. Spaghetti. Patterson's and Costcut.'

'Patterson's . . . oh-oh-oh-four . . . stroke fifteen. Costcut, um, P . . . twenty-three.'

'That'll do. Next time you're on sort room you can learn main brands.' Hutchinson moved on.

Baz looked up at the high dirt-streaked windows and saw the clouds gathering in the darkening skies, as usual. Funny how the weather was so predictable now. It nearly always rained in the evenings. He'd almost forgotten what proper weather was like. How different the seasons used to be. Summer. Winter. Those cold frosty mornings when you could see your breath as you stood waiting for the school bus. The long summer holidays, lying out on the dried-up front lawn, trying to get some last-minute homework done. Mum saying to come inside and put on some sunscreen or you'd be sorry later . . .

There was a rap on the main fire doors, and Baz could see vague figures through the reinforced glass. It was the jetty crew returning. The left-hand door swung back, and Dyson came in. Then there was some kind of struggle. The remaining figures didn't seem to be able to get through the gap. Dyson was already turning round, pushing at the second door. Baz couldn't catch what was going on at first, because Dyson was in the way. But then he saw.

Jubo stumbled awkwardly into the room, along with Enoch – and between them they were more or less carrying Ray. They had his arms slung about their necks, and his feet were dragging on the ground. Jesus. They'd killed him.

Baz immediately stepped forward, a ball of fury rising in his chest, but then Robbie was there – appearing in front of him – one arm stuck out to bar his way.

'Hang on,' Robbie whispered. 'Just wait a second.'

Steiner came through the fire doors, shoulders back, arms folded, a relaxed swagger. He looked at Hutchinson for a moment, pale eyebrows raised, then turned towards the sorry figure of Ray. He put one finger up to his chin as if in contemplation, all very theatrical, and made a sucking sound through his teeth.

'Cornflake Kid's had a busy day,' he said. 'Hey, you!' He looked towards Baz. 'Come and prop up this useless piece of crap.'

Again Baz felt a moment of restraint from Robbie's arm and heard his low whisper: 'Just watch out. Don't give him any excuse.'

It was good advice, and Baz managed to hold himself in control as he walked down the room.

'All right,' he said to Enoch. 'I've got him.' Baz put his head under Ray's arm, shifted his balance and took the weight. 'It's OK, Jubo, I can do it. Leave him to me.'

Enoch and Jubo stepped aside. They both looked exhausted.

Steiner said, 'Enoch, you're not done yet. Get me nine tins and put 'em down by t' bench. You know the drill by now: three meat, two spaghetti, two beans, two tomatoes.'

Baz saw the questioning look on Hutchinson's face, and heard Steiner mutter, 'Don't worry, Hutch. I've got it sorted.'

Ray's legs just weren't working properly at all, and by the time Baz had managed to get him down to the workbench area, the tins were already arranged on the floor. The other boys were gathered round. They'd left a gap so that Baz and Ray could join the circle.

'You first, Gene,' said Steiner. 'Go ahead.'

Gene stooped down and took his tin.

'OK.' Steiner looked at Hutchinson. 'Enoch's my top dog today. Who's yours? I'm guessing it could be Taps, right?'

Steiner held Hutchinson's eye for another moment, nodding his head slightly.

'Uh ... yeah.' Hutchinson seemed to catch on. 'You're right. It's Taps,' he said.

'OK, then. Top-dogs-ready-go.'

Enoch was sliding across the floor before Taps had even realized that he'd been picked as top dog. Dyson had to give him a shove. 'Go on, dummy.'

Taps stumbled forward. He hesitated over the tins, plainly bewildered at finding himself having to make such a decision. Finally he picked one up and stepped back.

'OK. Rest-of-you-ready-go.'

Baz stayed where he was, still propping up Ray, as all around him dived inwards. He hadn't even bothered to look at the tins or make any sort of plan. There was no point.

Once everyone was back on their feet again, the two inevitable tins of tomatoes were all that remained on the grimy sort-room floor.

'Oh dear.' Steiner was revelling in his triumph. 'Bit

slow again there, girls. OK, that's your lot. Get back to t' slob room.'

Baz turned to Amit. 'Pick ours up for us, will you?'

Amit glanced up at Hutchinson, perhaps to see if there might be any objection to this, then said, 'Yeah, sure.' His brown face looked a shade paler than usual, lips pressed together in a thin line.

Once the door of the slob room had closed behind them, Amit exploded.

'Right. *Sod* them, then. I've had it with this!' He strode off towards the sink unit, carrying the two tins of tomatoes, along with whatever he'd managed to get for himself. He reached up and grabbed a large saucepan from the shelf above the unit, then banged it down on the cluttered draining board.

Baz waited as Robbie got his shoulder beneath Ray's other arm, and then between the two of them they managed to get him to his mattress. They laid him on his back, and stood up to take a proper look.

'God, what a state,' said Robbie.

Some of the other boys began to gather round. Ray was deathly white, but not unconscious. His eyes were open now, and he raised a forearm to shield himself from the light. The palms of his hands were torn and bleeding.

Baz was trying to control his anger, trying to think practically. 'I'll get some plasters from under the sink,' he said. 'Disinfectant, whatever. Try and patch him up a bit.'

But Amit was still occupying the sink area, banging around with saucepans and can-openers.

116

'OK – listen.' He walked towards the group of boys, bringing the largest saucepan with him. 'If Steiner's going to keep doing this friggin' tomato thing then somebody's gonna end up starving every day. So the only fair way is to stick everything we get into one pot, and share it out between us, yeah? I've put my beans in here along with the tomatoes. Everybody else does the same, and we'll be OK. Come on. Open your tins and sling it all in together.'

'Yeah, good idea, Amit.' Robbie picked at the ring-pull on his tin. 'Should have done this before.'

But Robbie was the only one to immediately fall in with Amit's thinking.

'Whoa, whoa.' Dyson held up a hand. 'Who are you to suddenly start telling everyone what to do, Amit? Maybe not everyone wants to go along with this. Like me, for a kick-off. I'm not eating any friggin' tomatoes – not if I can help it.'

'So you're gonna stand by and watch other kids starve?'

'Hey, we all take our chances. If it's me that's too slow on the night, then it'll be me that ends up with tomatoes. Simple as that.'

'Too slow?' Amit pointed down at Ray. 'That poor bleeder can't even stand up. What chance did he have tonight?'

'OK, so Steiner's got it in for him, and that's tough. But whose fault's that? You go picking fights with a capo and you get what's coming to you – tomatoes!'

'So you're out.' Amit looked disgusted.

'Yeah, I'm out. Good luck with the Bleedin' Hearts Club.' Dyson walked away towards the sink area and began rummaging through the cutlery drawer.

Amit watched him go, then turned back to the rest of the group. 'Friggin' unbelievable. OK, well, let's see who's in. Baz?'

'Well, yeah, it's fine by me. And Ray'll be in for sure. I know we got nothing to lose tonight, but I think it's a good idea anyway.'

'OK, so that's three of us. Enoch? Jubo? Come on, we might as well just have a vote on it. But if we all stick together, then everyone gets fed the same. No more scrabbling about on the floor and hoping for the best. So who's in?'

Robbie's hand was already up. 'Yeah, OK. Me.' So now there were four.

But that was it.

Enoch and Jubo looked at each other as if for mutual assurance and then shook their heads. Taps just seemed to have gone blank.

'Dunno 'bout this, man,' said Jubo. 'Like Dyson say, it ain't our fault that Steiner got it in for these guys.'

'Sheesh. You try and make things fair . . . where's Gene?' said Amit.

'Gone to the jakes, I think.'

'*I* think' – Taps suddenly spoke up – 'that Dyson's correct. We must all take our chances. Sometimes you get tomatoes and sometimes you get meat. It all works out in the end. Tonight, for example, I was top dog—'

Amit turned on him, his voice rising with anger. 'Top dog? You weren't top dog, you dozy little retard! Steiner told Hutchinson to pick you because he wanted to make sure that Baz and Ray didn't get anything decent—'

'Hey. Leave him be, Amit.' Gene appeared from beneath the washroom curtain. 'Just because things aren't going your way, there's no need to take it out on Taps.'

'Oh, right,' said Amit. 'Here comes the big genius. Another one who knows when he's well off. Tin of meat every night, and never has to graft for it. Don't need to ask whose side you'll be on, then.'

'Well, yours, as it happens.' Gene already had his can opened. 'There you go. Chicken curry. Bung it in with the rest. Far as I'm concerned it's fair to share everything out, but what other people do is their business, OK? Let 'em make up their own minds.'

'Huh?' Amit looked astonished. He'd been completely wrong-footed, and all the bluster went out of him. After a few moments he said, 'Well . . . OK, then. Great. Thanks, Gene. And you're right – I shouldn't have gone off on one. Sorry, Taps.'

But Taps barely seemed to notice. He was holding his tin of food between both hands and looking down at the lid. CHIL. His forefingers tapped against the tin, first one side, then the other. One-two-three-four-five. One-two-three-four-five . . .

He wandered back towards his bed.

So the group was split, five for sharing and four against. Spaghetti and chicken curry were added to the tomatoes and beans, and a dubious-looking combination it made. The contents of the saucepan were doled out equally into the five tin cans.

'Bleedin' hell.' Amit took a spoonful of the mixture and pulled a face. 'Whose stupid idea was this?'

'Told you you'd be doing this for me,' Ray murmured. It was the first time he'd spoken. 'Christ, it hurts. How does it look?'

'Not good.' Baz knelt beside Ray's mattress and poured a drop more disinfectant onto the dampened sleeve of a T-shirt. Loose flaps of skin were hanging off Ray's palms, and beneath that the flesh was raw and pink, like uncooked chicken. 'And there's only a few plasters left. Gene's got some in the sort room, though. He might be able to get us a couple more tomorrow. OK. Here we go. It'll sting like hell.'

Ray's face was screwed up in agony as Baz dabbed at his hands. Baz saw that the wounds matched his own exactly – palms and fingertips – and he felt a shared and renewed pain as the disinfectant soaked into the grubby plasters he'd been wearing since this morning.

'Jesus . . .' Ray's breath hissed out of him. 'That dickhead Steiner . . . sheesssh . . . he was on at me all day . . . wouldn't get off my back. Thank God it's Sunday tomorrow. Ow.'

'Listen.' Baz didn't want to make things any worse, but he had to put Ray in the picture. 'The others told me something today, and it's scary. Steiner and Hutchinson get legless on Sundays. They drink all afternoon, and then they do this thing where they put you down into a sewer. A drain thing. The others reckon you and me are in for it.'

'What?' Ray tried to lift his head, but couldn't

manage it. He fell back on the blanket again. 'Ohhhh, great. That's all we need.'

'Yeah, and it's no good trying to hide, 'cos somebody else would just cop it instead.'

'What are we going to do? Get me up, will you?'

Baz put his arm around Ray's shoulders, levered him into a sitting position, then helped him to wriggle backwards so that he could lean against the wall.

'I'll tell you what we do. We refuse to work, and then we get sent back. Back to the mainland, I mean. I've had enough of this friggin' place.'

'You know what?' Dyson's voice interrupted them. He was over by the sink, getting rid of his empty food tin. 'I'm beginning to wonder about you two.'

Baz still had his arm about Ray's shoulders. He self-consciously withdrew it, but ignored Dyson's remark.

'And it's hardly gonna bother Isaac if we leave. Can't see why it would. There's plenty more kids trying to get here. It'd make no difference to him. Let's get out.'

Ray shook his head. 'Can't go.'

'Why not? You've still got a mum. Someone to—'

'Said I can't go, all right?' Ray had tears in his eyes, but his mouth was set firm. 'I need a pee.'

'Right. I'll give you a hand.' Baz took hold of Ray's wrists and pulled him onto his feet. 'Come on, then.' He lifted Ray's arm in order to help him into the washroom.

'It's OK. I can do it.'

'What? You can hardly stand, let alone walk.'

'I can *do* it. Stop fussing over me.' Ray disentangled

himself and staggered off towards the jakes. He was gone a long while, but Baz resisted the impulse to go and check if he was all right. You could only help people who were willing to be helped. Nevertheless, he went over to the cutlery drawer and found Ray a spoon. It would save him that journey at least.

Later, after Hutchinson had turned out the light, Baz was surprised to hear Ray whisper in the darkness, 'You awake, Baz?'

'Yeah. I'm too hot.'

'Sorry I got so stroppy. Thing is, though, I've got to stay here for my mum's sake.'

'Because of having to feed you? Well, it's the same for my dad. And it's hard on him, I know. But I figure he'd rather play an extra few hands of poker than see me wind up dead.'

'Yeah, that's right. A few games of cards. But it isn't so easy for Mum.'

'So what does she do? How does she get by?'

Baz heard Ray give a long sigh. 'It's just tough for her, OK? And so I have to stay. I got no choice.'

CHAPTER EIGHT

The assembly hall was huge, with a high curved ceiling and a wooden floor, once polished perhaps, now dulled beneath a thick carpet of dust and grime. Along one wall stood a line of metal racks, on which hung many folded chairs. A few of these had been placed in front of the darkened stage at the far end of the hall – just four rows, with five chairs to a row. The group of chairs looked like an island stuck out in the middle of such a vast empty floor space.

Baz trooped into the hall along with the rest of the boys, and together they filled the first two rows. The chairs were the kind that hooked together, aluminium, with grey padded seats. Baz sat next to Ray at the end of the second row. Directly in front of him sat Taps, his hair still wet from the shower. Then Enoch, Jubo and Dyson.

Perhaps it was just coincidence, but Baz realized that the rows had naturally split into the same two groups that had divided over the food thing. Dyson's group of four sat in the front row, with one spare space at the

123

end. The five who had agreed to share their food occupied the second row. Weird.

Nobody spoke, or even whispered. Baz took his cue from the others and sat in silence too.

There was dust everywhere. Long curtains that hung to either side of the high windows, rows of pictures lining the walls – the remnants of former art projects – even the wooden lectern that occupied centre stage – everything was furred in a coat of grey, all colours muted. It was like sitting in a black and white film. A piano stood at floor level to the left of the stage, its lid open. The bright shiny keys were the only things in the room that seemed to be in focus. Black side curtains framed the stage, and the backdrop too was black, so that the solitary lectern appeared to be hanging motionless in a dark universe of its own.

A wheezy gasp of breath came from the next row back, followed by a creaking of the aluminium seats. It sounded as though Cookie had arrived. Cookie had been last in the shower, entering the washroom just as Baz had been coming out. Ray, astonishingly, had once again been up first thing – already washed and dressed before the alarm bell rang – though he had collapsed onto his bed and gone back to sleep while everyone else took it in turns for the jakes.

Baz risked a quick look over his shoulder at Cookie, then saw that Steiner and Hutchinson had also taken their places at the far end of the same row. He hadn't even heard them come in. Steiner scowled at him, an indication that he should turn round. But now there was a murmur of voices from the back of the hall, and in walked a group of men. They were dressed in dark suits and ties, hair slicked back. It took Baz a moment longer to realize that it was the salvage crew – the Eck brothers and Moko.

He dared not keep his head turned any longer, but the impression that Baz got was of discomfort. Moko in particular looked all wrong in a suit, his burly frame threatening to burst out of the cheap shiny material, his hand already at his collar in an attempt to ease the strain.

Baz faced front again and waited. He became aware of his heart rate – not pounding exactly, but definitely out of rhythm. He had to keep taking extra breaths.

Into the settling silence came odd musical sounds – a faraway chorus of high peeps and whistles, tiny chirruping notes that went round and round. Baz turned his head slightly to listen, and realized that it was only Cookie, sitting behind him. Cookie's asthmatic wheezing sounded like a strange and distant birdsong. Baz felt a terrible urge to giggle, to shriek, to leap up from his chair and hurtle about the room, screaming at the madness of it all. But then there was a sudden stiffening of the bodies around him, an extra tension in the atmosphere, and Baz found himself instinctively looking towards the left-hand side of the stage. A flicker of orange . . . moving . . .

He thought for a moment that it was a flame – a fiery beacon gliding in from the wings. But it was a head. A great bearded head that appeared to sail through the void, alarmingly disembodied. The illusion held for a few moments longer, then the out-line of a figure became more distinct. Red-haired, black-suited, a huge man walked across the darkened stage. There was a familiar bear-like roll to his movements, a heavy swing of his shoulders and upper body, yet his footsteps made no sound. As he reached the lectern, he turned and took an object from beneath his arm, a black book that carried the emblem of a gold cross. He raised the book in his right hand, held it there for a moment, and then slapped it down hard onto the lectern. *Bang*. The sound was like a pistol shot, and Baz felt his neck jerk backwards. Dust flew from the lectern and continued to spread in a slowly descending cloud. The man reached into his breast pocket and took out a pair of gold-rimmed spectacles. He flipped them open with one huge red hand, gripped the lectern with the other, and looked out over the silent congregation. Every particle of him, every movement he made, seemed to give out the same clear message. Here was a man to be reckoned with. A man of power. A man who would be obeyed. Preacher John.

The preacher's gaze swept across the gathering like the light from a watchtower. Baz caught his eye momentarily, an eye that looked yellowish, as though stained by nicotine, yet with a stare so intense that Baz felt a shiver run though him.

'We'll start this morning's service with hymn number one-four-seven.' Preacher John's voice boomed around the hall.

Taps jumped to his feet as if he'd suddenly remembered something, and Baz blinked in surprise.

Preacher John looked down from his lectern. He had his glasses on now.

Taps ran over to the piano, snatched up a pile of books and scuttled towards the back row of the congregation. Three more times he did this, trotting to and fro in a flurry of confusion, delivering a stack of books to the end person on each row.

'One-two-three-four-five . . .' Taps was whispering to himself as he went, and Baz found himself the recipient of five cloth-bound copies of *Songs of Praise*. He kept one and passed the rest along.

And then, surprisingly, Taps was seated at the piano stool, an open hymn book before him. His ears, viewed from the back, were as red as tinned tomatoes.

'Isaac, I'll see you about this afterwards.' Preacher John's voice was quiet, but there was a hard edge to it. 'These boys should be ready. I don't expect to have to wait on them.' He lifted a hand to adjust his glasses. 'Very well. Hymn number one-four-seven. "For Those in Peril". All stand.'

Baz was still fumbling for the right page as Taps struck up the opening bars to the hymn. How extraordinary it was to hear the sound of a piano again. The bell-like notes rose to penetrate every corner of the room, filling the grey and cavernous space with colour, somehow.

> *'Eternal Father, strong to save,*
> *Whose arm hath bound the restless wave,*
> *Who bidd'st the mighty ocean deep,*
> *Its own appointed limits keep.*
> *O hear us when we cry to thee,*
> *For those in peril on the sea.'*

'Sing out! Sing out!' Preacher John raised his hands, palms upwards, and the voices of the congregation grew louder in response.

As the last line of the hymn died away, Baz found himself quite out of breath. He couldn't remember when he had last sung like that – if he'd ever sung like that at all. It made him feel dizzy.

'Sit.' Preacher John was looking down at the lectern, turning the pages of his Bible.

Baz followed the example of those around him, taking his seat once more.

'O hear us when we cry to thee. O Lord, hear our prayer . . . Dear Lord, we beseech thee . . .' Preacher John raised his head. 'This is how we carry on, forever pleading and begging for God's help, but then expecting Him to do everything Himself. Save us, we cry. Deliver us from our enemies. Sort it all out for us, Lord, so that we don't have to. But God helps those who help themselves, and despises those who will not lift a finger in their own defence. Turn the other cheek? These are not the words of God! Eye for eye, tooth for tooth – this is the way of the true testament!' And Preacher John leaned forward, pulling down the lower lid of his left eye and rolling it around in its socket.

Baz flinched at the sight, but couldn't turn away. Preacher John's presence was overwhelmingly powerful, impossible to ignore.

'We allowed criminals to walk free and spared them the rod of justice, yet we prayed to God to save us from their evil ways. We put ourselves in the hands of moneylenders, yet we prayed to God to deliver us from our debts. We brought famine into the world, and then blamed God for it, even as we stood with our begging bowls held out to Him. And now we reap what we have

128

sown. God's fury upon us all. Hymn number seventy-one. All rise.'

Up again, a hurried rustling of pages, and Taps began to play.

> *'Lead us, heavenly Father, lead us*
> *O'er the world's tempestuous sea . . .'*

Baz was carried along as though hypnotized. He stood up, sat down, mouthed unfamiliar words from the book he held in his hands, and all in a kind of trance. He was so transfixed by the figure before him that the psalms and the hymns and the prayers became just background noise.

'. . . and the Lord said, *I will* destroy *man whom I have created from the face of the earth: both man and beast and the creeping* thing, *and the fowls of the air for it repenteth me that I have made them!*' Again and again the preacher banged his fist on the lectern, so that dust and dirt floated down from the underside to land on the toe-caps of his shiny shoes.

'*Gird up your loins like a man*. These are God's words to Job. We must act as men, not as whipped puppies. And we must look to the Old Testament in order to regain His grace. For I tell you this: God has not changed. The God that looks down upon me and speaks to me is the same God that looked down upon Job, aye, and Jacob and Moses and Abraham. And he demands the same of me as he did of them. Worship! Sacrifice! Not the feeble whimperings of a lost child, but the actions of a man!'

By now Preacher John's slicked-back hair had dried.

It circled his head like a fiery halo, a burning bush, so that he might have stepped from the pages of the very book that lay before him. His high glistening forehead looked solid enough to batter down the walls of Jericho.

'Men have died, and have always died, for the greater glory of God. Where there are great leaders, those who speak directly to God, there will be those whose lives are sacrificed in order that His word be obeyed. So will I build my altar to Him. And so will I make my sacrifice to Him, whatever He sees fit to ask of me, even to my own. Rejoice then, my sons, that we have been spared the coming of this second flood, and be glad that the good Lord has given us meat and shelter. But understand this: while the floods remain we've not been forgiven. God may ask for more of our blood before he draws the waters back into the fountains of the earth, and we must be prepared to pay in blood. Now let us pray.'

Then everyone leaned forward and bowed their heads. As Baz closed his eyes, he felt that a spell had been broken, that he'd been released at last, though the dark-suited figure still filled his inner vision.

'We thank you, God, for this day. We thank you for the harvest you bring to our nets, and for the comforts you deliver to us. We beg only for the chance to earn your forgiveness. Show us how to atone for the sins of the world, O Lord, that we may live in your good grace once more. Amen.'

'Amen.'

Preacher John closed his Bible. 'Hutchinson, Steiner, stay behind as usual to receive your duties for the week. The rest of you, dismiss. Go and take some of God's good air. Isaac, I'll speak to you directly.'

'Quick, then. Let's grab the swipes while we've got the chance.'

Freed from the assembly hall, the boys hurried out of the main entrance, Amit leading the way. They rounded the corner of the building towards where the washtubs stood.

'Who's got the bags and the spoons? Robbie? Got the tin-opener?'

'Yeah, all here.' Robbie pulled two or three scrunched-up carrier bags from his pocket.

Several pairs of hands delved into the filthy water of the first washtub. Out came a dozen or more tins, dripping wet, and these were quickly put into two of the carrier bags.

'Come on, then. Don't hang about.'

Baz and Ray followed as the boys ran towards the part of the school building that had collapsed. They began stumbling across piles of rubble, broken window frames, upturned desks – a landscape of devastation. Baz looked up and saw the remains of what had once been a spiral staircase, now partially exposed on the outside of the building. Its metal railings were kinked and twisted as though they had been made of coat-hanger wire.

'Where are we going?' Baz was out of breath.

Jubo pointed vaguely. 'Up to da sports centre. But we goin' da back way, so they don't see us.'

'How do we . . . ?'

But Jubo was forging on ahead. There was a dirt

lane beyond the mounds of rubble, overgrown by hedges and nettles but still just passable, and this rose in a steep winding pathway to the playing fields.

In a few minutes the boys were all gathered at the rear of the sports centre building. A quick glance around to make sure that they hadn't been followed, and they emptied out the two carrier bags onto the ground.

'What did we get in the swipes then?'

'Ten . . . eleven . . . thirteen, I make it.' Dyson crouched down beside the pile of tins, counting them. 'Means we've got one each and some spares for next time. Let's give 'em a swill, then, and put them in the sack. Whose turn for Santa?'

'Me,' said Jubo. He reached behind the nearest water butt and produced a black plastic bin liner.

The boys sat round in a circle, and it was apparent from the trampled-down patch of bare earth that they had visited this spot many times. Jubo put all the tins in the sack, shuffled them around a bit at his feet, then passed them out to the group one by one.

'Merry Christmas, Taps. Merry Christmas, Gene . . .'

This was obviously another little ritual. As each boy received his gift from 'Santa', he looked at the end of the tin to see what he'd got.

Baz studied the numbered code. Mincemeat? Yes, he thought so. Savoury mince. Too much on its own, and he didn't feel much like eating in any case.

'Merry Christmas, Amit.'

'I already told you about twenty million times,' said

Amit. 'I'm Muslim. We don't do Christmas. Rats,' he added. 'I got friggin' tomatoes.'

'Ha, ha! Bad luck.' Dyson taunted Amit by waving his tin at him. 'Beef curry, mate. Go, Santa!'

'Share mine, if you like.' Baz felt that he owed Amit a favour. 'I don't think I could eat a whole tin of mince. We'll mix the two together. Be like a spag bol.'

'Yeah? OK, then. Thanks.'

'Have some of mine as well,' said Ray. 'Look – I got spaghetti. Be even more like a spag bol then.' He glanced across at Baz and pulled a face. It seemed that Ray didn't feel hungry either. The thought of what was hanging over them would ruin any appetite.

'Yeah, come on. We'll just do the sharing thing again.' Robbie was up for it too. 'Gene?'

'All right,' said Gene. 'I don't mind. But we've got no saucepan here to mix it all up in, only spoons.'

'Well . . . we can just put the tins on the ground and take a bit of each, can't we?' said Baz. 'Like tapas, or sushi.'

'Tapas?' said Jubo. '*Sushi*? Ey – you rankin' me? What kind of life were you leading, guy?'

Baz shrugged. 'Dunno. Normal, I s'pose. We used to eat out sometimes, that's all.'

'Yeah, we eat out too. Pizza Hut and KFC.'

Everybody laughed.

'Tell you what, though. I could kill a pizza right now.'

'Yeah. Or a kebab . . .'

'Fish and chips . . .'

'Proper Christmas dinner, with all t' trimmings . . .'

'Don't! You're killing me!'

'Let's face it,' said Amit. 'Anything'd be better than this crap.'

But it was kind of fun to dip spoons into one tin and then another, and to share everything around. At least it gave a bit of variety, and Baz had the impression that the others might have liked to join in if Dyson would swallow his pride.

But Dyson said, 'God, it's like watching a chimps' tea party. Your guts are going to be worse than ever on that mixture.' He took a spoonful of curry and made an elegant show of chewing it slowly and carefully.

'Yeah, yeah.' Amit changed the subject. He looked across at Baz and said, 'So what did you reckon to Preacher John? Told you he was nuts.'

Baz thought about it for a moment. 'It was scary,' he said. 'That bit at the end . . . with the sacrifices and everything. What was all that about?'

Amit shrugged. 'Dunno. He's getting worse, though. He really believes that the floods and everything are a punishment. From Allah. God, whatever.'

'Yeah, well, we already know that,' Robbie said. 'But he's never said anything about sacrifices before. I didn't like it . . .'

'Nah, it's just Bible talk,' said Dyson. 'It doesn't mean he's gonna start killing people. Not us, anyhow. That'd be mental.'

'Wish somebody kill that Preacher John, man,' said Jubo. 'Wish somebody kill the whole lot o' them.'

'Blow their heads off.'

'Yeah. Steiner, Hutchinson, Isaac . . . those other tossers.' Amit grabbed an imaginary machine gun.

134

'Line 'em up against a wall, grab their guns off 'em and: *duh-duh-duh-duh* . . .'

'I'd start with Steiner. *OK, Steiner*, I'd say . . .'

'*You freakin' pervert . . .*' Robbie joined in.

'Yeah! *OK, Steiner, you freakin' pervert. Let's see how tough you look with* this *pointing at you!* Then – *Boof!*'

'Right in the nuts.'

'Ha! Yeah. The ginger nuts!'

Amit made a leap for Robbie and the two of them rolled around the dusty patch of earth in mock struggle. It was clear that Amit was the stronger of the two, and in a few moments he was kneeling astride Robbie's chest. He put an imaginary gun to Robbie's forehead.

'*And now, Mr Steiner . . . you die!*'

'Aargh! Gerroff me, you freak!'

Dyson looked up from his tin. 'It's all very well *saying* it, Amit. But you couldn't actually do it.'

'Could if I had a gun,' said Amit. '*Badoomff!*' He fired his weapon and then rolled sideways, apparently thrown off balance by the powerful recoil. His slaughtered victim sat up and rubbed his nose.

'Know how to use one, do you?' Dyson said.

'What's to know? You point it and pull the trigger.'

'Huh, it's not like it used to be in the movies, Amit. What're you going to do – run around and shoot the lot of 'em? You're crazy.'

'So how would you do it then?'

'Wouldn't even try,' said Dyson. 'And nor would you if it came down to it. You couldn't do it – not actually kill someone. Don't think any of us could.'

'I could.'

Everyone turned towards Ray. He was sitting with his legs tucked under him, staring down at the palms of his injured hands, and there was a bitterness in his voice that stopped all other conversation.

'You give me a gun,' he said, 'and show me how to use it, I'd kill 'em all.'

Dyson looked at him for a few moments longer, before putting another spoonful of food into his mouth.

'Listen, Ray,' said Gene. 'Try not to worry too much about later on, OK? The hole, I mean. As long as you don't panic, you'll be all right. And at least you've been warned, yeah? At least you kind of know what to expect. Eat something, and drink some water. It's better to have something in your stomach to begin with.'

Nobody spoke for a while.

'So how long before we have to go down?' Baz felt like a condemned prisoner waiting for execution.

Robbie shuffled backwards towards where the grass grew thicker. He lay on his side, head propped on his hand, and yawned. 'Couple hours or so yet. They'll sit around the sort room and drink together for a while. Then they'll come out looking for a bit of fun. It's better if you just make it easy for 'em – don't try to run away or anything.'

Another spell of silence. Baz looked up at the sports centre, squinting against the hazy brightness of the sky. 'I can't believe there's nowhere better that we could all hide,' he said. 'I mean, what if they couldn't find any of us for the whole day and we didn't turn up till night time? What would they do?'

'I already told you,' said Amit. 'There's nowhere to go. The main stairway's totally collapsed, so you can't get up into the building. And the only other stairs are through the divers' bit, so nobody's gonna be daft enough to try that. I think they might be blocked off anyway. The sports centre's all locked up. Forget it.'

'What about the back stairs?' said Ray.

'Huh?'

'You know, the, er . . . that spiral staircase thing. You can see a bit of it where the wall's come away. Round the back of the building.'

'Oh, that. Yeah. Don't even know where it goes to. But if it's round the back then it must start somewhere down in the divers' bit, and so who's gonna go looking for that?'

No answer.

'Just imagine, though' – Robbie came back to the earlier subject – 'if it *was* only us here. No divers, no Preacher John, no capos. Be great, wouldn't it?'

'Yeah.' Dyson's voice was dismissive. 'Till the food ran out. What then? We don't know anything about diving.'

'We could learn,' said Robbie. 'Bet I could. Or we could, I dunno . . . grow stuff, maybe.'

'I used to have an allotment.' Enoch joined in the talk – a rare thing for him. 'My old man did, anyhow. He used to take me up there with him. I liked it.'

'There you go,' said Amit. 'Enoch could grow us some spuds. Problem solved.'

'Problem solved? Ha. I don't think so.' Dyson's was the gloomy voice of reason again. 'There'd be a bit more to it than that. You're dreaming.'

'Why don't you butt out, Dyson?' Amit sat up and leaned forward. 'OK, so I'm just dreaming. But maybe we shouldn't be just dreaming. There's trouble coming, that's what I reckon, and it's starting to scare me. The divers aren't pulling in anything like the amount of food they used to. That boat used to come back full of tins, but not any more. What's gonna happen to us once the salvage runs out?'

All faces stared inwards at the empty cans on the grass.

'Nah. Preacher's not daft,' said Dyson. 'He'll have some angle.'

'Angle? The bloke's a nutter. The only angle he's got is trying to make God get rid of the floods! How's he gonna do that?'

Dyson said, 'I still don't reckon the trading's that bad, or why would he take on new kids?'

And those around Dyson – the non-sharers, as Baz had started to think of them – seemed ready to take their cue from him.

'Yeah, him find another little Tesco or somet'ing,' said Jubo.

'Bound to,' said Enoch. 'And the floods'll have to go down in the end.'

The two of them glanced at Dyson for approval.

'Yes. Perhaps by next Sunday.' Taps seemed to be up to speed on the conversation for a change. But then he said, 'I don't know why everyone thinks that the number seven is lucky. Sunday's the seventh day, isn't it?'

Nobody could see the connection. They waited for Taps to explain, but he hung his great dark head and said nothing more.

'This is what I'm on about, though.' Amit plucked at little bits of grass near his feet. 'When it comes down to it, all you'll actually do is just sit here and hope that things are gonna get better. Well, they aren't. They're gonna get worse.'

'So what are *you* gonna to do about it? Or Robbie, or Gene? Or these newbies here?' Dyson was scowling now, arms folded, closed off to all argument.

'I don't *know*.' Amit looked equally angry and miserable. 'I don't know. But we ought to be seriously thinking about it. Trying to make some proper plan, instead of just . . . just . . . wishing.'

But nobody had any immediate suggestions. The silence that followed was eventually broken by Jubo. He leaned sideways and let out a long fart.

It cracked everyone up.

'Uh-oh . . .'

'*Uh*-oh . . .'

'Ha, ha! Good one, Jubes! That's the answer! We'll just use rocket power to blast our way out of here!'

'Yeah, jet-propelled. Fly to Australia, see if it's any better down there.'

The mirth soon died away and the group settled into a gloomy truce. Baz slumped backwards and rested his head in the crook of one arm. He was suddenly too exhausted to even think. But then he half sat up again.

'Hey – what happens to Cookie on Sundays?' he said.

'We already told you,' Robbie murmured, his eyes closed. 'We don't have anything to do with Cookie. He doesn't know about this, and it's best it stays that way.

He has to work on a Sunday in any case. The divers still have to eat.'

'Oh.'

Baz lay back and allowed himself to drift away, launching himself into an amazing flight all the way around the world to Australia. Rocket-powered. His own internal jet-pack. *Frrrrrrt*. It was such a great idea. He could feel himself chuckling as he soared to freedom.

The sky was darker when he woke up, misty rain clouds hanging close around the tiny island. It was later than anyone had intended, and now the others were worried that Steiner and Hutchinson would already be on the prowl.

Last-minute advice was offered as the boys hurried across the playing fields.

'Don't let on that you know what's gonna happen,' said Robbie. 'It makes it more fun for them if you act scared.'

Yeah, thought Baz. Act scared. I'll try and remember to do that.

As they neared the main building, the boys split up, drifting away in twos and threes. Dyson, Jubo and Enoch wandered down towards the jetty. Taps had gone off by himself somewhere. Amit and Robbie said they were going to have a kick around the ruins, see if there was anything interesting to find.

'I got a biro last week,' said Robbie. 'Works too.'

'I'll just hang around with you guys for a bit.' Gene, surprisingly, stayed with Baz and Ray. 'Keep an eye on you. Thing is, it's always best to try and— Oh, look out. Here we go.'

Steiner and Hutchinson had appeared. They came out of the main entranceway and stood for a moment at the top of the steps, eyes squinting against the daylight.

'Oi! Where've you lot been?' Steiner turned and spotted them.

'What? Nowhere.' Gene came to a halt, edging slightly in front of Baz and Ray. The three of them stood on the cracked tarmac driveway and waited.

'We been looking everywhere for you. Wha'f . . . wha' friggin' hell you been doing?' The two capos began to descend the steps. Neither looked very steady on their feet.

'Sunday, isn't it?' said Gene. His voice was calm, innocent. 'Do what we like, can't we?'

'Hey – none of your lip, Genius. You can shove off.'

'All right. I'm going.' Gene moved a couple of paces to one side, giving the impression that he was doing as he was told. He didn't go far though, and remained as a half-presence, just out of the capos' line of vision.

'Right then, you two.' Hutchinson's face looked flushed and sweaty, his words dribbling out from between loose wet lips. 'Gorra li'l job f' you.'

'Us? What job? I thought we didn't have to work Sundays.' Baz tried to keep his voice normal, cheerful even, but inside he could feel his stomach begin to quake.

' 'S not work,' said Steiner. He'd reached the bottom of the steps now. 'Jus' need a coupla volunteers f'r a minute, thass all.' His eyes had gone a pinkish colour, a look of dull cunning in them that would fool no one.

'Oh. Volunteers. OK, then.' Again Baz forced himself to sound as though he was willing to help, not about to argue. Ray had said nothing as yet.

'Gotta inspec' the drains, see. Only a li'l job. Go on – jus' round there.'

'What? Where?' Baz looked at Steiner, unclear as to where he was supposed to be going. Ray turned and moved away, as though he'd understood what was expected.

'Jus' there. Roun' the corner.'

Baz caught up with Ray, and the two of them hung close together, walking in front of the capos as they were directed round the side of the building. Glancing once over his shoulder, Baz saw that Gene was still watching from a distance.

'Whoa. Stop there. Stay where y'are.' Hutchinson slurred out his instruction.

There was a circular manhole cover set into the tarmac a couple of metres out from the side of the building. Black metal, with a diamond pattern. A word cast in plain bold letters across its centre: NUNEATON.

'I'll get t' levers.' Steiner put one hand flat to the concrete wall of the building. He wobbled, steadied himself, then stooped to retrieve a couple of short iron bars that were propped against the wall.

'OK.'

The capos took a lever apiece and inserted them into the manhole cover, a clink of metal upon metal as the bars locked into position.

'Ready? Two, three, lift. Hup . . . oof.'

The iron lid made a hollow ringing sound as it came away from its seating, and the capos both gasped with the effort of raising it, staggering as they lifted it across onto the tarmac. They dropped it with a heavy clunk.

'Foof! Chuffin' hell! Mus' be getting weaker or something. Weighs a friggin' ton, that thing.' Steiner stood up straight and brushed a gingery forearm across his face. His freckles had turned almost purple.

'C'mon – don't just stand there gawking. Get over here.'

Baz and Ray moved cautiously forward, and already the smell of sewage was in the air, a great waft of it coming up from the open drain.

'What for?' This time Baz couldn't keep the suspicion out of his voice.

'Show you,' said Steiner. 'Look down the— Get *closer*, for Chrissake! Can't see anything from there. Look down the bloody hole!'

The two of them leaned over and looked. Baz was certain that at any moment one of the capos was going to give him a shove. He could see . . . orange. The inside of the drain was orange, the iron tube streaked and heavily scaled with rust. A vertical metal ladder descended into the gloom, and this too was a deep orange colour . . . dripping wet . . . filthy . . . and – oh God – the smell . . .

Baz glanced across at Ray, and was shocked to see how white his face had gone – an awful ghostly colour. God, he looked like he was about to throw up on the spot.

'See that handle down there?'

Baz held his breath and peered deeper into the fetid

hole. Yes, there was some kind of mechanism, a winding handle . . . but he could also see the slurry of foul liquid from which the handle protruded. Christ. Was he supposed to stand in that? How deep was it?

'All you have to do is wind t' sluice handle. Turn it to the right till it won't go any more.'

'Yeah? To the right. OK, then.' Baz nodded, but he made no move. 'So . . . I just turn it to the right, yeah? How long does it take?' He couldn't go down there. He knew it. His stomach was already starting to heave, and no way could he climb down that ladder.

'Not long,' said Steiner. 'Maybe a minute. Couple minutes. But I wasn't talking to you, was I?'

'What?'

'I said, I wasn't talking to you, you friggin' freak. Don't worry, it'll be your turn next. But right now it's this *other* little maggot that's going down there.'

And then in a sudden move Steiner had hold of Ray, grasping him by the upper arm and shaking him.

'Oh yeah! *Ohhhh* yeah! You thought you'd bloody got away with it, didn't you? Thought you could come it with me, and after a couple days it'd all be forgotten, didn't you? Well, I don't forget, pal! I don't forget that friggin' easy. I told you there'd be payback, and this is it. You're goin' down the hole.'

Ray gasped, but made no further sound. He seemed almost to have fainted on his feet, limply allowing himself to be shaken back and forth, no resistance in him whatever.

Baz's first instinct was to rush at Steiner, but some fragment of reasoning held him back. It was no good trying anything physical. He wasn't big enough – and

144

in any case Hutchinson was there as Steiner's support. Insults were the only weapons he had.

'You friggin' coward!' he shouted. 'You dozy prat-faced gingah! Yah – look at you! So drunk you can hardly stand up! You ugly piece of cr—'

But then Hutchinson had him round the neck, and he was struggling to break free – still yelling for all he was worth, half choking at the same time.

'Dickhead! You useless . . . thick . . . tanked-up . . . bullying—'

'Get him down the hole!' roared Steiner. 'That one! Chuck him down there instead! Go on, Hutch – do it!'

'I'm trying . . . I'm try— C'm 'ere . . . you friggin' . . .'

Baz was kicking and wriggling for his life now, but Hutchinson still held him by the neck.

'I can't . . . gah . . . you little f— Gimme some bloody *help*, Steiner!'

Baz caught a glimpse of Ray, falling to his knees as Steiner flung him aside, and then there were two pairs of hands grabbing him, dragging him, lifting him . . .

'Ahhh!' He was dangling over the open manhole.

'Want us to drop you? Want us to drop you straight down there? Yeah?'

'No! No! Don't!'

'Stop friggin' around then! Keep still!'

'OK . . . OK . . .' Baz ceased to struggle, got his feet to the edge of the manhole and regained his balance – the capos still gripping his arms.

'Right. You're gonna climb down that bloody ladder, get in the tank and turn that bloody handle, yeah?' Steiner's ugly face was close to his, and Baz could smell

145

alcohol even through the foul fumes that came up from the drain.

'Yes! Yes – I'll do it.'

'Do it then, you little turd. Now!'

The capos let go of Baz. He crouched at the side of the manhole, shuffled round and awkwardly lowered one leg over the edge, searching for the ladder. His arms were shaking, hardly able to bear his weight. He got a foothold on one of the rungs, took a step down . . . then another . . .

The rusted metal felt wet and slimy and rough all at the same time, agony to his blistered palms, and yet he needed to hold on so tightly. Mustn't let go. Another step down – urgh, the stench – the unbearable filthy stench. He forced himself to go a bit further, and a bit further, and then the world was gone. He was all alone, descending step by step into an echoing tube of rust and scale and stinking waste.

'Keep going.'

Baz looked up at the confused shapes, silhouetted in the narrowing circle of light – looked up because he hardly dared look down. Time and again his stomach heaved, and he knew that he wouldn't be able to control the gagging at the back of his throat much longer. God, the smell was unbelievable. Ugh – his foot was wet . . .

He had to look down. Oh . . . Christ. The ladder disappeared into liquid sewage, and his foot was already submerged in it. Ugh . . . ugh. He quickly pulled it out again. God, this was horrible.

The drain had opened out, and surrounding the ladder was a circular tank, an underground chamber.

Brick walls running with slime. Baz could see the winding mechanism, a kind of gate or paddle, with a handle on top. It was only a couple of metres away, but the mechanism protruded from the middle of the slurry. There was no way he could reach it and still remain on the ladder.

'Go on, you little toad. You have to get in there.' Steiner's voice boomed down, echoing around the stinking cavern. 'Wade across. It's not deep. Go and turn that chuffin' handle.'

Not deep? Baz thought he remembered somebody saying it came up to your armpits. He couldn't do this. He just couldn't.

'Oi! If you don't hurry up and get in there, I'm gonna put this chuffin' lid back on and leave you to it!'

The threat made Baz jump. Being shut down here in pitch darkness was the one thing that could make it worse. *Help me. Someone help me . . .*

Dad. Come and help me . . . Please *come*. Baz felt the tears rushing to his eyes, great gulps of emotion choking him. He lowered himself, sobbing, into the tank. *It's OK, Dad. I can do it. I can. I bloody well can. But help me.*

He was waist-deep when his feet touched bottom. Baz didn't pause. In a blur of tears he forced himself to let go of the ladder, forced himself to wade straight towards the winding handle, crying openly now, not caring.

'Urrghhhhhh . . .' A continuous gurgling wail came out of him. *I'm doing it, Dad. I'm getting there. I'm reaching out. I'm reaching out. I'm holding the handle. I'm turning it.* Round . . . round . . . round. 'Urrghhhhh . . .'

More. More. More. It's done. Go back, then. Back through the stinking filthy . . . urrrggghhh . . . urrrghhh.

Baz fell against the ladder, still sobbing, and began to pull himself out of the foul slurry. *I did it, Dad. I did it. I did it . . .*

'Oi! Where d'you think you're going? Who said you could come out? We're not done with you yet!' Steiner was shouting at him. Baz gazed up at the blurred and broken circle of light. He heard murmurs – the capos in some kind of discussion. Someone said the word 'lid', and Baz was terrified that he was about to be left down here in the darkness after all. *No . . . not that. Please don't.*

'. . . better idea.' Steiner's voice again, drifting down in deep rebounding echoes. One shape had returned and now remained motionless, almost blocking out the light. Baz waited.

Something splattered onto his arm, then his face. A stream of liquid, bright drops raining down on him. It took Baz another second to realize what it was, and he tried to duck out of the way, lowering his head, scrunching up his shoulders. But there was nowhere to go, and so he simply clung to the ladder and waited for it to stop.

And eventually it did stop. The last few drops splashed down onto his knuckles.

'Ahh. That's better! *Now* you can come up.'

He could come up, and for the moment nothing else mattered. The shame, the tears, none of it mattered. He wasn't going to be shut down here in the reeking darkness. Baz climbed the ladder as fast as his aching body would allow, hauling himself upwards rung over rung, desperate to escape. He reached the top, threw himself forward and scrambled over the lip of the drain. On all fours he remained, crawling away from the hole, ready to tear his fingernails into the tarmac if anyone should try and drag him back.

'Ha, ha! Look at that! Like a bloody dog. Get up, you pillock!'

The capos' voices sounded flat after the booming echoes of the drain. Baz stumbled to his feet, turned round, backed away a few paces. He saw that Ray was still on the ground, close to the manhole.

Hutchinson said, 'D'you wanna leave this other one, then? 'Cos I got better things to do.'

Steiner looked down at Ray. 'Yeah, OK. It's getting late and I need 'nother drink. He's gonna be in the hole for a lot longer anyway – a helluva lot longer. It can wait till next Sunday. Gives him a week to think about it. Gerrup, you mongrel!' Steiner kicked out at Ray.

Ray rolled sideways, got to his hands and knees, then stood up. He moved towards Baz uncertainly, still keeping his eye on the capos.

'Right. Sod off, the pair of you. Go on – crawl back to where you come from!'

They were apparently free to leave. Stunned, directionless, Baz had no thought of where he was going other than away from this spot. His legs were moving, but his eyes were focused on nothing.

Then Gene was there, standing in front of him. 'You all right?'

The concern on Gene's face brought Baz back into

the present. He looked down at his clothes – T-shirt, shorts, trainers – all running wet and covered in filth. His bare arms and legs were streaked and glistening . . . urine trickled through his hair and down his neck.

Awareness of his foul and stinking self brought him to tears again, so that he was unable to speak. He couldn't even wipe his eyes, his hands and arms were so disgusting.

'I can't . . . I'm . . .'

'Don't try and talk,' said Gene. 'Let's just get you cleaned up. We'll see if the slob room's open, yeah? Sneak you in there and you can have a shower. You'll feel better then. Come and keep a lookout, Ray.'

Baz stumbled along between the two of them, the world around him a blur of utter misery.

Later he did feel a little better, but still not completely clean. The awful smell seemed to hang in his nostrils and at the back of his throat.

His shame was eased by the fact that others had suffered in the same way. As they sat around the slob room, the boys recounted their own tales of how they'd been put in the hole. Only Gene and Dyson, those who had been on the island the longest, had escaped the ritual.

'It could've been worse, mate,' said Amit. 'At least you didn't get the lid treatment like Jubo here. Or Taps. God, he came out screaming, Taps did. Remember that?' Amit lowered his voice as he glanced across to where Taps was sitting on his mattress. 'I mean, it was like . . . I dunno, a breakdown or something. Poor guy wet his bed for a week after that.'

'You can still smell his mattress,' said Robbie. 'Come on. We'd better get some sleep.'

It was late in the evening, and the windows of the slob room had grown dark, but nobody had come to switch out the light.

'The capos'll be flat out by now,' said Gene. 'Not likely to see them on a Sunday night. You feeling all right, Ray?'

Ray had been silent for hours, pale and withdrawn. He'd been sympathetic to Baz – helped him out with the offer of a clean T-shirt – but it was clear that his mind was elsewhere. Now he sat on the floor, his legs tucked beneath him, head lowered.

Without looking up, he said, 'I can't do it. I'm not going down there.'

It was a flat statement, and Baz knew that Ray wasn't hoping for words of reassurance, or persuasion, or argument. He'd made up his mind. And maybe everyone else could see that, because nothing was said for a while.

'Well . . .' Gene eventually gave a short sigh. 'You've only got one other choice, Ray. Refuse to work, and get yourself shipped back.'

'Can't do that, either.'

'I'm telling you, mate, there's no other way.'

'Course there's another way. There's always another bloody way.' Ray began to get to his feet. 'What if I killed them both while they were asleep? That'd be another way, wouldn't it? What if I stuck a bomb under their pillows?'

'Oh yeah, right.' Gene's mouth went a bit crooked. 'Hadn't thought of that.'

'What if I poisoned them or . . . or filled the drain with concrete . . . or glued their stupid eyelids together so they couldn't even see me? That'd be another way, wouldn't it?'

One or two of the boys were openly laughing now, but Ray was obviously furious. He stormed off towards the washroom and disappeared.

'Nutter,' said Dyson. 'You put up, or you shut up – that's what you do.'

'Yeah, well, you've never had to go down there,' said Amit. 'And it's right, though, what he says. There does have to be another way. What d'you reckon, Gene?'

'Hey, don't ask me,' Gene muttered. He stared towards the washroom, chin in his hands, a slight frown on his face.

Baz looked over at Taps. He was playing with a bit of plastic, some scrap of a thing that he'd found in the rubble. Poor kid. Taps wasn't exactly shunned, not like Cookie, but he was outside the circle, somehow. A circle that Baz was beginning to feel part of, perhaps the more so after today's experience.

Ray came back into view, pushing aside the wash-room curtain. He flopped straight onto his mattress and lay gazing up at the ceiling. Baz decided he'd better go down there and try and talk to him.

He glanced at Taps in passing. Taps sat alone on his bed, fiddling with whatever it was that he'd found – a red and grey plastic thing that rested on his knee. He kept pressing buttons and making half-whispered sounds to himself. *'Peeow-peeow! Zz-zz-zz-yow!'*

Baz felt a sudden warmth towards him – a child with

no friends playing all by himself. 'Hey, what you got there, Taps?'

'A present. Gameboy. *Peeowww!*'

'Wow. Haven't seen one of those in ages.' Baz drew closer and peered at the Gameboy screen. It was blank. The thing had no batteries in it. Or maybe it was broken altogether. Either way Taps was playing some game that existed only in his own head.

'*Peeeeowwwww. Zt-zt-zt.*'

Baz left him to it.

CHAPTER NINE

On Monday Baz and Ray got lucky. Taps had chosen them both for the sort-room crew.

'At least it'll give our blisters a bit more chance to heal up,' Baz muttered afterwards.

'Yeah.'

They had a fairly easy day of it. Hutchinson was so hung over from his Sunday drinking session that he disappeared at the first opportunity, and as there was no new salvage to put through the tubs, Baz and Ray were at least able to keep their hands dry. They spent most of their time standing at the workbench next to Gene, learning codes.

Taps and Dyson sat outside, cleaning and polishing a few odd bits and pieces. There really wasn't much to do. Dyson appeared to be giving Taps a hard time over how the teams should have been picked. Baz overheard him say, 'Can't you get it into your head? From now on it's me, you, Jubo and Enoch. Yeah? We gotta stick together over this.'

It was the food thing again, Baz realized. Dyson was trying to keep his supporters close.

'You gonna make us another rocket, Gene?'

Baz wandered over to Gene's workbench.

'Nah. I need to try and get this Seagull working.' Gene was fiddling around with engine parts.

'What's a Seagull?'

'Outboard motor. For a boat. A few weeks ago the divers dredged up some old tub from out where the reservoir used to be. Sailing dinghy. The mast's kicking around out the back there. They're not gonna sail it, though. They want a motor on it instead. They're gonna get it patched up a bit, see if it still floats, and in the meantime I'm supposed to be trying to get this old thing going. It's pretty basic, but it's also pretty knackered.'

'What – so the engine fits onto the boat?'

'Yeah, you can fit a Seagull to anything. It just clamps onto the transom at the back, then you got yourself a motor boat.'

'How'd you *learn* all this stuff?'

'You mean mechanics?' Gene shrugged. 'My dad started me off, I suppose. He was always fiddling around with motorbikes and scooters, and I got interested. He taught me a lot. And these old two-stroke engines aren't that complicated. Seen one, you've seen 'em all.'

'Reckon you could make a bomb?' said Ray.

'A *what*?'

'A bomb. Baz told me you made some kind of rocket thing on Saturday, out of cigarette-lighter bits. I just wondered if you could make a proper bomb.' Ray's big brown eyes were full of innocence, as if he were asking whether Gene knew how to repair a bicycle puncture.

'What are you, nuts? No, I don't know how to make

a "proper bomb". You'd need all kinds of stuff – explosives, detonators . . . God knows what else. Why? Thinking of blowing the place up, are you?'

Ray didn't reply immediately, and Gene said, 'Oh, look out. The kid's gone crazy. First he wants to put a bomb under the capos' pillows, and now he wants to go the whole hog and blow up Preacher John. Yeah, I get it. This isn't just about the hole, is it, Ray? You've been listening to Amit, haven't you? Well, listen to me instead – it's never gonna happen, OK? I can see where Amit's coming from, and how things could be different – and better. But the Eck brothers, you really don't want to think about messing with them. They're grown men, for Chrissake. Big guys. With real guns, yeah? You're not just gonna wipe them out like it's some friggin' video game.'

'But let's say you *could* make a bomb. Just say you *could* . . .' Ray obviously had some idea buzzing around in his head.

'Hey – give up, willya?' Gene was having none of it. 'I got work to do.' He took a heavy file from his toolbox and began rasping away with it, attacking a rusty piece of angle bracket that was held in the vice.

Ray looked as though he were about to say something else, but Baz shook his head at him. Enough. Leave it.

'Where did those divers come from, anyway?' he said, changing the subject. 'And the boat? We're miles away from where the sea used to be.'

Gene took a while to reply, cautious now as he spoke. 'The Eck brothers ran a scuba diving club on Clough Reservoir,' he said. 'But they used to hire the swimming pool at the sports centre to practise some-times, when the school was closed for the holidays. So they were up here with all their gear when it happened. That's what I heard. Dunno what Preacher John was doing here. Moko worked at the school, though.'

'What – he was a *teacher*?'

'Nah. Caretaker, I think. And he had this old boat he was doing up at weekends and in the holidays. It was on dry land at the time. I think he was allowed to keep it at the school. Or maybe he lived here. Dunno. So Moko and the divers all got together, I suppose. He had the boat, they had the scuba gear.'

'Oh.'

'So . . . this rocket thing you made—' Ray started again, but he got no further.

'Look.' Gene put down the file he was holding. 'I'm not interested, OK? This is a cushy number for me, and I'm not gonna blow it. I'm definitely not teaming up with some idiot kids who're gonna get me shot, yeah? 'Cos that's what'll happen to Amit, and that's what'll happen to you if you carry on the way you're going.' He lowered his voice. 'OK, anyone can see that things'd be a dam' sight easier round here with no divers and no capos. Yeah, and if I thought we had any chance of making it happen, then I might go for it. But there's no chance. And you've got no idea what you're dealing with. Now get back to your codes and gimme a break.'

The jetty gang were covered in grey powdery dust when they returned that evening.

157

'We bin mixin' concrete,' said Robbie. 'God, it was a killer.'

'*Concrete?*' said Dyson. 'Didn't know we had any. Where'd it come from?'

'The storeroom. Luke went in there and came out with all these bags of cement on a trolley. Never seen that before. Then we had to bring a load of sand and chippings down from the building site. Mix it into concrete on the jetty.'

'What for?' Dyson took a spoonful of spaghetti from his tin. The boys spread themselves around the seating area of the slob room, some draped across the chairs, some lying on the floor.

'Well, we've been building, like, some kind of platform,' said Robbie. 'Or a concrete base. You tell 'em, Amit.'

'Yeah, it's right at the end of the jetty,' said Amit. 'Steiner made us put four planks in a square, stood up on their edges like we were making a sandpit or something. Yeah? Then we had to hammer in bits of wood at the corners and along the sides so the planks didn't fall over. And then we had to mix all this concrete and spread it around in there.'

'You forgot about that pipe t'ing,' said Jubo.

'Oh yeah. There was this piece of pipe about a metre long, like a metal drainpipe or something. We had to hack through the rubble at the end of the jetty and stick this pipe in the hole and concrete round it. So's the end was poking up out of the ground. Then we built the platform thing in front of that. There's not enough concrete in there yet. Got to skim it off flat tomorrow, Steiner says.'

'Did he say what it's gonna be?'

'He don't say much at all today.' Jubo had a big grin on his face.

'Ha, ha! Feeling a bit poorly then, was he?'

'Sick as a dog, guy. T'row up twice in da first hour.'

'Good.'

'So what's with all this bomb business?' Baz wanted to know. 'Where did that idea come from? Was it Amit?' He and Ray were lying on their mattresses, waiting for lock-up. Ray rolled over sideways and propped himself up on one elbow.

'Not really. It was yesterday, when we were up by the sports centre,' he murmured. 'When Enoch said about growing potatoes. I thought – we could do that. We really could. This place'd be great if it was just us. Or as good as anywhere we'd ever find. It's safe, and nobody else can get here. And then . . .' Ray looked down at his palms, picking at bits of loose skin. 'I kind of went to sleep on the grass, and it was like it had already happened. I saw it. Everything had changed. It was sunny and we were all up on the playing field, kicking a ball around. And then you kicked the ball really hard and it went into the cabbages—'

'Cabbages?'

'Yeah. And you said, "Oh, we'll never find it now. Never mind, we'll play with a cabbage instead." And so we all started kicking this big cabbage around. It was . . . fun. And then I woke up again, back to all this.'

Ray's big eyes glanced around at the shabby room. 'It could be different,' he said. 'We could make it perfect.'

'But a bomb? I just don't get it . . .'

'Nor do I, really. I was just trying to think of a way to make it happen. Like in one go. We can't fight those guys, or get their guns or anything. But, you know, with a bomb . . . I dunno . . . maybe we could get 'em all in one place and just blow 'em all up at once. Then they'd be gone.'

Ray spoke as though killing people was nothing. Baz was shocked at the idea.

'So . . . say there was a button,' he said, 'like on a cigarette lighter, and all you had to do was press the button, and that would kill all the divers and Preacher John, and Steiner and Hutchinson. You'd do that, would you?'

Ray turned towards him, a steady look from beneath thick dark lashes, eyebrows raised in mild surprise. 'Well, yeah. Wouldn't you?'

Baz almost laughed. Ray looked at his most innocent when he was making the most outrageous statements.

'Um . . . don't know. Don't know whether I could.'

'Depends on what you care about, doesn't it? You'd do anything for people you really care about.' Ray looked at Baz for a long moment. Then he said, 'I mean, you've got a dad, right? So say Preacher John had a gun to your dad's head. Wouldn't you press the button on a cigarette lighter to save him?'

'Course I would. Yeah.'

'Well, then. Same thing.'

Same thing as what? What was the same thing?

On Tuesday Baz was back on jetty duty, along with

Taps, Dyson and Jubo. Together they climbed the steep path that led up to the playing fields.

When they reached the construction site, Dyson said, 'OK. We need water, sand and chippings. Taps and Baz do the water cart. Me and Jubo'll do the barrows.'

The water cart stood at one end of the sports centre building. It was a big oval-shaped drum, galvanized metal, fixed into a tubular frame. The frame had two wheels, and had a handle at the front to pull the cart along. Baz noticed that the tyres looked a bit flat.

'How do we fill it up?' he said. 'Buckets?' There were a couple of these lying around – yellow plastic ones.

'Yes,' said Taps. 'But not right to the top, or it becomes too heavy. We put ten bucketfuls in.' Then he looked at Baz and added, 'That's five buckets each.'

'No kidding?' Baz picked up one of the plastic buckets and went over to the nearest water barrel. He hopped up onto the stack of concrete blocks that the barrel stood on, intending to dip his bucket over the side, but Taps said, 'No. You must fill it from the tap.'

'Huh? Oh, right.' Baz hadn't noticed the plastic fitting on the side of the barrel. He jumped down to the ground, put his bucket under the tap and turned it on.

Taps came and stood beside him as the bucket began to fill up. 'One, elephant, two, elephant, three . . .'

'What?'

Taps was counting under his breath. 'Thirty-one seconds,' he said hurriedly. 'That's what it should come to . . . seven, elephant, eight . . .' He continued to count, but on his fingers now, nodding in time as he tapped the end of each finger.

'Yes. Thirty-one.' He leaned forward and quickly switched off the tap. 'That's enough now. You can put it in the water cart.'

Baz blew out his cheeks. 'OK,' he said, and picked up the bucket. He could see that this might take some time.

But Taps seemed to like filling the buckets, and Baz was happy to let that be his job. He stared out across the overgrown playing field and watched Old Bill, the white goat, as Taps counted his elephants. It was a rare moment of peace, if a slightly weird one, and Baz thought about Ray's dream with the cabbages. He could see the field with things growing in it, potatoes maybe, and beans, as well as cabbages. And Old Bill could be there too, munching away at the grass, with no worries. Just as he was now. Lucky Old Bill.

Taps was still filling the bucket. Baz suddenly felt that he wanted to reach out to this strange kid, to try and be a bit kind to him.

'Taps,' he said, 'is everything OK? You getting by all right?'

Taps carried on counting, and Baz wasn't sure that he'd heard the question. 'Twenty-nine, elephant, thirty, elephant, thirty-one.' Taps had finished filling the bucket. He stood up straight and looked at Baz, his pale-grey eyes serious and troubled. 'They made you go down the hole, didn't they? Yes. They did it to me too. When I first came here. And they put the cover on and left me down there in the dark. It was just a joke – a bit of fun. But I was so scared that I . . . well, you

162

know. It was all in my shorts. I didn't think anyone would know, because my clothes were all so messy anyway, but they did know. Everybody knew. Your friend Ray, he's not going to go down there, is he? I heard him say so.'

'Well . . .' Baz started to speak.

'I shan't go down there again either.' Taps looked up at the sky. 'I wish I could make the days longer,' he said. 'Like in summer. The days are longer in summer because the heat makes them expand. Did you know that? The heat makes everything expand and the cold makes everything contract. Like distances. Most people don't know that, but the distances between places keep changing with the temperature. It's never quite the same.'

'Er . . . right. Yeah, you're probably right, Taps. Come on. We'd better go.'

'I was just going to say that! Yes. We'd better go.'

Taps walked round to the front of the water cart. He grabbed the handle and waited for Baz to join him.

'I try not to forget things, you know, but sometimes I can't help it. Like with the hymn books. It's not my fault, is it?'

'No. Course not.' Baz pulled experimentally at the handle of the water cart. God, the thing was heavy.

'That's what I said to Hutchinson. But he said it was my fault, and that it was my fault that he got into trouble with Isaac.'

'Yeah?'

'And the days are shorter than they used to be. Now that it keeps raining and cooling everything down. It makes the time go faster.'

Baz was having difficulty understanding Taps at all. He could think of nothing else to say, and so he kept quiet for a bit.

It was hard work pulling the water cart around the perimeter of the playing field. The load was heavy, and the tyres needed more air. But once they got to the top of the steep pathway that led down to the jetty it became a matter of holding the cart back rather than pulling it along.

Baz and Taps both clung to the handle, leaning backwards in order to keep the water cart from running away with them, and struggling to steer it at the same time.

All of this was bad enough, but Baz realized that Taps was barely concentrating on the job in hand. He was whispering to himself once again, counting his footsteps as they staggered down the hill.

'Four-forty-four, four-forty-five—'

'Whoa – look out, Taps! Watch where we're going!' The cart veered into the side of the path and rocked to a halt. Water slopped out of the galvanized container, splashing down onto the tarmac.

'What are you *doing*?' Baz was getting annoyed.

'Sorry,' said Taps. 'I was just working something out. I like to know, you see.'

'Working what out?' Baz pushed down on the handle of the water cart in order to try and slew it round.

'It should be eight hundred and forty-two steps from the pile of chippings to the end of the jetty. Must be further, though, from the sports centre. Subtract the two, you see, and then you have the distance from the sports centre to the chippings.'

Baz was about to ask what the hell difference that should make to anyone – or at least to anyone who was sane – but he managed to stop himself. There was no point in getting mad at Taps. The poor kid obviously had problems. And if it was important to him to know how many footsteps between one place and another, or how many elephants it took to fill a bucket, then so what?

At any rate, he just sighed and said, 'It's OK, Taps. Come on. Grab the handle.'

The others were waiting for them by the time they got down to the jetty.

'Where've you been, you little freaks? We've been stood here ten minutes.' Steiner sounded as though he was in another great mood.

Baz and Taps dragged the water cart along the jetty, bringing it right up to where the new concrete platform was being built.

Steiner stood pointing at the ground with his finger, indicating where he wanted the cart to be. As they came to a halt, Baz heard Taps whisper, 'Eight-thirty-seven. Phew.'

A grey pile of sand and chippings and cement stood ready mixed and waiting on the flattened stone pathway in front of the platform construction. It looked like a volcano, its centre hollowed out so that water could be added.

'Where're the buckets?' said Steiner.

'Er . . . didn't bring any,' said Baz. 'Do we need some, then?'

'Course we *need* some, you rat's fart. How do you think we're gonna tip the water into t' mix if we've got no buckets?'

'Oh, right. Sorry . . .'

'Jesus. Have you got chuffin' bricks for brains, or what? Right – I've had enough. Get back up top, the lot of you. Fill t' barrows up again, four o' chippings and one o' sand, and this time don't forget the friggin' buckets. I want this batch mixed and another ready to go by the time I'm back. Ten minutes.' Steiner strode off along the jetty, shoulders slumped forward, hands in the pockets of his shorts.

'The guy make an early start today,' said Jubo, once Steiner was out of earshot.

'Yeah, right.'

The four boys climbed the hill once more, Dyson and Jubo pulling their barrows behind them, Baz and Taps carrying the shovels. When they got to the top, Dyson said, 'Taps, there's a couple of buckets over by that pile of sand. You might as well grab those – quicker than going over to the sports centre. The rest of us'll fill the barrows. See you back down there.'

'Yes. All right then.'

Baz said, 'What shall I do, sand or chippings?' and Dyson replied, 'Sand. We only need one barrowload of that.'

'OK.'

Baz took one of the barrows, put a shovel in it and wheeled it over to the pile of sand. Taps was already there, holding a bright yellow bucket in each hand, but looking confused.

'You OK?' said Baz. He picked up his shovel.

Taps blinked up at the sky as if he were searching for some answer up there. 'I've forgotten it now,' he said. 'Was it nine-thirty-seven? I think it was nine-thirty-seven.'

'What?'

But Taps didn't reply. He put both feet together, and then stepped forward, walking purposefully away from Baz as though he was pacing out the length of a cricket pitch.

'One, two, three . . .'

There was something about the way his head wobbled from side to side, the way his big red ears stuck out, that made Baz feel another pang of sorrow for Taps. But then he shrugged and turned towards the pile of sand. He had problems enough of his own.

The barrow was heavy, and Baz struggled to keep up with Jubo as he descended the hill. Already his hands were starting to hurt. The skin on his palms hadn't had a chance to heal properly, and Baz knew that he would be bleeding again before long.

But at least there was some air. A rare breeze had sprung up, and the distant sea looked choppy, flecks of white visible on the surface, almost like real waves.

Jubo, just in front of Baz, half turned his head and shouted, 'Ey, Dyson! What this t'ing supposed to be we building?'

'How should I know? Nobody tells me anything.' Dyson's voice from some way behind.

The concrete platform looked tiny from this height. It stood at the end of the jetty, a square of grey against the pinkish-coloured chipping pathway that led up to it. Maybe it was the foundation for some new building, Baz thought, although it seemed hardly big enough to put a shed on. He saw the little figure of Taps appearing far below, carrying a bucket in each hand, milkmaid-fashion, as he stepped out onto the jetty.

Taps wore shorts and sandals, and a red, white and blue striped T-shirt. With his two yellow buckets he looked quite colourful, a sunny kid who might have been on his way to the beach to look for crabs. In another life.

The sound of a voice drifted up – a faint shout – and Baz looked over to the right. He saw Steiner coming across from the direction of the school building, not hurrying, just strolling along the tarmac pathway, hands still in his pockets. Maybe the shout was for Taps and maybe it wasn't. Shouting came naturally to Steiner. He probably did it in his sleep.

Either way, Taps took no notice. He kept on walking along the jetty. Baz could almost hear him counting his footsteps.

Taps was approaching the water cart, but he didn't stop to put his buckets down. He walked straight past it, stepped up onto the square of concrete, and kept on going.

'Oi!' This time the shout from below was louder.

Jubo came to a halt, lowering the handles of his barrow so that the metal supports grated on the tarmac. 'What the guy doin' now . . . ?' He stood up straight. 'Ey – Taps!' he yelled.

Baz hauled backwards on the barrow, his feet slithering on the gritty surface of the pathway as he tried to avoid colliding with Jubo. But he was completely out of control, and the load tipped sideways, yellow sand slewing down the pathway as the barrow was wrenched from his grasp. Baz felt the skin of his palm split open, a stab of pain, but he dared not look at the damage. He clapped his hand to his mouth, the taste of blood metallic and salty on his tongue. And in the distance, through splayed fingers, he saw the figure of Taps disappearing over the end of the jetty . . .

'Oh, *man!*' Jubo took a hesitant step forward, then turned to look at Baz – his eyes wide in disbelief. 'You *see* that? Taps just . . .' Another moment of shock, and then Jubo seemed to come alive. He raised his arms into the air, waving frantically to Dyson. 'Dyse! Taps jus' gone off the jetty!'

Baz followed Jubo, running as fast as the steeply sloping path would allow.

The landscape below him danced crazily around, his vision shaken out of focus with each jarring foot-step. Steiner was hurrying along the jetty, then running, and Baz expected him to disappear in search of Taps. But when Steiner got to the end of the bank of rubble he came to a halt. He just stood there with his hands on his hips, looking down towards the water.

It seemed to take an age to get there. Baz caught up with Jubo at the point where the tarmac pathway came to an end, and together they ran along the top of the jetty, their feet scrunching in time on the chippings. They divided where the water cart stood, Baz to the right, Jubo to the left, then hopped across the half-finished square of concrete. From here it was only a few more steps to the crumbling edge of the jetty. Steiner turned to look at them, scowling, hands still on his hips.

'What the hell was *he* playing at?' he shouted. 'And where d'you think you're going?'

Jubo took no notice. He immediately began to clamber down the steep bank of rubble and concrete blocks, and after a moment of hesitation Baz followed, stooping to steady himself as he looked for solid footholds among the angular protrusions.

'Oi! Get back here!' Steiner kicked at the edge of the jetty and a scattering of chippings descended upon Baz, the sharp stones stinging him through the thin material of his T-shirt. He ignored Steiner and kept going.

There was no sign of Taps. The choppy waves smacked against the jumble of concrete blocks in random and unpredictable motion, sending gouts of foaming water shooting in all directions. Jubo was already thigh-deep in the waves, his hands cupped to his mouth, trying to keep his balance amidst the flying spray.

'Taps!' he shouted. 'Taps – you there?'

Baz was soaked long before he reached the water's edge. He put an arm up to shield himself and took another step downwards, searching for firm ground as his legs disappeared into the oily froth. Steiner was yelling something from above, but his words were lost in the surrounding rumble and splatter of the waves.

There was no rhythmic pattern to the current, nothing to work with. The waters rocked this way and that, battering Baz from all sides, and as he lowered himself yet further down the steeply shelving bank, he lost his balance. A wave caught him in the chest, threatening to throw him over backwards, and as he pushed against it in a desperate effort to stay upright, he was just as suddenly yanked in the opposite direction. He tumbled forward, sucked headlong into the soupy filth, eyes and mouth wide open with the shock of it . . .

Millions of dark fibrous threads swam before him, like little pieces of frayed cotton . . . and there were flakes of yellowy brown stuff . . . scaly sequins . . . all shooting away into the gloom. Down through a world of muted echoes he fell, swallowed up by the murk, until he was in utter darkness. His breath came out of him in a great sickly belch of terror, and foul water forced its way into his nose and throat and lungs, filling his mouth with nameless textures – gloops of slime – hairy things that brushed across the back of his tongue. He was choking, gagging, descending into a black and bottomless void. He was going down to his death. Oh God, it was really going to happen. Then his shins scraped against something solid – the hard edges of concrete blocks – and the pain of it came as a burst of relief, a stab of hope, because he hadn't disappeared into complete nothingness after all. The world was still here. Baz scrabbled blindly about, reaching out for something, anything, to cling to, the roar of panic in his ears. His fingertips found the bank of rubble, and the slope of it gave him direction. He clung frantically to the sharp corners of the blocks, pulling himself upwards, fingers, knees, toes. The water grew paler in colour – a glimpse of daylight – gone – there again. And then he was gasping in the roil of froth and foam, spitting, gulping, but still crawling. Still alive. He stumbled forward, hauled himself a little higher up the bank in a last effort to get clear of the waves, and then collapsed onto the rubble.

Almost immediately his stomach went into spasms of retching, so that he had to somehow get onto all fours once more in order to keep from choking. Black water spewed out of him, pumping so violently that he thought his very insides must come up through his throat. Oh God. Oh, God . . .

'That'll teach you, you dozy pillock.' Steiner's voice drifted down from above. Baz couldn't even look. His whole body was thrown into gasping convulsions again and again, although there was no longer anything to bring up.

He was aware of hands upon his shoulders, and he heard Jubo say, 'You OK, guy. You OK.'

Baz wiped his streaming eyes, coughed and spat, and spat some more. He couldn't get the awful taste out of his mouth. His stomach gave another dry heave, and another, but gradually his juddering breath became calmer. He looked briefly upwards to see that Jubo was standing beside him.

'No . . . no good?' he said.

'Taps?' Jubo shook his head. 'Nah. Him gone, man. Come on. We get you on your feet.'

Baz needed all the help Jubo could give him to get back up the rubble bank. The pair of them were dripping wet, and it was difficult to get any kind of grip on each other. Time and again Baz slipped from Jubo's grasp and fell. But somehow they got there, staggering over the lip of the jetty at last and onto level ground. Jubo still held him upright, and now the pair of them were confronted by Steiner.

'Satisfied?' Steiner's lips were pursed in cold anger, his upper teeth protruding slightly. He stepped forward and caught Baz with a stinging slap on the side of the head. As Baz rocked sideways, Steiner lashed out again – this time at Jubo. But Jubo managed to dodge what was coming, letting go of Baz's arm in order to protect himself. With no further support, Baz collapsed in a heap. He looked up to see Steiner and Jubo in a brief circling dance on the brink of the jetty, Steiner's arms outstretched like a goal-keeper's, Jubo dodging from left to right, trying to get past. Then Steiner suddenly lifted his foot and kicked Jubo straight between the legs.

Jubo doubled up and fell to the ground, rolling this way and that in gasping agony.

'What the hell d'you think you're playing at?' Steiner's freckled face had turned red with fury. 'Just 'cos one little nutter decides to go for a chuffin' swim doesn't mean you all have to. You're not much use to me alive, but you're no chuffin' use dead!' He whisked at the ground with the side of his boot, sending a shower of stones flying towards Baz.

'Get up! Yeah, *you*! Come on. You've wasted enough chuffin' time already.'

Baz rolled over onto his hands and knees and struggled to stand up. 'Now get that other useless tosser onto his feet. Drag yourselves down to t' sort room and tell Hutchinson I need a couple of replacements. Now!'

Jubo was still lying on his side in the dust, clutching at himself, tears of pain streaming down his face. Baz staggered over, his stomach in turmoil. He crouched beside Jubo.

'Come on, Jube. Better see if you can get up.' He managed to lift Jubo into a sitting position, then grabbed his wrists and hauled him onto his feet.

'Ah . . . ah . . .' Jubo's breath escaped in short bursts.

'Come on. You're OK.' Baz got one of Jubo's arms around his shoulders.

'Oi – shift yourselves!' Steiner took a step towards them, and Baz made an effort to start walking.

'Come on,' he said to Jubo. 'We can do it.'

They began to stumble slowly along the jetty. As they passed Dyson, he gave them a slight nod.

'See you later, Jubo,' he muttered. But Jubo said nothing.

About halfway back to the main building Jubo called a halt. 'Gonna have to stop.' He disengaged himself from Baz and leaned forward, his hands resting on his knees, head down.

Baz was glad of the breather. His insides were knotted up in pain and he felt dizzy. The putrid taste was still in his mouth, a reminder of his underwater terror, the moment when he really thought he was going to die. To die. And that was what had actually happened to Taps. Poor guy. Poor, poor guy . . .

The sudden splatter of falling liquid made him jump. Jubo was throwing up. Bits of yesterday's spaghetti festooned the tarmac, thick white worms in a pinkish juice, watery patterns trickling through the dust.

Baz felt his stomach lurch, and he too leaned forward, retching a couple of times in sympathy. But though his guts heaved and the back of his throat felt as though it would split open, there was simply nothing there. He got a grip on himself and stood up again.

'Jesus, man.' Jubo's voice was thick and muffled. He let out a deep breath, took another. Eventually he stood up too, wiping his chin with the back of his hand.

'Ey.' He looked directly at Baz, his dark face covered in a film of sweat. 'I gonna kill that Steiner. I don't care who say what – it already happen, man. Yeah. And not 'cos him kick me, but 'cos him stand there and watch Taps drown. Don' lift a finger. So I gonna take him – and *rass*, man, to what Dyson or anyone else t'ink. Yeah?'

Baz nodded. Yeah.

The hum of the sort room died down as they walked in, everyone turning to look at them. Hutchinson was slumped in a low chair close to the fire doors, one foot resting on his knee, a magazine spread across his lap.

'What do you two want?' he said.

'Been an accident,' said Baz. 'Down at the jetty.'

Hutchinson took in their bedraggled appearance, glanced at Baz's bloody shins. 'Get Gene to give you a plaster or something.' He flicked the pages of his magazine.

'No. It was Taps . . .' Baz didn't know what to say. 'Taps fell in the sea. He's gone.'

'How d'you mean, "gone". You mean like . . . drowned?' Hutchinson sat up straighter, paying attention now.

'Yeah.' Baz hung his head, aware of the dead silence

that had fallen upon the room. 'He fell off the end of the jetty. We tried to get there – me and Jubo. But he'd gone. And then I fell in as well – and I nearly drowned too. And then Steiner beat us both up and—'

'Christ.' Hutchinson stood up and flung his magazine onto the chair. 'So what's the matter with this one?' He looked at Jubo. 'Did he nearly drown as well?'

'Steiner kicked him.' Baz was embarrassed. The way Jubo was standing made it obvious where he'd been hurt. 'For trying to help,' he muttered.

'Ha.' Hutchinson was unmoved. 'For acting like a prat, you mean. OK, so what does Steiner expect me to do about it?'

'He wants two replacements,' said Baz. 'To mix the concrete.'

'Do what? He loses one of his own, and so now he wants two of mine? We'll see about that.' Hutchinson took off his lab coat and hung it on a peg next to the door. As an afterthought he picked up his magazine, folded it and stuffed it in the pocket of the coat. 'Right, you two. Stay here. Mark up some tins while you're waiting. And the rest of you – keep working!'

Hutchinson pulled open the fire door and left.

'Ffffffff . . . ffff. Me got serious grief here, man.' Jubo hobbled over to Hutchinson's chair and gingerly lowered himself into the seat. The other boys began to gather round, their mouths open, eyes wide with shock.

'What happened? What happened?'

'Taps was . . . on the jetty.' Baz stared blankly at Amit, trying to remember exactly what he'd seen. 'Just walking along the jetty, carrying his buckets. But he didn't stop – he kept right on going.'

'What, like, on *purpose*?'

'Maybe. I dunno. We were miles off – just coming down from the playing fields with the wheelbarrows. And Taps . . . you know that counting thing he does? He was counting his footsteps, seeing how many from the sports centre, how many from the sand pile. Maybe he got his numbers mixed up. But he just kept . . . he just kept on walking . . .'

Baz's voice faltered as he saw it again in his mind, the distant little figure, so colourful, disappearing over the edge of the jetty. *Had* Taps known what he was doing? Had he really decided to try and kill himself? Or was he just unable to stop until he'd reached the right number?

Ray came and stood next to him, put a hand on his shoulder. 'Are you all right?' he said.

'Well, I'm still alive,' Baz said. 'And I'm in better shape than poor old Jubo here. Don't think he'll be riding a bike for a while.'

It was a stupid joke and nobody smiled.

Amit put both hands up to his temples, his eyes staring wildly at the floor. 'God, I can't believe this place,' he said. 'Just can't believe it. Taps has gone and we're all standing here. What're we gonna do? Something's gotta happen before we *all* end up jumping off the jetty.'

'Yeah, I tell you wha' gonna happen,' Jubo croaked. 'I gonna take a hammer to that Steiner. I gonna wait till him in his crib and den clat him so hard his brain jump out.'

'Do Hutchinson as well, then,' said Amit. ''Cos he's as bad. Neither of 'em could give a stuff about Taps.'

'Hutchinson'll be back in a minute,' said Gene. 'So watch what you're saying. But you're right. Things are getting bad, and we're gonna have to talk about it. Later, though. Come on, Jubes – let's get you on your feet and give you some tins to play with.'

Gene's prediction was correct. Within a couple of minutes Hutchinson came back into the sort room.

'OK,' he sighed, apparently calm and unconcerned. 'A couple of you better get down to the jetty. Amit, Robbie, stop what you're doing. Go and give Steiner a hand.'

Baz had been going over things in his mind, and now he remembered something that Taps had said earlier about Hutchinson. The boys were in the slob room, grouped around the seating area as usual, and they listened as Baz tried to recall the conversation.

'It was to do with the hymn books – forgetting the stupid hymn books in chapel. I think maybe Hutchinson got into trouble over it with Isaac, and then blamed it on Taps. Anyway, Taps told me he wasn't going down the hole again, and said something about how he wished he could make the days longer. Oh, God . . .' It all became clear. 'Hutchinson was going to put him down the hole, wasn't he? Next Sunday. He must've said that to Taps.'

'What?' said Robbie. 'After what happened to him last time? Taps couldn't have gone through that again.'

'The bastard!' said Amit. 'I reckon it was

Hutchinson that drove Taps mental in the first place. And Steiner. It's their fault he's dead now.'

'It's kind of our fault too,' said Gene. 'We should've tried to help before it ever got to this.' He sighed. 'Too late now.'

'Ey – *some* of us try to help,' said Jubo. It was obvious to Baz who these words were intended for, but a few of the others looked puzzled.

'Huh?' said Amit. 'What are you getting at?'

A few moments of silence and then Dyson spoke.

'He's getting at me. It's because I stayed up on the jetty – didn't go down into the water to look for Taps. And you wanna know why? 'Cos I already knew it was no good, that's why.'

'Nah, it 'cos you scared, man,' said Jubo. 'You scared of Steiner.'

'I'm no more scared of Steiner than you or anyone else.' Dyson leaned forward in his chair and looked directly at Jubo. 'But I'm not going to get myself beaten up for no reason, OK? Look at you. Baz nearly drowned, and you got a kick in the bollocks. You reckon it was worth it? Taps had already gone, so what was the point?'

'If you don't know, guy, then I ain't gonna tell you.'

'They tried,' said Amit. 'That was the point.'

'Hey – you weren't even there, Amit, so butt out!' Dyson was looking beleaguered, his face reddening as he tried to defend himself. 'You're all mouth. And since when did you care so much about Taps, anyway? You were the one that called him a retard, not me.'

Amit said nothing.

'*I* ain't all mout'.' Jubo raised a fist. 'I say I gonna

179

take that Steiner an' it be done. I got him in the bag already, man. Body bag.'

'Yeah, sure.' Dyson's voice was a sneer of dismissal. 'Whatcha gonna do, Jubo? Choke him to death with one of your farts?'

The tension in the room broke and everyone laughed.

'Ey – whatever it necessary, guy.'

CHAPTER TEN

At Sunday chapel Preacher John gave another raging sermon, and this time, surprisingly, he mentioned Taps. At first the boys didn't know who the preacher was talking about, and it took them a while to twig.

'Heavenly Father, in as much as it has pleased you to take from us our brother Paul' – Preacher John lifted his eyes and hands to Heaven – 'and have gathered him unto you, let his body and soul be as a sacrifice for our sins.'

Paul? Who was 'our brother Paul'? What was he on about? Baz glanced sideways at Amit, who just shrugged and pulled a dumb face.

'Give us a sign that his young life has been accepted by you as an acknowledgement of our guilt and as a payment against our debts. Draw back the waters, O Lord, then we shall know that we live in your sight once more.'

Preacher John looked towards the vacant piano stool. 'And thus shall we give, and give again, until the tally is met, and all our sins have been washed away. Amen.'

Only then did it dawn upon Baz that Preacher John was talking about Taps.

'Hymn number one-three-one. All stand.'

Baz rose automatically amid the general shuffle of feet, and began to flick through his hymn book.

'*When I survey the wondrous cross . . .*' The voices sounded ragged and unmusical – naked somehow – without the piano.

At the end of the service Preacher John said, 'Capos, stay behind as usual.' Then he pointed at Gene and said, 'And you, boy. I want to see you as well.'

'I never knew his name was Paul.' Enoch was sitting cross-legged on the grass. He dipped his spoon into a tin of beans and passed it on.

'Yeah,' said Dyson. 'We only started to call him Taps because . . . Well, it was obvious why. He was always ruddy well tapping something. Like, if he did five on one knee, he had to do five on the other.' Dyson accepted the tin of beans from Enoch. He had agreed at last that sharing their food was the only way. The loss of Taps had drawn the boys together, healing the rift between them. The atmosphere behind the sports centre was less strained than it had been the previous Sunday.

But if the disagreement over food had been settled, the bigger worries had not.

'So . . . I didn't get it,' said Enoch. His pinched little face was creased into a frown. 'Taps was like a sacrifice? But it was just an accident, wasn't it? I mean, he wasn't pushed or anything. So how could he be a sacrifice?'

'Dunno. Maybe Preacher John's asking God if poor old "brother Paul" could be like a gift or something.'

Baz remembered the way Steiner had stood at the end of the jetty, just looking down at the water. Watching.

'Do you reckon Steiner was told not to help?' he said. 'Like maybe those were his orders?'

'Nah,' said Jubo. 'Nobody know what Taps gonna do.'

''Cept maybe Hutchinson.' Ray balanced a tomato on his spoon, and paused with it in mid air, as if struck by the meaning of his own words.

'What – you think Hutchinson *made* him do it? Told him to?' said Amit.

There was a moment of reflection as everybody considered this possibility.

'Come on. Even Taps wasn't that crazy.' Dyson dismissed the idea.

'What d'you mean, he wasn't that crazy? He soddin' well *did* it,' said Amit.

'But not 'cos someone told him to.' Dyson still wasn't having it. 'You think we're all going to get told to jump off the jetty like good little sacrifices?'

'Next time someone might get pushed,' said Amit. 'And what was that thing that Preacher said? Right at the end he said something about doing it again, or giving again. He was looking at where Taps used to sit, at the piano, and said, "We're gonna keep on giving." Something like that. "Till all our sins have been washed away." Gave me the bleedin' creeps, that bit did.'

Gene appeared round the side of the sports

building. He walked over to the flattened patch of earth and plonked himself down.

'Right,' he said. He pushed back his long curly hair and let out a deep breath. 'This is serious. Hey – did you save me any food?'

'Yeah,' said Amit. 'We kept back a tin. Here. Lamb stew. So what was all that about?'

Gene took the tin of food from Amit. 'Preacher John had a special job for me,' he said. He picked up the tin-opener, but just sat there staring down at it, turning it over and over in his grimy hands.

'Get this. He wants me to build him a crucifix. A cross. So I said, what, like something to go in here? On the wall? I thought he wanted to make the assembly hall look a bit more like a chapel, maybe. So Preacher John said, no, it had to be bigger. So I said, how big do you want it? Know what he said to me then?'

Gene raised his head and looked around at the puzzled faces. 'Lifesize.'

It took a while for that piece of information to sink in. The circle of faces remained blank.

'What do you mean, *life*size?' Dyson was the first to speak. 'How big's that? You mean big enough to . . .' His voice trailed off.

'Yeah, that's right, mate,' said Gene. 'Big enough to crucify someone on. He didn't say that was what he was gonna *do* with it, but that's how big he wants it.'

'Christ!'

'Exactly. Christ. And Christ knows what he's thinking. But if he's really going off his head, then we need to be coming up with some kind of plan. Today. 'Cos this has got me worried, I can tell you.' Gene applied the tin-opener, the soft click of engaging metal clearly audible in the surrounding silence.

'You don't really believe he's gonna start crucifying people,' said Dyson, and there was the trace of a plea in his voice, as though he were looking for reassurance rather than stating a fact.

'I don't want to hang around to find out,' said Gene.

Baz wondered if he was the only one to have noticed the faint smile that passed across Gene's face, and to have seen the grim little joke.

'We gotta be getting outa here,' said Jubo. 'Teef that salvage boat or somet'ing . . .'

'And go where?' Gene took a mouthful of stew. 'Mainland's as bad as this place. Worse.'

'Maybe another island somewhere. Where there no Preacher, ey?'

But there were no other islands as far as anyone knew, and stealing the boat would first mean stealing the keys from Isaac. Who would risk that?

'I wish we just had a bleedin' great tank or something,' said Amit. He squinted up at the sports building. 'Like, hidden in there. Wouldn't that be great? Drive down the hill and blow the whole place apart. Divers, capos, Preacher John – the lot.'

'Yeah, right.' Gene made a little sucking sound with his teeth. 'You're dreaming again, Amit.'

'I know,' said Amit, and for once he looked beaten. He hung his head. 'We got nothing, have we? No way of looking after ourselves and nowhere to go. Whatever happens to us, we just gotta sit here and take it.'

And that was the core of the problem: they were

helpless to defend themselves against whatever danger might lie ahead, and unable to escape.

Baz could find nothing new to offer, and so he came back to Ray's original crazy idea: building a bomb.

'Gene,' he said, 'I know it was just a toy, but that little rocket thing you made – it was so amazing. I mean, it really *worked*. Couldn't we, you know, build a bigger one somehow?'

'What the hell for?' said Gene. 'What would you do with it? Look, Baz, something seriously weird is starting to happen round here, and it scares me. We need to come up with some way of protecting ourselves, looking after ourselves, and you're just thinking like kids all the time. Tanks . . . bombs . . . rockets. OK, in theory you could build some kind of weapon, something big that would explode. But here's what you'd need: number one, a whole lot of propane – that's the liquid they put in cigarette lighters. Number two, a heavy-duty casing. And it'd have to be airtight. And then you'd have to have some way of lighting the gas that was in the casing.'

Baz thought about it for a minute. 'So if we had one of those big things of calor gas, like they used to use for camping – well, that's already a bit like a bomb, isn't it?' he said. 'Metal casing and everything. Wouldn't that work?'

Gene shook his head. 'Calor gas'd explode if it was mixed with air. But you'd have to get the mixture right, and then find some way of setting it off. And anyway – where are you gonna get calor gas from? I've never seen any come off the boat and I've never seen any go onto it. There's none around here.'

'Oh.'

So that was a non starter. But then Amit seemed to perk up a bit.

'What about petrol?' he said. 'Could you build a bomb if you had some petrol?'

'Well, yeah, maybe. But you'd still need a really heavy metal container, 'cos the heavier it is the bigger the explosion. You'd have to put the petrol in – just the right amount, and so there was the right amount of air in there as well. And then you'd have to have some way of sealing the container, and then some way of lighting what was in there.' Gene put his head on one side, his interest momentarily engaged. 'Like a spark plug, I suppose . . .'

'But that's . . . brilliant,' said Baz. He could see it happening. 'That'd really work, would it?'

Gene shrugged, dismissive again. 'Well, that's the way an engine works. Engine cylinders are just metal containers, really. 'Cept they have pistons in them, and the exploding petrol makes the pistons go. So yeah, it'd *work*. But we don't have any petrol, and we're not likely to be able to get any. And what would you do with a bomb anyway? You can't just blow everyone up.'

'Yeah, but' – Baz was full of enthusiasm now – 'it *could* be done.'

'That's all I was ever asking, really.' Ray spoke up, and he sounded a bit miffed. 'It was *my* idea in the first place. I just wanted to know if it could be done, that's all.'

'Ha. Anything can be done in theory.' Gene chuckled at his own thoughts. 'We could leave here and go to the *moon* in theory. But first you'd need an actual rocket. Yeah, and some actual rocket fuel to put in it. So you bring me a load of explosive – like propane, or methane, or petrol, or gunpowder – and maybe I'd start taking you seriously. Maybe. But till then it's not even worth talking about.'

'Yeah, but—'

'Listen, Ray. I've already done you a *big* favour this week, yeah? So do me a favour in return, and gimme some peace.'

Gene slumped back on the grass, arms folded across his stomach, and sighed.

Baz looked at Ray. What big favour was that, then? The frown of annoyance on Ray's face gave no clues, and Gene looked like he was already asleep. His tin of food lay half eaten beside him.

Baz woke up with a jump, fragments of troubled dreams still shooting around his vision. How could he have possibly forgotten about today? The hole! Ray was going to be put down the hole! Nobody had said a word about it, not even Ray. And there was Ray, apparently snoozing on the grass. Jesus . . .

'Ray! Hey – wake up!' Baz reached out, whispering urgently, and gave Ray a shake.

'Wassa . . . matter? What is it?' Ray sat up, and others began to stir too.

'The hole, that's what's the matter! How can you just lie there? We gotta do something.'

Ray rubbed his eyes. 'Oh yeah,' he said. 'The hole. Well, we'll see about that.'

'What do you mean, we'll *see* about it? Last week you

said there was no way you could go down there. You were crapping yourself.'

Had it really been a week? So much had happened since then that Baz hadn't given any thought to Ray's plight. How could he have simply forgotten about it? Possibly because the subject hadn't been mentioned again . . .

'They're not putting me in any blinkin' hole,' said Ray. He stood up and smoothed down the front of his shorts, brushed his hands through his hair and shook it back.

'Oh, right. So you just decided you didn't fancy it, then?'

'Something like that.' Ray sounded as though he were being deliberately vague. Or evasive.

One or two of the others had picked up on the conversation. There was a general stirring as they all got to their feet, and Robbie said, 'Well, if you manage to talk your way out of it, you'll be the first that ever did.'

'Oh yeah?' said Ray. 'Anyone wanna take any bets?' He sounded almost cocky.

Too cocky for some, because Dyson immediately said, 'Yeah, me. I'll bet you . . . uh . . . water duty for a month. OK? My water duty against yours that you're in that friggin' sewer before slob-down tonight.'

'I'll bet the same,' said Enoch. 'But I tell you what . . .' He hesitated for a moment. 'I hope I lose. Yeah, I do hope I lose. I been down there – I know what it's like.'

He was a nice little guy, thought Baz. Not too bright and never said much, but Enoch obviously had a kind heart. Betting, and hoping he'd lose . . .

'OK, done, then,' said Ray. 'Anyone else? Baz? *Gene?*'

There was a positively mischievous look to Ray now.

Gene gave a grim chuckle. 'You better start saying your prayers, mate.'

Baz shook his head. 'I don't even wanna joke about it.'

The smile faded from Ray's face. 'Yeah, well. If you didn't laugh you'd cry. And I am saying my prayers. I really am. Come on, then, let's get it done.'

Some of the confidence seemed to go out of Ray as they walked down the hill, and he went very quiet. Baz didn't push him into conversation. When they got to the main entrance and saw the capos already sitting there on the steps, Ray said, 'Stay with me, yeah?'

'Yeah, course.'

The capos had other ideas, though.

'Been on a Sunday stroll?' said Steiner. He stood up. 'That's nice. Well, you can just keep right on walking. All except . . . *you*.' He pointed at Ray. 'You stay where you are, maggot. We've got a li'l 'pointment, haven't we?'

Ray said nothing.

The rest of the boys began to move away, some of their faces angry, some fearful. Baz stayed where he was, right next to Ray.

'I'm not going anywhere,' he said.

'Oi – sod off.' Hutchinson was on his feet now, pointing the neck of a wine bottle at Baz.

'What're you gonna do with that?' Baz said. 'Stain my T-shirt?' But then Gene put a hand against his back.

'Come on,' he muttered. 'Better just do as they say. It'll only make things worse for Ray if you stir it up.'

'Yeah, you too, Genius.' Steiner was lurching down the steps. 'We don' want any sh-shpectators this time.'

'It's OK,' said Gene. 'We're going.' He leaned towards Baz's ear and murmured, 'But you and me'll come back in a bit and check, yeah?'

Baz thought about that for a moment, and gave in. Gene was right. There was no point in aggravating the capos, especially not when they'd been drinking. 'OK, then. Sorry, Ray. Probably best for you if we go – but we won't be far away. Good luck.'

Ray gave him a wan little smile.

The rest of the boys had wandered down towards the jetty, and now Baz and Gene headed off in the same direction. Baz looked behind him after a few paces, but Ray and the capos had already disappeared round the corner of the building.

'Don't know how he thought he was ever gonna get away with it,' Baz said. '*God*, I hope he comes through this OK.'

'Yeah, me too. Smart lad, though, is Ray. Some of his ideas are pretty crazy, but' – Gene spread his palms as he walked – 'some of 'em aren't. And at least he *has* ideas.'

They joined the group at the end of the jetty and mooched around for a bit, kicking at the shuttering that supported the concrete platform. The platform had been finished over the last few days, and some building work had begun – a rectangle made of concrete blocks. So far it looked like a big open-topped box, about two metres long, a metre deep and a metre high. Nobody could figure out what this thing was supposed to be. The whole construction was a mystery.

Two or three of the boys began throwing stones out into the muddy waves to pass the time. Baz felt that there was something wrong in skimming stones over the spot where Taps had drowned, and he didn't join in. It also seemed wrong to be doing anything vaguely entertaining while Ray was suffering. And he would be suffering, thought Baz. Probably down there right now, in that dark stinking pit and all alone . . . oh God . . .

'Four, man! Was definitely a four!'

'Yah, it was three. You can't friggin' count!'

Jubo and Dyson were in earnest competition, skimming their stones and arguing over the results. Baz watched them for a while, his mood growing darker. Idiots. He wanted to yell at them to stop, wished they cared more about what was happening to Ray. Or maybe he just wished he cared less.

'Now that gotta be a five!'

Jubo threw his arms out in appeal, a broad grin on his face. 'Ey, you saw it, Baz! Was a five, yeah?'

What an oaf he was, really. What a shallow, useless, unfeeling, ignorant—

'Gimme some back-up, man! It was a— Hey. That him already?'

Jubo's sight line had changed. Baz frowned at him for a moment longer, then turned to look.

It was Ray. Strolling along the jetty, hands in his pockets, as though he was out for a promenade along the seafront. If he'd been whistling he couldn't have looked more pleased with himself.

'Woo-hoo!' A ragged cheer went up. 'Wow! That was quick! What happened, Ray?'

The boys remained where they were, stamping and whistling, as Ray approached. Baz noticed Gene and Jubo bumping fists in a power salute.

'Right, Mr Dyson. I believe that's a month's worth of water duty you owe me.' Ray lifted his arms and performed a little twirl in front of the group. 'Not a spot on me, as you can see.'

'God, Ray. How did you manage it? What did you say to them?'

'Didn't have to say anything. Seems they had a bit of trouble getting the lid off the drain. They must be getting weaker or something – or maybe they were just too sloshed. Either way, they couldn't shift it. So after about ten minutes they had to give up. Poor darlings, I felt quite sorry for them.'

'Ha, ha! No! Seriously? What – so they let you go?'

'Yeah. I think they got embarrassed in the end. So they just gave me a kick and told me to naff off.'

'But . . . I still don't get it. How come they couldn't open it up?' Baz had watched the capos lifting the drain cover only last week. It had been a bit of a struggle, but they'd managed it OK.

'You gonna tell 'em, or shall I?' Ray was grinning at Gene.

'We stuck the lid down,' said Gene. 'Couple of trowelfuls of cement, and the job was a good 'un. Take a crane to shift it now.'

'Whaaat?'

'Yeah, Ray came to see me about it on Tuesday

night. One of his *better* ideas.' Gene gave Ray a look. 'Simple, yeah? And practical. Something we could actually do. We had the cement, we had the water, we had the levers. Took about five minutes. Lifted the lid off, shoved some cement in there, put the lid back on. And after we'd finished you couldn't see we'd even touched it.'

'Brilliant! Why didn't we ever think of it before?'

'That lid looks like it'd weigh a ton, though,' said Enoch. 'Don't think I could've lifted it off to get any cement in there.'

'No,' said Ray. 'I couldn't either. Thanks, Jubes.'

Jubo grinned and raised a hand. 'No worries, guy. You cool.'

So Jubo had been in on it as well. Jubo, Gene and Ray. The three of them together.

'Well, you could have told the rest of us.' Baz felt as though he'd been left off the party guest list. 'I mean . . .' He stopped himself from saying how worried he'd been over Ray. 'We could all have been in on the joke, then.'

'Yeah,' said Gene. 'But it was best not to say. If everybody had been standing round sniggering, the capos would've twigged. See, you kicked off nicely, Baz, and that looked more natural, yeah? Besides, we didn't want to risk Cookie hearing about it, 'cos you never know with him.'

'Anyway,' said Ray, 'it worked. And so – no more water duty for me for a while. Eh, Dyson?'

'Yeah, yeah.' Dyson took it amiably enough. 'You win. And I reckon it was worth it. Hey – but what about Enoch? He bet you too.'

'I'm gonna let Enoch off,' said Ray. ''Cos he's such a sweetheart. He hoped he'd *lose*. Awwww. How nice of him was that?' Ray put an arm around Enoch's shoulders and patted his cheek.

'Gerroff!' said Enoch, and the boys all laughed, but Baz felt an unaccountable stab of pain, as though he'd been betrayed. His own friendship had been used as a tool in this escapade. He'd 'kicked off nicely', as Gene had put it. Well, you *would* kick off, wouldn't you, if something horrible was about to happen to someone you cared about? Wasn't that what friends were for? And now Ray was prancing around and calling people sweetheart, and—

No, this was being ridiculous. Ray had come up with a brilliant plan, and it had worked, and he had a right to his moment of triumph. The capos, for once, had come off worst. It was something to celebrate, not get all sniffy about. Join in then, and be glad while you could.

The atmosphere at lights-out was more subdued. Taps's empty bed was a constant reminder of how vulnerable they all were, despite today's success. Whose bed might be lying empty tomorrow, or the day after that?

Baz lay on his, and stared up at the ceiling. The trouble with Sundays, he was beginning to realize, was that there was time to think. And thinking could bring more pain than pushing wheelbarrows. Today had brought a little victory, but tomorrow would surely bring payback.

Eventually Gene, who was nearest to the slob-room door, said, 'Everybody done?'

'Yeah.'

'Yeah.'

Gene clicked the switch and the light went out.

The room smelled worse in the dark, somehow. Baz spread himself out in a star shape and breathed in the foetid air. God, it was like living in a dustbin full of rotting cabbage stalks. He heard the sound of a muffled fart about halfway down the room, and someone murmured, '*Uh*-oh . . .'

'The blue angel flies again . . .' Another voice. But there was no subsequent flick of a cigarette lighter, and even if there had been, Baz wouldn't have bothered to look. The blue angel game had lost its appeal lately.

His own guts felt bloated and uncomfortable. A diet of nothing but tinned food was having its predictable effect. And what might it be doing to his teeth? he wondered. Having rotten teeth was a big worry nowadays.

The door clicked down at the other end of the room, and Baz raised his head slightly. Was that Cookie? Yes. He heard someone murmur, 'Hey . . . Sir Plus . . .' and after a few moments the bulky figure came padding down the middle of the room and into the jakes.

How strange Cookie's life must be. And how unhappy. He had no friends – everybody either ignored him altogether or just hooted his name whenever he appeared. Was he used to it? And what did the guy do all day, anyway? Nobody really knew.

Baz felt guilty about the fact that he just went along with the crowd. He'd never joined in the general mockery, but he'd never taken any stand against it either. Didn't want to make enemies. Didn't want to put himself outside the circle. Too much of a coward to suggest that such treatment was bullying. And wrong . . .

The curtain rustled, and the shadow of Cookie passed by again, running the gauntlet of murmured sneers and insults.

'Yo. Truck boy . . .'

'Mm. I smell lard . . .'

Baz frowned in the darkness. Maybe tomorrow he should make an effort. Say something.

The room settled into silence, but Baz didn't close his eyes. He could feel the perspiration, prickly on his forehead, a suspicious itch in the middle of his back. God, this place was a nightmare. What was going to happen to him? He brought his legs together, but kept his arms outstretched and imagined that he was being crucified. High up on a cross he was nailed, looking down upon a desolate world. Nothing before him but the endless floods, and the smoking ruins of far-off cities. The image was so vivid that it scared him, and sudden tears sprang to his eyes. It could happen. It really could. He let his jaw fall open, tried to get some air past the lump at the back of his throat. There was no future. There was no one to save him. He was all alone.

Something touched the palm of his hand, and Baz immediately closed his fingers. Another hand. In the moment of realizing what it was, he should have let go. But he didn't. He grasped the offered fingers in his own and held on tight.

'Baz? Are you OK? Listen – I've had another idea.'

Ray's voice, whispering in the darkness. Baz didn't care what the idea was, not right now. He had something to hold onto, something real, and he wasn't alone after all. Ray didn't withdraw his hand, or show any surprise. He returned Baz's squeeze as though it was the most natural thing in the world, and leaned a little closer.

'Listen . . .'

CHAPTER ELEVEN

Gene said it was about the stupidest thing he'd ever heard. He looked at Baz as though he were mad.

'Where the hell did this idea come from? Tell me you're not serious.'

'You said to bring you some explosive,' said Baz. 'Propane or methane, you said. Or gunpowder. Something that would explode.'

'Yeah, but I didn't mean *farts*, for Chrissake!'

It did seem crazy when you said it like that, but Baz persevered. 'It's methane, though, isn't it? We must be pumping it out by the gallon. Or by the bucket load, or the . . . however you'd measure it. And it explodes if you set light to it. You've already shown us that.'

Gene stood up straight. He'd been sawing through a wooden mast – a long tapering pole propped up on a couple of makeshift trestles outside the back door of the sort room. But now he left the saw stuck in the wood and wiped his hands on his T-shirt.

'OK,' he said. 'So how do you figure on collecting all this gas, then? Do we take it in turns to fart into a dustbin? Or do we run about trying to catch farts in a butterfly net? You're bloody nuts, kiddo. I don't know how you think 'em up.'

'Wasn't actually my idea,' said Baz. 'It was Ray's. He's on jetty crew today.'

'Ray's idea.' Gene rolled his head around and pulled a wide-eyed loony face. 'Should've guessed. Well, tell Brother Ray no chance, OK? Not this time. The blue angel will *not* be flying tonight. Or any other night. Now let me get on with this.'

'Yeah, OK.' Baz knew Gene well enough by now not to push too hard. And today Gene seemed to be in a particularly unreceptive mood. 'What're you making, anyway?'

'I told you,' said Gene. 'A cross.'

'What? So this . . . this is going to be it?'

'Yeah. And I'm not too happy about doing it either. Gives me the creeps.'

Baz nodded. Maybe there was a little extra leverage to be applied here. 'We really need to come up with something pretty quick, don't we?' He sighed. 'Pity there isn't any way of . . . I dunno' – he half recalled some school chemistry experiment – 'collecting gas underwater or something. Still, if you reckon it's impossible, then that's that. 'Cos if *you* can't figure it out, then no one can.'

But before Gene could comment on this, Hutchinson suddenly stuck his head round the back door. He looked very pale and puffy-eyed.

'Oi! Who said you could come out here? Get back inside!'

'Sorry,' said Baz. 'I just wanted to check one of the

codes. You weren't around, so I thought I better ask Gene.'

So it was a disappointment – another great scheme that looked as though it was going nowhere – and Baz had to report as much to Ray when the jetty crew returned that afternoon.

'Did you ask him?' Ray said, under his breath. They were all in the sort room, waiting for the food tins to be set out on the floor.

'Yeah.' Baz glanced across at Gene. 'No good, though. Not interested.'

Ray looked annoyed. 'But did you *explain* it properly?'

'Hey, I tried. Why don't you have a go? It's your idea, and he listened to you last time.'

But then Steiner said, 'OK, Hutch. Top dogs?' and it was time to play the food game.

The boys still made a daily show of diving for the tins, even though all would now be shared out equally. They guessed that if Steiner knew that it no longer made any difference who was top dog, or who managed to get which tin, he would soon devise some other way of humiliating them or making them suffer. So they played along.

Once they got back to the slob room, the tins were opened and all the food tipped into the biggest of the saucepans. Everything was thoroughly mixed and then measured out into the tins once more. It made for strange eating, but at least no one could complain that he wasn't getting his fair share.

The boys lolled around the seating area amid the debris of their evening meal.

'Whose is that?' said Amit. One of the cans was still full. It stood on the low formica-covered table, untouched, a spoon lying beside it.

'Must be Gene's,' said Dyson. 'Gone to the jakes, I think.'

'Oh, right. So. What's been happening at the jetty?'

Dyson leaned back in his chair and crossed his ankles. 'Well, it's weird,' he said. 'We've been mixing concrete again, barrowloads of the stuff, but now we're just tipping it over the end of the jetty. I mean, I s'pose it'll help hold everything together once it's set. The rubble and the blocks and that. But it sort of felt like we were just doing it for the sake of it, yeah? Like there's nothing much else on at the moment.'

'So there's been no more work on that box thing?'

'Nope.'

It had been a quiet day in the sort room too. This was hardly something to complain about, but the general lack of activity brought a sense of unease. Equally worrying was the fact that Taps had not yet been replaced. Perhaps Preacher John was thinking of gradually winding down his operation. In which case, what would happen to his workforce? Would everyone be sent back to the mainland? Or did the preacher have other more sinister plans for them?

Gene appeared from the washroom. He was carrying a plastic Coke bottle. The boys idly watched him as he walked over to his bed and reached under his rolled-up blanket. He grabbed some object, and brought it over to the table.

Baz recognized it as being the home-made rocket launcher.

'Hey – is this that thing that everyone was going on about the other day?' Dyson and a few of the others hadn't seen Gene's rocket toy in action, and now they sat up to take notice.

'Yeah. Gonna try a new experiment with it.' Gene set the square wooden platform in the middle of the table, and took the film canister from his pocket.

'Well, I hope you're gonna use someone else's lighter,' muttered Amit. ''Cos I'm nearly out of gas.'

'Don't need any lighter gas,' said Gene. 'Not if this goes to plan.' He placed the Coke bottle next to the square wooden platform. It was filled to the top – or nearly to the top – with what appeared to be plain water.

Gene took the little film canister in one hand, and held it near to the top of the bottle.

'OK. Here we go.' He unscrewed the Coke cap, and quickly placed the film canister over the mouth of the bottle. Then he gave the bottle a brief squeeze and immediately transferred the canister to the wooden platform, pressing it down onto its own original cap.

'Right,' said Gene. 'We're ready. Hey, Enoch – just check the corridor, will you? Make sure there's no one about.'

'OK.' Enoch jumped up and opened the slob-room door. He stuck his head out, glanced from left to right, and then came back in again. 'All clear.'

'Countdown, then,' said Gene. He put his finger on the lighter button that was mounted in one corner of the piece of wood. 'Ten . . . nine . . . eight . . . Oh, forget it.' He clicked the button.

Bang!

It was an even louder explosion than before. All heads jerked backwards in surprise as the film canister flew up into the air and hit the ceiling.

'Wow!' Jubo stuck out a hand and neatly caught the black canister as it tumbled back down towards the group.

'Hey – good one, Gene!'

'What the hell was *that*?' said Dyson.

'That,' said Gene, 'was one-hundred-per-cent pure rocket fuel.'

'What – you mean, like petrol or something?' Dyson picked up the Coke bottle. He cautiously passed it to and fro beneath his nose.

Gene laughed. 'Careful. That's powerful stuff.'

'But what is it? What's in there?'

'Just water – now. But what *was* in there was methane. Home-produced by yours truly.'

'Huh?'

'A fart, mate. It was a fart.'

'*Whaaat*?'

Some of the boys began to catch on, their faces splitting into wide grins.

'Yay! The blue angel!'

Baz looked across at Ray, caught his eye.

'But how did you get a fart into a bottle?' Dyson was still puzzled. 'And what's the water for?'

Gene took the bottle from Dyson and said, 'It has to be done underwater. The bottle has to be underwater, with no air in it, and your bum's gotta be underwater as well. Then when you fart into the bottle, there's just water and gas in there. You screw the cap on – while it's still underwater – and then you've got pure methane in a bottle. Like a genie. The blue angel.'

'Wow. Is that what you've been doing out in the jakes all this time?'

'Yeah, and it's friggin' impossible, nearly. I kind of sat down in the washtub and used a plastic funnel to try and make the bubbles go up into the bottle. I still lost most of it, though, so I gotta figure out a better way. Yeah. If we're going to go into serious production, then we need a proper system . . .'

Gene was racing ahead in his own mind, while others were still at the starting blocks.

'Serious production?' said Amit. 'What – you want *all* of us farting into bottles? Are we gonna get a factory going or something?'

'Yeah,' said Gene. 'That's exactly it – a factory. A fart factory. It sounds like a joke, right? But methane's a super-high explosive, and if you had enough, you could blow up this whole soddin' island with it. You just need enough of it, that's all.'

Gene looked around at the doubtful faces. 'Look. Pretend it was gunpowder. Let's say we'd been collecting gunpowder, just a pinch at a time, until we'd got a whole great barrel of it stashed away somewhere in secret. Now, that could be useful, yeah? I mean, if we really needed to protect ourselves, wouldn't we feel safer if we had a barrel of gunpowder to play around with?'

'Yeah. Too right.'

'Well, we already got one. We're sitting on it. See what I mean?'

'Ha, ha! Yeah! We're *sitting* on it!'

'You're a genius, Gene!'

'Yeah, yeah. I know,' said Gene. 'But it wasn't my idea. It was Ray's. He's been going on about building a bomb for ages now, and I kept ignoring him 'cos I couldn't see how. I still don't know what we'd do with a bomb even if we had one. But a load of explosive could be some sort of protection at any rate. Something to work with. And I reckon if we start collecting a big store of methane now, just a bit at a time, then we can figure the rest out later. So . . .' Gene reached forward for his tin of food, and lifted it as though making a toast. 'To Brother Ray, yeah?'

'Hey – Brother Ray!' The boys grabbed empty food tins and clanked them together.

'Brother Ray!'

The laughter died down to a general chuckle, and everyone looked at Ray – perhaps expecting him to say something. But in the pause Jubo rolled sideways in his seat and performed his party trick. *Frrrrrttttt!*

'There you go, man,' he said. 'Sound of freedom.'

'Ha, ha! Yeah. The sound of freedom . . .'

It was the beginnings of a plan, and with Gene onside it had a chance of working. As they made their way to their beds, Baz felt a sudden wave of admiration for Ray. He wanted to put his arm around Ray's shoulders and give him a hug, but he thought better of this, and gave him a kind of punch in the back instead.

'Result!' he said. 'You're brilliant.'

'Thanks. I'd never have thought of the water-thing, though.'

'Yeah, well . . . it was still down to you.'

By the following evening the plan had moved a stage further. There was a new atmosphere in the slob room, a buzz of excitement and interest, and the boys were more than willing to follow Gene into the jakes when he called for a meeting there.

'Have a look at this,' he said. 'I made it today.'

He was carrying part of a blue plastic crate. It looked like one of the loading crates, sawn in half. Gene went over to the shower and placed the sawn-off piece of crate in the tin bath, lowering it beneath the surface of the water.

'It's like a stool,' he said. 'It means you can sit in the water without falling over backwards, or having to hold onto the sides of the bath. OK? But here's the good bit.' Gene was holding a small white plastic funnel in one hand. He rummaged in his pocket with the other and brought out a balloon. Baz recognized it as one of the big party balloons he'd seen amongst the box of plasters in the sort room.

'So watch. Here's what we have to do. Take the balloon and push the end of it over this plastic funnel – like this.' Gene demonstrated, and the balloon hung limply from the tube of the funnel. 'Then you sit down in the water, and you make sure there's no air in the balloon or trapped in the funnel. Lean back and get the funnel as near your bum as you can. Then fart into the funnel. So now we've got a balloon with nothing but gas in it, yeah? And then have a plastic bottle with you, and put that underwater, no air in it. Take the balloon off the funnel and let the gas up into the bottle. Put the cap on the bottle, still underwater, and that's it. Fart in a bottle. We keep doing that until the bottle's full, and then—'

'Strewth, Gene,' said Robbie. 'You're gonna have to start again. You lost me about halfway through that.'

'Probably easier to do it than it is to explain,' said Gene. 'It's a doddle.'

'Go on, then,' said Amit.

'What?'

'Give us a demonstration.'

'Ha, ha! Yeah, come on, Gene.'

'Well, hang on a minute – I can't just fart any time I want to. Not like Jubo here.'

'Let Jubo do it then. Come on, Jubo!'

'Yay! Ju-*bo* . . . Ju-*bo* . . . Ju-*bo* . . .'

The chanting voices echoed around the washroom, until Jubo shrugged and stepped up to the tin bath.

'*I* got nothing I ashamed of,' he said. He pulled down his shorts, amidst much jeering and cheering, and lowered his backside into the bath.

'Comfy?' said Gene.

'Yeah,' said Jubo. 'It kind of . . . *soothe* me little bit.' He wiggled around in the water, and some of it slopped over the side of the bath.

'Right. Here you go, then. Try and put the funnel as close to your bum as you can.' Gene handed over the balloon and funnel, and Jubo submerged it beneath the water. His head was bent downwards in concentration, and by this time most of the boys were clutching themselves with laughter.

'Make sure all the air bubbles are out.' Gene's voice rose above the hoots and shrieks. 'OK? Let 'er rip, then. But gently. Gently, Jubo . . . don't rush it . . . maintain control . . .'

Jubo's ears began to turn red with the effort, and everyone laughed all the more. Baz and Ray were holding each other up, and Robbie was actually on the floor, writhing around and gasping for air.

'Jus' lemme concentrate . . . we on the way now . . .' Jubo's head was still down and his voice was muffled. There was a kind of glooping sound, and after another couple of moments he raised his head.

'Ey,' he said. 'It worked! Me got one!' He fiddled about beneath the water and brought up the balloon – held it aloft for all to see. It had partially inflated, a quite respectable bladderful.

'Wow,' said Gene. 'You're a one-man gasworks, Jubo. Quick – someone grab a plastic bottle. We need to save this.'

Finding a bottle was no problem, and Enoch was out of the door and back again in a few seconds.

'Out you come then, Jubo. Let's do the final stage.'

'But now me all wet, man!' Jubo stood up, water streaming down his legs and all over his shorts and trainers.

'Yeah, well,' said Gene, 'that's water for you. We just need to get hold of some extra rags or something to use as towels. So. Put the bottle in the bath and make sure there's no air in it. Then push the balloon underneath it . . . actually, that's not so easy . . .' Gene struggled to submerge the now buoyant balloon. 'OK. Just gotta be careful, that's all. And then we let the gas up into the bottle. Like . . . that. Put the cap on . . .'

Gene pulled the dripping bottle out of the bath. It was about three-quarters full of water.

'That gap you can see at the top – that's pure explosive, guys. Gotta make sure the cap's on good and tight, so it doesn't leak out. And there we have it. Our first instalment.'

'Hey, that's great, Gene! How much do you reckon we're gonna need?' The boys stood around admiring Jubo's efforts.

'Dunno. A good few litres. I don't even know what we're gonna put it in yet, or what the best gas-and-air mixture should be or anything. But it's a start. OK. Who's next, then?'

It gave them a sense of purpose, and over the next few days the fart factory went into full-scale production. The hour or two between supper and lock-up became known as Fart Club, the boys experimenting with various techniques, and competing to see who could produce the most gas. Jubo set the benchmark in this respect. Nobody else could match the volume and frequency of his contributions.

There were some who were too shy or too intimidated to perform in the spotlight. They needed privacy. Dyson was one of these, and Ray another.

'Anyway, I'm better in the mornings,' Dyson said. 'Get more of a build-up.'

'Yeah, me too,' said Ray. 'Maybe I've got a slow met . . . metathingy . . .'

'Metabolism,' said Gene. 'That's OK. But no cheating! I got calculations to do, and I don't want them mucked up by anyone just blowing the balloon up a little bit and then pretending it's a fart in there.'

Between them the boys were capturing about a half-litre of methane per day – one small Coke bottle – and soon the question of where to hide the stuff came up.

Gene had already thought of this.

'The water butts,' he said. 'Up at the sports centre. We'll get some big two-litre bottles and hang 'em upside down in the barrel we use for cleaning the tins – chuck a concrete block in there and tie 'em to that. Then we can put the gas from the little bottles into the big ones whenever we get a chance.'

'Maybe the water crew could do it?' said Robbie. 'Whoever's on that week could take the small bottles up to the sports centre. They got an excuse to be goin' up there.'

'Brilliant.'

CHAPTER TWELVE

On the morning following the first session of Fart Club, the jetty crew stood in the corridor outside the sort room, ready and waiting for their orders. Baz was there, along with Amit, Jubo and Dyson – all the bigger boys, in accordance with Steiner's instructions from the night before. There had been no picking of teams this time.

Steiner eventually showed up. He was carrying a steel tape measure, its bright green casing vaguely luminous in the dim light of the corridor.

'OK. You're gonna need pickaxes, and you're gonna need shovels. Wait here while I go and see Isaac.'

Steiner walked away, pulling out the end of the steel rule as he went, and brandishing it like a rapier. As he reached the corner at the far end of the corridor, he allowed the rule to snap back into position, an urgent whizz of the mechanism followed by a sharp click. Then he was gone.

What lay beyond that darkened corner was still unexplored territory to Baz, a mysterious otherworld known only to the salvage crew and the capos – and to Preacher John himself. None of the boys had ever been further than the slob-room door, and could only wonder at how they lived, those hulking giants who controlled the lives of so many. Down there was the centre of all power, the palace of the mighty, a kingdom. With Preacher John as its king.

There was a murmur of sound and Isaac appeared, emerging from the gloom, with Steiner following close behind. The boys stood in silence as the skipper approached. He was dressed for a day on the salvage boat – grey fisherman's smock, navy tracksuit bottoms and cut-off rubber boots. The sleeves of the smock were pushed up above his elbows, bits of thread dangling down. It looked as though the seams had either split or been deliberately unpicked in order to accommodate his huge forearms.

As Isaac passed by the line of boys, Baz caught the indefinable aroma of adult male, threatening and powerful.

The storeroom door was a little further along the corridor, on the opposite side, and here Isaac stopped.

'How many do you need?' he said to Steiner.

'Er . . . just three pickaxes, Skip. We've already got shovels.'

'OK. Here . . .' Isaac handed Steiner a bunch of keys. 'I want these back at the end of the day, and I'll be here to watch you check everything in again.'

Steiner undid the two heavy padlocks to the store-room, drew back the bolts and entered the room. Isaac positioned himself just inside the doorway, so that any view of the interior was effectively blocked.

'You got ropes?' the boys heard him say. 'Take two off that hook. And I don't want them disappearing, either.'

Steiner emerged after a few moments, carrying a couple of pickaxes. He stood them against the corridor wall and went back inside the storeroom. Isaac turned and glanced at the line of boys. Baz quickly dropped his eyes and stared at the floor.

Then Steiner came out again, this time with one more pickaxe, and some skeins of blue nylon rope looped over his shoulder. 'OK. That's the lot,' he said.

Steiner padlocked the door once more. As Isaac waited, he took another look along the line of boys. Baz felt as though they were being judged, examined. He instinctively stood up a little straighter, in case he should be found wanting in some way, but then he regretted this because Isaac said, 'Getting a bit *big*, aren't they, some of these kids? Who's that one?'

'Er . . .' Steiner looked across. 'Dyson. Been here a while now.'

Isaac nodded. 'Hm . . . long enough, maybe.'

There was a low rumble of other voices, a distant accompaniment to Isaac's own, and the rest of the salvage crew came round the corner at the far end of the corridor.

They were carrying their diving gear. Luke and Amos each had aqualungs hoisted loosely upon their shoulders, while Moko, bringing up the rear, carried a bundle of wetsuits over his arm. As they came to a halt in front of the line of boys, Baz realized that this was the first time he'd been in the presence of the entire crew, and so close up, with an opportunity to study them properly. He'd noticed before how similar the shaven-headed brothers were, and now he guessed they might actually be twins. He could tell them apart though, the one called Luke having a broken nose, a white scar across the misshapen bridge. Moko was shorter and stockier than the brothers, maybe a bit older. All of them were tough-looking guys, their broad frames and stubbled faces a reminder of the vast difference between boys and men. One swipe from Moko alone could have sent the entire group of boys spinning away like skittles.

'What's going on?' said Amos. 'Trouble?'

Isaac continued to stare at the boys, looking into their faces, one at a time. 'No, just weighing up stock, Amos. Weighing up stock. Haven't taken much notice for a while, and we need to be careful. A boy gets to a certain age . . . things start to change.' He rubbed at the underside of his bearded chin as his attention passed from Dyson to Baz. There was no emotion in his expression, nothing beyond professional interest, a cool observation of the specimens before him. He might have been at a county fair, appraising sheep or cattle. Baz kept his head up, and found that he could meet the skipper's gaze after all – if only for a few moments.

'Pups grow into young dogs before you know it, and that's when they begin to get ideas. They start to get that look in their eye—'

'They do indeed, Isaac. They do indeed.'

Isaac jumped – actually jumped – as the words came booming along the corridor. Baz reacted almost simultaneously, jerking backwards in alarm, the wall behind him thudding against his shoulder blades. He turned his head, and saw all the other heads do the same, swivelling to the right as if yanked by a single thread.

Preacher John!

From the direction of the main entrance came the preacher, bearing down upon the assembly. His vast rolling bulk seemed to take up all available space, and to soak up the very light itself. Bright particles of dust flew towards him, as though magnetized, sucked headlong into the black hole of his being.

He drew so close that Baz could smell him. A vague musty aura, like stale tobacco, or burning wax. And now Baz saw for the first time just how huge and awesome Preacher John was. The man was a giant. He dwarfed his sons. Even Isaac looked insignificant by comparison, shrunken, deflated.

Baz felt a terrible urge to reach out and touch the black cloth of Preacher John's jacket, pick at the motes of dust, examine the shiny seams. It was like wanting to reach through the bars of a cage and tug at the fur of a sleeping lion or a mighty gorilla, knowing full well what the consequences would be.

'Yes, Isaac. They get that look in their eye . . .'

Preacher John's own rheumy yellow eyes looked down upon Baz . . . held him for an intense and terrifying moment . . . and then moved on. Baz felt as though he'd been momentarily pinned against the wall, searched, and then released, his guilty thoughts now in the possession of Preacher John.

'The world might have changed, but boys don't.' The preacher was looking at Amit now. 'I know them for what they are. Pack animals. Aye, and every one of them wants to be pack leader. They're like dogs, are boys. Each of 'em chasing the one in front, ready to tear at his heels and bring him down. And they'll go for you too, the one holding the whip, if you should ever turn your back on them. The bigger they get, the more dangerous they become. So dogs need to be kept in their place, and the whip needs to be cracked. Isn't that right, Isaac?' He pointed a huge red forefinger at Amit. 'You. How long have you been with us?'

'Um . . . 'bout six months.' Amit kept his head low.

'Six months. And you reckon yourself top dog here, yes?'

Amit said nothing.

'I see I'm right. I'm always right. Get down on all fours, boy. On your knees, then, like a dog.'

Baz glanced to his left and saw Amit's look of confusion, hesitation.

'Down! On your *knees*, I said!'

Amit dropped to the ground and placed his hands before him, fingers spread.

'Right then – you!' This time Preacher John pointed at Dyson. 'Kick him.'

'What?'

'Kick him, I said. He reckons himself to be top dog – but then so do you, don't you? So kick him while he's down. Here's your chance.'

'But I don't—'

'*Kick him!*' Preacher John's voice rose to a roar, and Dyson hesitated no longer. He stepped past Baz and gave Amit a kick in the ribs. There was no real force behind it, but Amit grunted nevertheless, and lurched sideways.

'Again!' the preacher shouted. 'Kick him! And the rest of you – get stuck in! Come on!'

There was no choice but to obey, or at least pretend

to. The boys gathered around the kneeling figure of Amit, and Dyson led the way with another half-hearted kick – this time to Amit's shoulder. Hesitant and bewildered, the others followed suit. Feet snaked out from all directions, and Baz found himself aiming a gentle tap at Amit's thigh, determined to cause as little pain as he could.

But such restraint didn't suit Preacher John.

'*Kick* him, you scum, before I strangle the lot of you!' The preacher stepped forward, an open hand raised, and in the face of such a threat all fellow feeling had to be set aside. The corridor became a jostling scrimmage of bodies, a football game with the curled-up figure of Amit at its centre. Kick after kick landed upon the boy, and still Preacher John demanded more. There could be no holding back, and the game quickly escalated into a kind of blind violence. Baz was caught up in its ferocity, lashing out at any part of Amit that became exposed – arms, legs, buttocks – conscious only that his own skin depended upon it. He was underwater again, choking to death, and it was the same desperate struggle for survival. Whatever it took . . . whatever it took. And now he had to kick even harder – because he really *was* choking. There was something around his neck and he couldn't breathe. Kick for your life, then. Kick yourself free . . .

He was being dragged backwards, a hard muscular arm yanking him away from the bundle of bodies, shaking him back into focus.

One of the divers had grabbed him – Luke – and now the other boys were being hauled off too. Baz was shoved roughly aside. He careened into Dyson, and together they fell against the corridor wall, panting, coughing. Wild-eyed faces danced around him, each bearing the same hungry look that he had seen on the day of his arrival. And he was no different. No different to anyone else.

'Dogs.' Preacher John looked calmly down at the prostrate figure of Amit. 'And dog'll eat dog, if that's what it comes to. Pick him up, then, and set him on his feet. He'll take no harm from this. It does a dog good to be kicked every once in a while. Reminds him of what he is – a dog. And the rest of you had better remember it. This could have been any one of you. Wouldn't you say so, boy?'

'Eh?' Steiner realized he was being addressed. He looked at Preacher John, his face still half smiling from what he'd just witnessed.

'Don't you dare grin at me. They'd do the same to you, given half a chance. Or to me. They're getting too dam' big. But I've got no time to make any changes, so just watch 'em. And you' – Preacher John turned to his eldest son – 'see that you take a lesson from this.'

There was no explanation as to what this lesson might be. Instead Preacher John raised his right arm towards Isaac, then brought it sharply down, snapping his great fingers together as he did so. The sound echoed around the corridor like a pistol shot. Like a whipcrack . . .

Perhaps that was the lesson. They were all dogs – boys, capos and salvage crew alike. And Preacher John held the whip.

'Now get these kids working,' he said. His tone towards Isaac was cold, utterly in command. 'I want this job finished by Saturday night. If you can manage that.'

A final glance along the line of boys and Preacher John moved away, continuing his progress towards the dark end of the corridor, footsteps as silent as the shadows that eventually closed behind him.

Isaac watched him go, his eyes narrowed and resentful. Then he turned abruptly and walked in the opposite direction. The divers picked up their gear and followed him. As they passed through the main entrance doors, someone muttered something, and there was a low chuckle. Baz got the impression that it wasn't Isaac who was laughing.

'Get him up then.' Steiner seemed subdued for once.

The boys began helping Amit to his feet.

He didn't seem to be too badly hurt – able to stand at any rate – but his face was streaked with tears, and Baz felt sick with the shame of what they'd just done.

'God, Amit . . .'

'Man, are you OK?'

They spoke as though Amit had just had an accident or something. Everyone gathered round their dishevelled companion, apparently to dust him down, check him for injuries, but what they were really doing was finding an excuse to touch him, looking for a way of saying sorry without actually using the word.

Baz was the first to attempt any kind of apology, or to admit any blame.

'Amit . . . I'm really sorry. Sorry, mate. We didn't . . . we couldn't . . .'

'Yeah, sorry, Amit.'

'Sorry.'

Everyone was joining in, then, saying sorry and shaking their heads as though they couldn't understand what had come over them. And it was impossible to explain. Whatever had just happened had been beyond their control, and apologies seemed pointless. It almost came as a relief when Steiner cut them off short.

'Oi! We've got work to do. He'll live, so quit your blethering. Grab those ropes and pickaxes, and follow me. Come on – stop sodding about!'

So they let Amit be. Baz picked up one of the ropes, and the crew trooped out of the main entrance in silence.

They didn't have far to go. Instead of leading the way towards the jetty, Steiner walked just a short distance along the tarmac path and then came to a halt next to the school sign – the tall slab of stone that rose from the overgrown grass verge. He waded through the grass and took out his tape measure.

'Right,' he said. 'We're digging this up.'

Steiner paid out the metal rule until he was able to hook the end of it onto the top edge of the stone monolith.

Baz stared up at the neatly carved words. TAB HILL HIGH SCHOOL. Digging it up? Why?

'Two and a half metres tall,' said Steiner. 'Metre wide – just over. Probably another metre underground. That'd be about right. OK. You . . . and you' – he pointed at Dyson and Baz – 'you use the picks. The other two get digging with the shovels. Come on.'

Baz had never held a pickaxe before. It was heavy

and awkward, and it quickly became apparent that it was the wrong tool for digging through thick grass. The point of the pickaxe head simply disappeared into the vegetation, and either got stuck or failed to even reach the earth beneath.

'All right,' said Steiner. 'Pull up the grass first then.'

Progress was slow and painful. Come midday there was a roughly circular trench surrounding the stone, dug down to a depth of about thirty centimetres. This was a job that was obviously going to take some time, and there had been no explanation as to why they were doing it. When someone had ventured to ask Steiner about it, he simply said, 'Orders.'

And then things got worse. They discovered that the huge sign had been mounted in concrete. For the moment it was impossible to see just how much concrete there was – how far it extended or how deep it went. There could be a ton of it down there for all anyone could tell. But there was no going through it. The only option was to dig around it.

'Great,' said Amit. 'Welcome to Treasure Island.' These were the first words he'd spoken since the morning's incident.

'Shut up and keep digging,' growled Steiner.

Later, in the slob room, as they sat on their mattresses, Baz tried to explain to Ray what had happened.

'It was like we'd all gone mad,' he said. 'And it was like . . . like it wasn't really Amit at all. Once he was on the ground, he was just this . . . thing.' He looked down towards the other end of the room, where Amit sat with some of the others. The group were talking quietly among themselves – probably about the same subject. Baz tried to recall the moment when he had been hauled off by one of the divers; the sense of . . . disappointment?

'Yeah,' he said. 'It was like we were kicking at something else. This place, maybe. Yeah, this. All of this.' He shrugged it off. 'Hey, I think I've got a fart coming on. Better go and add to the store.'

'I wouldn't have done it,' said Ray. 'Not if it had been you. I couldn't have.'

Baz had no reply to that. He wanted to say, *Well, you weren't there*, but then he wondered if he would have acted in the same way if it had been Ray who was down on the floor. He tried to picture that. Would it have been any different if it had been Ray?

He changed the subject. 'So how's it been in the sort room?' he said.

Ray stared down at the palms of his hands. 'Scary,' he said. 'Hutchinson told me that Steiner's gonna smash the drain cover in.'

Baz forgot all about his rumbling gut, the build-up of gas that he'd been carefully harbouring. 'What?'

'Yeah. With a sledgehammer. Isaac said he could. Steiner told him it's got jammed somehow, and the handle has to be turned. So the thing is, Baz, the drain'll soon be open again. Probably by next Sunday . . .' Ray's voice faltered. 'And that scared me, but I didn't say anything. And then you know what Hutchinson said? He said, "I hope for your sake we don't find that that cover's been stuck down somehow. 'Cos if someone's been damaging Preacher John's property, then they're really for it." Looks like they

223

figured it out. So now I reckon it's gonna be even worse than before – what they do to me . . .'

Ray brushed the back of his hand across his eyes, and Baz felt his heart lurch within him. He reached out, not caring how his actions might be interpreted by anyone watching, and grasped Ray's hand, feeling the smear of dampness on his own palm.

'It's not gonna happen,' he said. 'So don't even think about it. We're gonna win. We're gonna do what we said we're gonna do, and get rid of the lot of 'em. We've just got to hang on, yeah? Hang on till we get it figured out. Just a bit longer, yeah?'

Ray nodded. His head was down.

They sat like that for a while with their hands clasped in each other's. And though the light flickered above them, and other boys came and went, passing by on their way to the jakes, and though there may have been whispers and a few quizzical looks, neither of them made any attempt to pull away.

It was Gene who eventually broke them up. He walked past waving a green balloon. PARTY TIME!

'Hey,' he said. 'Fart Club. Come on, you guys – no backsliding.'

Baz laughed. 'OK.' He looked at Ray. 'Are you in?'

Ray shook his head. 'Maybe in the morning. That's the way it works with me.'

'OK.' Baz let go of Ray's hand and stood up. 'You all right?'

'Yeah, I'm all right.'

* * *

By Friday Isaac was becoming impatient. He came out to see what progress had been made on digging up the school sign.

'What's keeping you?' he said to Steiner.

'It's this chuffin' great lump of concrete,' said Steiner. 'We've dug all around it, but we can't get the chuffin' thing to budge. We—'

'Oi. Watch your language.' Isaac looked down into the broad pit that now surrounded the stone sign. The boys worked on, conscious that they were being watched. Three days it had taken to reach this point. The huge lump of concrete that the tablet had been set into was now exposed – like the root ball at the base of a tree – but the stone itself stood as firm as ever.

'Have you tried the ropes?' Isaac said.

'Nah. These kids couldn't pull a twig out of the ground. They'd never shift this.'

Isaac grunted. 'Right. We've wasted enough time on this dam' nonsense already. Wait there.'

He went back into the building.

Ten minutes later he returned, and this time he had the salvage crew in tow. The boys clambered out of the pit, and Isaac set about looping ropes around the top of the stone slab.

'We'll take her out edgeways. It'll be easier to get at the concrete then. Amos, Luke, get on that rope. I'll take this one with Moko.'

The men spat on their hands and grabbed the nylon ropes.

'After three, then.' Isaac leaned back and got a foothold on the trampled-down earth. 'One, two, *three*.'

The men threw themselves into action, straining

against the ropes, and the top of the stone began to shift sideways – just a few centimetres at first, but it was enough to encourage an even mightier effort. Jaws set, eyes bulging, the salvage crew kept up the pressure, leaning almost horizontally, repositioning their stances as the stone continued to move.

'OK. Stop for a moment and take another grip. She's coming – though God knows why we're killing ourselves like this.' It was clear that Isaac's heart was not in the job. 'Poxy thing. Right, let's go again, then. After three.'

Baz watched the men, and once again felt a sense of his own feebleness. This display of brute power was another reminder of just what they were up against.

The stone lay sideways at an angle of about forty-five degrees. It would go no further, the edge of it now against the rim of the pit it stood in. But the lump of concrete had lifted to the point where most of it could at least be seen. A fringe of blue material was visible, protruding from where the slab had been set into the concrete mix. Isaac jumped down into the pit for a closer inspection.

'Polythene,' he said. 'Should be able to knock this stuff off all right, then. Steiner, bring the pickaxes back to the storeroom and get these kids some hammers instead. Sledgehammers, lump hammers, whatever we've got. Break up this concrete. And keep the ropes tied on – you'll need them later.'

'OK, Skip. Do you want me to break up that drain cover too while we've got the sledgehammers out? Might as well.'

'Nope. Leave it alone until I tell you. Get this done first.'

Baz felt his heart rate rise, and then subside again.

They found that the concrete had been made to a fairly loose mix, not as rock hard as it had first appeared. The fact that the base of the slab had been sheathed in polythene meant that the concrete broke away in satisfying chunks beneath blows of the sledgehammers.

But the job itself was difficult and dangerous. The boys stood two to each side of the pit and took it in turns to attack the slab, bits of stone flying in all directions. Baz was dizzy with fatigue, muscles aching, head swimming. He raised his sledgehammer for the hundredth time and prepared to swing . . . but then the spot that he was aiming at seemed to move. Baz blinked the sweat out of his eyes, and realized that the slab was tilting, coming towards him. Everyone was suddenly yelling his name. '*Baz! Baz!*' He dropped the sledgehammer, stumbled sideways to avoid the on-coming slab, and tripped. As he rolled over onto his back, he saw that the stone sign was closing down upon him like the lid of some huge box. Too late to think straight, too late to do anything but follow instinct – Baz pushed backwards on his elbows, frantically wriggling towards the edge of the dug-out pit. The stone heeled over in a kind of awful slow motion, blocking out the sky, the chiselled words bringing their message of doom: TAB HILL HIGH SCHOOL . . .

There was just time for Baz to get the palms of his hands flat against the huge monolith as it came, pressing him to the earth, the big red letter S looming straight at his face. Gasping, screaming at the terror of being crushed alive, Baz turned his head sideways and pushed at the stone. He felt his elbows and shoulder blades digging into the soil beneath him, the air in his lungs being squeezed out of him, and heard the sound of his last hopeless cry, amplified in the confined and shrinking space.

Then, as he shoved with all his might against the weight crushing down on his body, the pressure eased, and the slab began to rise upwards. For a moment Baz thought that he'd found some superhuman power, that he really was lifting a ton of stone from his chest with his own bare hands. His terror had given him the strength of ten men – twenty men – strength far beyond that of Isaac and his crew . . .

But the stone carried on rising until it floated out of the reach of his fingertips, and Baz realized that it had simply tipped up like a seesaw, pivoting on the edge of the pit to lie flat on the ground above. The shorter end of it had been raised, and was now suspended over his head. Baz rolled sideways, preparing to scrabble out of the way, and in that moment the last big lump of concrete fell from the underside of the slab. It landed with a dull and heavy thud, right beside him.

As Baz emerged from beneath the great tablet, heart thumping, he saw a ring of pale faces staring down at him, all of them wearing the same horrified expression. All but one.

'Ha. I always said he looked like something that just crawled out from under a stone.' Steiner's slack-jawed face split into a grin.

They had been told to bring fencing posts from the stacked pile outside the sort room, and these were now inserted beneath the slab.

'Right,' said Steiner. 'Get on those ropes and start pulling.'

The round posts were apparently supposed to act as rollers. But though the four boys heaved on the ropes again and again, the stone wouldn't budge. Eventually Steiner gave up and went off in disgust. He returned with Hutchinson and the sort-room crew, including Gene. Now there were eight of them, and they found that if they all pulled in unison, they could just about move the slab. It took a good twenty minutes to manoeuvre it off the grass verge and onto the tarmac pathway, but here things became a little easier. The rollers started to work properly, and the smallest of the boys – Enoch – could be spared from the haulage team. It became his job to run from the back of the slab to the front, continually replacing the fencing posts.

Like Egyptian slaves they worked, pulling the slab along, a few centimetres at a time, with Enoch keeping the rollers in position.

'What are we doing?' Gene asked. 'Building a bloody pyramid?'

'You'll see,' said Hutchinson. 'Tell you what, though – it makes a change seeing *you* break into a sweat.'

'Yeah,' said Steiner. ''Bout time you did some proper work, kiddo.'

Once the tarmac path began its downward slope the slab became more difficult to control. The crew was split – three boys to the front, steering the slab from left to right, and four at the back, hauling on their ropes to act as a brake. When they reached the point where the tarmac ended and the jetty began, Steiner just said, 'OK, keep going.'

So now their destination became clear. At the far end of the jetty stood the box-like construction built out of concrete blocks. It didn't take a genius to guess that the big stone slab might be intended as a lid for that box, but still nobody could guess what its purpose might be.

Progress along the top of the jetty was far slower than it had been on the tarmac, and it was late afternoon by the time the boys had managed to position the slab parallel to the concrete platform. The nylon ropes had blistered their hands, and they were exhausted.

'Had enough?' said Steiner – but he was speaking to Hutchinson.

'Yeah, I reckon.'

'Right then, you lot. Everybody back to the sort room. Today's Friday. We've got till tomorrow night to get this baby up onto the box. Preacher John's orders.'

'How are we supposed do that?' said Gene.

'How?' said Steiner. '*I* don't care how. You're the chuffin' smartarse, you figure it out. But it'll be done by tomorrow night, OK? Now get back to the sort room.'

CHAPTER THIRTEEN

Saturday morning, and the entire crew were down at the jetty. On Gene's instructions they had barrowed a few dozen concrete blocks down from the building site, together with three long scaffolding poles.

'First thing we're gonna do,' said Gene, 'is try and get the slab up onto the platform. We'll use the scaffolding poles as levers – two of us on each pole.'

Steiner and Hutchinson looked on, their arms folded. They had adopted the air of schoolmasters, or competition judges – those who understood perfectly well how this task should be accomplished, but were testing the boys to see whether they could work it out for themselves. They were fooling nobody, however. This was Gene's show, and everybody knew it.

The stone slab was still on its wooden rollers from the night before. Two of the fencing posts were removed from one end, and the scaffolding poles inserted in the gap beneath.

'Right then, lift!' said Gene, and eight boys began to raise the tubular steel poles. These were heavy enough in themselves, and Baz had little faith in their ability to lift the weight of the stone as well. So he was amazed when the front of the slab began to rise up and separate from its bed of rollers. The boys shuffled to one side, and the front corner of the tablet slewed across to the concrete platform.

'Now the back corner.' Gene seemed to have it all planned out. He laid out three concrete blocks in a row on the platform, and with a lot of lifting and levering the slab eventually lay balanced like a seesaw on the line of blocks.

'We put blocks under each end,' said Gene, 'and keep going like that – levering it up and building three stacks of blocks, yeah? So the stone rests on the three stacks. Once we get it high enough, we'll jiggle it across onto the walls. Job done.'

Steiner looked at Hutchinson. 'Yeah, that's one way. It was either that or a ramp.'

'Yeah. Or block and tackle.'

'We need a couple of guys doing the concrete blocks,' said Gene. 'How about Enoch and Ray? You OK with that? Have to watch your hands, though.'

'All right,' said Enoch.

'Yeah, I don't mind.' Ray glanced at Baz and pulled a slightly crooked face.

The slab had to be jacked up at quite a steep angle in order to get the blocks into position. One slip and fingers could easily get crushed under there. From where he stood, at the furthest end of a scaffold pole, it was difficult for Baz to see what was going on. He kept peering anxiously over Jubo's shoulder as Ray and Enoch crawled around beneath the construction.

The supporting stacks of blocks grew higher, until the slab was almost level with the top of the wall, but by now the whole thing was beginning to feel creakily unstable, groaning beneath its own massive weight. Baz could smell the perspiration of those around him. The slab seemed darkly threatening, poised, a slumbering monster that had been poked and prodded once too often.

Gene let go of his pole and stepped back to inspect, wiping his forehead. 'Just one more level,' he said, 'and we're there.'

Baz looked across at Jubo and let out a long shaky breath. Even Steiner and Hutchinson had dropped their pretended lack of interest, and now watched with frowning concentration.

'Come on,' said Gene. 'We're OK. Ready, Enoch? Ray? Middle blocks then.'

The boys inserted the scaffolding poles, and gingerly began to apply some force. The end of the slab rose up, but then Gene seemed to lose his nerve.

'Whoa . . . whoa . . . lower it again.'

'What's the matter?' said Steiner.

The slab came back down to rest and Gene shook his head.

'I dunno about this. I think it's too much.'

'What do you mean "too much"?' said Steiner. 'It's the same as all the other times.'

'No,' said Gene. 'I'm worried about the stacks. They're starting to wobble.'

'Hey – we can see what's going on from here. You can't. Now get it done. Come on – we'll keep an eye on it. It's fine.'

Gene bit his lip and hesitated, but then Hutchinson joined in.

'Listen, if we think it's looking dodgy we'll tell you. Now stop friggin' about and get this job finished. I've laid off the sort-room crew long enough.'

'OK . . .' Gene still sounded uncertain. 'Well, just you keep watching that end stack, that's all. If it starts to lean, then you better bloody tell us.'

'Oi, watch your lip! We don't take our orders from you, OK?'

Gene shrugged. 'Come on, guys. It'll be all right.' He positioned himself on the scaffolding pole again. 'Gently does it.'

Once more the boys began to push down on the scaffolding poles.

'We're OK . . . we're OK . . .' Gene leaned outwards to get a better view of what was happening. 'That high enough, Ray?'

'Bit more . . .' Ray's muffled voice came from beneath the slab.

Baz could hear Ray muttering something to Enoch. 'Got it? Shove your end in then . . . bit further . . .'

And then Baz felt the metal pole being wrenched from his grasp, dragged sideways with a force far beyond his control. There was a horrible grinding crunch, a hollow echo of it in the tube that he was gripping. He lurched forward against Jubo, pulled by the unbelievable weight of collapsing steel and stone. Down it all went, the metal poles clanging out their warning amid a rumble of exploding concrete. The stone tablet crashed into the billowing grey dust like some giant oil tanker belly-flopping into a raging sea.

Baz somersaulted over Jubo and landed on top of

the slab, oblivious to his own danger even as he fell. All his thoughts were for Ray – Ray, who had been under the huge monolith as it collapsed . . . and was under there now. Baz scrambled sideways, trying to get off the slab, his head filled with the panicky notion that he was only adding to the weight, that he might somehow be making matters worse. He slithered down amongst the rubble, banging his knees and elbows on the rough corners of broken blocks, his heart pumping as though it would burst.

Baz hauled himself into a kneeling position, grabbing uselessly at lumps of concrete, throwing them aside . . .

'No! No! Ray . . . he's under there!'

And then he saw that Ray was sitting right next to him.

Ray's face was damp with sweat, dark patches of grey on his forehead and chin where the concrete dust had stuck to him. His eyes were wide with shock, his gaze fixed on the stone slab.

'God . . .' Baz dropped the piece of concrete that he was holding, the breath collapsing out of him. 'Ohhhh . . . God. You got out. I thought you were . . . thought you were still under . . .'

But Ray said nothing, wasn't even looking at Baz. Open mouthed, he began to struggle to his feet, and as Baz squinted up at him he saw that all the other boys were standing, a loose and silent group staring down at the slab.

Enoch! Baz rolled over and pushed himself upright. He'd forgotten all about Enoch.

Gene picked his way forward through the rubble

and crouched beside the slab, his head tilted as if to listen.

'Enoch?' His voice was higher than normal, on the verge of panic. 'Enoch! Can you hear me?' No reply. 'Oh, God . . .' Gene stood up again. 'Uh . . . right. Grab the scaffolding poles.' He looked around at the mess of rubble. 'Oh, Christ. Let me think for a minute. OK. Um . . . just two poles then. One at each end. Let's see if we can lift it right up and tilt it back against the wall.'

But it couldn't be done. There was only room for two boys to effectively get a grip on each of the two poles, and that was too few to be able to raise the slab. After a couple of attempts they gave up.

'We're gonna have to put a pole in the middle as well, then,' said Gene. 'But watch what you're doing. He's under there somewhere.'

'Christ,' groaned Steiner. 'What a friggin' mess.' Neither he nor Hutchinson offered any help.

Baz got ready on the middle pole, sick at the thought of what he was about to see. His hands were trembling and sweaty. He quickly wiped them on his shorts before stooping to grasp the rusty scaffolding pole.

'. . . two, three, *hup*.' Gene gave the signal to lift.

Amid the sobbing gasps and grunts of the boys, the slab began to rise. As Baz staggered forward to reposition his grip, he glimpsed pale shapes flickering around the edges of his vision. He knew that it was Enoch, lying on the ground to his left, but he deliberately kept his eyes averted. All his strength and concentration were needed for the job in hand.

The slab was almost upright. One more push took it

beyond its balancing point, and it toppled against the blockwork wall with a grinding thud. The heavy scaffolding poles were lowered, hand over hand, and only then did Baz take a proper look at Enoch.

There didn't appear to be a mark on him. He was on his back, shoulders flat to the ground, head and legs turned to one side. His arms were raised above his head. He could have been a sunbather lying on a beach and stretching himself, wondering if he could be bothered to go and buy an ice cream. The piles of rubble to either side of him had kept his body from being crushed. There was no blood.

Yet they all knew that Enoch was dead. Gene knelt beside him and raised his torso from the concrete platform. Enoch's head lolled backwards, hanging down at an impossible angle. His neck was broken.

Baz had seen dead bodies before – many many dead bodies. Some stood out in his mind more than others . . . Mrs Kenwright, his saxophone teacher, floating past the bathroom window. She looked so young, like a child in her starry blue pyjamas, her hair all undone, her skin impossibly white against the dark waters that bore her along. And Mr and Mrs Gavindra from the paper shop, both dangling upside down in the same lilac tree, as though they were performing a trapeze act together . . .

It didn't matter how many you'd seen. Nothing prepared you for the next one. You could never get used to it. And Baz knew what it felt like to be trapped beneath that slab . . . the terror of seeing it coming down . . . knowing that it was all over . . .

Baz stood motionless, his hands hanging uselessly

at his sides, just staring at Gene as he cradled Enoch in his arms.

'Get 'em all back to t' sort room,' muttered Steiner. 'I'll deal with this.'

'Sure?' Hutchinson didn't seem inclined to move.

'Yeah. Done it before.'

'Right, then,' Hutchinson said. 'Back to the sort room, you lot. Go on.'

'What are you going to do?' Gene laid Enoch gently down and looked up at Steiner.

'What am *I* gonna do? Don't worry about it,' said Steiner. 'I'll tell you what *you* can do, though, smart-arse; get back to the chuffin' drawing board. 'Cos that little idea of yours didn't work too well, did it?'

Baz thought he could never have hated Steiner more than at that moment. Now he was certain that if he had that magic button to push, then he would push it, and have no regrets. Yes, he could do it right now – blow that toe-rag sky-high. And maybe now *was* the time. Forget about bombs – just grab whatever came to hand . . . a shovel . . . a lump of concrete . . .

As Gene rose to his feet, Robbie stepped in front of him, quick as a squirrel, ready to head off trouble. 'Come on, mate,' he said. 'Let's go. Gene? It's OK. Let's go.'

And Gene allowed himself to be turned round, though his face was taut and set, dark eyes blazing with anger.

'Yeah, come on.' Dyson had seen the danger too, recognized how close things were to kicking off. He crowded in on Gene, kept him from turning to face Steiner again. The boys began to disperse, splitting up as they made their way along the jetty. Baz walked alone, not wanting to speak to anyone for the moment. He glanced round at the scene they were leaving behind them. Steiner was watching them go, legs apart, hands on hips.

A crowd of emotions jostled for space in Baz's head, too many to be able to cope with. Rage burned him from the inside out – flaring torches of hatred for the capos. And terrible sadness for Enoch. But then he imagined that it was Ray lying dead back there amongst the rubble, Ray instead of Enoch, and relief flooded through him. It was shocking. Frightening.

It was frightening about Gene as well – Gene who was supposed to be their hope, their saviour. Gene had showed that he could be wrong, just like anyone else. His plan hadn't worked. He could make mistakes after all.

As they wound their way up the pathway that led to the school buildings, Baz turned once more to look down at the jetty. Just before it all disappeared from view he caught a last glimpse of Steiner. He was pushing a wheelbarrow. It didn't look as though disposing of Enoch would take very long.

CHAPTER FOURTEEN

Having the time to think, to keep reliving the moment, made Sunday almost unbearable.

Only Gene had anything to say – and he said it over and over, in the same distraught voice. This was all his fault. If only he had been more careful, thought things through, taken everything more slowly, then Enoch might still be here now.

Lost in their own grief and anger, none of the boys gave Gene much reassurance or argued against him. His plan had been a screw-up, and now Enoch was dead. Perhaps Gene was not such a genius after all.

Eventually Dyson spoke up in Gene's defence.

'What were you supposed to do?' he said. 'They didn't give you enough time, they didn't give you the right gear, they didn't give you the . . . the watchamacallit – the manpower. And when it all started to go wrong, the capos wouldn't let you stop and think 'cos Isaac says it's gotta be done now. And Isaac's only doing what he's told in any case. It's Preacher John's fault, not yours.'

Dyson was right. There was no point in blaming Gene, or in Gene blaming himself. They were all slaves, and they had no choice but to obey orders.

Preacher John sickened them all by giving another pious Sunday sermon, regretting the sad loss of their 'brother', Enoch, and once again asking that Enoch's life be accepted as a sacrifice to God's will. *Draw back the waters, O Lord*, was Preacher John's plea, *and let the world be made whole again*. It was horrible.

Ray spent a tense Sunday afternoon trying to dodge the capos. In the event nothing happened. The drain had not been reopened, and both capos had made a very early start on the wine. Or maybe they'd just decided to lay off for once. At any rate they collapsed into a stupor long before evening, and Ray was safe. But his luck couldn't hold out indefinitely.

Trudging along the jetty on Monday morning, the work crew came upon a strange sight. Preacher John was there, all alone and staring out to sea. He stood beyond the platform, right at the edge of the jetty, with his arms raised high. It was as though he was greeting the day, his head thrown back, long ginger hair curling down over his shoulders.

As the boys approached, Preacher John lowered his arms. He stood with his head bowed for a moment, then straightened up again. When he turned to face them, they saw that he was smiling.

That smile was the most extraordinary thing – open mouthed, fixed, like an opera singer reaching a last rapturous note. And he looked as out of place as an opera singer might have done, standing amidst the heaps of sand and rubble and upturned wheelbarrows. Dressed in immaculate black, shoes polished, his great red face beaming, Preacher John was of another world.

He walked towards them, one hand in his pocket, and as he passed by, he waved his free arm in the general direction of the sea. 'The power of prayer, my sons,' he said. 'We have made a beginning at last.' He walked on.

Baz lowered his barrow and looked out to sea. It was unchanged as far as he could tell, the water level as high as ever.

But then Ray said, 'What's that?'

The day was clear for a change, and the horizon visible. Far away to the left the ocean abruptly changed colour, a definite line separating the familiar dull grey of the coastal water from the broader expanse that stretched towards the skyline.

'Whoa . . .' Baz put a hand up to shade his eyes. 'It's *blue*.'

Even the capos stopped to look. Something had undoubtedly happened out there, or was in the process of happening. The difference between the two colours was remarkable, a strip of blue water melded to the murky grey, like new plasticine attached to old. *The power of prayer*, Preacher John had said. Did he believe that this was somehow down to him?

There was no time to consider further, because Steiner turned away from the sight with a shrug and said, 'Come on. Stop hanging about.'

The boys began the process of trying to lift the stone slab once again. They hated the thing now, and they worked in glowering and resentful silence, ignoring the remarks of the capos and listening only to Gene.

Gene refused to be hurried. This time he constructed the three supporting stacks from builders' planks instead of concrete blocks, so that the angle of leverage wasn't as steep. It took a lot longer, but with six boys working the scaffolding poles and Gene directing operations, the slab was gently raised and then shuffled sideways, inch by inch, until it rested on top of its box. At last the job was done. And still nobody had the slightest idea of what this thing could be for.

Later that evening, when Hutchinson came to the slob room to lock up, he said to Gene, 'Hey – Isaac wants to know when that cross is going to be ready.'

Gene kept his head down. It was plain that he wasn't going to answer Hutchinson, or even look at him.

'Listen, you. Just because some dozy kid—'

Whatever Hutchinson said next went unheard. From outside in the corridor came a high wailing sound, almost a scream, mingled with the more distant cursing of a man's voice. Hutchinson moved towards the doorway – then had to immediately dodge sideways as Cookie came crashing into the room.

'Ahhh-ahhh . . . !' Cookie was bent over double, one hand extended, palm upwards, obviously in agony. He lumbered around in circles, his hand stuck out, rocking up and down as though performing some wild dance. The effect was somehow comical, and a few of the boys laughed out loud.

'Oi!' Hutchinson snatched at the collar of Cookie's white jacket. 'What the hell are you bawling about? Shut up and keep still!'

But Cookie fell against Hutchinson, grabbing him around the thighs, wailing and crying all the louder.

Hutchinson shoved him away in disgust and Cookie fell heavily to the floor. He crouched forward, head low, still with one hand extended.

'Jesus! I better find out what's going on. Get this idiot sorted, some of you.' Hutchinson backed away and left the room.

Nobody made any move towards Cookie. The boy remained on his knees, swaying to and fro, his grubby white jacket stretched tightly over his rounded back. He looked like a big mushroom.

Baz couldn't stand by any longer without at least trying to find out what had happened. He went over to Cookie and crouched down on the greasy carpet tiles beside him.

'Hey – what is it? What's wrong with you?'

Cookie made some gulping sound, but his head was almost touching the floor and Baz couldn't understand him.

'What?' He reached out and put a hand on Cookie's shoulder – aware that he was crossing some sort of boundary in doing so. 'What did you say?'

The pimply rolls of fat on Cookie's neck became more deeply creased. He raised his head, turning his face sideways to look up at Baz.

'They . . . they . . .' Cookie struggled to get the words out, tears and snot dribbling down his wobbly chin. 'They shoved my hand . . . in the . . . in the . . . *soup*!'

Baz heard the explosive sniggers of some of the boys around him. He might even have been inclined to join in – but then he looked properly at Cookie's hand. It was awful. The back of it was one huge blister, like a big yellow jellyfish, full of fluid, the surrounding flesh mottled red, fingers swollen as though they would burst. Baz winced at the sight. He could see strange little orangey bits here and there, as though globules of fat had bubbled up through Cookie's skin.

'What are those things?' Then he realized. 'Oh. They're lentils. Hey – shut up, willya?' He frowned up at the snorting onlookers. 'This is serious. Ray, come and take a look . . .'

Ray stepped forward and bent closer. 'God,' he said. 'That's horrible. Uh . . . we better see if we can get him over to his bed or something. Then get his jacket off.'

Cookie seemed helpless, almost unable to move, and it felt strange to be making such direct contact with him – touching the untouchable. It was only Baz and Ray who were doing any serious lifting. The others hovered around, vaguely sympathetic now, but they stopped short of physical assistance.

With Cookie on his bed at last, Baz began trying to remove his jacket. Every jerk and tug brought a fresh wave of agonized howls from the patient, and Baz began to wish he hadn't taken this task upon himself. Cookie was so big and so awkward, that was the trouble. The jacket stuck to his heavy nakedness, seemed to get caught in the folds and creases of sweaty flesh.

Ray said, 'I'll go and get a wet T-shirt or something. Wrap it round his hand.' It was a good idea, but Baz felt that it was partly an excuse to leave all the hard work to him.

'Come on, Cookie. Almost there.' Baz gritted his teeth and hauled on the sleeve of the jacket.

Ray came back with a white T-shirt dripping water, and wrapped it around Cookie's hand as gently as he could. 'That's gonna have to do for tonight,' he said. 'Maybe in the morning . . .' His voice trailed off. There was no guarantee that the morning would bring anything more in the way of assistance. Cookie lay back on his bed, still crying, but silently now, as though withdrawn into a private world of pain. He looked like a defeated boxer, naked from the waist up, one huge paw all swaddled in a bandage.

Baz glanced across at Ray, and then around the room, realizing that most of the others had disappeared. Only Dyson remained in the vicinity of Cookie's bed.

'Where the hell is everybody?' said Baz.

Dyson just shrugged and said, 'Fart Club, I guess. Not that anyone's really in the mood. Better hurry up, though, if you want your turn. Hutchinson'll be back in a minute.'

Cookie kept up a low moaning throughout most of the night. Usually he was the first to depart the slob room, but in the morning he was still there, struggling to get his jacket on as the other boys were lining up.

Hutchinson came by. 'Cookie,' he said, 'gimme a look at your hand.'

Cookie unwound the T-shirt that bandaged his damaged hand. Baz caught a glimpse of red raw flesh, the glistening crustiness of burst blisters. He knew something of what that felt like.

Hutchinson looked briefly down at Cookie's hand. 'OK. Isaac said to send someone else with you if you

weren't gonna be able to work properly. So . . . er . . .
you' – he pointed at Baz – 'get on down to the kitchens
and give this idiot a hand. Ha! Give him a hand . . .'
Hutchinson chuckled at his own feeble joke. 'Rest of
you line up outside the sort room.'

So Baz found himself unexpectedly accompanying
Cookie, walking towards the dark end of the main
corridor, about to enter a world that few of the X Isle
boys had ever seen.

CHAPTER FIFTEEN

The kitchen was huge. Baz's first impression was of stainless steel – acres of it – and blue ceramic tiled flooring. The floor might have been swept sometime in the last month, but the rows of cooker hobs, ovens, dishwashers and steel cabinets had a dull and long-disused look to them. Baz ran his finger along one of the grimy metal surfaces as Cookie showed him around.

'Yeah, none of it works of course,' said Cookie. 'All gas, see. This is what I have to make do with.' He came back to the first section of the room, where a small two-ring electric cooker stood on one of the work surfaces. The cooker looked pretty ancient.

'I've got this and a microwave, and that little fridge over there. You can only use one of 'em at a time, 'cos that's all the generator can cope with. The microwave's a bit dodgy in any case.'

'Hot food, though,' said Baz. 'Can't remember the last time I had anything hot.'

'A lot of the time I'm just heating up tins.' Cookie pulled open the door of a steel cabinet. 'But I got all this other stuff too.'

The cabinet shelves were full of jars, bottles and packets. Baz could see flour and salt, powdered milk, herbs, sauces . . . stock cubes . . . jam . . . marmalade . . . tea . . . coffee . . .

It was like a treasure chest to him, and he was sorry when Cookie closed the door again. He could have stood and gazed all day at the array of foodstuffs.

'Don't often get anything fresh.' Cookie walked over to the fridge, wheezing. 'Maybe a lettuce'll come in, or some mushrooms. Had some cooking apples a few weeks ago – scared the life out of me. Look . . .' He stooped to open the little fridge door. Baz stared at the sole contents – a bundle of greenstuff with orange roots. 'The fridge doesn't work most of the time. It's just a place to put stuff.'

'Is that . . . carrots?'

'Yeah. I'm still thinking about them. Isaac'll expect something good, and I'm panicking a bit.'

'So, like, you just have to make something up?'

'I got recipe books.' Cookie waved his swaddled hand at a row of perhaps half a dozen books that stood next to the microwave. 'But it's the ingredients, see. Got no potatoes, no butter, no cheese. No eggs, or not very often. Got no fresh milk. Not much pasta. I had a big sack of rice, but that's half gone. Dried lentils – half gone. Flour's running out, and I gotta watch that. I worry all the time.'

To Baz the whole set-up seemed quite wonderful, despite Cookie's gloomy outlook. 'Wow,' he said. 'It's pretty amazing, though. I always wondered what you did all day.'

'All day?' Cookie looked at him, his eyes still puffy

from a night of pain and weeping. 'I don't just work in here all day. I spend more time cleaning than cooking. I clean their rooms, I clean the bogs, I clean the kitchen. I do all their laundry – wash it all by hand – and that's a crappy job. I do their mending. I rinse out their wetsuits, hang 'em up to dry. Oh, and I press their Sunday suits. Iron 'em with an old flat iron that I heat up in here on the electric ring. And all the time I'm doing those things I'm thinking about what I'm gonna cook for supper. Tell you what' – Cookie paused for breath, his chest straining against the material of his jacket – 'you ever want someone to write a book on what it's like to be a friggin' housewife, you send 'em to me. About one day a week I might get a couple of hours off, and then they lock me in the slob room.'

Baz was astonished at this list of duties – and astonished to find that Cookie was actually quite a likeable person. Or even a person at all. He'd gone along with the rest of the crowd, ignoring the boy completely, treating him as though he didn't exist. He felt ashamed, and decided that now was the time to try and make up for it.

'OK,' he said. 'So where do we start? What do you want me to do?'

'We start with the bogs. Give 'em a scrub down. But first I need to do something about this.' Cookie waved his wrapped-up hand. 'Get a bandage on it.'

'What – you've got real bandages?'

'Yeah. There's a first aid cabinet – need it for the divers. They'll be gone by now, so I can get one from there.'

*　*　*

250

It was weird to see inside the divers' living quarters. They each had their own room, with proper beds and duvets, along with clothing racks, shelves, magazines, bedside cabinets – total luxury. The spaces were quite small – studies, perhaps, when this had been a school. A couple of the rooms were incredibly messy, a couple were tidy. Baz felt nervous as he peeked through the doorways of these private sanctuaries, as though he had strayed into enemy territory. At any moment one of the divers might return, and then what would happen?

'Don't worry,' said Cookie. 'It's part of my job. You're gonna have to help me clear up in here later on, in any case. Along that other passageway we got Hutchinson's room, and Steiner's. Worst of the lot, those two are. Total pigs. But at least I don't have to cook for them. They eat in their rooms – there's tins everywhere.'

'What about Preacher John?' asked Baz. 'Where's his room?'

'Round the corner on the other side of the corridor.' Cookie's voice sank almost to a whisper as he pointed. 'I've never even been in there. Don't think anybody has. He eats by himself – hardly ever comes out. I have to leave his meals on a little table outside. I just knock on his door, leave his food, collect the plates later. Every Sunday morning I pick up his washing and leave the clean stuff outside the door. That's it. Come on. We've got work to do.'

Baz took another quick look around before following Cookie.

There was a fire exit just past the divers' quarters,

the doors partially wedged open by a mound of junk on the other side. Baz could see a stairway. This was completely blocked, stacked up with boxes and piles of chairs, and obviously not in use. It must lead to an upper part of the school, though . . . and perhaps to a hiding place? Somewhere they could go on Sundays? No, it would take ages to clear any sort of pathway through that lot, and the risk of being caught was far too high. Sneaking around the divers' quarters would be a deadly game to play.

Cookie hadn't been exaggerating the extent of his duties, and long before evening came Baz felt that he'd already put in a solid day's work. The toilets had been cleaned, rooms tidied, clothes washed and hung up to dry. There was a small sluice room to one side of the kitchen. Here were a couple of sinks, and in these the divers' clothes had to be washed and rinsed. The drainage worked, but of course the water had to be bucketed in. This meant a long journey right around the building, the back door to the kitchen having apparently being blocked by falling rubble.

Their last job, apart from cooking, was to fill the generator with diesel. The generator was housed in a galvanized metal hut just outside the kitchen window, but again it could only be reached by going the long way round. Baz was surprised to find that Cookie had the key to this hut.

'Why would they worry?' said Cookie. 'What am I gonna steal? There's nothing I need I don't already have. And if something did go missing, they'd know exactly who to blame. Wouldn't be worth the risk.'

It was dark inside the metal hut, and the smell of diesel was strong. Baz saw that there were three large jerry cans in one corner. The generator itself was an old-fashioned-looking thing, a big greasy machine with a flywheel on the side, and there was some other mechanical contraption standing next to it. This was basically a horizontal cylinder, maroon coloured, with some sort of motor attached, and a gauge mounted on top of it, which looked a bit like a clock.

'What's that thing?' Baz asked.

'Compressor,' said Cookie. 'That's what they use to fill up their air tanks from. It's driven by the generator. OK – this is the filler cap for the diesel.'

'Do they keep petrol in here as well?' Baz watched as Cookie picked up one of the jerry cans.

Cookie shook his head. 'It's all locked in the armoury.'

Baz tried to take note of everything he saw. Gene, he thought, would be interested in hearing about this.

'You can eat whatever you want, as long as it's not the carrots.' Here was another surprise for Baz. Back in the kitchen he and Cookie were beginning to pre-pare the divers' evening meal. Cookie had decided to make lamb stew with carrot rissoles. The carrots had been chopped and rice measured out according to Cookie's instructions, and now the smell of it all boil-ing away on the little electric stove was making Baz hungry.

'Just grab a tin of something,' Cookie said. 'Heat it up if you like.'

'What – they don't mind?'

'Nah. They figure that as long as they feed me I don't need to steal anything. And it'd be hard for me to smuggle stuff out of here in any case, wearing this stupid outfit.'

Baz looked at Cookie's tight-fitting white jacket.

'Got no pockets,' said Cookie. 'That's why they make me wear it.'

'Oh.' Baz picked up a tin of corned beef. 'So – I could eat some of this if I wanted?'

'Sure, go ahead. Eat it all if you like.'

Baz began to understand how Cookie had got to be the size he was.

The boiled rice and carrots were mixed together with some seasoning and a little milk powder, then divided up into ten patties. An outsized frying pan had been put to one side, at the ready, and five tins of stew decanted into another big saucepan. Baz did all the work, while Cookie stood by and gave instructions. He kept his bandaged hand tucked under his arm. It was obviously causing him a lot of pain.

'So . . . how did it happen?' Baz asked.

'Luke got fed up waiting,' said Cookie. 'I hadn't put the lentils in to soak early enough, and so everything was late.' He looked down at his bandaged hand. 'Luke came into the kitchen, and he was in a right friggin' mood. They'd had a bad day, I s'pose. The soup was boiling on the stove. He just grabbed my arm and shoved it in the pot . . . held it there . . .'

'Christ . . .' Baz tried to imagine what that must have been like. It occurred to him that he might be in danger of the same thing happening to him. He looked doubtfully at the rissoles. What if the divers decided they didn't like them?

The kitchen door opened, and Isaac looked in.

'Ten minutes,' was all he said, and the door closed again.

'Damn, they're back early. We need to be quick.' Cookie began rattling off orders.

'Put the rissoles in the frying pan. I'll start heating the stew. Get 'em evenly spaced. That's it – don't let 'em touch.' Cookie stirred the pot of stew for a minute. 'OK. Now swap.'

Back and forth went the two pans, Baz turning the rissoles over, Cookie stirring with his wooden spoon. The ten minutes were surely up, and Baz began to panic. He expected Luke to come raging through the door and do to him what he'd done to Cookie.

'Isn't it ready yet?' Baz felt the sweat trickling down his face.

''Nother minute. We're OK . . . we're OK . . .'

At last Cookie judged the rissoles to be sufficiently browned and the stew hot enough. 'I'll ladle,' he said. 'You dish out those onto the plates, two each.'

Another minute and the food was all plated up and on the metal serving trolley.

'OK, showtime. You push the trolley.'

Cookie held open the kitchen door and let Baz through.

Directly opposite the kitchen was a dining area, an open space that contained a formica-topped table and four chairs. Isaac was at the head of the table, Luke and Amos to his left and right, Moko at the other end.

Baz felt the eyes of all upon him as he wheeled the trolley towards the table.

'Put out the knives and forks first,' muttered Cookie, 'then the plates. I gotta take Preacher John's food down. Back in a minute.'

Baz's hands were shaking as he leaned across the salvage crew to distribute the cutlery. He automatically began with Isaac, and then worked his way round the table. By the time he'd got to the fourth person, Luke, his brain seemed to seize up altogether. He laid the knife and fork the wrong way round, realized his mistake, and in fumbling to reverse them he dropped the fork. It landed in Luke's lap. Baz hesitated, wondering whether he should try and retrieve the fork. He was spared this embarrassment when Luke picked it up and said, 'Just give me the knife, idiot, and get on with it.'

But even this simple action was fraught with danger. As Baz offered the steak knife blade first, he knew that he had made another mistake. Luke looked at the sharp blade, then at Baz.

'What's this, you soddin' little apache? Are you trying to mug me or something?' There was a chuckle from Amos on the other side of the table, but Luke wasn't laughing. His eyes were cold, ice blue, in a hard and unshaven face, his broken nose an ugly indicator of past violence.

'Gimme that.' Luke grabbed Baz by the wrist. His grip was unbelievably strong, and Baz's fingers immediately sprang open. Luke snatched the knife from Baz's palm, but continued to hold onto his wrist, squeezing so hard that it felt as though the bones were being crushed.

'Don't you ever point a blade at me, fella. Got it?' Luke held the steak knife an inch from Baz's chin, kept it there for a long moment. '*Got it?*'

'Yes! Argh . . . yes . . .' Baz gasped in fear and pain.

Luke let go of his wrist. 'Now get those plates on the table.'

Baz wanted to collapse in a heap, but he managed to hold himself together long enough to dole out the food. Once everybody had a plate in front of them, Baz drew away from the table, feeling very shaky. Cookie had returned and Baz supposed the two of them would now be going back into the kitchen. But Cookie stopped at the kitchen door and stood there with his hands behind his back, feet apart.

'You have to wait here,' he muttered. 'Case they want anything else.'

'Oh.' Baz stood beside him.

For a while the only sound was the clatter of knives and forks. The first remark came from Amos.

'Bank Bottom again tomorrow, Isaac?'

Isaac nodded. 'Not much left there, I know. But the old fool reckons things'll improve soon. I'm for going over to Skelmersley, try our luck there, but he wants us to wait for the water to clear first.'

'So things are really on the turn, then? The sea's gonna get clearer?'

'Hah. According to him it is. And all thanks to the miraculous power of prayer.' Isaac gave a sardonic little grunt. 'Load o' crap. The power of a good south-easterly, more like.'

'Hey – whatever works . . .' Amos took another mouthful of stew.

Isaac looked at his brother. 'Yeah, well, that's you all over, Amos. Keep your head down and don't ask questions.'

Amos stopped eating and returned Isaac's stare. 'Oh? That's me, is it? I don't see you putting up too many objections – not when he's around to hear you, anyway. You do as you're told, same as the rest of us.'

'While it suits me, maybe. But not for ever.'

'Yeah, right. You're all talk, Isaac. When the old man says "jump", you jump. Always have, always will.'

Isaac leaned back in his chair and pushed his plate away. 'We'll see who's all talk. I can bide my time.'

The Eck brothers were plainly in the power of their father, but Isaac seemed the most resentful of the three, his tone full of bitterness. Baz was surprised that the men would talk so freely in front of Cookie and himself. But then he and Cookie were just servants. They were nothing. They didn't exist.

'And I'll tell you this.' Isaac was on his feet now. 'The old man's losing his grip. Either that or his ruddy marbles. We've got a good business going here, or did have, and I don't intend to see it go under because of that nutter. So maybe you two should be thinking about the future – like I am.'

He took his jacket from the back of his chair and went out of the room.

'He's getting worse,' Luke muttered, once Isaac was out of earshot. 'Why does he have to keep rocking the boat?'

''Cos he wishes the boat was his,' said Amos. 'Always has.'

* * *

258

As Baz and Cookie entered the slob room, Cookie said, 'Thanks for helping me out today. Can't remember the last time I got off this early.' He walked towards his bed.

'That's OK. Hey, Cookie . . .' Baz was aware of the other boys looking at him. He waited until Cookie turned round. 'How's your hand?'

There was silence for a moment, and then Cookie said, 'Dunno. It still really hurts. I'm gonna leave the bandage on for a couple of days before I take a look.'

Baz said, 'Yeah. Good idea, mate. Maybe . . . er . . . maybe see you tomorrow then. Do the same again.'

'Maybe. Depends on what Hutchinson says.' Cookie didn't seem inclined to push the conversation any further.

'Yeah, OK. Er . . . later, then . . .' Baz put his hands in the pockets of his shorts and walked over to the seating area, where most of the boys were lolling around.

'Hiya.' He tried to sound casual, but was aware of the attention focused upon him.

'Been having *fun*, dear?' Amit grinned up at him and there were several sniggers.

'Wouldn't call it fun exactly.' Baz sat down on the floor. 'More like hard graft actually.'

'Well, it's nice to see you making some new friends, love.' Amit had obviously cast himself in the role of concerned mother. 'But make sure you don't let the big boys fall on you, all right?'

Baz waited for the laughter to die away. 'Listen – just cut it out, OK? We're all in the same boat here . . .'

'Must be a friggin' big boat then,' murmured Amit, and there were more giggles.

Baz felt his temper begin to rise. 'Hey – how would you like it, Amit, if everyone was picking on you all the time? Huh? What if we all started calling you "Paki"? Or started calling Robbie "Gingah"?'

'Well, you could try.' Amit looked at Baz, his dark eyes narrowed, challenging. 'But then I'd just have to start calling you "Gayboy", wouldn't I?'

'What?' It took a moment for Baz to grasp what was being said. Then he understood. He glanced quickly at Ray – too off-guard to avoid doing so – and felt the colour flooding into his cheeks, a burning embarrassment that all could see. He began to scramble to his feet, fists clenched, and saw that Amit was already out of his chair, equally prepared for violence.

'Hey, knock it off, Baz! Don't be stupid.' Gene grabbed hold of Amit and held him back. 'For Chrissake . . . Amit . . .'

'I'm not taking any of that "Paki" crap from him!' Amit threw a punch over Gene's shoulder, missed, and overbalanced.

'I didn't say that! I said how would you *like* it . . .' Baz lashed out, trying to get to Amit, but now Robbie was in the way.

'Whoa, whoa . . .' Robbie was doing his peacemaker bit as usual, and after another brief bout of scuffling the momentum was lost. Baz and Amit were kept apart long enough for them both to calm down.

'What's the matter with you two?' Gene hustled Amit back towards his chair. 'We got enough to worry about without trying to kick each other's heads in.'

Baz waited until Amit was seated before lowering himself to the floor once more. He knew that his face was still red, and that nothing had been resolved.

'Now let's get back to what's important' – Gene was talking – 'and try and figure out what they're up to, and what we're gonna do about it. After today . . . I just don't know . . .'

Baz dragged himself from his own angry thoughts. 'What do you mean – "after today"?' he said. 'What's been going on?'

'Yeah, I forgot,' said Gene. 'You weren't there. We've been working down on the jetty. You know that big cross Preacher John told me to make? Well, we had to carry it down to the jetty today, and put it up.'

'Put it up where?'

'It fits into that bit of drainpipe at the back of the platform. Might have been made to measure. Isaac's obviously had it planned all along.'

'Preacher John has, you mean,' said Robbie. 'It'll be his orders, not Isaac's.'

Baz pictured the tall wooden cross, standing upright at the edge of the platform – immediately behind the concrete box-thing, with its huge lid . . .

'But what's it supposed to be?' He still didn't get it. 'What's the box for?'

'Box?' Gene looked at him. 'It's not a bleedin' box, mate. It's an altar.'

CHAPTER SIXTEEN

Baz spent another day in the kitchen, helping Cookie out. He found that he didn't mind it. The hours were long, but the work was more interesting than labelling cans in the sort room, and a lot less strenuous than barrowing stone and concrete. Cookie was easy enough to get along with, and was obviously proud of his domain. He was also proud of his ability to conjure something out of nothing, to be inventive with whatever ingredients came his way, and happy to share the knowledge that he had. This was clearly his world, and in the kitchen at least, he was king.

But even Cookie looked a bit panicky when Moko entered the kitchen on Wednesday evening carrying a cat box. The big Japanese man opened the swing door, put the cat box on the floor and gave it a shove with his foot. The plastic box slid across the tiles, turning in a half-circle so that the entrance flap ended up facing away from Cookie and Baz. Moko said nothing – or at least nothing audible. He simply grunted and left.

'Strewth,' said Cookie. 'What now?' He went over to take a look at the cat box, and Baz followed – images of cats and cooking pots already beginning to flash through his head.

Cookie lifted the box and placed it on a work surface. He and Baz peered through the grille of the entrance flap, cautious lest the occupant of the box should hurl itself at them in a spitting ball of fury. But it wasn't a cat in there. It was rabbits – two of them.

They were white, the domesticated sort, and unusually big. Fresh meat was scarce, and it was rare for rabbits to be allowed to reach this size nowadays. Hunger and impatience normally got the better of their breeders.

'Oh God,' said Baz. 'Are we supposed to cook 'em?'

'Probably not tonight,' said Cookie. 'But yeah, that's why they're here.' He opened the door of the cat box in order to get a better view. The rabbits looked calm enough, nibbling away at a few handfuls of dandelion leaves that someone had thought to provide. They made no attempt to escape.

'So . . . we've got to kill them?' Here was a thought that Baz didn't relish.

''Fraid so. It's OK. I've done it before.'

'Yeah? How?'

'Well, you *can* do it with a chop of your hand. You hang 'em upside down by the hind legs, and whack 'em across the back of the neck. I've never tried it that way, though – not sure I could hit 'em hard enough – so I use a meat hammer.'

Cookie went over to a drawer, pulled it open and took out a metal hammer. It was shiny, with a black rubber handle, and one face of the hammer-head was cast into sharp little pyramids. He handed it to Baz.

'Jesus.' Baz hefted the hammer, tapped it experimentally against his palm. 'You hit them with this?' He tried to imagine himself doing such a thing, and knew for certain that he wouldn't be able to.

'Yeah. Hang 'em upside down and knock 'em over the head. The thing is, if you're gonna do it, you really have to do it. You can't bottle it, or have two or three goes at it, 'cos that'd be cruel. You have to do it in one, and that means making a proper job of it – one really good thump. It's not easy.'

Cookie's voice was matter of fact.

'But you know what's really daft? We've got rabbits already – here on the island. The copse is full of 'em. I dunno why the divers trade for them when they could catch their own. Same with vegetables – why not just grow some? There's plenty of room. They don't think that way, though. Easier to trade a few tins, I guess. But see' – Cookie continued his lesson in butchery – 'the tricky bit is paunching and skinning, 'cos if you mess that up it's a hell of a stink. You have to get all the guts out in one. Look . . .' He reached inside the cat box and got hold of one of the rabbits, swinging it out of the box so that it hung upside down by its back legs. The rabbit was big and amazingly long. It didn't struggle.

'You lie it on its back, and press the guts down with your thumbs—'

'Oi!' The kitchen door was open, and Isaac was standing there. 'What're you doing? You're supposed to be cooking in here, not yakking.'

'Sorry,' said Cookie. He cradled the rabbit.

'Put that thing back in its cage and get some food on the table. Ten minutes.'

'OK. Um . . . when do you want the rabbits, then?'

'What? Just feed 'em and leave 'em alone. We're saving them for Sunday. Now get moving.'

The swing door closed behind Isaac, and Cookie put the rabbit back in the cat box. Baz wasn't sorry to see it go, or for Cookie's lecture to be brought to a close. When the time came, he thought, he would have to leave the butchering to the expert.

'Better get the rice on,' said Cookie. 'The water's already hot, and basmati only takes ten minutes, so we're OK.'

As they served the divers their supper – chicken curry and rice, with hot chapatis – Isaac looked up and said to Cookie, 'If you've got time to be playing around with rabbits, then there's nothing much the matter with you. Tomorrow you're on your own again. This one can go back to the sort room, where he belongs. All right?'

'Yes.' Cookie sounded miserable and Baz threw him a sympathetic look. The two boys took up their positions by the swing door, hands behind their backs, feet slightly apart.

Returning to sort-room duties at least gave Baz the chance to catch up with the outside world.

'What's happening?' he said to Gene. 'Is that the motor you've been working on?'

'Yeah. Just about done.' Gene stepped back from the workbench, wiping his hands on an oily rag. There was an outboard motor clamped to the bench, a complicated-looking thing with a brass flywheel on top, and a small black fuel tank with the word SEAGULL on it. A long alloy tube led to a propeller down below.

'Does it work?' said Baz.

'That's what we're gonna find out. We'll just give the carburettor a quick tickle . . .'. Gene pressed a little button up and down, and moved a couple of levers. He took a length of nylon cord and wound it around the flywheel on top of the motor.

'OK. Stand back.' Gene yanked on the rope and the flywheel spun round. There was a kind of hollow sucking sound, but the motor didn't fire. Gene pumped a little more petrol into the carburettor and readjusted one of the levers. Then he wound the rope around the flywheel again and gave it another pull.

This time the engine caught. It fired a couple of times, stuttered almost to a halt, picked up momentum again, and then burst into sudden roaring life. The sort room rang with the high-pitched yammering of the motor, and clouds of blue exhaust fumes spread from the workbench. Gene turned back the throttle lever and slowed the motor to a tickover.

'Just going to check the drive!' he shouted above the din. He pushed at a longer metal bar, and the engine engaged the propeller. This began to spin, and after revving it up and down a few times Gene shut off the motor altogether.

'Nothing wrong with that.' His voice cut through the ringing silence.

The rest of the sort-room crew had gathered round, and Robbie put out a hand, tracing his grubby fingers over the embossed word on the petrol tank. 'Wow. It's great, isn't it?'

There was something hypnotic, exhilarating, about the smell of exhaust fumes that hung in the air. To Baz it was an instant reminder of the world that had gone, the very street where he'd lived before the floods. There had been a group of lads that used to whizz up and down on their scooters in the evening, parking up on the corner, laughing and talking late into the night. The neighbours all complained about the noise, but Baz had envied the bigger boys and secretly hoped that someday he would be able to join them, have a scooter of his own and plan weekend trips to faraway seaside towns. And this had been the same smell that drifted in through his open bedroom window. Exhaust fumes. Freedom . . .

'I didn't have to do that much.' Gene was talking. 'Stripped it all down, gave the head a de-coke, unblocked the carburettor jets. Had to put in a new spark plug and new HT lead – Hutchinson found me a big roll of that, which was lucky. And the petrol was ancient, all gummy, so I put some fresh in. That was it.'

'Hey,' said Dyson. 'You mean you got *petrol*?'

'A cupful, that's all. Just enough to get it going. Hutchinson brought it – don't even know where it came from. Storeroom, I s'pose. No chance of any more, though.'

This reminded Baz of Cookie, and his key to the generator shed. 'Hey, Gene,' he said. 'If we could get hold of diesel, would that be any good? For a bomb, I mean?'

Gene shook his head. 'Nah. Not really. Doesn't

explode in the same way as petrol does. Methane's way better . . .'

But then Hutchinson reappeared, brought hurrying back by the noise no doubt, and the boys dispersed. Baz stepped sideways and pretended to study the list of codes on the wall. FB. French beans . . .

The methane production was going well. Four litres – two big Coke bottles – were now stashed up at the sports centre, both full of gas, and a third bottle was well under way. It hung upside-down in one of the water butts, anchored by string to a concrete block, a plastic funnel fitted into its neck. The water duty crew added to it whenever they could, taking a small bottle with them and releasing the contents underwater into the larger container.

Fart Club was observed religiously, evening and morning, so Gene had no cause for complaint. And yet he worried.

'We got nothing to actually put the gas in yet,' he said. 'We gotta find a big heavy casing of some sort. And I still don't know what the mixture should be.'

Gene's attitude had shifted since Enoch's death. His thinking had gone beyond just accumulating a store of explosive. He was definitely planning to build something now, a working weapon. A bomb.

But to Baz it all seemed less real than it had been. A wild pipe-dream. He thought about his queasiness over the rabbits, and suspected that if he was incapable of killing an animal, he'd find it a whole lot harder when it came to killing men.

Baz sat on his bed and watched the other boys going

about their business, finishing their suppers, hanging bits of washing on the lines that criss-crossed the slob room. He could hear voices echoing from the jakes, Jubo and Robbie laughing – Fart Club in full swing by the sound of it. Ray was down at the other end of the room in deep discussion with Gene, both their faces frowning and serious. Probably working on some new aspect of the big plan. Amit and Dyson were having an arm-wrestling match, kneeling at the low table in the seating area. Here were his companions, his fellow captives, his brothers. His family. A pang of guilt accompanied that thought. He missed his dad, missed him every day, but his family was here now. And he cared about them all.

But he cared about Ray the most, and he wasn't sure why. He knew that it wasn't in the way that Amit had hinted at. He liked girls – had always liked girls . . .

The door opened at the far end of the room, and Steiner came in. He looked around briefly, located Baz and pointed a finger.

'You!' he shouted. 'Kitchen. Now!'

Kitchen? What had happened? There was no point in asking questions, so Baz scrambled to his feet. He hurried out of the slob room, past Steiner, and down the corridor towards the divers' quarters.

Isaac and crew were sitting at the table in the dining area, arms folded, and judging by the sour expressions on their faces they were none too happy. As Baz approached, Isaac leaned back in his chair. He nodded towards the kitchen door.

'Get in there and help that fat slob out. He's ruddy useless.'

Baz pushed at the swing door and entered the kitchen.

Cookie was in a state. Beneath the dim flicker of a single bulb he was rushing around, clouded in steam, a long strip of bandage trailing from his injured hand. There were two saucepans on the stove, a frying pan to one side, an onion on a chopping board. An onion! Baz wanted to stop and stare at this marvel, but there was no time.

'Oh . . . gawd . . .' One of the saucepans started to boil over, and Cookie made a grab for the lid. 'Chop the onion!' he shouted. 'Use that knife with the white handle. Quick as you can!'

Baz picked up the knife that Cookie had indicated, and prepared to tackle the onion. But how did you begin? Weren't you supposed to peel it or something?

'Cut it into quarters' – Cookie took the saucepan off the cooker ring, and replaced it with the frying pan – 'the skin'll come off easier. Then just chop it up.'

By the time Baz had finished his eyes were streaming.

'Sling it all in the frying pan!'

Baz blindly scraped the onion into the massive frying pan and felt the sharp sting of boiling fat pricking at his fingers. 'Ow! What are you making?'

'Onion-fried rice and peas . . . tin of boiled ham. OK. Rice is done. Empty the water out and tip it in with the onions. You look after that bit; I'll sort the ham out.'

So Baz mixed the rice and peas in with the fried onions, while Cookie retrieved the tin of ham from the other saucepan.

'God. I can't do it . . . can't get the blimmin' thing open . . .' Cookie was struggling.

It was no good. Baz had to leave the stirring of the rice and onions to Cookie, and take over control of the ham. The tin was boiling hot, and he scalded his fingers on it several times trying to get it open.

'Tip it onto a plate and cut it into slices. Then we're done.'

At last everything was plated up and ready to go. Cookie held open the kitchen door for Baz, and he pushed the trolley through.

The grumbling voices of the divers ceased as Baz and Cookie drew near. They'd been talking about their teeth, it seemed, because Isaac muttered, 'We'll get it all sorted next week. Dentist on Monday.' It sounded funny, the idea that Isaac and his crew had dental appointments.

Cookie disappeared with Preacher John's tray of food, leaving Baz to deal with the divers. He doled out the plates without mishap, although his whole body was shaking with nerves. When Cookie returned, Isaac said, 'Oi. Come here.' He reached out and grabbed Cookie by the arm.

'Take off that filthy bandage,' he said. 'Let me see your hand.'

'It – it's OK,' Cookie stammered. 'It's almost better now.'

'Take it off, I said!'

Cookie began to unwind the long strip of grey and greasy bandage. His big round face was already crumpling as the flesh became exposed, and Baz could hardly bear to look.

The skin on Cookie's hand was almost purple, with puffy weeping areas of bare flesh, fingers swollen into a soggy mass. Baz had had no idea that it was that bad. The poor guy must be in agony.

'What's your name?' Isaac's voice was flat; no emotion there.

'Matthew.' Tears rolled down Cookie's face.

'Matthew. Right then, Matthew, you're no good to us now—'

'I'm fine. I'll be all right. I just need a bit more time . . . bit more help—'

'Don't interrupt. I said you're no good to *us*. Understand? So you'll go back tomorrow. Preacher John wants you down on the jetty and ready to leave first thing.'

'Please . . . oh, please . . .' Cookie was shaking, near to collapse. He dashed his forearm across his streaming eyes. 'Don't. I can't go—'

'You're going.' Isaac turned his attention to Baz. 'And you're taking over. From now on you're Cookie, understand?'

Baz couldn't find his voice.

'I said *understand*? Are you lot deaf or something?'

'No! I mean, yes! I . . . I understand.'

'You start tomorrow, then. Now hop it. I don't want you talking to this kid again. Get back to the slob room.'

Baz looked once more at Cookie, hesitated, and then turned and walked away. As he left the dining area, he heard Isaac say to Cookie, 'Take the trolley back to the kitchen and get the place cleaned up. Then you're done.'

*   *   *

Cookie stumbled into the slob room after lights-out, a confused and shadowy figure. Baz heard his shaky breathing as he made his way into the jakes. Everybody knew what had happened, and for once there were no sneers or jeers following the boy's progress. But there were no words of comfort either.

As Cookie came out of the jakes, Baz was surprised to hear his voice – a throaty whisper in the darkness.

'Baz – got something to show you. Early tomorrow. 'Fore I go.' Cookie passed on, his feet thumping softly on the carpet tiles.

But by the time the boys were up in the morning, Cookie had already disappeared.

As Baz hurried down to the kitchen first thing, he bumped into Moko, carrying a bundle of wetsuits over his arm.

'Has Cookie—?' Baz began to ask, but Moko walked by without even a sideways glance. Whatever it was that Cookie had wanted to say, he'd left it too late.

The busy day took over, and there were enough worries and moments of panic to keep Baz from dwelling too much on Cookie's departure. He found himself thinking about the rabbits in the odd spare minutes that he did have, and wondering how on earth he was going to cope with preparing them for the pot. At around midday he slipped outside the main building and pulled up a few handfuls of grass and dandelion leaves to feed the creatures, and as he stood upright he took a moment to stare out over the seascape. The line of blue water he'd seen on Monday

273

seemed to have moved further away. It was still visible, but surely more distant than it had been. So much for Preacher John's ideas on the power of prayer, then.

Back in the kitchen he fed the rabbits, watching the silent creatures as they nibbled their way through the fresh fodder. The fate that awaited them hung far more heavily over his head than it did theirs.

Time to think about the cooking. Baz decided to play it very safe. He went to the store cupboard and sorted out some tins of I/STEW. Irish stew. Couldn't go wrong with that. And for pudding he would just open some tins of stewed fruit. Maybe he would try his hand at custard, made with milk powder. If it went wrong he could simply leave it out – not serve it – and nobody would be any the wiser. As Baz pulled open the utensils drawer in order to find a tin-opener, he saw the shiny metal hammer winking up at him. He snatched at the tin-opener and quickly pushed the drawer shut.

That evening he delivered Preacher John's supper for the first time. Walking down the dim corridor, carrying the aluminium tray of food, Baz felt as though he were approaching a dragon's lair . . . an ogre's castle. Well, at least he wouldn't have to face the monster within.

He turned the corner and came to an immediate halt, rocking forward on his toes in an effort to keep his balance – and almost dropping the tray. Preacher John was standing in his open doorway, a dark and solid mass against the eerie light from the room beyond. The smell of burning wax drifted out into the corridor. Candles.

Baz stood completely still, too shocked to move.

The huge bulk loomed before him, awful in its silence. Then it began to alter shape, shifting, diminishing, as it moved back through the door frame. Preacher John's face became visible, cracked and weather-worn, the orange hairs of his beard glowing like electric filaments in the flickering light. He motioned Baz into the room with a wave of his hand, and pointed to a far corner. Here stood a small table and a single wooden chair. The table was covered with a white cloth, laid diagonally, and at the centre of the tablecloth a candle burned in a glass jar. Baz hesitated for a moment, then stepped across the threshold.

A dark wooden bed with a white coverlet. A wooden cabinet next to the bed. A Bible – the same black leather Bible that was used on Sundays; a crucifix hanging on the wall above the bedstead. Baz took in the sparse features as he crossed the room. The candle flame danced away from him at his approach, sending forth a twisted plume of black smoke. Baz rested the tray on the tablecloth. He noticed that there was a kind of cushion-thing lying on the floor, just beneath the table. It was covered in thick carpet material, heavily embroidered. Baz recognized it as being a kneeler, or a hassock. Like you'd see in church pews . . . or before an altar—

'And before the altars of God, the righteous lay their offerings.'

Baz jumped at the deep sound of Preacher John's voice – and at how his own thoughts had been snatched from him. It was as though his head were transparent, everything in it visible. He was aware of

Preacher John's towering presence behind him, black and threatening as a tidal wave. A creeping coldness flooded his insides, ran like icy needles through his veins, pricked at the very roots of his hair.

'So the other one has gone.' The room seemed to vibrate as Preacher John spoke again. His words made no sense, and yet an answer was demanded.

Baz turned his head, instinctively cowering, still unable to properly face the monstrous figure behind him.

'Other one?' He just about managed to get the sounds out.

'The other boy.' Preacher John pointed to the tray. 'The other purveyor of these . . . offerings.'

'Oh.' Baz risked a quick glance up at the great battered face above him. 'You mean Cookie? Yes. He's gone home.'

'Ah. He has gone home – as all must, in the end.'

Baz found himself looking directly into Preacher John's fearsome eyes, drawn beyond the bloodshot rims and pale grey irises to deeper and darker places within. And then it was as though he was being sucked forward into that darkness, pulled into the night, unable to resist. Like a moth he fluttered, directionless, beating his way through the ruined cities, shattered belfries, slimy streets. Ugly things were hidden here . . . amidst smoke and fire . . . wild dancing creatures—

'Take the tray.'

'Ah . . .' Baz blinked, and the terrifying visions whirled away into nothingness. 'What? Oh . . . yes.' In a daze he turned once more, and lifted the shimmering plates of food from their tray, slid them across to the table. Oh God. His hands quaked, beyond his control, so that the knife, fork and spoon that he'd brought clattered onto the white cloth in a heap.

'Leave them be!' Preacher John's voice pulsed at the very walls, too big for such a confined space. 'Go.'

'Yes. Thank you. I'll pick . . . later – I'll . . .' Baz was gibbering, stumbling, backing away across the room, desperate just to get out. As he groped behind him for the door handle, he saw Preacher John stoop to retrieve the hassock from beneath the table. Baz wriggled round the door and pulled it shut. His last glimpse was of the dark-suited figure going down onto one knee, a heavy palm already covering his brow.

'O Lord, look down upon your servant . . .' The muffled sounds drifted away as Baz fled down the empty corridors, the scent of candle smoke lingering deep in his nostrils, the taste of it upon his panting breath. It was still with him as he burst into the kitchen.

For a while Baz leaned against the stainless steel cooker, head down, gripping the cool metal with both hands. Now he understood. Now he saw why Isaac and his brothers were so in awe of their father, so completely at his command. Only when he looked at you, deep into your eyes, could you experience the full weight of his power. The terrifying hypnotic power of Preacher John.

It was late by the time Baz had finished his duties, and he felt completely shattered. The atmosphere in the slob room seemed unusually gloomy. Nobody was saying much. Baz lay on his bed and waited for Ray to come back from the washroom.

'Everything OK?' he said. 'What've you been doing?'

Ray fell onto his mattress, rolled over and looked up at the ceiling. 'Collecting wood,' he said, 'is what we've been doing. We had to go up to the copse and find dead wood – branches, whatever. Drag it all down to the jetty. Then we've been sawing it up.'

'Yeah? What's it for?'

Ray turned his head to look at him. He had a smudge of green across his brow, and scratches on his forearms – evidence of his day working in the copse.

'The altar. That's what we reckon, anyhow. To burn on the altar. What the hell's Preacher John gonna be burning on there? That's what we want to know. There's that blinkin' great cross sticking up – it's scary. Yeah. So that got us all worried. And . . . I dunno. We've all been feeling bad about Cookie as well, I s'pose. Really bad about that. He didn't deserve what happened to him. And maybe if we'd kind of stuck by him a bit . . . you know . . . he might still be here. Poor guy.'

'Yeah. Poor old Cookie. I sort of liked him. Still' – Baz tried to be positive – 'maybe he's got family – friends – whatever, back on the mainland. A home. He might be better off there than here, for all we know.'

'What?' Ray looked at him as though he'd said something particularly stupid.

'Well, you know . . .' said Baz. 'I mean, it might not be as bad for him over there as—'

'Baz, it's Friday. Don't you get it?' Ray lay back on his mattress and stared at the ceiling again. 'Friday's a diving day.'

Baz had a brief memory of Moko, then, coming along the corridor, carrying wetsuits over his arm . . .

'Ohhh . . . God,' he groaned.

'Yeah, that's right,' said Ray. 'They took Cookie out on the boat this morning, but it came back this afternoon loaded with salvage. The boat never went over to the mainland, and neither did Cookie. He never got there.'

CHAPTER SEVENTEEN

Sunday. Baz had been dreading it. He'd sorted through his recipe books and found a number of interesting ways of preparing rabbits – rabbit stew, rabbit pot-roast, rabbit jointed and deep-fried – but the books didn't say anything about slaughtering the beasts to begin with. Nobody around him had much in the way of advice or sympathy to offer. What he served up to the divers, or how he did it, was none of their concern.

And that was another thing. He was beginning to feel separated, estranged from the other boys. His role and his position had changed. He worked alone now, and ate alone, and was no longer part of the general crew.

'Yeah, but it's not your fault.' Ray at least was understanding. 'You got no choice but to do as you're told. None of us have.'

Ray was up and dressed early as usual. Baz was still pulling on his trainers. One of the soles had come away from its upper – the things were completely rotten – and this didn't help improve his mood.

'It's like I'm ... like I've changed sides or

something. It's horrible. I've got to wear this stupid white jacket – look like a prat – and you know what's worse? I don't even get Sundays off. The divers need feeding whatever day it is. While you're all up at the sports centre this afternoon, I'm gonna be strangling rabbits.'

Ray laughed at that, and it made Baz madder than ever.

'Listen, it's not funny, OK? It's all right for you – tucked away for the afternoon. I'm still gonna be hard at it, *and* doing some pretty nasty work, and getting treated by everyone like I'm a traitor or something.' Baz looked around the room as he said this, making sure that those nearby were fully aware of his grievances.

'Nobody thinks you're a traitor.' Ray got serious. 'And don't forget the rest of us are having a pretty hard time too. I am, anyhow. That Hutchinson, he keeps needling me. And once Steiner gets permission to smash that drain cover – which could easily be today . . .'

'Yeah. Yeah, sorry.' Baz immediately backed down. Ray had more problems than he did, that was for sure. A lot more. 'I just . . . oh, I just wish I didn't have to do this. And I don't want you – anyone – I don't want to be treated like Cookie was, that's all.'

'Hey, don't worry.' Ray stood up and pulled at the waistband of his shorts. 'I still love you.' He smiled, dark eyes looking down at Baz for a moment. 'Come on. We'd better get lined up for chapel.'

He wandered off down the room, hands in his pockets. Baz stared after him. Then he realized that

Dyson was looking his way, and he quickly returned his attention to the split in his shoe.

The boys were all standing outside the slob room, lined up and ready for chapel, but for some reason they were being made to wait.

'Just shut up and keep still,' was Steiner's only comment. The two capos moved further away, standing by the main entrance and looking out through the glass doors. They muttered to each other in low voices.

Eventually there was some activity down at the dark end of the corridor, and Preacher John appeared, striding towards them, followed by the diving crew. They were all dressed in their Sunday suits – suits that Baz had watched Cookie pressing only a few days ago. That job would be his now, he supposed.

The capos quickly returned to take up positions at the head of the line of boys.

'Send somebody for the hymn books.' Preacher John spoke to Steiner as he marched by.

'You' – Steiner nodded at Ray – 'run down to the assembly hall and get the hymn books.' After a blink of hesitation Ray was off.

Isaac stopped outside the storeroom door. He undid the padlocks, drew back the bolts and pushed the door open. Then he reached round it, picked up some object and stepped back into the corridor. Fuel can? Yes, it looked like a plastic fuel can – black, with a red screw-on spout. Isaac snapped the padlocks back into place and then turned to face the line of boys.

'Get down to the jetty,' he said.

As the bewildered boys began to shuffle off, following the capos' lead, Isaac spoke again.

'Oi, you – Cookie.'

It took Baz a moment to realize that Isaac was addressing him. He came to a halt, stumbling slightly as Dyson bumped into him.

'Me?'

'Yes, you. Where are those rabbits? I told you to look after them.'

'Rabbits? Uh . . . they're in the kitchen.'

'Well, go and get them, then. No use to us there, are they?'

Baz stared up at Isaac's black-bearded face, trying to find some connection, some meaning to what was being said. 'You want me to bring them down to . . . ?'

Isaac wasn't going to ask him again, that much was plain. Baz hurried away.

There was a definite atmosphere to the kitchen now, the smell of living creatures overlaying the everyday staleness of food scraps and cooking oil. It reminded Baz of Saturday morning trips to the petshop when he was little – buying food for his guinea pigs, or a new water bottle to strap to the side of their cage . . .

Baz peered into the cat box and watched the rabbits for a few moments, their pink noses snuffling around the few limp scraps of greenstuff he'd provided. Then he grabbed the carrying handle. Better go.

The school building was eerily quiet as Baz hurried along the corridors. He had to hold his arm out at an angle in order to keep the cat box from banging against his legs. This took effort and concentration, and so the sudden sound of a voice made him jump.

'Baz!'

It was Ray, entering the main corridor from another direction, and struggling to stay in control of the hymn books that he carried, his chin resting on top of the tall pile. 'Where is everybody?'

'Down at the jetty,' said Baz.

'Well, I wish someone'd told me. I've been wandering about like an idiot. What've you got there?'

'Rabbits,' said Baz.

'*Rabbits?*'

'Yeah.'

It was a strange cargo they carried between them, hymn books and rabbits. But it was also a rare moment of peace, to be the only ones in the building. They walked side by side along the empty corridor towards the light of the main entrance.

'Hang on,' said Baz. 'I'll get the door.'

As Baz and Ray rounded the bend in the steep pathway, the jetty below came into view. Gene's wooden cross stood tall and imposing behind the stone construction of the altar, making the jetty itself look vaguely like a boat being launched into the waves. The boys were throwing wood onto the altar, piling up logs and twigs and branches under Preacher John's direction.

Baz and Ray reached the jetty and hurried along it as quickly as they could. Preacher John stood on the concrete platform before the altar. His congregation were now arranging themselves into their usual rows, boys at the front, then the two capos, then the divers. There were no chairs.

Baz and Ray hovered to one side of the gathering,

uncertain as to what they should do next. Preacher John looked at Ray and said, 'Hand out the hymn books.' Then he pointed to the concrete platform, indicating to Baz that he should lay down the cat box beside him. 'Take your places.'

Baz added himself to the end of the second row, and Ray stood directly in front of him.

'Hymn number three-three-three. "Lord Behold Us with Thy Blessing".'

Preacher John waited for the hurried flipping through of pages to die down, and then he began to sing, his voice deep and powerful on the muggy air.

> *'Lord behold us with thy blessing,*
> *Once again assembled here . . .'*

The ragged crew joined in, uncertain of the tune. Baz was glad to be hidden away in the second row, where he hoped that his feeble mouthing of the words would go unnoticed.

The last line of the hymn was 'With thy choicest gifts array', and Preacher John took this as the first line of his text.

'*With thy choicest gifts array*,' he said. 'Aye. To us the choicest gifts are given. But God expects gifts in return . . .'

Baz avoided looking directly at Preacher John. He was wary now of that all-seeing gaze, but also horrified by the thought that whatever had happened to Cookie would have been on Preacher John's orders. The man was a monster.

Instead Baz stared up at the cross that Gene had

made, and studied its construction. The cross-piece itself had been fashioned from one of the round fencing posts they'd used as rollers, split in half and then let into the upright. His eyes dropped to the pile of brushwood that festooned the top of the altar. There was something vaguely Christmassy about this – bits of holly and ivy poking out here and there, as though someone in the local church had gone a bit overboard with the festive decorations.

Finally he looked down at the cat box, standing at an angle on the concrete platform, a metre or so away from Preacher John . . .

'. . . the Promised Land!' Preacher John swung his arm out in a broad and dramatic gesture towards the seascape behind him. Baz was dragged from his thoughts as all turned their heads to where the preacher was pointing.

'There it lies, within our grasp, a clear and visible sign from God. What must we do to bring it closer?'

Was he talking about the line of blue water? It seemed further away than ever now, a glimpse of brightness on the horizon, fading before the overwhelming force of a murkier tide.

'God has given us a sign that we are doing right in His sight, and shown us what our reward might be. Clear blue water. Aye. In clear blue water are God's choicest gifts arrayed. No more shall we be left to grope in the darkness, but shall see our way to all that God has in store for us, his chosen people.'

He was talking about *diving*, Baz realized. Preacher John wanted the waters above the cities to clear so that he could find more supermarkets! He was bargaining with God for the chance of another warehouse or two.

'And on this spot we shall light our beacon. Here we shall guard our altar' – Preacher John raised his arms as he spoke – 'and thus we shall make our sacrifice – whatever God shall ask of us – until the waters become clear or draw back altogether.'

Before the silently watching congregation the preacher stepped to the side of the altar and picked up the black plastic fuel can. He unscrewed the lid and began to pour the contents over the piled-up brushwood that festooned the giant slab. Up and down he walked, and when the last few drops were shaken from the can, he took a cigarette lighter from the pocket of his long black coat.

Baz instinctively braced himself for an explosion of fire, narrowing his eyes, head turned to one side. If it was petrol that had been poured onto the brushwood, then those nearest might do well to shield themselves.

Preacher John flicked the lighter and held it to the pile of wood. Was he crazy?

But nothing seemed to be happening. Again and again the lighter clicked, and still there was no sign of fire.

Eventually there came a wisp of smoke – a crackling of twigs – and the brushwood began to catch. There was more smoke than flame at first, thick white plumes that swirled up towards the cross. Perhaps the wood was too damp, or too green, or perhaps it was diesel rather than petrol that Preacher John had doused the altar with. Either way, it took a while for the fire to get going properly.

Baz was caught up in the hypnotic effect of the

rising smoke, the sinuous forms that grew and intertwined. With no breath of air to break it down, the smoke wreathed itself into a single corded column, a gently twisting tornado, rising from the altar to reach for the heavens.

When Baz lowered his gaze again, still in a half-trance, he saw that Preacher John had hold of one of the rabbits. There was barely time for this to register, or to question why this should be. The preacher's stooping bulk was turned away from the congregation, so it was difficult to see exactly what was happening. He appeared to be holding the rabbit across his knee. His elbow gave a sudden jerk, a sharp backward movement, and he straightened up. The rabbit dangled lifelessly in his grasp. Preacher John dumped it on top of the cat box as casually as if it had been a scarf or a tea-towel, then he leaned forward again and reached inside the open flap . . .

This time Baz knew what to expect, and so did those around him. He saw Ray turn his head to the left, obviously intending to look away, and heard Robbie's gulp of dismay at his shoulder. Baz shifted his own focus, concentrated on Ray's yellow T-shirt in front of him, the raised bumps of vertebrae showing through at the base of his neck. But still he caught that quick jerk of movement at the corners of his vision, the twitch of Preacher John's dark bulk, and he knew that the second rabbit was dead the instant it happened. The merciful crackling of the fire hid any sound there might have been, but as Baz continued to stare at Ray's slim neck, he imagined how easily such bones would separate, how frail was the cord of life within.

They were hardened to the sight of sudden and unwarranted death, all of them, though not yet immune. The revulsion that Baz felt in the pit of his stomach was less a horror of the two dead creatures before him than of Preacher John himself. In his long black suit, and with a white rabbit dangling from each of his beefy hands, he looked like some monstrous conjuror. He might have pulled the rabbits from the flames that now roared behind him.

As if in contradiction to this thought, a final twist to his performance, the preacher turned and tossed the rabbits onto the fire. In lazy swinging arcs their extended bodies rose and fell, graceful dancers, momentarily silhouetted against the blaze. They disappeared into the brushwood and the smoke thickened around them, veiling them from sight.

Preacher John raised his arms high once again and threw back his mane of hair. 'O Lord,' he cried, 'here is a token of our faith, a sacrifice to thee! Give us a sign that we do right, and lead us forward from this new beginning. Clear our path and let us see the bounty that you have given, the world that you have created. And we will give in return whatever you ask, all that you think fit, until our debt is paid. Amen.'

'Amen.'

The response came automatically, a collective and embarrassed mumble.

Preacher John lowered his arms and said, 'Hymn number three-three-two. "We Give Thee But Thine Own".'

Another long and unfamiliar hymn, but in it Baz

thought that he could see the message that Preacher John was trying to get across.

> *'We give thee but thine own,*
> *What e'er the gift may be:*
> *All that we have is thine alone,*
> *In trust, O Lord, from thee.*
> *May we thy bounties thus*
> *As stewards true receive,*
> *And gladly as thou blessest us,*
> *To thee our first fruits give.'*

As the last line died away, Preacher John turned towards the far horizon. If he had been wearing long robes and carrying a staff he could not have looked more like a prophet, his great beard jutting out, long red hair lifting slightly in the onshore breeze . . .

The breeze. How strange that this should suddenly have sprung up, when a few moments ago the air had been so thick and still. From the bright line of the horizon the cooling vesper blew, playful as a kitten's paw, batting the smoke from the fire into wispy clouds and rolling them down among the congregation.

Baz caught a glimpse of Preacher John's beaming face through the smoke, and heard him give the order to dismiss. Not a moment too soon. Hurrying along the jetty with the rest of the boys, Baz was forced to let out his breath at last, and so take another. The smoke was still all around them, following them, teasing them with the smell that it carried. It was a smell that was simultaneously delicious and disgusting: that of roasting meat.

Halfway up the hill Baz realized that he was being summoned.

'Oi – Cookie!'

Cookie. He would never get used to that.

It was Isaac, roaring up at him from below. The divers and capos had walked the length of the jetty and were just beginning their ascent of the pathway. Preacher John remained by the altar, gazing out to sea.

'Oh, hell,' said Baz. 'Now what?' There was no choice but to go back down again.

'Bad luck,' said Ray. 'Catch you in a bit.'

'Yeah. Actually, no. I'm gonna have to start cooking, aren't I? Go on, though. Get to the playing fields, quick as you can.'

Down the hill went Baz, meeting Isaac and the crew coming up.

'You forgot the cat box.' Isaac's voice was sour.

'Oh. Right. Sorry.'

'Keep it in the kitchen. We might need it again. And another thing – we'll have wine with our meal tonight. Red.'

'Yes, OK.'

Isaac and the divers strode on, the capos close behind.

Baz took his time retrieving the cat box. He didn't want to run the risk of bumping into the capos if he could help it. When he got back to the school building, all was quiet, but as he came to the main entranceway he paused. Isaac was just down the corridor, standing outside the open storeroom door, the black plastic fuel can in his hand. He was in conversation with one of his brothers, Amos.

'Do you reckon?' Isaac said. 'Hang on.' He thrust the fuel can through the gap in the storeroom door and pulled it closed. 'Well, let's get the maps out and have a look. Soon see if you're right.' He put his hands in his pockets and strolled down the corridor, side by side with Amos.

Baz waited until the low voices faded into the distant darkness. He had stopped in the entranceway simply because it was generally wise to avoid contact with Isaac if at all possible. But he had remained there for another reason.

As he walked past the storeroom, he glanced at the door. The padlocks were hanging open on their bolts. Isaac had forgotten to snap them shut! Baz kept on going for a few more paces, wondering what he should do. Dare he go back and take a look in there? No, that would be suicide. But perhaps he could improve matters a bit. He turned round and walked back to the main entrance, once again taking note of the padlocks as he passed by. Yes, definitely undone.

Baz closed the glass door of the main entrance so it looked as though this had been his reason for coming back. There was still nobody about, as far as he could see. But the end of the corridor was obscured in darkness, and one of the divers or capos might appear from the gloom at any moment. Or Preacher John might return from the jetty . . .

As Baz walked down the corridor, he glanced with feigned surprise at the storeroom door. He paused in his stride, took a step backwards and casually put out a hand. Pretending to examine the padlocks, he squeezed the hasp of first one and then the other until both were just short of clicking shut. To the passing eye they now looked as though they were locked as usual.

There were no sudden shouts or accusations, no sounds of running footsteps. Baz continued on his way to the kitchen, a hundred ideas bouncing around his head.

The Sunday meal that he cooked was a success in as much as nobody actually threw it back at him. Isaac's only grumble was that five bottles of wine as an accompaniment seemed over-generous.

'Garn – the old man can afford it, Isaac. Cheers!' Amos raised a glass and took a noisy slurp.

'I'm not worried about him, or what he thinks. But we've got things to do tomorrow.'

'What, the dentist?' Amos attacked his glass again. 'We're just taking our anaesthetic in advance, that's all.'

The general mood was good, despite Isaac's warnings, and the divers made the most of it. They got through their five bottles with no trouble and Isaac didn't object when another was called for. Consequently it was a very mellow and relaxed crew that finally staggered off to bed, and a very late hour by the time Baz had finished clearing up in the kitchen. He was pleased with himself, though. Thanks to his generosity with the wine, he didn't expect any of the men to have much trouble sleeping.

It didn't sound as though the capos were having much trouble sleeping either. As he left the divers' quarters and approached the main corridor, Baz could hear loud snoring coming from Steiner's room. Good. Perhaps Ray had managed to keep out of their way once again.

Moonlight shone through the glass entrance doors at the far end of the corridor – enough to see by – and down there lay the unlocked and unguarded store-room. To Baz it seemed too good an opportunity to miss, although there was still one danger from which there could be no protection: Preacher John. Was the preacher likely to be up and about at this hour? Wandering the corridors, perhaps, alone in the darkness . . . silently watching over his domain, while all around him slept . . . Baz shivered at the thought. He would get a second opinion on it. Gene.

The atmosphere inside the slob room hit him in a warm fetid wave. God, it stank in here. Baz knelt by Gene's mattress and put out a fumbling hand in the semi-darkness.

Gene responded instantly. 'Who's that? What is it?'

'Gene – it's Baz. Wake up!'

'I'm already awake. What's happened?'

'The storeroom's unlocked,' Baz whispered. 'The divers are drunk, and so are the capos – sparked out, the lot of 'em. And the storeroom's been left unlocked. Can't tell about Preacher John, but what do you reckon? Worth a look?'

'Unlocked? You sure?' Gene threw back his blanket and scrambled to his feet.

'Definite.'

'Hang on, then.' Gene padded down towards the sink area, rummaged around in the cupboard for a minute and returned carrying some chunky object.

'What's that?'

'Wind-up torch. Clockwork thing.'

'Brilliant.'

'Hey . . .' Another shadowy figure was up and about, appearing from the other end of the room. It was Ray. 'You going somewhere?'

'Yeah,' whispered Baz. 'Storeroom's unlocked. Me and Gene are going to take a look in there.'

'Wow. Want me to keep a lookout?'

'Yeah,' said Gene. 'Good idea. Just stay here by the door, Ray.'

He took a quick glance up and down the passageway. 'Come on, then.'

They were off, Gene leading, Baz following, and in a few seconds were outside the storeroom. Baz gently drew back the bolts, pushed at the door, and slipped through the gap.

The room was big. Baz could see tall dark columns – stacks of pallets, he would guess, their outlines broken up by thin vertical strips of moonlight. These faint illuminations fell from above, perhaps from windows covered by closed blinds. Other heavy silhouettes that he couldn't make out. Machinery? The place smelled airless, musty . . .

'OK. Here we go.' Gene stopped winding the torch, and a broad beam of light shot through the darkness. He swung the torch around, just to get a quick impression of the place – floor, walls, ceiling – and then did a slow-motion replay, allowing the beam to pause here and there. It looked as though this might once have been a sports hall or gym. There were wall bars along one side, and the remains of painted markings on the wooden floor, high windows protected by closed metal shutters.

And the place was packed full, a warehouse of spoils. Rows of pallets filled the major part of the room, each of them stacked three high. Baz couldn't even estimate how many thousands of tins of food this represented. The stacking work had apparently been achieved by use of a small fork-lift truck, the piece of machinery he'd seen. It stood on the window side of the room, a bright yellow object in Gene's torch beam.

'Electric,' whispered Gene. 'Charge it from the generator probably.'

Then there were bottles and bottles of water, still shrink-wrapped in their plastic packaging, crates of wine, beer-packs, soft drinks. Baz could see piles of cardboard boxes, dry foodstuffs, gardening tools – seeds, even. Bags of cement. Electrical stuff, cables, light bulbs. Furniture. Chairs, tables, new mattresses . . . bedding . . . Preacher John's superstore.

How many diving trips, Baz wondered, had it taken to accumulate this lot? How many trading deals with the mainlanders? The two boys wandered around in awe, pointing out to each other this object and that, surrounded by wealth that was barely imaginable.

And yet amongst all this treasure there seemed to be hardly anything worth the risk of stealing. A few tins of food perhaps, the luxury of a bottle of Coke, but nothing to actually aid their cause. Gene picked up a couple of spark plugs, still newly boxed, but that was all. Baz stole a penknife. It was nothing special, just a cheap single-bladed knife, and so the kind of thing that would probably not be missed. But there were no real weapons here, no explosives, and certainly nothing that looked like a bomb casing.

'Damn,' said Gene. 'You'd have thought there'd have been *something*.'

'Well, where do they keep the guns?' whispered Baz. 'And the petrol? And the ammo?'

'Dunno.'

They found a galvanized metal door at the far end of the room, heavily fortified with solid-looking bolts and padlocks to the top and bottom. Whatever lay beyond there was obviously thought precious enough to require a lot of extra security.

'Bet that's the armoury,' said Gene. 'Where the weapons are. Gotta be. Look at those locks.' He gave the door a cursory push, just to check that by some miracle it hadn't been left open. No such luck.

Baz rested his forearm on a metal shelving rack to the right of the door. 'Yeah. And even if we had a crow-bar or something, it wouldn't be any good. Too much damage. They'd know we'd been in there.'

'Unless we found the guns. Then it wouldn't matter whether they knew or not.'

'We can't use guns, Gene. You said so yourself.'

'Yeah, I know. You're right. The thing is – we got rumbled today. Steiner came up to the playing fields just by himself, looking for Ray. Shouting and carrying on.'

'Oh my God,' whispered Baz. 'Did he get him?'

'No. We heard him coming and ran round the sports centre. Just managed to keep out of his way. But he'll have found all the food tins and everything – so now that little secret's out. We're not gonna be able to smuggle anything much from now on.'

'Ohhhh . . . no.'

They stood there a little longer. Gene wound the handle of the torch a few more times to keep the light going. Baz idly tapped his fingernails against a cardboard carton that stood on the shelving rack. He imagined himself – him and Gene – walking down the corridor with machine guns . . . bursting in upon the capos and the divers . . . mowing them down . . .

Baz chopped angrily at the carton with the edge of his hand. The box didn't move – a surprise, considering that it wasn't very big. Baz closed his fingers over the box and tipped it sideways. The solid weight of the thing was familiar. He'd seen it before.

'Gene! Look at this. Cartridges!'

'What?' Gene shone the light on the shelving.

The same two boxes of shotgun cartridges that had bought Baz his passage to the island were here right next to him, stacked on the shelf. Eley Imperial.

'Shotgun cartridges,' he said. 'Fifty of 'em. It was me that brought them here! Gunpowder – that's gotta be worth nicking, yeah?'

'Woo! Too right,' said Gene. 'We're having those. Hey – and what's that other box?'

Next to the Eley cartons stood another container. It was military looking, green-painted metal, with a carrying handle on the top. In white lettering on the side were stencilled words and numbers.

'Christ,' said Gene. 'It's an ammunition can! M sixty? That's machine-gun bullets! Is it full?' He reached out for the carrying handle. 'Yeah –

result! Come on, Baz – that'll do us. We're out of here.'

They gathered up the heavy boxes, excited now, and headed back to the entrance. Gene fumbled at the door, and quickly stuck his head out to make sure the coast was clear. A mistake. In his haste, he'd forgotten to switch off the torch, and the light beam flashed across the corridor.

'Wassat? Who's there?' They heard a mumbling voice from just a few metres away.

'Oh, God . . . no!' Gene whipped his head back into the room and switched off the torch. 'Hutchinson!' His voice was a hiss of panic. 'He's out there!'

'Jesus . . .' Baz felt a cold wave of fear at the back of his neck. That was it. They were dead.

More voices. They could hear Hutchinson's slurring mumble, but now there was someone else speaking as well.

'Hey – are you OK?' It was Ray.

Baz pushed his head past Gene's and peeped round the door, desperate to know what was happening. He saw that Ray had come out of the slob room and was now talking to Hutchinson, standing in front of him, trying to divert his attention.

'You don't look so good. You want a hand?'

'Wha'? Summat . . . down there . . . summat going on . . .' Hutchinson leaned heavily against the wall. His shoulder slipped forward and Ray put out a hand to try and steady him.

'Hey, you need to lie down, mate. Let's get you to your room, yeah?'

Hutchinson reeled backwards, obviously struggling to stay upright. He seemed to focus on Ray for the first time. 'Hey – itsh you . . . Yeah. We been looking for you. 'S you, innit . . . yeah . . .'

'Yeah, it's me. Come on, then. Better get you back to bed.' Ray was trying to turn Hutchinson round, to get him facing in the other direction.

'Ughhh . . .' Hutchinson got an arm around Ray's shoulder, almost falling on top of him. 'Back to bed . . . yeah. Goo' idea. But you're . . . you gotta help me. Come an' have a drink.'

'Yeah, that's right. I'm coming with you. We'll have a drink.'

And then Ray was leading Hutchinson away, keeping him upright somehow, the two of them weaving and staggering back down the moonlit corridor. Baz peered round the door, watching. Thank God for Ray. *Get him out of here, Ray. Just get him out.*

But in another moment Hutchinson had collapsed. The drunken capo was crumpled against the wall of the corridor, lying in a dark heap, motionless. Ray stepped away from him. As Baz hurried towards the scene, the slob-room door swung open and one or two of the others emerged – Jubo, Robbie . . .

They gathered around the sprawling figure, speaking in whispers.

'Is he down?'

'Yeah. Out for the count by the look of him.'

'You all right, Ray?'

Gene switched on the torch. Hutchinson looked as though he'd tried to dive through the very floor, his face all squished up and distorted against the tiles, dribble running from his mouth.

'Look at him. What a pig.'

'Ey – we could stomp him right now.' Jubo's idea. 'Stomp him so him wake up an' wonder wha' happen his kidneys, man. Like where they go.'

'Nah. Leave him. With any luck he'll choke on his own puke,' said Gene. 'And if he wakes up in the morning, he'll feel like he's had the crap kicked out of him in any case. Come on, Baz. We better get the store-room door back to like it was.'

'Whatcha find in there?' said Robbie. 'Anything good?'

'Yeah. Tell you about it in a bit. Let's get the job finished, Baz, before anyone else shows up. Then we're done.'

CHAPTER EIGHTEEN

The following morning a particularly bleary-looking and foul-tempered Isaac came into the kitchen looking for Baz. There was an art room on the next floor, directly above the kitchen, he said, that had to be made habitable.

'Empty all the crap out and stack it in the corridor,' Isaac said. 'You'll need to clear the staircase before you can get up there, so get some help.'

Baz managed to wangle it so that Ray was sent down from the sort room to give him a hand, and the two of them made a start on clearing the blocked stairway next to the kitchen.

'What's this all about?' said Ray. 'Why are we doing this?'

'Dunno. Maybe the divers just need some extra space or something. So . . . have you seen Hutch this morning?'

'Yeah. And he was pretty bad, even for a Monday. Only showed up for a few minutes, though. He didn't say anything.' Ray yanked at a broken chair. 'Prob'ly doesn't remember much. God, I'm starving. We didn't get to eat the swipes yesterday 'cos that pig Steiner caught us and they never left us any tins out last night.'

'Yeah, I know,' said Baz. 'I'll get you something in a bit – just wait till the divers are properly out of the way.'

They eventually removed enough clutter from the stairwell to be able to reach the next level. Here they found just a single corridor, empty and featureless, a pair of double doors at the far end. There were windows down one side of the corridor, and doorways on the other – three of them. Presumably these opened into classrooms.

'OK, it must be one of these,' said Baz, and walked towards the first door.

'Yeah, but hang on a minute. Let's just see if we can get any further . . .' Ray hurried down the corridor. Baz saw him try the double doors, pushing and pulling at the handles, peering through the glass.

He came back shaking his head. 'Damn. I was hoping we might be able to get further round the . . .' He didn't finish the sentence. 'Anyway, it's all locked up. Take a sledgehammer to break through those. Well, where are we supposed to be, then?'

'Isaac said it was an art room. Above the kitchen.'

Ray began to move away, but Baz said, 'Hold on,' and pushed open the first door. This turned out to be a small washroom – just a sink and two cubicles.

'Oh, right.' Baz glanced about him. 'Well, we've got to sort out the jakes as well . . . bring some stuff up . . .'

Then he realized that he was talking to himself, and so he stepped back out into the corridor. Ray had already opened the next door down.

'Found it.' Ray's muffled voice. Baz went to join

him, feeling that he was a step behind somehow. He entered the room and saw lines of desks and stools, a big paint-splattered sink with upturned jam jars on the draining board – a few paintbrushes that had been left to clean in a jar of white spirit, very sticky. And pictures, brightly coloured pictures, all around the walls.

'So what've we got to do?' said Ray.

'Get rid of all the desks and that. Just shove 'em along the corridor, and stack 'em up at the end. Bring up some buckets of water and put 'em in the jakes. And we gotta haul three mattresses up here. Isaac said they'd be left outside the storeroom, with some new duvets.'

'Yeah? Wonder what's going on. Who it's for . . .'

'Dunno. Come on. We'd better get started.'

It really didn't take that long, and with just one more mattress left to install, Baz reckoned it was time for a break.

'Come on,' he said. 'The divers'll have gone by now. I'll sneak you into the kitchen and we can get something to eat. Then we can sort the last bed out, and that'll be it.'

'Yeah? Wow. I'm starving. Let's go then.'

Baz was right. The salvage crew had long disappeared, and all was quiet downstairs. He opened the kitchen food cupboard and grabbed a couple of tins. 'What do you fancy, then – tuna fish? Peaches?' It made him feel proud all of a sudden, to be in charge of all this, and to be able to offer such luxuries.

But Ray didn't appear to be as interested in food as

he had been a moment ago. He was looking towards the far corner of the kitchen, and said, 'You know, I'm sure this must . . . What's through that door down there?'

'Huh? Oh, you can't get out that way. It's all blocked up with rubble.'

This was what Cookie had told him, but the truth was that Baz had never actually looked. The far end of the kitchen was where the gas ranges were, and as none of these worked there was rarely any reason to go down there. But Ray was already trying the handle, putting his shoulder to the door and repeatedly shoving against it.

'What are you doing?' Baz felt vaguely annoyed. 'We haven't got time to be mucking about.'

'Hah. Yeah, I *thought* this must be right.' With a final thump and scrape of masonry, Ray had managed to shove the door open far enough to wriggle round it. 'Come and have a look.'

Baz sighed and wandered down to see what Ray had found.

It was a stairwell. From amidst a pile of concrete and broken glass rose a spiral stair – white-painted railings and wooden steps. Shafts of daylight shone from above. Baz picked his way amongst the rubble and looked upwards. He could see where the wall had crumbled away high above him, a great section of it having collapsed. The spiral stairway was exposed to the outside world at this point, its railings all kinked and twisted. But it seemed to be more or less intact. Climbable perhaps . . .

'Blimey,' said Baz. 'How did you know this was here?'

'Well . . .' Ray reached out to grab one of the railings. 'I saw it from the outside. You know, when we went up to the playing field. I just reckoned it had to end up around here somewhere.'

'Yeah? Wonder where it goes.'

'Well, let's take a look. Might not get another chance.' Ray was already clambering onto the first accessible step. 'Come on. It'll only take a minute.'

'Blimey, Ray . . .' Baz wasn't prepared for this but felt that he was being given little choice in the matter. If Ray was determined to go, then he would have to follow.

About halfway up they reached the point where the stairway was effectively outside the building. From here they had a rear view of the tiny island and the lane that led up to the playing fields. Baz hadn't realized that the lane was at the very boundary of the land. Beyond its overgrown hedge was nothing but the grey and endless sea.

'Better keep going,' said Ray. 'Don't want to risk being seen.'

Higher they climbed, round and round, and into the dim shadows of the building once more. Eventually they could go no further. The spiral staircase opened out onto a broad landing. Ray didn't hesitate or pause to look about him. He turned left.

'Phew, this is a bit of a mess.' Baz caught up with Ray, and they walked side by side. Part of the roof was missing here, a huge section of it ripped away by the storms, and the interior of the building was soaking wet as a consequence. Black mildew grew on the walls, and the corridor was deeply puddled, awash with floating debris. The place stank. Baz splashed along, saying no more for the moment. He realized that he was still carrying the tins of tuna fish and peaches.

They turned a corner, climbed a short flight of stairs, and now the floors were dry. Another corridor, another corner. They appeared to be going round in a circle, or rather a square.

'What are we looking for?' said Baz. He would have been interested in stopping here and there, the better to take in his surroundings, but Ray seemed to be walking with a purpose, ignoring the classroom doors, the passages that led off in other directions.

'I just got a hunch about something,' said Ray. 'Schools are all pretty much the same, aren't they?'

It was true. This was all very familiar to Baz. And how weird it was to see again the signs of a former life – the notice boards, the photographs, the trophy cases with their various cups and plaques.

But no bodies, thank goodness. It had been half-term, Baz remembered, when it happened. All the kids at this school would have been at home for half-term. Just as he had been . . .

'Aha – what's this?' Ray had stopped in front of a glass door. Sellotaped to the inside of the glass was a printed sheet of A4 paper. ALL LIBRARY CARDS MUST BE SHOWN. REMEMBER: NO CARD, NO BOOK!

A library.

'Yeah. I guessed it,' said Ray. 'Had to be up here somewhere. Come on, let's take a look.' He pulled open the glass door, and the two of them stepped inside.

Baz stood still and gazed about him. A *library*. God.

And it all looked so perfect. The room was large and airy, full of light, with windows along two of its sides. And amazingly it seemed to be completely intact. Not smashed or burned or looted, as all such places on the mainland now were, not torn apart by hurricanes or torrential rains. Everything preserved just as it should be, everything still in place. Books stacked properly on their shelves, a row of computers with their monitor screens neatly covered, the librarian's desk cleared and tidied for the holiday. All had been made ready for the second half of the summer term.

But then the second half of that summer term had never come . . .

Baz put down his tins of food and wandered over to the nearest set of bookshelves, a science section, touching the neat rows of volumes, running his fingers along the spines. How wonderful it would be to just sit here and read for the rest of the afternoon. How fantastic to be able to do that. To sit and read . . . or maybe just look at pictures. His fingertips traced the embossed silver lettering on *The World's Greatest Inventions*, and after a moment he pulled the book from the shelf. The first thing he did was sniff it. He let the pages fall open and brought them close to his face, burying himself in the heady smell of paper and ink, something he had never expected to do again. Amazing.

He put the book back in its place and roamed around some more, looking at the pictures on the walls, photos, the various projects that had been going on. There was a display area set out, with a big photograph of a bald man sitting in a chair. He was holding up a book. An author perhaps. A group of girls looked over the man's shoulder, bending slightly in order to get in the frame, obviously posed. Big smiles all round, although none of them could have been very comfortable.

'What do you think? This could be great, yeah?' Ray was standing with his back to one of the windows, arms folded.

'How do you mean, *could* be great? It *is* great.'

'I mean as a hiding place,' said Ray. 'Like, if we could manage to sneak up here on Sundays. Nobody'd ever know we were here.'

'God . . . yeah! I hadn't even thought about that.'

'Well, let's think about it now, then. Hey – what did you do with those tins? Are they ring-pull?'

'Huh? Oh, yeah. I'll go and get them.'

'D'you really think it can happen? I mean, the bomb-thing. Or is it just stupid?'

They sat on two stools, side by side, at the opened windows of the library, finishing off the last of the peaches. This had definitely been the best morning that either of them could remember since the day they'd arrived. No Isaac, no capos, no Preacher John. Nobody to push them around or beat them up or put them down the hole. Or kill them. Here was a glimpse of another life, a tomorrow free of all the horrors that surrounded them today.

'It's not stupid,' said Baz. 'This is what it could be like.'

'Just us.'

'Yeah.'

They gazed out across the view, their elbows resting

309

on the windowsill. Everything seemed . . . lighter up here. Yes, a different kind of light. They might have been in a restaurant, thought Baz. Or a café, maybe. A bright bookstore café, with paintings on the walls – nothing to do but drink coffee and talk . . . and be happy.

And though the view was undoubtedly strange – what with the church tower poking up out of the waters, along with the rusting crane – and though the sun didn't shine properly like it used to, and the rain came pounding down most days, it could still be beautiful. It could be . . .

Baz stared lazily down towards the jetty, watching the gentle rocking motion of the salvage boat, and it was another moment before realization exploded within him. The boat was back! It was bumping against the jetty wall, and there was Luke, throwing a rope towards Steiner.

Oh my God . . .

'Ray!' Baz grabbed at Ray's shoulder. 'Look – they're back. Quick! We've gotta get out of here!'

'Oh hell . . .' said Ray, and in another few moments the two of them were out of the door, racing along the echoing corridors, splashing through puddles and flying down the spiral staircase towards the darker world that waited for them below.

Isaac was coming in through the front entrance just as they arrived at the storeroom. He glanced at the mattress that was propped against the wall and said, 'Haven't you finished that yet? Well, it can wait a second. Just leave it for now.'

His voice was calmer than usual, more polite, and

Baz could see why. Isaac wasn't alone. A little group of people had followed him in through the entrance – a woman and two girls.

'Here we are, then,' said Isaac. 'It's pretty basic, but we can make you comfortable.'

The trio put down the holdalls they were carrying and looked about them. Their very presence was so bewildering, so utterly unexpected, that it took Baz a long moment to realize that he knew one of the girls. Or rather, he knew who she was. Tall, fair-haired, pretty, dressed in a blue denim skirt, white T-shirt and sandals: Nadine Wilmslow, the girl from downstairs in the building where he'd last lived! *Nadine Wilmslow?* What was she . . . how could *she* be here? Baz's gaze must have been so fixed that it couldn't go unnoticed. At any rate Nadine looked at him, held his eyes for a second before turning away. There had been no sign of recognition.

The woman, perhaps the girls' mother, said, 'I'm sure it'll be fine, Mr Eck. Thank you.' She was fair like the girls, professional-looking somehow in a navy-blue tracksuit. Not the sort of woman who would be shipped across on the notorious Ladies' Days, Baz thought. So why *were* they here?

'Good,' said Isaac. 'Right – you, lad.' He pointed to Ray. 'Take our guests up to their room, show them where everything is. Help them with their bags, and then you can come back for the other mattress. And you, Cookie, go down to the jetty and get the rest of their things off the boat. You'll find some equipment in the cabin locker. Bring it all up.'

Baz began to move, but he was hesitant and

uncertain, Isaac's instructions still not having had a chance to sink in properly. Ray brushed past him, stooping to pick up one of the holdalls, and Baz noticed that the younger girl was staring at him, frowning. She tipped her head sideways, as if to get a better look at Ray's face.

'He might need some help,' the woman was saying. 'Some of the equipment's rather heavy.'

'No trouble,' said Isaac. 'Cookie – get someone from the sort room to give you a hand. You'll be cooking for eight tonight, by the way.'

'Eight? All right.'

Baz started to walk towards the entrance, then remembered that he was supposed to get help from the sort room, so he turned round again. Ray was standing upright now, a bag in each hand. He flicked the hair off his forehead. And then Baz saw the expression on the younger girl's face. Her eyebrows shot up and her mouth simply fell open – a look of complete astonishment. And yet she said nothing. In fact she seemed to deliberately and quickly look the other way. Why? Had there been some signal from Ray? Did the two of them know each other?

'What's the problem?' Isaac was becoming impatient.

'Nothing,' said Baz. He went off to the sort room.

By the time he came out again, accompanied by Gene, the corridor was empty.

It was strange being on the *Cormorant* with none of the capos or crew overseeing them. Baz and Gene felt they ought to be making the most of the opportunity, but

312

they'd taken a look around and could find nothing worth pocketing. And Baz, still in his white coat, had no pockets in any case.

'We could nick the boat,' he said, 'if we had the keys.'

'Yeah, and then what? Sail off to the Bahamas? Don't s'pose there *are* any Bahamas any more. Anyway, there's a disabler thing on it. A bit that they take away. The keys are no good without that.' Gene was crouching down and examining the engine that powered the winch. 'Couldn't even hot-wire it.'

'What're you doing?' said Baz.

'Nothing, really. Just checking this out. I did a bit of work on this motor when the winch was first rigged up. Come on. We'd better get back.'

They gathered up a couple of black canvas bags, smaller and slimmer than holdalls, but heavy none-theless. It felt as though these contained equipment of some sort rather than clothes. There was also a large flat-packed object on wheels, a bit like a suitcase, with an extending handle to pull it along.

'So is that the lot?' said Gene.

'Oh – Isaac said there was stuff in the locker as well.'

The big wooden locker was built into the side of the cabin – the same locker that Baz and Ray had sat upon while waiting for the boat to leave the mainland. Gene lifted up the lid.

It was a much deeper space than it appeared from the outside, the floor sunk some way below deck level. A couple of aluminium cases lay amongst a tangle of ropes and other assorted rubbish – old fishing lines and big lead weights.

'S'pose it must be those things.' Gene swung his legs over the side of the locker and jumped in.

'Sling 'em up to me, then,' said Baz.

But Gene's attention had been drawn by something else. 'Whoa – look at that,' he said. 'There's a trap-door.' At the rear of the locker well was a square trapdoor with a ring handle mounted into the floor. Gene picked at the metal ring, raised the trapdoor and peered down. 'Yeah. It's so you can get at the bilge pump. I can see the stopcocks.' He looked down into the dark hole a little longer, then closed the trap again. 'Hm.'

'Come on,' said Baz. 'It stinks in here.'

'Tell you what, though . . .' Gene hoisted the cases over the lip of the locker and clambered out. 'Just gimme a moment.' He stepped through the doorway and took another look at the winch, walking around the tripod construction, glancing back towards the wheelhouse once or twice, as if measuring the distance. 'Yeah . . . this could be good. This could be perfect.'

'What are you on about?' Baz watched from the cabin doorway as Gene crouched down and ran his fingertips over the grooved decking.

'The boat.' Gene looked up at Baz, his dark curly hair falling across his eyes. 'If we ever *could* build a bomb – I mean, if we really had to – then this'd be the place for it. Here on the boat. In that locker. Maybe even get something down through the trap and into the bilges. Perfect. We could blow 'em out of the water, the whole friggin' lot of 'em in one go. Just like Ray said.'

Baz turned round and looked at the locker again,

a dark shape in the gloom of the wheelhouse. 'Blimey . . .'

'The thing is, though' – Gene stood up and gazed blankly out to sea – 'I *still* got no idea what the gas and air mixture's supposed to be, to make methane explode. The proper formula. And I got no way of finding out. It could be ten to one, could be fifty-fifty. Could be anything.'

'Bring back the internet,' murmured Baz.

'Yeah, right.'

Then Baz thought of something. He waited for a moment before speaking, savouring the feeling of power, anticipating the look he was about to bring to Gene's face. 'So,' he said, 'would a few chemistry books be any good to you? Like maybe a whole library shelf full of them?'

The woman who had arrived earlier in the day was a dentist. A makeshift surgery had been set up in the dining area, and as Baz went about his afternoon chores, he found excuses to pass through here several times and observe what was happening.

What had looked like a suitcase on wheels turned out to be a folding table or couch. It had chrome legs, and a base that was padded in white plastic material. One by one the divers took turns to lie upon the couch as they had their teeth checked by the dentist lady. It was strange to see the great burly men looking so vulnerable.

'That's going to have to come out, Mr Moko.'

'Ahh!' Moko struggled to sit up, but the dentist put a hand on his chest and pushed him down again.

'Yes, I'm afraid it will hurt a bit. Sorry.'

Baz hurried into the safety of the kitchen to hide his sniggers, delighted to see the mighty Moko on the receiving end for a change.

But now he'd better get serious and start thinking about cooking – and cooking for eight, at that. Eight! Baz took one of the recipe books from the stack beside the microwave and began thumbing through it, looking for inspiration. Why did so many recipes call for potatoes, and cheese, and onions, and all the things he didn't have?

'Er . . . Cookie?'

The kitchen door opened, and Nadine Wilmslow stood there. The fact of her being on the island was still such a shock that Baz didn't know how to cope with it. He was too astonished to do anything but stare.

'All right if I come in?' Nadine didn't wait for an answer but came in anyway, letting the door swing to behind her. She'd swapped her denim skirt for a pair of pink jeans, and looked altogether amazingly fresh and clean. 'Only we brought over half a dozen eggs, and Mr Eck said to give them to you.'

'Uh?'

Mr Eck? Half a dozen eggs? This was just too weird to be really happening.

'Oh. Um . . .' Baz had found his voice. Just about. 'Er . . . OK. Thanks.' How stupid he sounded. And how stupid he must look, in his shorts, and his split trainers, and his oversized white jacket.

'What are you making?' Nadine smiled at him and came closer. She was clutching a carrier bag, rolled over at the top.

Baz put down his recipe book and tried to pull himself together. 'Well . . . I haven't made up my mind yet.'

'Oh. And is this your job, then? Is that why they call you Cookie?'

'They don't call me Cookie.' Baz felt that he had to make this much clear, at least. 'Nobody calls me Cookie, except the divers. My name's Baz.'

'Oh. Sorry. Mine's Nadine.'

'Yeah, I know. I've seen you before. I . . . we . . . used to live upstairs from you. In Canal Street.'

'*No!* Really? What – not in the Brindley building?' The girl laid her carrier bag on the worktop.

'Yeah. Me and my dad. I saw you most days . . .'

'Seriously? How amazing!' Nadine opened her green-brown eyes extra wide. 'We just moved out a while back, and went over to Golthwaite. But are you sure it was me? It was a big building – loads of people lived there. Plenty of other girls . . .'

'No, it was definitely you.'

And Baz could see that Nadine wasn't in any serious doubt that he might have mistaken her for someone else. She looked like a girl who was used to being noticed. Her blonde hair was loosely scrunched up into a high ponytail, but so casually perfect that it must have required a mirror. And her clothes weren't just clean, they were uncreased. Almost like they'd been ironed.

'So . . .' She stood back slightly, as if trying to place him. 'Would you have been wearing your white jacket then?'

'This? No, course not. They only make me wear this stupid thing for working in the kitchen.'

'Oh, but it's so *sweet*. Makes you look like a proper chef.' And to Baz's horror, Nadine reached out with both hands and straightened his grubby lapels, her lips pursed as she took in the effect. Baz could do nothing but stand there and endure the indignity.

'Er . . . so you've brought some eggs then.' It wasn't what he wanted to say, but it gave him an opportunity to pull away.

'Yes. A little present. Preacher John's been so kind . . .'

Kind? Preacher John? Baz couldn't swallow that idea at all. 'So, what . . . what're you doing here? I mean, I can see your mum's a dentist, but—'

'She's not our mum. We call her Aunt Etta, although she's not really even our aunt. She's our dad's cousin. She's been looking after Steffie and me ever since . . . well, you know . . .'

'Oh. So . . . Steffie. That's your sister?' Baz remembered the way the younger girl had stared at Ray. 'I think maybe she knows my friend Ray,' he said. 'The guy that took your bags up.'

'Mmm . . . wouldn't have thought so. Let's make sure these eggs have survived, then.'

Nadine began to unroll the top of the carrier bag.

'So your aunt's a dentist . . . but why are *you* here?'

'Preacher John invited us!' Nadine began to take the eggs out of the bag, placing them on the work surface, one by one. 'He sent a message – a letter. He said that he wanted Aunt Etta to come to the island for a few days and give all his workers a check-up, but Aunt Etta sent a message back saying she couldn't leave me and Steffie by ourselves. And so then Preacher John invited all of us! He said that me and Steffie could come to the island too, so that we could be with Aunt Etta. He sent the boat over specially! We couldn't believe it, 'cos girls aren't usually allowed here, are they? So, what's he like?'

'Who?' Baz was getting a bit lost.

'Preacher John, of course. We've never met him. Everybody says he's like a guru – or a saint from the Bible or something. Anyway' – Nadine carried right on talking – 'Aunt Etta jumped at it. It's given her some extra work, and for me and Steffie it was like we'd be coming away on a real holiday.' Nadine looked at Baz, and her hazel eyes seemed to cloud over. 'We were so excited about seeing the place again. But now—'

'What do you mean,' said Baz, 'seeing the place again? You couldn't have been on the boat before.'

'No. Me and Steffie went to school here. Tab Hill High. It was a girls' school.' Nadine's voice brightened. 'Tell you what, though, it's still a lot better than back on the mainland. We've got our own room here, and proper mattresses . . . toilets all to ourselves – can't believe that. You know what I hope?' She lowered her voice. 'I hope their teeth are so bad we get to stay here for a month!'

Was she nuts? Couldn't this idiot girl see what a hell-hole she'd landed in, and what these men were really like?

'Were you ever around on trading days?' Baz said. 'You know, when the boat came over to the mainland at Linley? Did you ever go down and watch?'

'No. We'd have liked to, 'cos it seemed like it might be fun, but Aunt Etta would never let us. Too many

319

Teefers about. Aunt Etta said the Ecks were a good family, just trying to run their business and keep people fed, but the Teefers – they could get nasty. Best to keep away. It was one of the reasons we moved, the Teefers.'

So Nadine had never seen the Ecks in action, by the sound of it. They were just a jolly sailor crew as far as she was concerned. Baz thought of Preacher John tossing the rabbits onto the altar fire, of Enoch, crushed beneath that same altar slab . . . the disappearance of Cookie . . . Taps . . .

But Nadine knew nothing of these things. She'd turned up in her pink jeans and white blouse like a tourist, ready for a holiday, eager to see how the natives lived.

And now she was continuing that tour, poking around the kitchen, delighted with all that she found.

'Oh, is this your little cooker? How sweet. And how amazing to have electricity – can I make a cup of tea?'

'Er . . . well, I ought to be thinking about cooking.' Baz looked doubtfully at the eggs. These were a real bonus, but how was he going to stretch six eggs between eight people?

'OK. Can I help?' Nadine had drifted down to the far end of the room, and her voice was less distinct. 'What's this then? *All you need is her.* What does that mean?'

'Huh?'

'On this metal cupboard thing. *All you need is her*, it says.'

Baz wandered down to take a look. He seldom had any reason to be in this part of the room, the defunct gas cooking ranges being of no interest to him. Nadine was standing in front of a tall metal cabinet, and she was right: scrawled across the two doors were the words . . . Awkward fingermarks in the dust.

'Did you start to write a poem or something? Who's it for – your girlfriend?'

'What? *I* didn't write it!' Baz was indignant. 'Nothing to do with me.'

'So what's in there?'

'Dunno. Just pots and pans, I think.' Baz had a vague memory of Cookie showing him where all the bigger utensils were kept. Was it Cookie who had written the words on the door? Why?

He grabbed the cabinet door handles and pulled. The doors opened with a judder, and yes, the inner shelves were stacked with large metal cooking pots – some of them very large indeed. Here was all the para-phernalia necessary for mass catering: deep metal trays with carrying handles at either end, round pans that fitted one inside the other, sieves, colanders, cheese graters. On the bottom shelf was a truly massive pot, a veritable cauldron of heavy-duty stainless steel, and resting against it stood a complicated-looking lid. The lid had big clamping devices all around the edge of it, and a gauge mounted on top – a bit like the gauge Baz had seen on the air-compressor in the hut where the diesel was kept. 'Nothing here,' he said, 'so I dunno what all that's about.'

Nadine had already lost interest. She was fiddling with the knobs on one of the big gas ranges.

'Hard to remember what it was like,' she said, 'when stuff like this all worked.'

'Yeah.' Baz started to close the doors of the cabinet – but then he noticed something tucked between the huge cooking vessel and the lid. A piece of paper? He stooped to pick it up, and found that it was a half-page torn from a recipe book. A pudding recipe – *Bombe Surprise. Ingredients: 6 meringues . . . 250ml double cream* . . . what was that doing in there?

Baz looked at it for a moment, then shrugged and screwed it up. Not a recipe he was ever likely to have any use for. He pushed the doors of the cabinet closed.

All you need is her. The dusty fingermarks relayed their puzzling message to him once again. *All you need is her*. All you need is . . . *here*? Could that be what it meant?

It had to be Cookie who'd written these words. The fingermarks were too fresh for it to have been anyone else. *All you need is here*. Had Cookie been trying to leave him a message? But what *was* here? The huge cooking vessel . . . the torn recipe page . . . 'Bombe Surprise' . . .

Baz opened the doors again. *Oh my God* . . . He felt the back of his neck tingle as he understood. He'd finally got it. The thing they'd been looking for was right here – in this very cabinet – and Cookie had led them to it. That big cauldron with the clamp-down lid. Baz remembered then that Cookie had whispered something to him, the night before he was taken away. *Baz . . . got something to show you . . .*

And this was that something. But there had been no time to explain, no time for Cookie to even finish writing his message. He'd tried to help them, even though they'd all treated him so badly. Poor Cookie.

322

'We could make kedgeree.' Nadine was back down at the other end of the room, looking through a recipe book.

'What?'

'Kedgeree. It's dead easy. Rice, smoked fish and hard-boiled eggs. Got any kippers?'

Baz couldn't help but laugh. Kippers? This had to be the weirdest day ever.

'Er, don't know. Might have something in a tin.' He searched through the food cabinet, and he was still smiling when he brought a large flat tin of kipper fillets over to where Nadine was standing. She'd put a pan of water on the two-ring cooker, and was getting ready to boil the eggs. Taking over the operation, just like that.

'You look cheerful all of a sudden,' she said. 'Suits you.'

'Well . . . maybe things are looking up.'

'Really? Is that since I got here, then?' Nadine gave him a sideways glance, her tongue pressing against the inside of her cheek, her eyebrows raised.

Was she flirting with him?

'That's right,' he said. 'Ever since you got here. You and the eggs.'

Nadine pushed out her lower lip in an expression of mock-ruefulness. 'Well, that's put me in my place,' she said.

Yeah. This was definitely the weirdest day ever.

CHAPTER NINETEEN

'Sounds like it's a pressure cooker,' said Gene. 'Gotta be. Wow – I'd *never* have thought of that. How deep is it? D'you reckon the big Coke bottles'd stand in there upright, with the lid on?'

Baz pulled on his white jacket, getting ready for the morning's work, and tried to recall the size of the metal container. 'Yeah, I'm pretty sure they would.'

'Great. Maybe we're in business then. OK, two things. Number one: can you get me the lid? Just the lid, so I can take a look at it? And number two: can you see if there's anything on the casing that tells you how big it is? Like, how many litres it holds.'

'Er . . . I can try,' said Baz. 'The lid's huge, though. Don't know how I'm gonna smuggle it out of the kitchen.'

But within a couple of hours he'd managed it. The dental surgery was in morning session, but Amos was the only one there apart from the dentist – and Amos seemed to have plenty of other things on his mind, judging by the noise he was making. Baz was able to hurry out of the kitchen with the heavy lid tucked under his left arm and partially out of view. He got it safely to the slob room and hid it in the jakes before scurrying back to the kitchen.

Later that evening the boys gathered in the wash-room to inspect their prize.

'Wow, that's some piece of kit.' Gene knelt on the floor and lifted the edge of the lid.

'So what is it?' said Amit. 'How does it work? What's that clock thing on the top?'

'It's a pressure gauge,' said Gene. 'See, the lid bolts down onto the pot – that's what all these clamp things are for: to make it totally airtight. Then the food in there's cooked under steam pressure. There's a safety valve on top – this thing here. Releases the steam if the pressure inside gets too high. Have to have one of those or the thing'd explode.'

'But that's what we want it to do, isn't it – explode?'

'Yeah, we do. So we're gonna take that safety valve out and block up the hole. In *fact* . . .' Gene turned the lid over. 'Yeah, I reckon I can get the valve out and put the spark plug in there instead . . .'

'Huh?'

'OK.' Gene seemed to realize that he was going to have to explain properly. 'This is just the same as that little rocket toy I made, yeah? No different. The gas is in the container, and the spark plug is fitted in the lid. Then we clamp the lid down. Make the plug spark, the gas explodes, and *whoosh* – up she goes. I mean, I'm gonna have to think about it a bit more, but that's basically it.'

'And we're gonna put it on the boat?' said Ray.

'Well, I dunno. But it's the best plan we got. We'd never do it like you reckoned, Ray. Trying to get 'em all gathered round the thing and then let it off – that wouldn't work. But if we could blow a hole in the side of the boat while Isaac's lot are all out on it . . . see what I mean?'

'But they'd be miles away,' said Robbie. 'How would we set it off?'

'We wouldn't.' Gene grinned up at him. 'They would. Here's what I've been thinking. Say we hide this thing in the cabin locker – Baz knows where I mean. Yeah? And say we ran a lead from the winch motor to the spark plug that's on the bomb. And say it was a diving day, not a trading day. Now, they've got no reason to start the winch motor until they're miles out to sea, and the divers are down below the water, and they need to haul something up. So then Moko pulls the rope to start the winch motor. But instead of the spark plug being in the winch motor, it's in the bomb, see? So up she goes. *Boom*. Boat sinks, job done.'

A wondering silence fell on the washroom. All were lost in the same vision, the same magnificent thunderous explosion playing and replaying in their imaginations. Great waterspouts rising from the sea . . . the *Cormorant* splintering into a million pieces . . . Isaac and his band of thugs flying through the air . . . blown into the stratosphere . . . vanishing without trace. And they, the X Isle boys, blasting their way to a heroic and righteous freedom. It was a brilliant plan. Utterly brilliant.

'Oh, *man*,' Jubo breathed at last. 'You a genius, Gene. You the real Spartacus, man.' He gave a long sigh. 'Eyyyy.'

'But what if—?' Dyson began to speak.

'Yeah, I know, mate.' Gene raised a hand to interrupt him. 'I know. There are a helluva lot of "what ifs". Like what if one of them opens the lid of the locker box and sees the bomb? What if they spot the HT lead? What if they try to start the motor and the bomb doesn't go off? They're gonna come sailing back here and they're gonna kill us, that's what if. Yeah, and I don't mean just beat us up. Kill us.'

How quickly that brave vision of freedom then disappeared, fleeing to the corners of the room to hide among the cobwebs, a timid and insubstantial thing. And in its place came another image: the dark shadow of the *Cormorant* returning through the mist, solid and intact, its outraged crew vowing bloody revenge.

'Yeah, you see?' said Gene. 'It's still just an idea, that's all. Only an idea. Whether we'd really have the guts to go through with it, I don't know. And the other thing, the other *big* thing is . . . what about Preacher John? He's not gonna be on the boat, is he? He never goes on the boat. *But*' – he stood up and dusted off his bare knees – 'what I say is this: let's at least build it. We don't have to use it, but we've come this far, so let's get the job done. I'll take this lid into the sort room and work on it, and we'll think about it some more. Try and make it so we're not dead if it all goes wrong.'

He looked around at the thoughtful faces. 'Anybody got any objections? No? Anybody got any questions, then?'

'Yeah, me,' said Jubo. 'When is old Baz gonna start sharing these girls around, hey? That's what me wanna know, man. Me keep hearing 'bout them, but me don't even *see* them yet! When he get so lucky?'

Which made everyone laugh of course, and changed the subject of discussion entirely.

Jubo soon got his wish, because within twenty-four hours the two girls, Nadine and Steffie, had been seen by all. They were spotted up on the playing fields feeding the goat, and again a little further along the coastline from the jetty, sitting beside the wooden dinghy that was beached there. It seemed that they more or less had the run of the island, although they never came near where the boys were working, or made any contact with them.

'They've been told that we're very busy and that they must try not to disturb us,' Baz said. He was speaking to an open-mouthed audience on Tuesday night in the slob room. 'It's important that we continue our good work without any interruptions, Mr *Eck* says. If it wasn't for us, the poor mainlanders would starve, and so we must all do our best not to let that happen.'

'You what?'

'Yeah, I know. They think Isaac's a friggin' hero. And they can't *wait* to meet the wonderful Preacher John.'

'Well, I hope you put 'em straight,' said Amit.

'Don't get a chance,' said Baz. 'I have to take their meals up to their room, but there isn't time to say anything much. Nadine – that's the older one – she came down to the kitchen and helped me do some cooking. But I haven't really talked to her since.'

'Woo-hoo – Nadine! "She helped me do some cooking." Get you!'

'Yeah, yeah.' Baz could feel himself blushing. It was ridiculous, but once a blush began it was impossible to stop. He tried to divert attention from himself. 'So what's been happening, Gene? You got any further?'

'Yup,' said Gene. 'I already told the others before you got here. I've fitted the spark plug into the lid, and it's as tight as you like. The end pokes through to the other side, and that's given me another idea. Tell you about it later. The other thing I had to do today was make some torches – like firebrands. Long sticks with a load of oily rag tied round the ends. Preacher John's orders, and I can guess what they're for. The altar. I reckon he's planning on more sacrifices.'

But sacrificing what? More rabbits? Or something . . . else? It was a scary thought, and everyone was quiet for a minute.

'Yeah, well,' said Gene. 'Let's try and forget about that for now. But did you find out how big it was – the pressure cooker – how many litres it holds?'

Baz nodded. 'Sixty-five. Says so on the bottom. Sixty-five-litre capacity. I tipped it up to have a look, and I can tell you it weighs a ton.'

'Sixty-five?' said Gene. 'Blimey, that's a lot. I'm gonna have to check some calculations – soon as Baz can get me up into that library.'

'I can get you up there tomorrow night,' said Baz. 'No problem. You've only got to get as far as the kitchen door, and from then on you're pretty safe.'

'Let's do it, then.'

'Wow. I'm telling you – it is *amazing* up there. Perfect hideout. You guys are gonna love it.' On Wednesday night Gene returned to the slob room, full of all that he'd seen in the library. As Baz had predicted, it had been easy enough to get him through the kitchens. Armed with his wind-up torch and some directions, Gene had spent an hour alone at the top of the building.

'Nice chairs, tables. There's pens up there. There's even *paper*. Yeah—'

'Yeah, but did you find the right books?' Baz was impatient to know whether the trip had produced any actual results.

'Yup. Working mixture's anything between seven and fifteen per cent gas to air. Found it in a chemi book. We've got enough methane for a ten-per-cent mixture. So that's it, boys – we're there. We've already got enough gas.'

'You sayin' we can stop blowing up balloons?' said Jubo. 'Good.'

'What, are you all out of breath, Jube? I hadn't noticed.'

'Ha, ha!'

But it was a sobering moment. They'd reached their target, according to Gene, and with it a turning point. They had the vessel, they had the explosive, and they had a way of detonating that explosive. They had the makings of a bomb.

On Friday morning Baz was in the little sluice room next to the kitchen, rinsing out the divers' foul underwear – his least favourite job. He heard voices outside in the corridor and was surprised when Nadine looked in at the door.

'Hiya,' she said. 'You're always so busy! What're you doing now?'

Baz resisted the temptation to say, *What does it look like?* and just grunted, 'Washing some clothes.' He was resentful of the easy life these girls led.

'Yeah? We're just seeing Aunt Etta off,' Nadine said. 'She's working over on the mainland this weekend. A couple of the men are taking her across in the boat. She's coming back on Monday . . .'

'Ooh – is this the laundry room?' The younger girl, Steffie, appeared. 'It's good, isn't it?'

Like her sister, Steffie looked unfeasibly neat and clean. She was maybe twelve or thirteen, her fair hair tied up in bunches.

Baz glanced up and said, 'Hey. Feel free to come and join in the fun.' But then he looked at Nadine and added, 'What – you mean your aunt's going back and you're staying behind?' This seemed a bit odd.

'Yeah.' Nadine put her hands in her jeans pockets. 'She's got some more patients to see. Mr Eck says Preacher John's given us special permission to stay on. It's only till Monday, when Aunt Etta comes back.'

'Oh. She, er . . . she trusts him, does she? I mean, to look after you OK? And to bring her back again?'

'Who, Mr Eck? Well, yeah, why wouldn't she?'

Then someone was shouting from the corridor, 'Aren't you going to come and wave me goodbye?' A woman's voice.

'OK!' Nadine shouted back. She turned and smiled at Baz. 'Back in a bit. We'll come and give you a hand.'

The girls disappeared. Baz heard them giggling as they ran off down the corridor. He slapped a soaking wet vest down onto the draining board and began to wring it out. Yeah, right, he thought, I'll save something special for you. Moko's underpants maybe.

But Nadine was as good as her word. In about fifteen minutes she was back again, along with Steffie, and both girls seemed willing to muck in.

'Where do you want us to start, then?' said Nadine. She grabbed a handful of clothing from the pile on the floor.

'Wow. You've got real soap powder.' Steffi picked up the box that stood beside one of the sinks. 'We've been having to use washing-up liquid for months now – and that's for our hair and everything. This is luxury!'

Baz had forgotten in the past few weeks just how hard life was back on the mainland, where there were no supplies other than those that could be bought on the black market. If you had nothing to bargain with, then you had nothing. And even if you had a skill, like his dad, or like the dentist, then you could only trade your skills for what was available – which still might be nothing. Life was tough here on the island, and deadly dangerous, but at least they had the basics.

These girls weren't rich, he realized. For all that they'd managed to keep themselves looking good, they were poorer than he was. Hungrier probably, maybe even more desperate. No wonder they were so delighted to be here. No wonder they wanted to stay. Wasn't that the very reason he'd been so keen to get here in the first place – for the promise of food every day, and a roof to sleep under every night? His attitude towards them softened, and he tried to be a bit nicer.

'Yeah,' he said. 'We got soap powder. I might even

be able to get hold of some proper shampoo. I'll ask the guys in the sort room.'

'It's OK,' said Nadine. She didn't look at him. 'Ra—Your friend Ray . . . he already said he'd—'

But whatever she was about to say went unfinished.

'What're you two doing here?'

Luke was standing in the doorway. His stubbled face was unsmiling, his eyes cold and threatening.

'Sorry?' Nadine looked at him, her arms still full of dirty clothes.

'Put that stuff down and get back up to your room. You don't talk to these other kids, and you don't show your faces down here again, got it?'

'What? But we were just trying to help. And Mr Eck said that we could go wherever we—'

'I don't care what Mr Eck said. Things have changed, girlie. Now get back upstairs and stay there. You keep to your room till you're sent for. Preacher John's orders.'

'But why should we?'

Don't argue, thought Baz. *You don't know these guys . . . you don't know them . . .*

'Don't question me, you gobby little slag! I already told you – Preacher John's orders! Now get upstairs!' Luke had moved forward, one arm raised.

Nadine dropped the clothes back on the floor and stormed out of the room. After another moment Steffie put down the box of soap powder and ran after her.

Luke watched them go. 'You keep away from those two,' he said to Baz. '*Well* away – understand?'

'OK.' Baz didn't question this.

'See that you do, then, fella.' Luke paused at the

door. 'Ladies' Night tonight,' he said. 'There'll be four of 'em coming back on the boat, so you're cooking for nine altogether, right?'

'Yes,' said Baz. But then he thought about this. 'Um . . . don't you mean eleven? There's the two girls as well.'

'You don't cook for them any more. You give 'em a can o' beans, same as the rest of you get.'

'All right.' Again Baz put up no argument. 'Am I allowed to get someone to help me in the kitchen for the night?'

'Do what you like. Just make sure you put some decent food on the table – and plenty o' wine. Nice and generous with the wine.'

Luke turned his back on Baz and left the room.

Tuna-fish curry, with rice and chapatis. Tinned mandarins for pudding, with condensed milk.

It wasn't the most dazzling of menus, and Baz knew it. But he had none of Cookie's finesse, none of his inventiveness with a limited range of ingredients, so he preferred to play things safe rather than get too adventurous and risk messing up.

Baz and Ray stood side by side, their backs to the kitchen door, and watched the meal in progress.

Four women had been brought over from the mainland, and it had been a squeeze to fit them all in around the dining table, but nobody seemed to mind that. The ladies were plainly here to enjoy themselves. They ate and drank everything that was put in front of them, screeched with laughter, clinked their wine glasses and called for more. Baz looked wonderingly at their made-up faces, their dyed hair, their shiny shoes . . . it was out of this world. You just didn't see women like that any more. He vaguely remembered Saturday nights before the flood, when girls would emerge from their houses, transformed into exotic creatures such as these, ready for an evening on the town. He would watch them from his bedroom window, groups of bare-limbed girls grasping at each other for support as they tottered down the road in their impossible shoes, the sound of high heels click-clacking on the summer pavements.

But now those tropical birds had disappeared, most of them, or shed their fancy feathers for something more practical. And for those few that remained, dressing up was no longer something they did just for fun. This was their job, Baz realized. This was their skill. Like his dad, and like Aunt Etta the dentist, these women had a trade. They were performers, actors.

And very good at it they were too. As Baz watched, he began to appreciate how cleverly the women controlled the situation. In between the loud laughter and the crude jokes, he saw the glances that passed between them, the subtle sign language that would result in a change of seating positions after a joint visit to the washroom. He saw that it was the girls who were making the choices, and how each girl then attended to the man she had chosen – keeping his wine glass full, engaging his attention, hanging upon his every slurred and leering remark. They were as good at their job as his dad was at poker, Baz thought, and probably made about as good a living.

He found his eye drawn to the woman who sat next

to Isaac. She acted – if acting it was – in a more sober and demure way than the others, a way that seemed fitting for the lady of a skipper. Her dress was flamboyant and colourful enough, a flower in her dark hair so that she looked vaguely Hawaiian, or Thai, but she didn't shriek or bang her wine glass down on the table or trade raucous insults with her companions. Instead she listened, smiling, to whatever Isaac was saying, and when he laid his heavy paw upon her slim brown arm, she put her own hand over his, squeezing it briefly. A friendly gesture rather than a provocative one. It was as though they had known each other for years – as they might have done, for all Baz could tell.

Moko was the only one who didn't seem to be enjoying the party. He sat beside a woman in a blonde wig, an outrageous confection of swirling ringlets that tumbled halfway down her back. And though the woman kept plying Moko with wine – which he drank – and kept up a steady chatter, Moko barely glanced at her. He stared into the distance, lumpy and uncomfortable in his shiny suit, looking more like a man who'd just been given a death sentence than one who was at a party.

'Hey, Cookie! More wine!'

Luke was calling him, and Baz took another bottle of red from the trolley beside him. He glanced at Ray and raised his eyebrows. They were in for a long night by the look of it.

But Ray's face was cold and set, with no emotion in his eyes or apparent interest in the proceedings. He seemed to be blanking out the whole experience.

* * *

Later Hutchinson turned up. He nodded in the direction of the party – by now a rather bleary and weary bunch – and spoke to Baz.

'I'm not waiting up any longer,' he muttered, 'so I'm gonna have to leave the slob-room door unlocked. But I'm warning you . . . any trouble . . .'

'What are we gonna do? Run away?' said Baz. The slob-room door was rarely locked, and he knew that Hutchinson had only shown his face out of curiosity. Come to leer at the girls probably.

'Watch your lip,' said Hutchinson. He glanced over at the revellers. 'Looks like fun. It'll be our turn on Sunday, eh?' This remark was addressed to Ray, but Ray made no reply.

Baz wanted to pick up one of the remaining wine bottles and smash it over Hutchinson's head, but the capo had already turned to leave.

'Yeah. Definitely this Sunday . . .'

He wandered off.

'Pig,' said Baz. But still Ray said nothing.

When the last of the drinking party had finally staggered off to bed, Baz whispered, 'OK, forget the clearing up. We're gonna have to risk leaving it till morning. Let's grab the pressure cooker while we can – might be our only chance.' He and Ray went back into the kitchen. But while Baz was concentrating on manoeuvring the huge cauldron out of its steel cabinet, he realized that Ray was rummaging through the food cupboard.

'Hey – what're you doing? Come and give me a hand with this thing.'

Ray didn't reply. Instead he reached in amongst the tins and boxes, and pulled out a packet of some sort.

'Ray!' Baz was getting annoyed. 'What're you playing at? Put that back and get over here.'

Ray closed the cupboard door, but he still had hold of whatever he'd taken from the cupboard. He walked over to where Baz was crouching and dropped the packet into the cooking pot.

'That's mine,' he said – the first words he'd spoken in over an hour. 'Wages, OK?'

'Wages?' Baz stared down into the pot, saw the reflection of cellophane in the dim yellow light. It was a packet of pasta quills. Unopened. 'How do you mean, *wages*? That's no good to you here. You can't spend it – can't even eat it. What the hell's the matter with you?'

'Just shut up and don't ask questions. They're my wages. Now come on.' Ray stooped forward and grabbed one of the handles of the massive pot. 'Let's go.'

'Ray—'

'You wanna make something of it?' Ray's mouth barely moved as he spoke. His face was rigid, eyes furiously determined.

Baz let it go. 'No.'

'Then shut up.'

Baz grasped the other handle of the pressure cooker, and together they hurried out of the kitchen and down the corridor, bearing their heavy cargo between them. When they got to the slob room they found that Gene was still awake.

'Hey – is that it? Did you get it?' His voice was an excited whisper in the darkness.

'Yeah.'

'Brilliant. Stick it in the jakes, then. We'll take a look at it tomorrow.'

They put the pressure cooker in the second cubicle. Ray reached down, took his packet of pasta and left the washroom without another word.

CHAPTER TWENTY

Dressed in scruffy jeans and T-shirts, hair tied back, their pale faces washed clean of make-up, the group of women who were gathered in the corridor next morning bore little resemblance to the gorgeous beings of the night before. The performance was over. Props and costumes had been packed away into holdalls, along with the bawdy jokes and raucous laughter, and now the players were silently awaiting their transport.

Baz and Ray had been detailed to carry bags and belongings to the jetty, and this took a couple of journeys. On the second trip the women followed them down, accompanied by two of the divers. Luke and Moko had turned up, having been given the job of ferrying the ladies back to the mainland, by the look of it. Nobody spoke.

Standing beside the pile of luggage, Baz waited for further instructions. The gangplanks were already in place, bridging the gap between the rocky slope of the jetty and the salvage boat. Ray stood looking out to sea, as uncommunicative as he'd been the night before. He was muffled up in a hoodie, his hands stuffed into the pouch pocket, even though the morning was warm. Maybe he had a cold or something.

Moko and Luke were first across the gangplank, their combined weight causing the boat to rock gently in the water. The instant their backs were turned to the shore, Ray stooped towards the collection of holdalls. He withdrew a hand from the pouch of his jacket, and quickly thrust it into the half-open top of one of the bags – a secretive and surreptitious movement. Baz couldn't see whether something was being taken from the bag or placed inside it, but he instinctively stepped forward in an attempt to shield Ray from view.

Both men were in the boat now, Moko heading towards the wheelhouse, Luke remaining by the gunwale. The women picked up their belongings and gingerly began to cross the gangplank. Luke offered no steadying hand, and each of them had to jump down into the boat unaided.

'Fire her up, Moko!' Luke's voice was a rough croak, the expression on his face sour. He looked like a man who had been dragged too early from his bed.

Baz watched the last of the women cross the gangplank. He recognized her as the one who had been with Isaac the night before – the dark-haired lady who had worn the Hawaiian dress, with an artificial flower behind her ear. She was tiny. Her shoulders, painfully thin beneath the fabric of her yellow T-shirt, seemed hardly capable of bearing the weight of the two bags she carried.

And it was one of those bags, Baz realized, that Ray had tampered with. What was that all about? He looked again at the dark-haired lady, Isaac's woman, her face visible now as she found a place on the transom bench beside her companions. *Ba-dub, ba-dub, ba-dubdubdubdub*. The diesel engine thudded into life. Then Luke was shouting.

'Oi – wake up, you two. Get that soddin' gangplank away!'

Baz and Ray scrambled down the rocky slope of the jetty and hauled at the planks.

'Right, cast off!' Another rough command from Luke. Baz dropped his plank and ran to the bow end of the boat. He unhitched the rope from its iron ring, and saw Ray do the same down at the stern. The engine revved and the salvage boat began to pull away from the jetty, churning up the waters into a grey froth that slapped greasily at the concrete blocks.

Huddled in a group around the stern sat the four women, their faces pinched and unsmiling, eyes staring blankly ahead. But then, as the boat swung to starboard, the woman in the yellow T-shirt altered her position slightly. She looked over her shoulder towards Ray, and although her expression didn't change, she made a curious little gesture in his direction, placing a forefinger beneath her chin and tilting her head up.

And still it took another moment before Baz understood. The woman was Ray's mum. It was the yellow T-shirt that finally reminded him of where he'd seen her before: standing on the bowling green with Ray on her shoulders, waving a packet of cornflakes . . .

Ray wouldn't talk about it. On the way back up to the school building Baz said, 'Sorry, Ray. I didn't know.'

But there was no reply, and so Baz tried one more time. 'What was that you put in her bag?'

'Her wages. What do you think?' Ray quickened his pace so that he was walking slightly ahead of Baz, his face hidden inside the hood of his jacket.

Wages? It took Baz another moment to realize what Ray had meant. The pasta . . .

The day didn't improve. When Baz got back to the dining area, he found Isaac surveying the wreckage of the previous evening – dirty plates and glasses and bottles still littering the table – and he knew that he was in trouble.

'What's all this crap?' The skipper was obviously in a foul mood. Before Baz could reply Isaac swept an arm over the table and sent glass and crockery scattering in all directions. Baz flinched as a spinning wine bottle cracked against his bare shin, the last of its contents slewing out in a pinkish arc across the sticky carpet tiles.

'Now get it cleared up! I don't pay you to slope off to your pit while there's still work to be done. On your hands and knees, boy, and pick up every bit.' And as Baz crouched down, fearful of cutting himself on the broken glass, Isaac walked past him, pausing in his stride to deliberately grind a shattered plate of half-eaten curry into the floor with his boot heel.

Baz spent the rest of the day trying to catch up on his other chores. To make matters worse, the divers decided to eat early that evening. Baz was unprepared, and the meal that he served up was nothing more than a hurriedly thrown together mess of corned beef and rice. He wheeled the trolley into the dining area and found that he had a plate too many. Moko was missing.

When Baz returned from delivering Preacher John's food, the three brothers were discussing the subject of Moko.

'What the hell was he thinking?' Amos was leaning forward at the table, questioning Luke.

'God knows.' Luke shook his head. 'One minute he was on deck, calm as you like. Next minute – soon as the gangplank was down – he was off. Shoved the women out of the way and made a run for it. By the time I realized what was happening, he'd gone. Never came back.'

The men sat in silence for a few moments as Baz distributed the food.

'So he was all right up until then?' said Amos.

Luke thought about it. 'Bit quiet, I s'pose. But then he never says anything anyway, so it's hard to tell. He looked pretty miserable last night, though. Anybody else notice that? In fact he's been a bit off for a day or two now.'

'Don't think he liked the old man's trick with the rabbits much,' said Amos.

'Who, Moko?' said Luke. 'He's done a lot worse than that in his time. And with bigger things than rabbits – if you know what I mean. Bit late in the day to start losing his bottle.'

'Maybe he decided he'd had enough,' said Isaac.

'What are you saying? That he was right? You reckon maybe it was against his religion, sacrificing little bunnies? The bloke went soft on us. He's left us in a ruddy hole, I know that much. We need four on the boat for diving.'

Baz retreated from the table and took up his place by the kitchen door.

'Soddin' hell.' Amos stared at his plate in disgust. 'What's this muck? Wish we hadn't got rid of the other kid now. At least the fat creep could make a decent hash.'

'Maybe we could do with another change of cook,' said Luke.

Isaac looked across at Baz. 'Maybe you're right. In fact maybe we need to have a general shake-up while we're about it. There's at least three or four we could do with getting rid of. Too big, some of 'em – it's time we got it sorted.'

Baz felt a cold lurch in his stomach. He kept staring straight ahead.

'Better talk to the old man, then,' said Amos.

'Hey – I don't have to ask his permission over every little detail,' Isaac muttered. 'And I don't have to keep dancing to his tune either.'

'No?' Amos sounded unconvinced. 'That'll be a first, then. I wouldn't fancy taking him on. And I don't see you doing it either.'

'Yeah, well. Maybe there's a few other things round here I'm thinking of changing . . .' Isaac's voice tailed off, as though he'd intended to say more and then thought better of it.

Baz listened, trying to get some spit into the dryness of his mouth. Boys were about to be got rid of – at least half of them shipped back to the mainland! And just like Cookie they might never get there . . .

'Seen the water today?' Luke moved on to another subject. 'I was looking at it when me and Moko took the women over – Jesus, I still can't believe he's done a runner . . . But that line of blue has moved closer. I mean, it's gone back a bit since last weekend, but not as far back as the week before. That means it's gradually shifting towards us. There's gotta be a tide out there – slow tide coming this way.'

'Yeah, it's working,' said Amos. 'And so the old man's been proved right. We've been here nearly two years now, and this is the first sign of any clear water. And when does it start to happen? The very day he makes a proper sacrifice to God. You can't argue with it.'

Isaac looked the other way and snorted. 'It would have happened in any case, you idiots.'

'So when does he say we can take a look out there?' Luke was still talking about diving. 'I'm getting fed up with hanging around.'

'Soon as the water clears above Skelmersley, he told me,' said Amos. 'It could be deeper over that way than it is here, and we don't know the area. Can't risk fooling around till we can see what we're doing down there. We have to wait for his say-so. Wait for the signs. Anyway, it's Sunday tomorrow, and the old man's got another service planned. Yeah. Special service. Special offer. This week only.' Amos chuckled and raised his glass. 'Here's hoping his prayers are answered.'

'Oh, give it a rest.' Isaac seemed agitated. 'You sound like you really believe his crap. We used to have a proper business here. A proper business. And I didn't care what I had to do when it *was* just business. But now it's all this ruddy nonsense. The old man's losing it.' He stood up as though to bring the conversation to a close.

But then Amos said something more. 'We're in this

together, Isaac, or we're not in it at all. And I'm with the old man. For better or worse we've done everything he's told us to. And it's working. So what's your problem? You can't go against him – nobody can. And you can't back out now, or do a runner like Moko. Not just over a couple of bleedin' rabbits.'

'I couldn't give a toss about rabbits,' said Isaac. 'But I can see where this is going – and it's bloody insane. Worse than that, it's a waste of time.'

Amos shrugged. 'Hey, you're the one that brings 'em over here for him. Don't forget that.'

Brings who over here? Baz didn't understand what was being said.

'Listen' – Isaac turned to go – 'he can chuck rabbits on a bonfire by the crateload for all I care, and chuck himself on as well. But when it comes to . . . the other things . . . and all this waiting around for "signs" . . . we're wasting time, is what we're doing. Losing trade and wasting time. Gah – I've had enough of it.' He stormed off.

The two younger brothers, Luke and Amos, remained for a while.

'I'm starting to wonder about him,' said Amos. 'He's not gonna try something stupid, is he?'

'Nah. He's all yak. Isaac knows who's boss around here.'

Baz had been so rushed that he'd not yet had time to take any food up to Nadine and Steffie. Once Luke and Amos had left the table he grabbed a couple of cans of beans from the kitchen and hurried upstairs to the next floor.

The door of the art room was open, and he saw that the two girls were sitting at the window, staring out at the dying day. They turned their heads towards him as he came in.

'Sorry,' he said. 'Couldn't get away till now. I've brought you some food, though. Here.' He crossed the room and put the cans of beans on the windowsill.

'Thanks,' said Nadine. 'We're starving.' She looked at the cans. 'Still on rations then, are we?'

'I've been told to give you what everyone else gets.' The words came out more defensively than Baz had intended, and so he added, 'But I'll see if I can smuggle something extra next time.'

'It's OK.' Nadine smiled at him. 'It's not your fault. And anyway, it won't be for much longer. Aunt Etta'll be coming back over on Monday, and we're gonna tell her what's been going on – how we've been treated. Stuck up here like prisoners . . . getting yelled at by those horrible men if we so much as show our faces. What have we done wrong? That's what we want to know. Why's everything changed? And what's happened to Preacher John? We haven't even seen him yet. I can't believe that he even knows about this. But anyway, we've had enough. We're going home as soon as we can.'

'Yeah,' said Steffie. 'And that lot are gonna get a right earful once Aunt Etta gets back. She's *fierce* when she wants to be.'

'Listen . . .' Baz scratched his head as he sought for the right words. 'Um . . . I don't wanna scare you . . . but I'm not so sure she's coming back. Your aunt, I mean. See, I'm wondering if maybe Preacher John planned it this way. Planned it just to get you here . . .'

'What?' Nadine didn't react with alarm, just puzzlement. 'Why would he do that?'

Her face was half in shadow as the evening light fell across it, bright sparkles in the corners of her eyes. She looked more beautiful than ever. Baz simply couldn't tell her what he was thinking – it was too awful, too shocking. *A special offer*, Amos had said. *A very special service*. And Isaac had brought these girls over on Preacher John's orders . . .

'Oh, I dunno.' Baz back-pedalled, tried to keep his voice from shaking. 'I've probably got it all wrong. Yeah, I'm probably wrong. But you got no idea what these guys are really like. And Preacher John's the worst of the lot. So just . . . just try and keep out of the way, that's all.' He'd only added to the girls' confusion, he knew that, but he could say no more. Not yet. 'Here . . .' He searched his pockets. 'I brought you a couple of proper spoons.'

When he got back to the slob room, he found that the others had been waiting for him.

'Hey, he's here! Come on, Baz. We're gonna do it!' Amit grabbed his arm.

'What?' Baz looked with bewilderment at the excited faces around him.

'We're gonna build the bomb! Tonight's the night!'

'Yesss!' Jubo and Robbie were jumping about, hardly able to contain themselves. Baz, dragged from the darkness of his own thoughts, felt as though he'd entered a noisy playground. He wanted to tell the boys everything he'd learned today, but saw that it would have to wait. He allowed himself to be hustled down to the jakes, where Gene and Ray were already kneeling among assorted bottles and explosives. The ragged curtain had been tied back, so that light from the main room spilled across the tiled floor, and in the middle of that floor stood the huge pressure cooker, with its lid propped up against it.

'Good. You're back.' Gene grinned up at him, and even in his face Baz could see a kind of childish excitement – a kid with a new toy.

'Right, gentlemen. Let us begin.' Gene picked up one of the big Coke bottles. 'We've only got about twenty minutes before Hutchinson's s'posed to turn up, so we're gonna have to take it in turns to keep a lookout. Coupla minutes each. Go on, Jube, take first watch.'

'No way, man,' said Jubo. 'I's stayin' here.'

Gene sighed. 'I don't care who goes first, but I'm not starting till we've got a lookout.'

'Well, OK.' Jubo gave in. 'But two minutes, and another guy better show.' He disappeared through the doorway.

'Right,' said Gene. 'First we're gonna get the water out of the bottles.' He tipped the Coke bottle upside down. 'Tear me off a bit of gaffer tape, Ray, like I told you. OK?'

'Yeah.' Ray had a roll of black plastic tape at the ready.

Gene picked up a wine cork that lay on the floor. There was a needle sticking out of it.

He pierced the upside-down plastic bottle, as near to the cap as he could, then gently began to squeeze the bottle. A thin stream of liquid leaked out, fine as a miniature water pistol. Gene kept up a steady pressure and said, 'Gimme the bit of tape, Ray. Here, on my thumb.' As the last drops of water turned to spray, Gene quickly pressed the scrap of black tape over the hole.

'Phew,' he said. 'I caught a whiff of that. There you go.' He held up the partially crushed bottle for a moment, before placing it upright in the steel cauldron. 'So that's pure methane in there, yeah? No water left, and no air can get in. OK – one down, three to go. Somebody go and take over from Jubo.'

'I'll do it.' Amit left the washroom, and Jubo rushed back in a few seconds later, just as Gene picked up the second bottle.

'All quiet out there.'

Once the same operation had started for the third time, Baz took over from Amit. He figured that this way he wouldn't miss anything that he hadn't already seen.

The corridor was silent and empty as Baz began his watch – no sign of anyone about. It was pitch black down at the divers' end, and Baz felt an increased sense of something awful hanging over the place. He couldn't shake the thought of Nadine and Steffie from his head. *A special service*, Amos had said; *a very special offering* . . .

Baz pictured the altar down on the jetty . . . burning fires . . . flames . . . screams . . .

'OK. My turn.' Dyson's voice made Baz leap sideways in fright.

'Jesus, you made me jump!'

'Hey. Sorry.'

Baz hurried down through the deserted slob room and back into the jakes, his head still full of troubled images.

The circle of dimly lit faces surrounded Gene as he moved to the next stage.

'Right,' he said. 'So we've put all the bottles in. Now we do the cartridges. I reckon if we open maybe half of them and tip the gunpowder into the pot, then that'll set off the rest. Grab a couple each and pick the ends open. Pull out the wadding, and then tip everything else into the pot.'

There was a general scrabble as everyone took a couple of shotgun cartridges from the two square boxes. Baz looked curiously at the smooth cylindrical objects in his hand: orange plastic casing, shiny brass ends. They felt pleasurable to hold, a satisfying weight to them. These had been his passage over here, he thought, won by his father in a poker game. Were they now to be his means of escape? Baz used the blade of his penknife to pick experimentally at the rolled-over lip at the end of one of the cartridges, levering it up and back. Beneath that was a small plastic disc, then some tightly packed wadding, like cotton wool. He pulled this out and gently tipped some of the remaining contents into his hand. Black gunpowder and a stream of little balls of lead. So tiny, they were, for such a deadly purpose. Baz sniffed at his palm and was instantly reminded of firework nights . . . sitting on his dad's shoulders . . . watching all the wonderful lights. His baby sister, Lol, sitting on Mum's shoulders and looking the wrong way completely, staring not at the

352

fireworks but at the moon . . . 'Look at *that* one, Mum . . . look at *that* one' . . .

'Come on. Don't muck about with the stuff. Just get it in the pot.' Gene was giving out orders. Baz quickly opened the second cartridge and knelt by the pressure cooker. As he added his small contribution to the mix, he took the opportunity to brush a forearm across his eyes, glad of the semi-darkness.

'Last ingredient,' said Gene, and dragged the ammunition box towards him, the metal case scraping across the gritty floor. He undid the hasps, flipped up the lid and drew out a long folded belt of machine-gun bullets. Baz had never seen such a thing in real life. He rubbed at his watery eyes again, and caught the sparkle of brass, the rows of bullets like teeth or miniature rockets, each neatly held in place by its clip.

'Are we gonna take those apart as well?' said Robbie.

'Nope. We're just gonna add them for good luck.' Gene lowered the belt into the cauldron, using both hands to weave it around the upright bottles.

'OK,' he said. 'So now we've got methane, gunpowder, shotgun cartridges and M sixty ammo. If that lot goes up, then it's gonna be a bloody big bang. *But* . . . we have to try and make sure it does go up, and that's where this little baby comes in.'

Gene held up a small plastic bottle. It might have once contained nose-drops or body lotion.

'What's in there?' said Robbie.

'Lighter fuel. It's like a detonator.'

Gene took the cap off the little bottle, and then gently pushed the mouth of it over the end of the spark plug. He looked up as Dyson came back into the room.

'Hey – someone else's turn,' Dyson said. 'I bin out there for bleedin' ages.'

'Sorry,' said Gene. 'We got carried away. Anyway, we're almost done. Just keep an eye out through the doorway, someone – we'll risk the last couple of minutes. OK, I need four pairs of hands – Whoa-whoa-whoa. Get back, all of you. I'll tell you who they're gonna be. Me, for a start, 'cos I know what I'm doing. And Ray, 'cos this was his idea. Baz, 'cos he found the pressure cooker, and Jubo.'

'Why Jubo?'

''Cos without that arse of his we'd never have got enough friggin' methane, that's why.'

'Hah! Good old Jubo.'

'Right,' said Gene. 'The tricky bit. We've got to loosen the caps of the Coke bottles, but keep 'em pressed down so the gas doesn't escape, yeah? Then when I say go, we whip off the caps, grab the lid of the cooker and get it on there as quick as we can – tighten up the bolts before any of the gas leaks out. Anybody smells farts then we've been too slow.'

Baz and Jubo and Ray knelt down next to Gene and took a Coke bottle each.

'After three, then,' said Gene. 'One, two, three . . .'

Baz took the cap from his bottle, threw it aside and grasped the rim of the heavy lid. He lifted in unison with the others, and in less than two seconds the lid was sitting snugly on top of the circular steel drum.

'Bolts! Tighten the bolts! Quick as you can . . .'

Their hands flew, flipping the hinged bolts upwards

into their slots and spinning the T-shaped wing nuts until they met resistance. Tighter and tighter they turned the wing nuts, until the lid was well and truly clamped down.

'My God,' said Gene. 'We've done it.' He sat back on his haunches for a few moments, then got to his feet. The others followed suit, and the washroom was silent as all stared at the object in front of them.

It was impressive. The heavy vessel stood well over knee-high, and was almost as wide as it was tall. With its pressure gauge mounted on top, and the white ceramic spark plug protruding from the metal dome, it looked deeply purposeful. A mighty engine of destruction. A weapon of vengeance. If they could truly make it explode, then what could withstand such a blast?

'See, the gas'll mix with the air in there,' said Gene, 'now we've taken the tops off the Coke bottles. It'll all mingle up together. So when the detonator bottle explodes, it should be like a chain reaction—'

'Oi! What are you lot all doing down there?' A voice coming from the slob room.

Hutchinson! He was heading directly towards the jakes – his square bulk just metres away – ugly face screwed up in a frown . . .

Oh God, no! Baz was too stunned to move. He swayed to one side as someone squeezed past him. It was Ray, already through the door of the washroom.

'Hey, Hutchinson.' Ray stood in front of the capo. 'You haven't got another shower-head, have you? A proper one?'

'What? What are you talking about?' Hutchinson came to a halt.

'That old garden-hose thing we've got – it's had it. The holes are all blocked up. We can't get the shower to work.'

God, the kid was sharp. Baz gawped at Ray in total admiration. But Gene was making better use of the delay.

'Quick,' he hissed. 'Help me drag this thing into the cubicle. Get rid of those cartridge boxes – and block the doorway, some of you.'

'*Shower*-head?' Hutchinson glanced down at Ray. 'What the hell do you expect me to do about it, you little tosser?'

'Well, I just wondered – you know, being a capo – whether you could get hold of a new one for us?'

'Eh?' Hutchinson still looked confused, but he stepped round Ray and continued towards the jakes. Baz, finding his senses at last, crowded himself into the doorway with one or two of the others.

'Get out of the way.' Hutchinson was trying to peer into the washroom. 'Christ, it's like a chuffin' mother's meeting in here.' He shoved Baz aside. 'Move yourself, arsehole.'

'See . . .' Baz pointed towards the shower, trying to deflect Hutchinson's attention from the heavy scraping sounds in the end cubicle. 'It's all blocked up.'

Hutchinson stood just inside the washroom and looked over at the hosepipe arrangement that dangled above the shower tray.

'Tough,' he said. 'Get Gene to fix it. Where is he anyhow?'

'In here.' A muffled voice from the second cubicle.

'Then get yourself out of there. And everybody else – hop it. Get into your nighties and slob down. I'm putting the lights out now. Come on. Shift it.'

Hutchinson stood in the doorway as the boys trooped past him, seeming to deliberately position himself so that they had to brush against his sweaty body.

'Hurry it up, Gene.' Hutchinson left the jakes and walked back down through the slob room. As he passed Ray, he said, 'Sunday tomorrow. And we're in business, 'cos Steiner's just smashed that drain cover in. Fun time!' He gave a horrible little double click of his tongue.

CHAPTER
TWENTY-ONE

The sense of something awful being about to happen remained with Baz. He walked in silence amidst the other boys as they trooped along the jetty on their way to Sunday service. The capos and a couple of the divers were close behind, and to Baz it seemed as though he was one of a herd of cattle being driven out to pasture. Or perhaps to the slaughter-house . . .

He felt the heavy atmosphere weighing down on him, a dull and sticky heat that blanketed the surrounding grey waters in steam. The altar drew closer – so grotesque and sinister, now that its purpose was known. Branches and brushwood covered the stone tablet, piled higher even than before, and beyond that rose the tall wooden cross, smoke-blackened against the featureless sky.

Preacher John was already there, waiting. The lectern had been brought down from the assembly room, and he stood behind it, dressed all in black as usual, his huge crack-knuckled hands gripping the edges of the tilted bookrest.

The boys took their places, shuffling into two lines.

Baz glanced up and saw that Preacher John was looking directly at him.

Ivory coloured, the whites of his eyes were, as though pickled in vinegar. Pale-grey irises, pink-rimmed lids beneath thick gingery brows. Unblinking, cold, emotionless. Yet that gaze was deeply piercing, and once again Baz struggled to look away, feeling that his every thought was being read.

Crack!

An explosion! Baz had no time to react before it happened again. *Crack!* Gunfire!

From where, though? All the boys were ducking low, bumping against one another, staring wildly about. Baz looked briefly towards Preacher John, half expecting to find that someone had assassinated him.

But the preacher was very much alive. He raised his arms and shouted, 'Stay where you are! Face me!'

More confusion, the boys still lurching this way and that in panic. 'Face *me*, I said!' Preacher John roared out his order, and this time everyone obeyed. Baz resumed his former place, between Jubo and Dyson, and faced forward.

'Now then. Let's have those hymn books handed out.'

The gunshots had apparently come as no surprise to Preacher John. He pointed at Ray, standing at the furthest end of the front row, and said, 'You – get moving.'

Ray passed along the lines, handing out the copies of *Songs of Praise*. He looked ill, terrified, his skin unnaturally pale.

Baz risked a quick glance back towards the school

building. Had the shots come from there? Horrible thoughts surged through his head, and he tried to pick out the windows of the art room . . .

No, it was impossible. Not even Preacher John could be that insane. But then Baz remembered Amos's words once again, about the special service. The special offer . . .

'Hymn number three-three-one. "Thine Are All the Gifts".'

> *'Thine are all the gifts, O God,*
> *Thine the broken bread:*
> *Let the naked feet be shod,*
> *And the starving fed.'*

Baz had never felt less like singing. The words stuck to his dry tongue, and judging by the feeble croaking of those around him, he wasn't the only one having difficulty. The hymn droned on, but Baz was scarcely present. He tried to hear once again the echo of the distant gunshots; tried to judge from which direction they had come. *Was* it the school? This was crazy.

'O Lord, we know that you hear our prayers . . .' Preacher John had begun his sermon. 'The clear waters draw ever closer, by your hand, and so we continue to lay before you all that we have. Whatever it may please thee to receive, so we shall give, even to our own. And for whatever is given to us, we shall offer our thanks in return.'

Preacher John leaned forward across the lectern. 'Yes, my sons! We understand that it is not enough to merely pray for deliverance. When such deliverance comes, we must offer up proper acknowledgement. From the deep comes the bounty we seek, and from the heavens the blessed rain. To the deep, then, and to the heavens, we send tokens of our gratitude.'

Something was happening on the other side of the gathering. Baz's vision was partially blocked, but he could see Luke moving towards the altar. Luke's back was hunched, his arms unnaturally straightened in front of him. He was pushing a wheelbarrow. Had he only just arrived? The wheelbarrow came to a halt, right at the front of the congregation. Baz saw Ray's jolt of alarm, a jerky sideways movement, his skinny shoulders bumping against Amit.

Baz stood on tiptoe, desperate to know what was in the wheelbarrow, yet terrified of discovering what that might be. He caught a glimpse of white . . . white like a T-shirt . . . white like a blouse . . .

No, not T-shirt material. It looked . . . hairy. White fur?

Preacher John was lighting a firebrand, one of the things that Gene had made. It was just a bit of oily rag wound round the end of a pole. Preacher John thrust the smoking torch towards the altar.

This time the fire caught quickly. A deep *whoosh* of ignition, and the flames were instantly leaping up, crackling and spitting on the still air. In seconds the altar was fully ablaze, the whole great pile of brushwood roaring furiously, tall yellow flames licking at the cross itself.

Preacher John stepped down off the platform. He nodded in signal to Luke, and the two of them leaned over the wheelbarrow, stooping forward to reach for whatever lay in there.

Legs . . . hooves . . . white fur. As the men hoisted the body over the lip of the barrow, a horned head appeared, and Baz recognized the creature at last. A goat. It was Old Bill.

Baz's throat tightened so that he was struggling for breath, his lungs heaving, dizziness sweeping over him. The sight of the small white goat was shocking, dangled upside down by its legs in the grasp of the two men. An awful image. Yet it wasn't what Baz had feared or expected.

Preacher John muttered something, and he and Luke began swinging the dead animal, once . . . twice . . .

At the height of the third swing the goat seemed to poise in mid air, its head and neck straining towards the congregation, its mouth open as though it would speak. In that moment of stillness Baz saw a glistening piece of meaty tissue protruding from the goat's forehead, long and tapered, like an extra tongue. Pinkish grey. Then the body of Old Bill swung downwards and away, flying from the grasp of the two men, limbs flailing, an awkward animated shape against the bright flames.

Baz stared into the roaring depths of the fire as Preacher John's voice rose in incantation.

'O Lord, in as much as it pleases thee to accept this beast, our sacrifice today . . .'

Our sacrifice today – Old Bill. A goat. But what would be next? Baz tried to breathe through his mouth rather than his nose. He'd already caught the first whiff of burning hair, acrid and unmistakable; the stench of it carried on a hot breeze that had sprung up from nowhere.

'Come on. Don't hang about.'

Baz hustled the boys up the hill. If he was going to get them safely to the library, then first they needed to enter the building unseen. He looked behind him. The men were still down on the jetty. Preacher John and Luke and Amos stood in a group looking out to sea. Isaac was walking away from them, hands in his suit pockets, head down. Steiner and Hutchinson were waiting to one side of the altar, half hidden by clouds of swirling black smoke, unable to leave until they had been given their weekly orders. Good.

Through the glass doors of the main entrance . . . down the corridor . . . and into the kitchen. The boys seemed stunned, disorientated. It was like trying to herd moths.

'God . . . poor Old Bill. What the hell was the point of that?'

'Never mind about Old Bill – what's next?'

'*Who's* next, you mean.'

'Jesus, man . . .'

Baz kept things moving. He shoved the back door open and hurried everyone through. 'Ray, take 'em on up. Listen, I'm gonna see if I can get you some food. I'll leave it on the staircase later on. Might just be left-overs, though. OK? Don't come down until it's dark at least. Go on – go go go.'

Baz pulled the kitchen door shut, leaned against it for a second. God, he felt dizzy. He went over to one of the plastic buckets, knelt beside it and scooped some water onto his face.

Washing, cleaning, refuelling the generator. Baz carried out his Sunday duties automatically. He felt alone, abandoned, and he longed to be up in the library with the others. They would be talking about what they'd seen, taking comfort from being together. He had no one to talk to, and no one to help chase away his dreadful imaginings.

Yet he forced himself to keep working. If he was to avoid Cookie's fate then he needed to concentrate on the Sunday meal. A marrow had been brought over from the mainland, and so Baz attempted to follow one of the cookbook recipes, splitting the vegetable in half and stuffing it with rice and tinned mincemeat. It was a disaster. The marrow collapsed into a leaky heap, its dark green skin splitting open so that the whole meal was swimming in a pool of pale liquid. A dog wouldn't eat it.

But by now the Eck brothers were in the dining area, and Baz's only choice was to serve up what he had.

'Soddin' hell. It gets worse.' Amos looked at his plate. He splashed at the food with his fork, dibbled it around a bit and pushed the plate away. 'Come back Fatso, I say.' He reached for the wine bottle instead.

'Aye, well. There are going to be some changes this week.' Isaac glared at Baz as he took a forkful of his own food. 'Come Tuesday or Wednesday we shall be saying a few goodbyes.'

Baz felt his heart jump at this remark, but there was

no time to stop and think about it. He had other things to do first. Preacher John would be waiting for his dinner. Baz lifted the aluminium tray from the food trolley, turned to go . . .

. . . and there was Preacher John, standing right behind him. Baz stepped backwards in fright, and bumped into the food trolley. He stumbled, but managed to regain his balance. Upright again, he held the tray out to Preacher John.

'Er . . . I was just . . .'

Preacher John looked down at the dish of watery mince as though it were river-mud. 'Isaac is right for once,' he said. 'There will have to be some changes this week. Take that muck away from me and get out of my sight.'

Baz did as he was told. He put the tray back on the trolley and wheeled it towards the kitchen door. But here he hesitated. Should he go into the kitchen, out of Preacher John's sight, or stand here and wait as usual? He decided to wait for more definite orders.

The Eck brothers were plainly surprised to see their father. They watched him in silence as he circled the table, Isaac in particular looking darkly sullen and suspicious.

'Aye, there will be changes!' Preacher John's voice boomed around the dining area. 'And we have waited long enough. The day is upon us, my sons, and a momentous day indeed!' He laid his hands on Luke's broad shoulders. 'The waters are finally clear over Skelmersley. Our prayers have been heard. Our sacrifice has been accepted.'

Luke twisted his shaven head in order to look up at

Preacher John. 'Clear?' he said. 'So we can take the boat out that way? Give it a try?'

'Yes, Luke.' Preacher John beamed down at him as though he were giving his son permission to go and play. 'You can. I have been down on the jetty all this time, praying, and I have seen a vision of what will be. Such a vision! I cast my nets across the water, like Simon Peter himself, and how those nets overflowed – filled with riches. The bounty of the Lord!' He raised his hands and gazed up towards the dusty ceiling tiles. 'And, Lord, if this vision be true, then I shall give thanks with the ultimate sacrifice. The ultimate! All that I have to offer shall be thine!'

'There!' Amos banged his hand on the table, caught up in Preacher John's enthusiasm. 'You were right all along, then, Father!' He looked meaningfully across at Isaac. 'The power of prayer.'

'Aye. Prayer and sacrifice.' Preacher John lowered his arms. 'And by tomorrow night you will see how right I am.'

But Isaac's face was as sour as ever. 'That's all very well,' he said, 'but you're forgetting about Moko. We're a man down now. We need two to dive and two to work the boat. It's not safe otherwise. And so all these wonderful riches and ultimate sacrifices are gonna have to wait a bit longer. Till we can get a replacement.'

'Ah, yes.' Preacher John seemed suddenly deflated. He gave a heavy sigh. 'Of course. We need a full crew. Isaac's right again, then, and we shall have to postpone our victory. Continue to have patience—'

'No!' Luke clearly had no patience at all. 'What

about . . . what about . . . you?' He looked up at Preacher John. 'I mean . . . couldn't you come out with us, Father? Just this once? To work the winch – or take the helm? It's not that hard.'

'Me?' Preacher John appeared insulted. 'You'd have *me* work on a salvage boat? No, I don't think so. My mission is here, praying for our salvation and communing with the Lord. I have nothing to do with the boat, nor anything that happens on it. The boat is Isaac's responsibility.'

Isaac had been sitting with his arms folded, scowling at his unfinished plate of food. But Baz saw the skipper's expression begin to change slightly, his narrowed eyes moving to the right, as if a new possibility had occurred to him.

'Deck work's not easy.' Isaac kept his head down as he spoke. He didn't look at Preacher John. 'Loading, and that. Swinging the nets onboard. It's heavy going. Yeah, and it can be dangerous too – takes a couple of good men to do it right. Young and strong. It's not everyone that's up to the job.'

'Hm.' Preacher John moved round to Moko's empty chair and pulled it out from the table. He sat on it sideways, one arm resting over the back.

'I see that you're trying to protect me, Isaac. And it would certainly be wiser to wait until we find a replacement for Moko. But that will take time. Meanwhile we ignore the will of God at our peril. Hm. Well. Let's suppose that I were to make an exception and come out with you tomorrow after all—'

'Yes!' Luke reached across the table and bumped knuckles with Amos.

'Good,' said Amos. 'You know, if the boat really is gonna be that loaded up, then I think maybe we'll need a tender.'

'A tender?' said Luke. 'But that'd mean another pair of hands . . .'

'So what about one of the capos? We could take Hutchinson maybe. Leave Steiner behind . . .'

Preacher John loudly cleared his throat to speak. '*If I were to make an exception and come out with you tomorrow, then it would have to be on Isaac's say-so. As he's already pointed out, I'm not used to hard labour and I'm not as young as I was. I wouldn't want to be a liability. Isaac – this decision is entirely up to you. Let me hear what you think.*'

'Yeah, well. I suppose if we were properly prepared . . .' said Isaac. He seemed to have brightened up, become more animated. 'Skelmersley's a good way off, and so it'd be a long hard day. We couldn't afford to waste time in the morning. Luke, you'd need to check all the equipment now, directly after we've finished here. See that the air tanks are full, the wetsuits are on board and the boat gassed up. Check the winch motor, and make sure there's plenty of petrol in it. Shove an extra can in the locker – maybe a can of diesel as well. I want that boat made ready this evening. Got it? No messing around in the morning – just straight up and away.'

'And what about a tender?' said Amos. 'Could come in handy. But that means dragging some kid along – one that's got a bit of sense. What d'you reckon? One of the capos?'

Isaac rubbed at his black beard. 'Hm. We could

take . . . Hutchinson, maybe. Make that ugly mongrel work for a change. Yeah, OK. Steiner can deal with these other snot-noses just for one day . . .'

Preacher John rose. With a vague wave of his fingers he indicated that the others should remain where they were. 'It seems that the question is settled then. Isaac, you're the skipper and so I shall leave the details to you. I'm sure I'm in capable hands.'

He flicked a speck of dust from the lapel of his long black coat, and walked away from the table. Before turning right towards the dark corridor Preacher John glanced across at Baz. It was only a brief look, but those eyes were as fierce and cruel as a hawk's, and once again Baz felt his insides begin to quake.

'Are you still here?' Preacher John's voice was a low growl. Baz could make no reply, but in any case the preacher had already passed by, leaving the faint scent of candle-smoke behind him. His footsteps made no sound at all as he disappeared into the gloom.

Luke let out a long breath. 'Bloody hell! The old man on the boat! *All* of us on the boat – the whole family. I can't believe it.'

'No, nor can I,' said Isaac.

And nor could Baz. It was the best chance they were ever likely to get, he was certain of that. As he cleared away the half-eaten plates of food, he was already thinking about the fishing boat, picturing it far out to sea, miles away from the island. All the Eck brothers onboard. And Preacher John as well, yanking at the starter motor . . .

But even better, Hutchinson would be there too! That was a last-minute bonus that couldn't have been predicted.

Back in the kitchen, Baz looked doubtfully at the remains of the marrow and mincemeat. He'd yet to take any food up to Nadine and Steffie. But how hungry would they have to be to eat this mess? Maybe if he drained off the liquid and gave it all a quick fry-up, it would taste better. It was something other than beans, anyway. Worth a try.

'Hey!' The back door of the kitchen opened and Ray stuck his head round. 'Is it safe to come back through? It's getting pretty dark out there – and we're starving!' More faces appeared in the doorway.

'What? Yeah – hang on. The divers have gone to their rooms, but I'll just check it's all clear. Grab yourselves some tins of food, while I have a look.'

Baz had almost forgotten about the boys up in the library, so many things were spinning around his head. There was nobody in the dining area, and so he waved the troop through.

'I could be another hour yet,' he whispered to Gene. 'Got lots to tell you. Were you OK up there?'

'Yeah, brilliant. See you later, then.'

The door of the art room was locked, or wedged somehow. Baz pressed down on the handle with his elbow, but it wouldn't open. He stood in the gloomy upstairs corridor, feeling like an idiot, a plate of hot food in each hand.

'Hey!' he shouted. 'Anybody in there?'

'Who's that?' Nadine's voice from the other side.

'It's me – Baz. What's wrong with the door?'

There was no reply, but Baz could hear activity just inside the art room. After a few scrapes and clunks, the door opened. Steffie was dragging one of the art stools back into the room. Nadine stood to one side. She was holding a broken wine bottle in one hand. Had there been an accident?

'What's going on?' Baz began to cross the dim room, intending to put the plates of food on the windowsill. There was still just enough light to see by, and as he passed Steffie he got a better look at her face: dirt-streaked, her eyes all red and watery – the girl had obviously been crying.

'Hey, what's the matter?' Baz took a couple more steps and put down the plates of food. Nadine was jamming the metal stool beneath the door handle, giving it a shove with her hip. She still had hold of the broken bottle.

'You're asking me what's the *matter*?' Nadine crossed the room. She jabbed the bottle towards the windows. 'After what happened down there today – that horrible . . . awful thing . . . and you're wondering what's the matter?'

Baz glanced through the open window. A moon-haze already shone on the endless expanse of water, glints of blue and green, a shimmering curve that stretched beyond the protruding crane and church tower all the way to the horizon. Over to the left stood the jetty. The altar and the cross were clearly visible, dark shapes against the failing light.

'Oh,' he said. 'You saw it, then. The sacrifice.'

'Yeah, we saw it.'

There was silence for a few moments.

'We thought . . . we thought it was nice at first. Watching you all down there. Singing hymns. We could hear you.' Nadine stood close to Baz, her free hand gripping the windowsill. 'But then we heard the shots, and we started to get . . . and then we saw the wheelbarrow . . . and that awful man. Preacher John. God, he's horrible! That poor animal. We just couldn't believe it.'

'Yeah. You know what? I wish you'd stop waving that blimmin' bottle around.' Baz edged away from Nadine.

'Sorry. Sorry . . . Hey, come on, Stef. It's OK. It's OK.' Nadine laid the jagged bottle on the windowsill and put an arm around Steffie's shoulders. 'Tomorrow we're out of here.'

The younger girl wasn't crying, though. She looked drained, exhausted, but her mouth was set firm and her voice was steady. 'I know,' she said. 'I'm OK, Nad. Just tonight to get through, and then we're gone.'

Baz had his doubts about this. He didn't believe that Preacher John had any intention of ever bringing Aunt Etta back to X Isle. But he said, 'You'd better eat something. Come on. You'll feel better.'

'Yeah.' Nadine gave a long sigh. 'Thanks.' She made no move towards the food. Instead she looked straight at Baz and said, 'What's going on here? I mean, it's like it's all just insane or something . . .'

Baz could see no point in lying. 'Well, that's just it,' he said. 'Preacher John *is* insane. I mean, madder than you could ever believe. He thinks he's like Moses, or someone from the Bible, and that if he prays – and makes sacrifices to God – then God'll reward him. He wants the water to clear so he can carry on diving and get richer. He reckons that if he makes enough sacrifices, then God's gonna do that for him. Or even make the floods go away. He talks to God, and he thinks that God talks to him.'

'Well, so do I talk to God,' said Nadine. 'I pray. Sometimes . . .'

'Yeah, but you don't make sacrifices. You don't throw goats and rabbits onto altars . . . or throw kids into the sea . . . you don't murder people—' Baz stopped. He was saying too much, too quickly.

'Kids into the *sea*?'

'Well . . . that's what we think.' Baz pulled back a little. 'It isn't Preacher John that actually does it, but it happens – and everything that happens around here is on his orders. Kids die. They disappear. They get shipped back to the mainland when the Ecks have had enough of them, and' – he shrugged – 'we're pretty sure they never get there.' He could find no way of making things sound any better than they were.

'Oh my God,' breathed Steffie. 'We knew something bad must be happening, but not . . . not that.'

'You haven't seen what they're really like,' said Baz.

'We were starting to guess. As soon as Aunt Etta left, everything changed. They all got nasty with us. And then, when we saw what happened today, we thought, OK, this place is wrong. We gotta get out of here. So we locked ourselves in to try and keep safe. Just till tomorrow.'

Baz didn't reply to that. After another few moments Steffie said, 'But she's not coming back, is she?'

'Who – Aunt Etta? Course she is.' Nadine sounded as though there was no doubt. 'She said she was coming back on Monday, and that's what she'll do.'

'Hey, I'm not a baby.' Steffie was defiant. 'I'm as old as Baz is, so you don't need to pretend to me. We're stuck here, aren't we? I know we are. And like Baz said before – it's almost like it's been planned this way.'

'What? How do you mean?'

'He *sent* for us.' Steffie's voice began to waver. She looked at Baz as she spoke, and in her hazel eyes he thought he saw something change, a moment of realization. 'Preacher John sent for us,' she said. 'And it wasn't just to be kind. I think he wanted us here.'

'Why? What good are we to him?'

'I don't know. But if he's really as crazy as Baz says he is, then maybe he's going to . . . going to . . .' Steffie sounded really scared now.

'To what?'

'To kill us.'

Baz could feel his mouth hanging open. He knew that Steffie was watching him, reading his reactions, searching for the truth.

'Like the goat . . .' Steffie's voice sank to a whisper. 'Like maybe we're next . . .'

'Whaaat?' Nadine sat down – or rather collapsed – onto the one remaining stool. She looked at Baz, helpless, speechless.

Her T-shirt glowed white in the dim light of the room, and Baz shivered, remembering the wheelbarrow, the little patch of white showing. And then there was that awful thing that Preacher John had said, about how he would be offering God the ultimate gift, the ultimate sacrifice. That had to be a human life. Had to be.

But Baz couldn't bring himself to tell Steffie that he thought she was right. He avoided looking at her, and searched instead for words of comfort, grabbing at whatever came into his head. 'Nobody knows for sure what Preacher John's thinking,' he said, 'or what he's gonna do next. Listen, though . . . it's gonna be OK. You're gonna be OK. Whatever Preacher John's got planned, it's not gonna happen.' Baz stumbled recklessly on. 'We've got a plan of our own. Yeah. Been working on it for weeks. We're gonna get rid of the lot of them.'

God, that sounded so stupid. And Baz could see the surprise on the girls' faces, the doubt.

'Get *rid* of them?' Steffie didn't try to hide her disbelief. 'How?'

'Doesn't matter how. You don't have to know.'

Because if I told you, thought Baz, *it wouldn't make you feel any better. We've built a bomb out of farts and gunpowder, and we're gonna blow the Ecks right out of the water. Oh really, Baz? That's OK, then. Our troubles are over.*

'Look, you're gonna have to trust us,' he said. 'We've been planning this for a long time. So just keep doing what you're doing and it'll be OK. Lock your-selves in and wait. You'll be safe enough.'

'All right, then,' said Nadine. 'So . . . when's this plan gonna happen? Will it be soon?' She seemed less sceptical than Steffie, more ready to believe. Or perhaps more desperate. Something in the way that she looked up at Baz made him want to act the hero. At any rate, the words came out before he could stop them.

'Tonight,' he said. 'We're gonna do it tonight. I promise.'

CHAPTER
TWENTY-TWO

'Tonight?' said Gene. 'Hang on a minute, Baz. We only just finished building the bloody thing yesterday!'

The wind-up torch had been switched to lantern mode. It stood on the floor between Gene's mattress and what had once been Cookie's, the pale tube of light a focal point for the boys who sat around it. The ring of solemn faces looked eerie, illuminated from beneath like kids at Halloween.

'It has to be tonight.' Baz had thought his arguments through as best he could before returning to the slob room. Most of the boys had still been awake, surprised at his urgent demand for a meeting. They were willing enough to gather round the clockwork lantern and listen, but Baz knew they were going to take some convincing.

'OK,' he said. 'I heard a lot of things today. First off, the Ecks are going out on a big trip tomorrow – over to Skelmersley. And Isaac wants the boat got ready this evening. He told Luke to make sure that everything was done, so they could be away first thing, yeah? Far as I can see, they got no reason to be messing around with gear tomorrow, or opening that locker again. In fact Isaac told Luke to put a coupla spare cans of fuel in there tonight. Petrol and diesel.'

'Petrol?' said Gene. 'You sure?'

'That's what he said. Next thing – get this – Preacher John's going out with them to work the winch. Yeah, really. And it gets even better. They're taking Hutchinson too. That means that there's only gonna be Steiner left here with us. Now when are we ever gonna get another chance like that?'

'Wow,' said Robbie. 'Well, we can deal with Steiner all right, if it's just him left. He's half dead on a Monday morning in any case.'

'What do they want Hutchinson for?' Gene sounded cautious.

'Preacher John thinks it's gonna be a big haul. The water's clear over Skelmersley way, and that's where they're going. They want Hutchinson for a tender or something.'

'A tender?' said Ray. 'What's that?'

'Dunno. Someone who attends?'

'I thought a tender had something to do with old railway engines,' said Gene. 'But Preacher John . . . are you sure he's going too?'

'Yup. The lot of 'em.' Baz leaned forward, bringing his face into the light so everyone could see him. 'The boat's all made up and ready for the morning, they're off on a long trip, and Preacher John and Hutchinson are going with them. It's never gonna get any better than that.'

'Maybe.' Gene clasped his hands together, brought

them up to his chin. 'But I dunno. It doesn't make it any less dangerous if it goes wrong and they all come back.'

'Well, there's other reasons why it has to be tonight.' Baz sought for a way of making his next point. 'This isn't just the best chance, it's the *only* one. They're getting rid of us. Some of us, anyway. I've heard Isaac say it a coupla times now, and Preacher John too. He wants shot of us 'cos we're getting too big. Or he just wants new kids so he can get paid more, or maybe he just doesn't need us any more. But we're done. By Tuesday or Wednesday half of us aren't gonna be here.'

'God. You mean sent back to the mainland?' Dyson looked across at Baz.

'Who says you're ever gonna reach the mainland, Dyse? Did Cookie? Or that Greek kid?' There was silence as this remark sank in.

'Yeah, I bin thinking about that,' said Robbie. 'And I bin wondering about that other kid too. The one that was supposed to have been sent back the same Saturday I came across. Everybody was still talking about it when I got here, this kid Sammy whose arm got broken. But nobody came off the boat on the mainland that day. I know, 'cos I was there.'

'He coulda been dropped off somewhere else,' said Dyson. 'Up the coast.'

'Funny how it *always* somewhere else, yeah?' said Jubo. 'Funny how every guy land up here, they always from da same place, Linley Top, but nobody ever get off da boat there.'

A new realization began to spread through the group.

'So . . . everyone here's from the same bit of main-land?' said Ray. 'Linley Top?'

A general nodding of heads.

'And did anyone ever actually see any kid get off the *Cormorant* on the day that they got on it?'

Silence.

'Hang on,' said Dyson. 'They send you back to the mainland as a punishment. That's what they threaten you with. But now you're saying *nobody* ever gets there? Why?'

Gene said, 'Think about it. Anyone who gets back to the mainland, they're gonna talk about this place, yeah? X Isle. They're gonna say what it's really like. And if people know what it's really like, who's gonna come here? Who's gonna pay to send their kids here if they know the truth? Nobody. And where's Preacher John gonna get his workers from then?'

Jubo said, 'So once you here, you done, man. No way out alive.'

'Jesus . . .'

'Yeah, and I'll tell you another thing,' said Baz. 'Those girls are never gonna get back alive either. Preacher John's got plans for next Sunday. He says he's gonna make the ultimate sacrifice. First it was the rabbits, then it was Old Bill. So what's next? The ultimate has to be a person, doesn't it? You know what I thought today . . . when Luke showed up with the wheelbarrow . . .' Baz could still hardly bring himself to say it. 'I thought it was Nadine in there.' He looked around the circle and knew he'd hit home. 'Yeah. And some of you did too. So if we're gonna save them from . . . from . . . what we saw today, then tonight's our only—'

'Right. That's it.' Ray didn't appear to need any more convincing. 'We gotta do it.'

'Yeah, but hang on a minute,' said Dyson. 'We're talking about serious stuff here. If this plan doesn't work, they'll just come sailing back and kill us. I mean, we could probably hide out for a little while, but they'd get us in the end.'

'Yeah,' said Robbie. 'We got no plan B, that's the trouble. If the bomb goes off, they might be dead. But if it doesn't, we definitely are.'

'We're definitely dead anyway,' said Amit. 'Unless we do something about it tonight.'

'OK,' said Ray. 'So we need a plan B. What about the dinghy?'

'Huh?'

'Say once the main boat was gone, we pack up the dinghy. We break into the storeroom and get a load of food, yeah? And put it in the dinghy. Then we keep watch. If we see the salvage boat coming back, we get into the dinghy and hop it. Gene? What do you reckon?'

Baz looked at Ray in wonder. The guy just seemed to be able to pull ideas out of nowhere. And since the mention of Nadine and Steffie, he seemed to have become instantly committed, instantly forceful. He'd made up his mind that this was going to happen.

'Hey,' said Amit. 'That's not bad. Seeing what you've just been through.'

Ray looked embarrassed, irritated almost.

'What?' said Baz. He was obviously out of the loop. 'What's he just been through?'

'Capos got him,' said Gene. 'Soon as we came down from the library. We broke the tin-opener.'

'What the hell're you on about?' Baz couldn't make any sense of what Gene was saying.

'We got back from hiding in the library, yeah? And we were starving. But none of the tins we took were ring-pull, and we broke the bloody tin-opener on the first one. So Ray said he was gonna go back to the kitchen to find you, see if you could get us another opener. I said don't be daft, but he wouldn't have it. He was off down the corridor before anyone could stop him. I watched him go – shouted after him. Next thing you know Steiner's come round the corner and grabbed him.'

'Christ, Ray!' Baz's head was reeling. 'What did they do to you? They didn't . . . put you down the hole?'

'No! Do I *look* like I've been down the blimmin' hole? I keep telling everyone that nothing happened! It was nothing. I managed to talk my way out of it, OK? Just leave it.' Ray was obviously exasperated, tired of having to explain. 'We got more important things to worry about than stupid capos. So forget about it. Come on, Gene. The dinghy idea – what do you reckon?'

Ray had deflected attention from himself, and though Baz had a hundred questions he wanted to ask, he could see they would have to wait.

'Er . . . well . . .' Gene blinked. 'Yeah, maybe. We got binoculars. We know the Seagull motor works. I suppose if we kept watch and saw that everything had gone pear-shaped, we could make a run for it in the dinghy. There'd be a chance of getting to the mainland without the Ecks catching us – or even seeing us. And being on the mainland's better'n being dead, I guess. Just about.'

'OK, then,' said Ray. 'We got a plan B. So let's do it.'

Robbie said, 'Hey, why not just take the dinghy anyway? We could get away in it right now if we wanted to! Tonight!'

Gene shook his head. 'Engine's locked in the store-room now that it's been fixed. We'll have to break the door down to get at it, and that's too risky with every-one around. Better to wait till they've gone. Then there'd only be Steiner to deal with . . .' His voice tailed off, and he sat staring into the lantern light.

The dinghy was the key. It provided an escape route, and it gave the boys a lot more confidence. They talked for another hour, picking apart this detail and that – what they would do with Steiner once they got him alone, how much petrol they were likely to need in order to get to the mainland. The one real risk was that the bomb would be discovered before the divers left. But even here they figured out that there might be a slim chance of escape. They could keep an eye on the jetty first thing in the morning, watch the divers as they boarded the boat, and if there was any sign of trouble they could run for it. Maybe hide up in the library, then creep down to the shore after nightfall, and still get away in the dinghy. Somehow . . .

Finally Ray said, 'Too much talk. Come on. Let's just do it.' He was impatient, pushing for a decision.

'Well, I'm in,' said Baz. 'The bomb's our only choice, far as I can see. If we wait any longer we've had it.'

'Count me in, man.' Jubo smacked a fist into his

palm. 'Me get a pop at Steiner, an' it all be worth it.'

'Yeah, OK. I'm for it,' said Amit.

'Me too,' said Robbie.

They all agreed. Even Dyson, probably the most cautious of all, said, 'Ah, screw it. We're dead anyway. Might as well go down fighting.'

'Yeah. Well said, Dyse. Let's have 'em.' Amit was looking belligerent, ready for anything. 'Gene?'

Gene had been quiet for a while. The scheme would never have got this far if it hadn't been for him, yet now he appeared to be hesitating.

'I dunno. It's not just about . . . whether it's gonna work or not. Or whether we get caught or don't get caught. I mean, this is murder, right? We're talking about murder here.'

'It's not murder,' said Amit. 'It's bleedin' *war*. It's whatdyacallit . . . *freedom* fighting. Yeah. Somebody comes at you with a gun, and you know they're gonna kill you, then you got a right to smack them first. That's how I see it.'

'But are we really sure that Preacher John *is* planning to kill us, that's the thing. See—'

'You know what, Gene?' Amit interrupted him. 'Wanna hear what I think? You're starting to back out 'cos you figure you're better off as you are. Better off than the rest of us. 'Cos as long as you just sit tight, you're gonna be safe.'

'What do you mean? Why am I better off than the rest of you?'

'You're not in any danger, that's why. Not really. Not like we are. Kids can get killed round here, drowned, dumped in the sea, chucked on an altar . . . whatever.

384

But it's never gonna be you, is it? They'll never touch you, 'cos you're too smart. Too useful to them. Whatever happens to the rest of us, you'll always be OK, yeah? Safe, like you've always been.'

Amit had hit on some truth, and it obviously stung. Gene stood up.

'Safe? You better hope I'm safe, Amit, 'cos if anything happens to me you've got *no* friggin' chance. Yeah. And if we ever get out of this *safe*, it'll be down to me, not you! I gotta try and think of everything. If we left the thinking to you, we'd all be stuffed! Right, then. I've had enough. Let's do it.'

Gene grabbed the lantern and started off towards the washroom.

'What, you mean now?' Baz called after him.

'Yeah, now.'

Amit looked at Baz and pulled a bug-eyed face. 'Result,' he said.

CHAPTER TWENTY-THREE

The pathway down to the jetty was steep, broken up by shadows from the hazy moon, and the pressure cooker was heavy. There were carrying handles, but Baz and Ray found it difficult to walk in time. The huge receptacle rocked around alarmingly.

'Hey – try and keep it steady.' Gene was following behind. 'I don't want lighter fuel splashing up onto the plug.'

'Sorry.'

Dyson was last man in the chain of lookouts. He remained halfway along the jetty, watching from above as Baz and Ray carefully descended the bank of rubble. They staggered and slithered among the loose lumps of brick and concrete. God, it was awkward. Gene was already standing on the gangplank below, anxiously regarding their progress.

'Keep it upright! Upright!' His voice was a hoarse whisper.

'For Chrissake, Gene. We're trying . . .'

The night was hot and airless, and by the time Baz and Ray reached the gangplank they were both sweating.

'Let's just put it down a second.' They stood the

pressure cooker on the end of the planks and took a breather. Baz wiped his forehead and glanced back up at Dyson – a shadowy figure, just visible against the night sky. So far, so good.

The slap of the waves against the jetty seemed amplified in the darkness, everything sharp and clear, as though a thousand sea creatures were feeding down there, sucking and slurping at the island itself. The effect was eerily hypnotic, and Baz jumped as another sound cut through the still air – a high whistling cry . . . *mee . . . mee . . . ma-mee-mee . . .*

A warning signal!

'What the hell's that?' Ray's eyes showed white in the darkness. The boys stood motionless, listening. There it was again, more distant now – *mee mee-mee* – fading into the night.

'Christ,' said Gene. 'I think it's a seagull.'

A seagull? Baz couldn't remember when he'd last heard such a thing, or where. Certainly never round here, not even before the floods.

'Yeah. It's a gull. Weird. Come on, though – we got no time for that.' Gene wanted to press on. Baz and Ray began to edge their way across the planking, facing each other over the lid of the pressure cooker. It was a short journey but an anxious one, the planks rising and falling unpredictably with the motion of the boat.

'Stay where you are a minute, Ray,' said Gene. 'Come on, Baz. Get in the boat.' Baz let go of the handle he was holding and jumped onto the deck.

'OK? Let's lift her down then.' The angle was awkward, but Baz and Gene managed to drag the pressure cooker towards them, tilt it forward and gently lower it on board.

'Your turn, Ray.'

Ray hesitated for a moment, then jumped. He landed with a thump and staggered against Baz.

'Whoa. You OK?'

'Yeah.'

'Come on, then.'

They picked up the bomb once more, taking a handle apiece.

Gene was already in the wheelhouse. The confined space smelled of oil and diesel and the familiar sickliness of the grey sludge that had become part of their daily lives. Salvage.

'Listen,' whispered Gene. 'I've got the locker open, and I've shifted the cans of diesel so I could get the trapdoor open as well. When I switch the torch on, I want you to lift the thing up and over, and then hop in and get it as far down into the trap as you can, yeah? Looks like it might be a tight fit. Ready?'

The light flashed on – dangerously bright, it seemed – and Baz and Ray immediately hoisted the pressure cooker over the lip and down into the well of the locker. Then they both clambered in and lowered the heavy vessel through the open trap as far as it would go. The base of the cauldron was resting against the inner hull, and only the lid now protruded up into the locker well.

'Yeah, that's great,' said Gene. 'It's below the waterline at any rate.'

He switched off the torch, and the inside of the wheelhouse was as black as ink.

'Come on. We need to go and wire it up.'

Outside again, Gene crouched down beside the winch motor. He laid a pair of pliers, two screwdrivers and a roll of thin cabling on the deck. 'OK,' he said. 'I've got to fix this new lead on. It's gonna take me a few minutes, so here's what I want you two to do. See these grooves in the decking? I want you to scrape all the crap out of one of them, so there's a clear channel from the motor to the cabin. Use one of these screwdrivers. We're gonna try and hide the HT lead down in the groove.'

Gene flashed the torch over towards the wheelhouse door, holding the beam steady.

'Yeah, start that end,' he said. 'Pick the nearest groove to the left-hand corner of the door, and just come this way. Clean it out with the screwdriver. Take the torch, but hide the light as much as you can. And keep an ear out. If we hear a whistle, we're gonna have to dump everything overboard and run for it.'

'Don't you need the torch?' said Baz.

'Nah. I can see well enough for what I gotta do. It's easy.'

So while Ray held the torch close to the decking, Baz cleaned out one of the square-cut grooves, using the screwdriver to lift up the continuous plug of dirt and grime that had been trampled in there.

By the time Baz and Ray had reached the winch, Gene was finished. He had his roll of cabling ready, and he began to press this down into the groove.

'Follow on behind,' he said. 'See if you can get some of that dust and muck to cover this over. Rub it around a bit. Yeah, that's right – scuff it in with your feet. Try and make it look like nothing's changed.'

It didn't take long to get the cabling in place. Once inside the wheelhouse, Gene ran the thin black rubber lead around the lower framework of the doorway and along the skirting, pressing it into the gaps wherever he could. Then he brought it up vertically at the back end of the locker, just at the point where the lid was hinged.

'That's about as good as we can get it,' Gene said. He measured out another couple of metres of cabling, and snipped off the remainder with his pliers.

'Nearly done. I've just got to strip the end and wire it to the spark plug.'

'Wanna use my penknife?' said Baz.

'Nah, it's OK. These'll do.' Gene used the pliers again, then climbed into the locker well. Kneeling beside what was visible of the pressure cooker, he unscrewed the little metal cap from the top of the spark plug.

Ray was holding the torch, keeping the beam low, shielding the light as best he could. There was nothing for Baz to do but watch. He waited for Gene to attach the lead to the plug.

But Gene appeared to have come to a halt. He leaned a shoulder against the inner wall of the locker, holding the wire in his hands, twisting the ends of it round and round. His head had dropped forward. Maybe he'd forgotten something, or maybe there was some detail he needed to go over in his mind. Whatever it was could be vitally important, so Baz wasn't about to interrupt his thoughts.

A deep stillness fell on the interior of the wooden cabin, the faint whirring of the wind-up torch the only sound.

In the end it was Ray who broke the silence.

'Want me to do it?'

The question took Baz by surprise. It hadn't occurred to him that Gene might be having last-minute doubts – was perhaps unable to make that final connection to the bomb.

But Ray had seen and understood.

'Here – hang onto the torch, Baz.'

Ray clambered into the locker. 'Come on, Gene. Give it to me.' He took the wire from Gene's un-resisting fingers. 'And the other bit – the little cap thing. So I just have to wrap it round the plug and screw the cap on, yeah?'

Gene nodded, but said nothing.

'Shift the light around, Baz. Can't see what I'm doing.'

Baz adjusted his position so that the beam fell directly onto the pressure cooker. Ray crouched down and wrapped the bare wire around the tiny screw-thread on top of the spark plug. He twisted the end over a few times, and then replaced the little metal cap, screwing it down tightly with his fingers.

'Yeah? That it?' He looked across at Gene.

'Yeah,' Gene sighed. 'That's it. Sorry . . . I just can't . . . just can't do it all. Can't be the one who . . .'

'I know. It's OK.'

It was like a death warrant, thought Baz. Like adding the final signature. A terrible thing to do, no matter how bad the crime, or how deserved the punishment. Did anyone ever have the right to sign away another life? Now that he saw it like that, he wondered if he could have done it himself. Maybe not.

Yet Ray could . . .

'OK.' Gene stood up. 'Nearly there. I'm just gonna shift those cans.' He hauled the two jerry cans across, tipping them over so that they lay against the protruding lid of the pressure cooker. Then he closed the trapdoor as far as it would go, resting it on top of the jerry cans. The pressure cooker was still partially visible, but it might escape a casual glance.

Gene climbed out of the locker well. 'Let's shut the lid, then,' he said. Baz put the torch down on the floor, and the three of them gently lowered the solid hinged lid. They stood there for a moment, six hands resting on the top of the locker.

'God help us,' Gene muttered, in such a way that it was hard to tell whether he was praying for forgiveness or predicting disaster. He lifted his head and took a last look around. 'Switch off the light, Baz. We're done. Let's go.'

The lookouts joined them one by one as they climbed back up the pathway to the school, and each boy whispered the same thing: *Have you done it? Have you done it?*

Yeah. We've done it.

But there were no expressions of jubilation at their achievement, no air-punches or excited slaps on the back. Rather it was a silent and thoughtful crew that entered the glass doors of the building and crept along the moonlit corridor.

A heavy sense of apprehension and fear hung in the stuffy darkness of the slob room. Baz tossed around on his mattress, knowing that others were doing the same, knowing that none of them would ever sleep. They'd done a terrible thing. And maybe it was the wrong thing after all. Maybe it was their own death warrants that they'd just signed, not Preacher John's. Maybe tonight would be their last night ever.

And who should take most blame for that? It had been Gene's genius that had built the bomb, yet Gene had never truly pushed for its use, thought Baz. That had been down to him. He'd been the one to insist that it must be done tonight. And there would never have been a bomb in the first place if it hadn't been for Ray. It was Ray who had started this. And it was Ray who had finished it.

'Ray? You awake?' Baz whispered.

A few moments of silence, then a long sigh.

'Yeah.'

'Ray, I'm really scared now. This is bad . . .'

'Yeah. I know.'

Baz reached out towards the mattress next to him, found Ray's hand and held it. He squeezed the slim fingers between his own, and was comforted by the brief pressure in response. But Ray was elsewhere, he could tell. Some distant place.

'Ray . . . what happened tonight? Tell me what happened to you.'

'Uh?'

'With Steiner and Hutchinson. You've gotta tell me.'

'Oh, that.' Another sigh. 'Forget it. Don't keep on at me. It doesn't matter now.'

'It does matter. It does to me.'

'Hey – I keep telling you. Nothing happened, OK? Nothing.'

But Baz couldn't believe that. He was being fobbed off, and it hurt.

'How do you mean, nothing? Why?'

'Just go to sleep.'

Ray withdrew his hand, then, and that hurt even more.

Baz felt the bridge of his nose tingle, and quick tears stinging his eyes. He rolled onto his back again, and stared up into the swimming darkness.

CHAPTER
TWENTY-FOUR

They'd made a huge mistake. It was Baz's first thought as he woke up. He lay on his side, eyes open, looking at the grubby wall next to his bed.

A bomb. They'd built a bomb. It was out there on the boat at this very moment, sitting silently in the darkness of the locker, armed and ready to kill. And that was wrong. It didn't matter how you looked at it, you couldn't just go around blowing people up. Murdering people. But then, if the only other choice was to be murdered yourself . . .

. . . drowned . . . sacrificed . . .

Baz rolled over to see whether Ray was awake yet. Yes, he must be, because his bed was empty. Baz sat up and pulled on his shorts.

Ray was just coming out of the jakes as Baz entered.

'Whoa – you're up early for once,' Ray said. His hair was slicked back, T-shirt damp here and there with splashes from the shower. 'You OK?'

Last night's coolness or exasperation had gone from his voice.

But Baz had come to a decision, and he knew it wouldn't be a popular one.

'No, I'm not OK,' he said. 'I can't do this, Ray. We're gonna have to get down to the jetty quick. Unwire the bomb before anyone else is up.'

'What the hell are you talking about?'

'We can't just— Hang on, I need a pee.' Baz ran into one of the cubicles and carried on talking. 'There's still time to sling it over the side of the boat. Dump it in the water right now, and no one'll ever know.'

'Jesus, Baz. Have you gone *nuts*? We've spent weeks on this, and now *you've* decided it's not gonna happen? What's the matter with you? It's gonna work. I know it is. It's gonna work.'

'Yeah, but that's not the point. It's murder—'

'Murder? What about *us* getting murdered, then? And what about all those kids that've been dumped in the sea? What about Nadine and Stef—'

'Just listen. Ray . . . just shut up and listen a minute.' Baz tried to summon up the right words, the right argument. But into the moment of stillness that fell on the washroom came the sound of other voices, men's voices, drifting through the open quarterlight window.

'So we're taking the little 'un with us. That's a definite now, is it?'

'Yeah. Gimme ten minutes and we'll get her tied up. Rope her to the transom.' Amos and Luke, passing by the rear of the building, their heavy feet scrunching on the loose gravel.

'It'll need two of us to sort her out, so just wait till I get there, OK?'

The footsteps faded away. Baz and Ray stared at each other. *The little 'un? Rope her to the transom?* What was going on? Who were the divers talking about?

'Oh my God . . .' Ray put both hands up to his face. 'They're taking . . .' He pushed his fingers up into his wet hair. 'They're gonna take Steffie! Ohhh no . . . no . . .' Then his eyes were furious, accusing. 'But you said Hutchinson! You said they were taking Hutchinson!'

'But that's what I heard them s—'

'Christ! Listen. Just don't do anything *stupid*, OK?' Ray was at the washroom curtain now, pulling it aside. 'If you tell, if you say anything about the bomb, or try to do anything *stupid*, then we're dead. All of us are dead. Got that?'

'Yeah, but—'

'Just tell me you've *got* that, Baz. You don't say *anything*, yeah? Not to anyone. 'Cos I'm really starting to worry about you.'

'Where are you going?'

But Ray had already gone.

Baz pushed his way past the swaying curtain, just in time to see the shadowy figure of Ray disappearing through the door at the far end of the slob room.

There were six of them lined up on the jetty – Baz, Amit, Dyson, Gene, Jubo and Robbie. Ray had gone missing, his absence soon noticed by the capos. And in the hunt for Ray it had been discovered that the two girls had vanished too, the art room empty. So now there was trouble.

Baz was so terrified of making matters worse that he had followed Ray's instruction and said nothing to anyone.

Steiner and Hutchinson patrolled the line, both

looking very white and shaky. Their eyes were all gummed up, puffy slits, narrowed against the daylight. It was plain that the pair were suffering from the previous night's drinking, and this provided some comfort at least to the others. Baz felt Jubo's elbow nudge at his ribs and he gave a little snigger.

'Right,' croaked Hutchinson. 'Somebody knows something. Where are they?'

No reply.

'Come on,' said Steiner. 'We're gonna find them in the end, so you might as well tell us now. Save yourselves some grief.'

Still nothing.

Hutchinson got specific, then, and poked Jubo in the chest. 'You. Where've they all got to?'

'Get off me, man,' said Jubo. 'I dunno what you talkin' 'bout. Wouldn't tell you if I did.'

'Eh? You cheeky little f—' Hutchinson aimed a slap at Jubo's head, but Jubo easily ducked out of the way.

'Yah. You still drunk. You stink like a pig.' Jubo danced backwards a couple of paces. He was on his toes, weaving from side to side.

Hutchinson lurched after him, but gave up almost instantly. 'Right,' he spluttered. 'You're in deep trouble, pal.' He pointed his finger threateningly at Jubo, then moved back to rejoin Steiner.

'Rass. You the one in grief, man.' Jubo was defiant, but kept his distance nevertheless.

'What did you say?'

'Hey, forget it, Hutch. We'll kick the crap out of him later. Don't worry about it.' Steiner's voice was seemingly casual, unconcerned. But as he walked down the line, he suddenly grabbed at Baz, yanked him forward and got him in a headlock.

'Right. *Now* we'll get some chuffin' answers. I'll teach you to laugh at me, you little sod! Where's your girlfriend, eh? The cornflake kid?'

Baz was doubled over, choking, Steiner's bony fore-arm pressed into his face. 'Ow! Let go . . . I don't know . . . I don't know anything!'

'Yeah? Well, here's a memory jogger!' Steiner gave a vicious sideways jerk with his arm, and Baz thought that his neck would break . . . like a rabbit . . . like Preacher John with the rabbits . . .

'Arggh . . . arghhh . . .'

'Oi! Are you at it again? I told you to go and find those other kids, not beat this lot up!' Isaac had arrived.

Baz dropped to his knees, gasping for breath. The skipper stood over him, an unlikely saviour, his huge sea boots planted on the gravel surface beside Baz's insignificant hand. Other feet passed by . . . *crunch* . . . *crunch* . . . *crunch*. Amos, on his way to the boat. The smooth sheen of metal caught Baz's blurry vision. He squinted upwards and saw that Isaac was carrying a shotgun, twin barrels pointing downwards.

'How many times do I have to tell you to lay . . . *off*?'

Baz heard the whack, and saw Steiner's bare knees buckling as he staggered backwards. Isaac must have hit him really hard this time, because Steiner fell to the ground and didn't move.

'What do you think you're doing, Isaac?'

Here was Preacher John – also just arriving – his unmistakable voice booming across the jetty. But it was

Preacher John as he'd never been seen before. He'd changed his long black garb for seaman's clothing: a grey smock and big rubber boots. Baz looked up at him in astonishment.

'I'm protecting our ruddy property,' said Isaac, 'that's what I'm doing.' He stepped away from Baz.

'Protection? Is that what you call it? The day's hardly begun and you've already lost three kids. Now I find another two injured. This hardly looks like protection to me. And I'll remind you that this is *my* property, not "ours".'

Baz cautiously stood up, wondering if Preacher John was now about to hit Isaac. Isaac carried the shotgun over one arm, the barrels broken for safety, the bright cartridge ends exposed. Baz was now familiar with those circular brass caps . . .

'Gaah.' The skipper was defiant. 'Steiner needs a good thump round the ear every once in a while. He'll live.' And it was true. Steiner was already rolling over and attempting to sit up – although his face looked horribly swollen and bruised.

'Maybe so. But he's not much use to me like that, is he? I can't trust him to look after this place alone, not in the state you've put him in. Thanks to you we'll have to leave both capos here now, and take someone else instead. Right. You' – he pointed at Hutchinson – 'get him on his feet. Get him up, and listen to me, the pair of you. By the time I'm back tonight I want those other three found, got it? No excuses. You find them, and you bring them to me – or so help me God, you're in trouble. Right?'

'Yes,' said Hutchinson. 'Right.'

'Right,' said Preacher John. 'And you' – he looked at Baz – 'get on the boat.'

'What?' Baz thought he must have misheard.

Preacher John stepped towards him, his face as red and raw as butcher's meat. '*On the boat*, I said. Go on – get down there. You're coming with us.'

Baz stared stupidly up at the preacher. This couldn't be happening. 'Me? But . . . what . . .'

'Hang on a minute.' Isaac looked confused. 'He's no use. We need someone who can work the tender. We'll take the mechanic.'

'We'll take this one,' said Preacher John.

'What the hell for? He's no good to us!'

Preacher John stood upright and turned towards Isaac. 'Are you questioning me, boy?'

Isaac held his ground. 'I think as skipper I have some say in who's gonna be on the boat – and why.' His shoulders broadened a little.

'Skipper you might be, Isaac, but I am Master. Do you understand that? I am Master, and I always will be.'

Isaac's expression darkened in anger, bearded jaw thrust belligerently forward. The two men faced each other. A long moment of deadlock followed, a silent clash of wills, but then Isaac seemed to sag before Preacher John's ferocious gaze. He turned without another word and walked away, heading towards the salvage boat. As he reached the edge of the jetty, he altered his hold on the shotgun. There was a sharp metallic sound as the barrels clicked into place.

Preacher John watched him go, his eyes still fierce and dominant. Then he looked down upon Baz once more. 'Why are you standing there, boy? Get on the boat.'

Baz had the sudden idea that this must be some kind of test; that what Preacher John really wanted was information about Ray and Nadine . . . and Steffie. The boat was being used as a threat. He tried to get as much sincerity into his quaking voice as he could.

'I don't know anything,' he said. 'I really . . . really, honestly don't know where they are. I'm telling you the truth.'

Preacher John leaned forward, bringing his horrible face so close that Baz could smell the sourness on his breath.

'And I believe you.' The words were filtered through a beard as coarse as Shredded Wheat. 'But I'm not talking about "they". I'm talking about you. And now I'm telling you for the last time. Get . . . on . . . that . . . *boat*!'

Preacher John's breath blasted forth like the hot stink of salvage itself, and Baz reeled backwards.

There was no choice, and no escape. Baz stumbled to the edge of the jetty, and began to pick his way down the slope towards the gangplank. He'd made this same journey just a few hours ago – a journey of hope then. Now it was one of despair. He crossed the gangplank and jumped clumsily down into the boat, his stomach lurching so badly he thought he would throw up. Amos and Isaac were already on deck, sorting out their gear. Amos glanced at him in mild surprise, but said nothing. Isaac ignored him completely.

Baz leaned against the gunwale for support, and looked up towards the top of the jetty. The other boys stared down at him, their expressions anguished, helpless. Preacher John was a little to one side, saying something to Hutchinson, jabbing his finger in the direction of the school building. But his voice made no sound. Baz's ears were filled with a hollow buzzing noise.

The boys shifted their gaze from Baz, and their eyes grew wider still. Baz turned to look. The wooden dinghy was rounding the end of the jetty in a plume of blue exhaust smoke. Luke sat at the tiller of the buzzing outboard, expertly guiding the boat around in a tight circle . . .

Baz looked at the little craft in disbelief. What was going on?

The engine noise shut down, and Luke brought the dinghy right up close, so that it disappeared from Baz's view beyond the transom of the *Cormorant*.

Amos was ready and waiting. He tossed a rope over the transom and shouted down to Luke, 'Tie her up then!'

Baz still didn't understand what was happening.

Preacher John lumbered across the gangplank. 'Don't forget what I said!' he shouted to Hutchinson. 'You find those girls by tonight, and that other kid as well, or you're both on the next trip out!'

There was a deep thudding sound, a shudder in the bowels of the boat as the diesel motor kicked into life. Then Luke appeared on the bank, jumped across the gangplank and shouted, 'Cast off!'

A cloud of black smoke arose from beyond the transom of the *Cormorant*. The engine speed increased and the jetty began to slip away.

Baz was still gripping the gunwale. He felt a twitch of movement through his fingertips, a slight jerk of resistance. The wooden dinghy appeared through the haze of diesel smoke, rocking from side to side in the churning wake of the main vessel. It was being towed away from the island. There was no chance of escape now for those who remained.

CHAPTER
TWENTY-FIVE

'Get out o' soddin' way.'

Amos brushed past him, carrying an air tank. Baz dumbly moved towards the stern of the boat and collapsed onto the bench seat. He stared back at the island, X Isle, visible now in its entirety. The boys had already vanished from the jetty.

A shadow passed over Baz's head, and the twisted frame of the hammer-head crane appeared to his right, rusting iron stanchions rising from the murky water. Then came the stonework of the church tower, lichen grey, sliding past the gunwale, close enough to touch as it had been before. Baz was aware of these things only at the corners of his vision, saw but didn't see, his blank gaze still fixed on the dark mass of land. Shrinking now. A blur of shapes and colours, the details gradually fading.

He watched the little dinghy bobbing along in the wake of the *Cormorant*. The little dinghy . . .

The 'little 'un'. And now he understood what the divers had been talking about – the conversation he and Ray had overheard. *Tie her up . . . rope her to the transom.* They meant the dinghy, nothing more. God, this was such a mess.

Amos and Luke were in their wetsuits now, or at least half in and half out. They hadn't pulled the tops on yet, the air being already hot and humid. Consequently they moved around the deck with their bare torsos exposed, hard and muscular men – another reminder to Baz of how small and feeble he was. After checking over their gear, the two divers disappeared into the wheelhouse. But Preacher John climbed up onto the foredeck and stood there, one hand resting on the roof of the cabin as he faced the horizon.

Baz sat on the transom bench and turned again to gaze at the receding island. It looked as insubstantial as a lump of driftwood now. Nothing there to cling to. He was lost in a fog of helplessness, his thoughts too jagged and jangled to fall into any proper order. Everything had failed, everything had come apart. He knew that much. The threads of how and why, and what it meant, were beyond his grasp.

When the true horror of his position finally struck him, it was in such a crushing wave that it took the breath from his lungs. He was on the boat, and the bomb was there with him. Death was just metres away, hiding in a locker in the wheelhouse. The bomb might go off, or someone might open the locker and find it first, but either way it would be the end of him.

The bomb would go off, and he would die. Or it would be discovered, and he would die . . .

Baz could see no other possibilities.

What if he could choose between the two? Which would it be? If he had the choice . . .

Here was a beginning, perhaps. A way of starting to think.

Baz looked at the scaffolding tripod, where last night Gene had knelt with his pliers and cabling, fiddling with the winch motor. One quick tug on the starter handle, and that could be the end of everything. But surely the winch wouldn't be needed until the divers were underwater and had netted their haul? They might not find anything for ages yet, so he had a little time to try and figure out his options.

Jump overboard right now, while nobody was looking – that was one thing he could do. But Baz knew that he had no hope of getting back to the island from here. He wasn't a good swimmer. Going overboard meant drowning.

He could try and cut the cabling, and disable the bomb. The penknife that he had stolen from the store-room was in his pocket. He kept it on him always now, tied to the belt loop of his shorts by a length of green garden twine. It was a puny little object, but reassuring nevertheless. He could just walk over to the winch motor, rip the lead up from the planking, and cut through it . . .

But even though that might save him from an explosion, it wouldn't save his life. The bomb would be found and Preacher John would kill him.

What if he simply confessed to everything and threw himself at their mercy? No. There would be no mercy.

So there was nothing he could do, after all. He had no choices.

Baz crouched back in his corner, numb with misery. An hour went by, maybe more. He wondered what they would be doing back on the island. Gene and Jubo, Robbie and Amit. Dyson. Nadine and Steffie.

That was the last he would ever see of them, he knew that. And Ray . . . he would never see Ray again . . .

Resentment burned through him. Why had he been picked for this trip? Isaac would have chosen Gene – the mechanic – which at least made some kind of sense. But Preacher John had definitely wanted him, not Gene. Why?

Baz stared down at the passing waves. They said that it didn't hurt. Not if you relaxed, it didn't. You just let go . . . closed your eyes . . . allowed yourself to sink peacefully into the blue-green world below . . .

Blue-green. The water had changed colour. It was clear, translucent, no longer murky grey. The thick soup that had been familiar to him for so long had given way to something different, something long forgotten. Sea water. When had that happened?

The engine note altered, slowing down to an uneven chug, and Baz sat up straight. He was alert again, trying to get his bearings. The mainland coast was visible now, far off to his right, a low line of hills. So they must have been travelling west. Baz gazed back over the transom, searching the horizon, but could see nothing. The island had long disappeared.

There was activity. The two divers came out of the wheelhouse, zipping up their wetsuits. Preacher John shouted something from the foredeck, where he had been standing for the entire journey. Baz could see the back of his head and shoulders, a raised arm signalling directions. The boat swung round and part of a large plastic sign came into view – tilting to the right, the top corner protruding from the choppy waves. BP in green letters. Petrol.

It looked as though Preacher John had got lucky. Wherever there was a petrol station there was likely to be a store. Perhaps even a supermarket.

Baz felt his bladder tighten, a sense of panic and fear rising within him. Something was about to happen, something was coming. And still he could do nothing but sit and wait for it.

The engine cut out, and Isaac appeared from the wheelhouse. He walked around the winch tripod, glancing behind him before joining his brothers. Preacher John was still up on the foredeck, alone, looking out to sea.

Luke and Amos hoisted aqualungs onto their shoulders as Isaac spoke to them. He kept his voice to a low mutter. 'We'll just have to see how this goes. If we'd brought the mechanic kid we could have sent him out to have a scout round in the tender. Covered a lot more ground and saved ourselves some time. But the old man had to bring that idiot Cookie instead. There's no way I'm letting *him* loose in a dinghy, so all we can use it for now is a bit of extra loading space.' Isaac glanced over to where Baz was sitting. 'God knows what the old fool was thinking of. He's ruddy lost it.' He spat over the side of the boat. 'But then he lost it a long time ago.'

The two divers began adjusting their masks.

'Where's he got to, anyway?' said Luke, his voice already muffled as he manoeuvred his breathing gear into position. Baz looked up towards the foredeck. Preacher John was no longer visible.

'Must be there somewhere.' Luke pulled at one of his cuffs. 'Look after him, Isaac. Try and keep him out of mischief.'

'Oh, I'll look after him all right.'

Isaac stepped back towards the winch motor. He reached up and tugged on a thin wire that was attached to the crossbeam. *Ting!* The single note of a small bell, very clear and bright in the surrounding silence. It seemed ominous somehow, a marker of time, or the signal for some ceremony to begin. The skipper then crouched down beside the motor to adjust some part of it, and Baz felt his stomach begin to churn. He shrank back against the transom, his head turned away, eyes narrowed . . .

But Isaac stood up again, wiped his hands on his greasy sweatshirt and made his way down to the stern. 'Hop it,' he said. 'Get in the wheelhouse, out of my way.'

Baz found that his knees would barely support him as he rose from the bench. The very last place on earth he wanted to be right now was in that wheelhouse.

'Can't I stay out here?'

'Wheelhouse, I said. Go.'

Baz kept one hand on the gunwale as he walked towards the darkened doorway of the little cabin. But the two divers were blocking his path, standing together between the winch and the side of the boat, doing something with a bundle of netting. Baz waited. One of them turned to look down upon him, an unearthly being in his suit and mask, the reflected glare of light on glass making him unidentifiable. They were like invaders from another planet, aliens or warrior gods, clad in rubber and glass and metal. Webbed feet. Strange tubular breathing apparatus, heavy weighted belts around their waists. The air tanks

410

on their backs could have been rocket packs. They might have lifted off from the deck there and then, and roared away into the heavens.

But instead, they moved to one side and sat on the gunwale. Then, simultaneously, without apparent signal or warning, they toppled backwards into the water. In another moment the alien figures had disappeared, not up into the skies, but down into another world far below. A fading string of bubbles accompanied their departure – that and a high-pitched whirring sound. Baz looked round. It was the winch. A thin steel hawser was spooling from a revolving drum. It passed through a series of pulleys, up and along the cross-member, and over the side of the boat. The divers were taking the hawser down with them, along with the loading net. They were obviously confident of finding something to bring back up.

Baz saw that Isaac was scowling at him, so he started again towards the wheelhouse.

At the doorway he hesitated for a moment. Bright beams of light flooded in through the main window ahead of him, but this threw the rest of the interior into confused shadow. Baz automatically looked to his left, where the locker stood – and felt his heart jump. Preacher John was there. Kneeling in front of the locker.

The bomb had been found! That was Baz's first thought. But then he saw that Preacher John's elbows were resting on top of the big wooden box. He hadn't opened it, and he wasn't trying to. Hands clasped in front of him, head bowed, voice muttering low . . . The preacher was at prayer.

'And for bringing this clear blue water, we thank you, Lord. We thank you for leading us to such a place, where we might find and receive all that you hold in store for us. We see that we are your chosen people, and that you look favourably upon our prayers and sacrifices. And to thee our first fruits shall be given. Therefore, in accordance with your will, I bring a gift . . . aye, as Abraham did bring a gift . . .'

Baz stood stock-still in the doorway, unable to breathe.

'. . . a lamb, returned to your fold. Here I make my covenant, then. As thou givest to me, O Lord, so I shall give in return. Amen.'

Preacher John remained where he was, kneeling in front of the locker as though it were an altar, the light from the porthole falling on his wild red hair. Baz saw that there was a gun – Isaac's shotgun – propped upright in the corner between the locker and the cabin wall. It was a strange and frightening scene.

'I said "Amen". Do you not know how to pray, boy?' Preacher John hadn't turned round, but he was clearly aware of Baz's presence – and perhaps had been all along.

Baz struggled to bring anything more than a squeak to his dry throat. 'Er . . .'

Preacher John placed his hands flat on the locker and tilted his head backwards, gazing for a moment out of the porthole. 'Then it's time you learned.' He turned to face Baz. 'Get down on your knees.'

'What?'

'Get down on your knees, boy, and pray to God.

Here, beside me.' He pointed to the filthy planking in front of the locker.

Baz sank forward onto his knees, partly because Preacher John had commanded it, and partly because his legs felt so weak they could no longer hold him up.

'God is in this place, as He is everywhere, looking down upon us. Place yourself before Him, then, and pray.' Preacher John had bowed his head again. Baz rested his elbows on the lid of the locker and put his hands together, clasping them tightly in order to try and stop their shaking. He stared at the upright shotgun, the blue-black smoothness of the barrels, the perfectly machined patterns in the wood. And beyond the shotgun he saw a piece of rubber cabling, just visible where it looped beneath the far corner of the locker. It was the cabling that he and Ray and Gene had laid only last night. It seemed like a thousand years ago now.

'Close your eyes and pray for forgiveness. Pray for your sins, and for all the sins of the world. And pray that God will find you worthy.'

Baz squeezed his eyes tight shut, his whole body shivering as he waited for what was to come, the blow that would surely fall. Because now he understood. He was the gift. The lamb. The sacrifice. That was why he was here.

'Oh God . . . oh God . . .' The whispered words came out of him without any conscious thought. Spoken automatically in fear and despair. But the sound of them hung there, and their meaning grew. *Help me. God help me. Don't let this happen . . .*

He'd never prayed before, not really.

Please, God . . . if you're there. I'm so scared . . . and I don't know what to do. Don't know what to do . . .

He'd helped to build a bomb. A wicked and murderous thing. It lay before him now, right beneath his elbows, even as he prayed to God to make it go away. And if he was killed, then it would be his own doing, his own fault.

Yet nothing happened. The boat rocked gently on.

Baz sank into his own inner darkness, no longer praying but just desperately hoping. Hoping for a sign, or an idea, or a miracle. Waiting. And at the same time he shrank from the overwhelming presence of Preacher John. He could sense the solid mass of the man who knelt beside him, could hear him breathing through his nostrils, deep and controlled and patient. As if he too were waiting . . .

Jump up and cut the cable. This was still the only thing that Baz could think of doing. It wouldn't save him, but it would take away his guilt – make it so that he wasn't going to be a murderer. But no. That didn't work either. If he exposed the bomb, or defused it, then his friends on X Isle would die, and he would be to blame. What was the right thing to do? Where could he find the answer?

There was a soft squeak of the planking behind him, a rustle of material. Oh God, it was coming. This was it. Baz opened his eyes wide. A huge hand crossed his vision, reaching out, thick hairy fingers closing around the barrels of the shotgun . . .

CHAPTER TWENTY-SIX

'Well, isn't this cosy?'
Isaac stood with his back to the open doorway, the shotgun in his grasp.

Baz looked at the barrels, and was then unable to look away. His eyes were fixed on those dark and sinister tunnels. Far into them he was drawn, his body cold, a bubble of sick-water rising at the back of his throat.

'Get up.'

Through waves of terror the words came, and Baz automatically raised one knee.

'Not you, you ruddy half-wit. Stay where you are. You – get up.'

What? Baz couldn't tear his gaze away from the shotgun, but he was aware of movement, another squeak of the planking as Preacher John rose to his feet.

'So it comes to this at last, then, Isaac. As I knew it would.'

'Oh, you knew it would. Well, you know everything, don't you? Pick up that diving belt.' Isaac waved the shotgun towards the other side of the cabin.

Baz grasped the fact that, for the moment at least, this had nothing to do with him. He turned his head and saw Preacher John stoop to pick up a tangled object from the floor. A webbed nylon belt – red and brown stripes – a series of what looked like big yellow buckles. No, they were weights. It was the same kind of belt that Baz had seen earlier on the two divers.

'Put it on.' Isaac's face was flushed, his voice slightly unsteady. He seemed the more nervous of the two men.

'What do you think you're going to do, Isaac?' Preacher John swung the heavy diving belt around his girth. He hitched up his seaman's smock, brought the ends of the belt together and searched for the fastening. At no time did he take his eyes off Isaac.

'I think I'm gonna watch you go for a dive,' said Isaac.

'I see. Well, I can soon take this thing off, once I'm in the water. Unless you intend to shoot me first. Is that your plan?'

'Just get outside.'

Baz sank back down onto one knee, horrified. Isaac was going to kill Preacher John! He'd seen and heard enough to know that there was deep animosity between the two . . . but murder . . . to murder your own father . . .

'What about Luke and Amos?' Preacher John seemed calm, in no hurry to move. 'What do you intend to tell them?'

'You had an accident. You must have overbalanced, fallen overboard. Just disappeared.'

'And you expect them to believe that?'

'You were out of sight, even before they left. You could have already gone. And I have a witness.'

Preacher John seemed puzzled for a second. Then he glanced down at Baz. 'The boy? You seriously think he'll be your alibi? Back up your story?'

'He'll say whatever I tell him to say if he wants to stay alive. That's why I brought him.'

'You didn't bring him.' Preacher John was still unflustered, matter of fact. 'I did. You would have brought the mechanic.'

'What's the difference? I've still got a witness.'

'Oh, I don't think there can be any witnesses, Isaac. And that's why I brought *this* boy. Not a capo, not a mechanic, but one that's worthless. One that I can easily afford to lose. You haven't thought this through at all, have you?' Preacher John's voice was even, controlled.

But Isaac began to look as though control were slipping away from him. 'Don't come that tone with me,' he said. 'I've put up with it for too long! You've always treated me like the fool of this family. The idiot! Always favoured the others over me . . .' He was spluttering now, his anger and hatred plain to see, all pretence at coolness gone. 'Always made me do your dirty work. Dump this kid, get rid of that one, bring these young girls across. And all the while you hide behind God, like you're so . . . so holy, like you're better than anyone else. Well, I've had a lifetime of listening to your crap, a bellyful, and now you'll listen to me for once. I've thought this through all right, don't you worry. I got you on this boat. Yeah, and I made sure there was a witness, and I brought this gun. I planned it all!'

'Really? And now you think you're just going to take me outside and shoot me. Hmph.' Preacher John was openly jeering. 'You haven't got the guts, Isaac. That's right. You're gutless, and Godless too. You have no God to guide your hand, and so your hand falters. I see it shaking even now.'

And it was true. The gun was raised, pointing towards Preacher John, but the barrels wavered around uncertainly. Sweat poured down Isaac's face, glistening droplets on his dark beard.

'You think *you* planned this moment?' said Preacher John. 'You haven't the wit. *I* planned it! I saw this day coming long ago. I saw how you would turn against me and try to rob me of what is mine!' His voice grew louder, booming around the little wooden cabin so that the windows vibrated. 'I prayed to God for guidance then, and God answered. *Send him to me! Send him to me and I will make him whole again, and all the world I will make whole! Build me an altar, like Abraham of old! Bring me Isaac, your firstborn! Put your trust in me, and I will draw back the waters into the fountains of the earth . . .'*

'What?' Isaac briefly took one hand from the gun to dash the sweat from his eyes.

'Sacrifice, Isaac! Sacrifice! This is what God demands! To Him our first fruits shall be given – and you are my first fruit! The sacrifice has to be *you*. It was always you! But' – Preacher John raised his eyes towards the ceiling of the cabin – 'I was weak-hearted. And though I built my altar as God commanded me, I could not offer up my firstborn there. Not in the sight of my other sons. It would have to be away from the island, and hidden from all but the eyes of God. Out

418

here, on the boat. A private covenant between me and my Maker.' Preacher John took a step forward, and Isaac backed away, stumbling against the door-post.

'But first I needed to see for myself what a traitor you were.' Preacher John glanced towards the port-hole. 'Aye. So I had you bring girls over from the mainland and let you think that they would be the next to go to the altar. I tested you, and all my sons, as God tests me. And Luke and Amos kept their faith. They would do whatever I asked of them, no matter what. But not you. You wanted me brought down, destroyed, so that you could take my place. Isaac . . . Isaac . . .'

A note of exasperation came into Preacher John's voice, as though he were tired of explaining. 'Don't you understand? I am an instrument of God! To defy me is to defy God Himself! Only a fool would try. Or a traitorous dog like you. But even a dog must have his day, and so I decided to let you have yours – out here on the boat, just the two of us . . .'

Baz shrank against the wall of the locker, plainly as insignificant to this scene as if he'd been a spider in the corner.

'You'd have been suspicious, though,' said Preacher John, 'if I'd invited myself out on a diving trip for no good reason. Much better if the invitation were to come from you. And that's why I got rid of Moko.'

'You . . . what?' Isaac seemed to almost drop the gun, the twin barrels momentarily dipping downwards before he hastily regained his grip.

'Aye, all my doing. I put the fear of God into that heathen – made sure he'd jump ship and not come back again. I wanted the *Cormorant* short handed. I knew it wouldn't be long before one of you asked for my help, once there was treasure within reach.' Preacher John brought one arm up to point a finger directly at Isaac. 'And there you saw your chance, Isaac. A chance to kill me. To do murder.' He nodded slowly as he said the word. 'Aye, murder. And how cunning you tried to be. Pretending that you didn't want me on the boat . . . having to be persuaded. This is work for *strong* men, you said. And you were right. This *is* work for strong men – men of God! But you have no strength, because you have no God! And so you can't do it, can you? Even though I've put myself at your mercy – even now – when all is yours for the taking . . . you can't do it . . . you just can't do it . . .'

Preacher John spread both arms and moved towards the raised gun. 'You're a fool, Isaac! A coward! A gutless . . . Godless . . . idiot . . .'

'Keep away!' Isaac stepped back through the doorway. 'Keep away from me, you mad bastard!' His voice was almost a scream. 'I'm warning you! I'm warning you! Get away! Gaah!'

There was a click – and another – sharp metallic sounds that cut through the high panic of Isaac's voice. Then silence. Isaac had pulled the triggers, but the shotgun hadn't gone off.

Preacher John sighed, almost as though he were disappointed. He put a hand in his pocket, withdrew it and held it out. Resting in his open palm were two cartridges. He kept his arm extended for another moment before Isaac's horrified gaze, then allowed the orange cartridges to tumble to the floor. They landed with a clatter and rolled across the planking, one of them coming to rest against the split toe of Baz's trainer.

'I see everything, Isaac. God grants me the vision to see into the soul of every living thing that passes before me. God grants me protection from my murdering enemies. And now may God grant me the strength to carry out His will.'

From his other pocket Preacher John drew a gun – a short-barrelled pistol, its chipped black paintwork somehow making it look all the more purposeful, all the more deadly.

'Now get out. Onto the foredeck. You've shown me all I need to know.' Preacher John moved forward.

Isaac had disappeared beyond the doorway, and out of Baz's sight.

'Don't. Don't do this . . . no . . .'

'Get on the foredeck!' Preacher John ducked as he left the cabin.

Baz looked towards the porthole and saw Isaac stumble past, moving backwards, still carrying the useless shotgun.

'No . . . no . . . no, you can't . . .' Isaac's voice was muffled now, but his terror was awful to hear. Baz remained on one knee beside the locker, pouring with perspiration, unable to get up. He dropped his head so that he would see no more of whatever was happening out there. Instead he kept his eyes fixed on the solitary cartridge that lay by his shoe, concentrating on that alone, watching it roll from side to side with the rocking motion of the boat.

'O Lord, behold Thy servant, and accept this

sacrifice!' Preacher John was roaring away outside. 'Thou hast delivered me from mine enemies! Thou hast brought me into Thy sight and shown me the paths of righteousness! Thy will be done, O Lord! *Thy . . . will . . . be . . .*'

The crash of the pistol drowned out the last of Preacher John's words, but through the booming echo that followed, Baz heard a faint splash. It seemed to him that the boat momentarily rocked a little more, the cartridge at his feet travelled a little further. Then silence.

For a long time Baz stared at the floor, his head empty of any conscious thought, a vague ringing sounded in his ears. Some kind of feeling returned to him, and at last he was able to move. He fumbled for the belt loop of his shorts, took hold of the piece of string and pulled the penknife from his pocket.

The blade was stiff, and Baz's hands shook as he struggled to get it open. His grubby thumbnail was too short and bitten-down to get a proper grip, his fingers too sweaty. Again and again they kept slipping. Ah . . . there . . . it was done.

Then the cabin darkened. Baz looked up to see Preacher John standing in the doorway. At the same time the ringing in his ears became more persistent.

Ting!

The sound had some meaning, but Baz couldn't think what it was. He kept staring at Preacher John.

Ting-tingggg.

A frown of irritation crossed the preacher's face, as though he'd been disturbed, interrupted. He looked at the penknife.

'What do you think you're going to do with that? Drop it.'

'No, I have to cut the wire . . . the lead—'

'Drop it!' Preacher John stepped forward. He reached down and grabbed Baz's wrist, twisting it back so that the knife immediately fell from his hand in a tangle of green string. Baz was yanked towards the doorway, dragged through it and out into the daylight.

'Aargh!'

Ting . . . tinggg . . .

The bell rang for a third time, clearer now on the open air. The bell! Baz remembered what the sound actually meant . . . the divers . . . signalling . . .

'No! Don't!' Baz kicked and fought against Preacher John's overwhelming power. It was too late though, too late to explain, too late to take any action. In another moment he was swept upwards, the world spinning briefly about him . . . deck . . . tripod . . . sky . . .

'No! No! There's a b—' Baz was still trying to shout, but his face was jammed into the back of Preacher John's neck and his mouth was full of greasy hair. He was aware of body heat, the musky smell of salvage and candle-smoke, horrible textures on his tongue.

He heard Preacher John's roaring voice: 'Away to your Maker! Gahhh . . .'

The sky whirled above him in white and grey patterns . . . spiralling clouds . . .

. . . and down he went. Baz felt the stinging slap of the waves across his shoulders, and the sky disappeared. He was instantly submerged, the unbelievable shock of cold water snatching his breath away, filling his mouth with bitter saltiness. Strange echoes . . . pressure in his ears . . . a booming green void. He kicked out at the darkness, sure that he was continually sinking. But then he found himself bumping into the slimy wooden hull of the boat. In another second he was thrashing around on the surface, and Preacher John's angry voice was in his ears again.

'Come on, you motherless heap of scrap!'

Who was he talking to?

Thunka-thunk . . .

An empty hollow sound.

Baz spat out a mouthful of water, coughed, tried to get some air in his lungs.

'What the hell's the matter with this thing? Graaggh!'

Tha-tha-thunkk . . .

Again the rhythmic half-familiar sound. Something turning. An engine failing to catch.

Oh God. Preacher John was trying to start the winch motor!

Baz threw himself forward in a desperate attempt at swimming, a frenzied bid to get as far away as possible from the prow of the boat. Arms pounding and clawing at the water, legs kicking, he struck out towards the stern. In his panic he was making more noise than progress – thrashing and splashing and spluttering – but he kept going.

Tingggg . . . t-tingg . . .

The divers' bell sounded its warning above him. But he was getting there . . . getting there . . . closer to the stern now.

Crack! Not an explosion. A gunshot! Baz ducked

beneath the water, breathed in a great mouthful of it, came up choking.

Crack! Another shot, and this time Baz heard the *zzzip* of the bullet in the water beside him.

'Should have shut you up before I threw you in!' Preacher John's raging voice again.

Crack! Crack! Crack!

Baz dug at the waves, trying with all his might to get beneath them, but only succeeded in rolling over onto his back. White sky above him . . . the dark stern of the *Cormorant*. The bow of the dinghy just beside him. Then Preacher John was shouting again, his voice muffled now, more distant.

'Gaaah! I'll deal with you in a minute. Soon as I get this damn thing start—'

Baz saw it before he heard it – a huge flash of light, the planking bursting outwards as though kicked from within by some mighty boot, a great gaping hole at the waterline. *Ba-DOOOMMM! Kkkkk . . . wowowowow . . . whoommFFF . . .*

His eardrums felt as though they had exploded, but then the sound was just as suddenly gone . . . dissolving into absolute nothingness. Up and away he floated . . . far, far away into the smoky void. So peaceful. Such wonderful silence. And there was the blue angel, just like in his dream, sailing across the horizon . . . a gentle smiling face. She put her hand to her chin, tilted her head upwards . . .

Whoooorrff . . .

The world tipped over, and he was surrounded by water again, roaring flames shooting from the salvage boat, great gouts of fiery liquid arcing across the waves.

Something banged against his shoulder blade – the dinghy – and Baz automatically reached upwards, grabbing at the rocking side. The boat yanked him out of the water, tearing at his arms, and as it fell once more Baz half tumbled, half scrambled over the lip. He was in the dinghy, cracking his elbows and shins against the ribs and struts, tossed this way and that, completely off balance.

As he got to his knees, facing the prow, he saw the transom of the salvage boat rising before him . . . and continuing to rise. It was coming out of the water, the green-encrusted propeller dripping, and Baz realized that he was being dragged towards it. The bow of the dinghy was still roped to the *Cormorant*.

Shhroomphhh! Another flaring explosion, scatterings of fire falling all around. The *Cormorant* was going down, and pulling the dinghy with it! Baz scrambled to the prow of the boat, grabbing at the piece of string tied to his belt loop. Miraculously the penknife was still dangling there, blade still open. The nylon tow rope tautened jerkily, ripped from his grasp again and again as he tried to saw through it. He couldn't do it . . . just couldn't do it. A sudden great lurch, and Baz was thrown sideways. The rope lashed at his face, whipping across his eyes. He was half blinded, in agony, but he knew that the rope had snapped. The rope had snapped.

Bits of vision came back to him . . . fountains springing up from the deep . . . whirlpools . . . the dinghy rocking and spinning . . . and the word *Cormorant* disappearing, fading, swirling down into the darkness below. A last great belch of smoke and steam, and she'd gone. Scattered flames still danced on the waves like floating tea-lights.

The waters calmed, and the lights went out one by one. Baz was all alone. He lay against the prow of the dinghy, rubbing his eyes, half deafened, too shocked and too exhausted to move. The horizon slowly revolved, and the distant hills of the mainland came into view, rocking gently, a roughly drawn pencil line between sea and sky.

'*Arrrk . . .*'

The sound made Baz jump, a harsh squawk, alarmingly close. He spun round. A bird! It was perched on the petrol tank of the outboard motor. Huge, it seemed – grey and white, its head to one side, regarding him with a cold yellow eye. A gull?

Yes, and there, beneath the curiously twisted grip of its claws, was the word SEAGULL, embossed on the petrol tank. As though the bird was a labelled exhibit: SEAGULL.

'Yaaah!' Baz waved his arms, a delayed reaction to his fright, and the gull hopped into the air. It rose vertically with no apparent effort, borne upwards on lazily hanging wings, calm and unflustered in contrast to Baz's own frantic flapping. The seagull banked and wheeled away, dipping down again as it headed off in the direction of the mainland, skimming low over the waves.

Baz watched it go, lost for a moment in the wonder of seeing such a creature.

Then the world came flooding back in, the horror of what had just happened, all that he had just witnessed. Were there bodies? Was that why the bird had descended – in the hope of easy pickings? Baz looked around, scanning the choppy waters. Two or three pink marker buoys bobbed about in the near vicinity. An upside-down wine bottle. Nothing more.

Baz clambered down to the stern of the boat and looked at the outboard motor. The starter rope lay coiled beneath the bench seat, along with a red plastic fuel can. He remembered how the rope worked. But what about the controls? What had Gene done exactly to get the motor going? Baz felt panicky now, frightened by the very silence that surrounded him. He had to get out of here.

Wind the rope around the flywheel, then. No. Something else first. Gene had fiddled around with this little pump thing, pressed it up and down a few times. Yes. Like that. And then there had been a lever. This one, with the cable attached to it? Open that up a bit. Now the rope.

He pulled it too timidly the first time. The flywheel turned, but only in a feeble half-hearted way. Baz tried again. He wound the rope around the notched fly-wheel and then gave it such an almighty wrench that he nearly overbalanced. The engine caught instantly, rapidly picked up speed, and in the next moment it was racing completely out of control, the screaming note of the exhaust causing Baz to panic even more. Which lever? Which lever? This one. Baz pulled the throttle lever right across, and the clamouring engine slowed to the point where it was firing only inter-mittently, in danger of stalling now. Try opening it up a bit more then.

Baz fiddled about with the throttle lever until the

428

engine sounded comfortable, a fast tickover. OK. But the boat wasn't moving. There was something else he needed to do. He had to put it into gear, make the propeller work. Baz searched around the brackets and the engine casing until he found the only thing that looked like it might be a gear lever. Which way did it go – left or right? As he hesitated, frightened of doing the wrong thing, he saw a swirl of turbulence beyond the stern of the boat, and then something came bursting up through the surface in a great eruption of froth and spray. Metal cylinders . . . glistening black rubber . . . the unmistakable flash of a diver's mask. Like tentacles the looped breathing tubes surged through the water, the diver lunging forward, arm outstretched, fingers clawing, reaching . . . reaching . . .

Baz cried out in horror and tumbled backwards, his hand still on the gear lever. He felt the clunk of the motor engaging, and then the lever was wrenched from his grasp as the boat leaped into reverse. There was a muffled yell, a horrible thud beneath the transom. The dinghy rocked sideways but kept going, slewing round stern-first in an increasingly tight circle. *Oh God . . . oh God.* Baz scrambled to his knees and struck out at the lever, banging it across with the heel of his palm. An awful graunching sound – the screech of suffering gears – and the boat gave a violent jerk in the opposite direction. Baz was thrown towards the transom.

He fell onto the seat next to the outboard and grasped the tiller bar, swinging it wildly back and forth in an attempt to steady the boat. At the same time he was trying to look over his shoulder, terrified that the diver was about to come shooting up from the depths once more. Nothing there. *Oh God – just concentrate. Stop panicking and concentrate. Left this way . . . right that way. Left . . . right. OK, then. Go. Get this thing moving. Open up the throttle lever and get out. Get out, get out, get out!*

Baz looked behind him, still fearful that some great hand would rise up, that Preacher John's huge red fingers would appear over the edge of the transom. But it didn't happen. The marker buoys receded into the distance, bright spots of colour riding the swell.

For a while he simply kept going, heading in the direction of the mainland, engine running flat out. But once he felt relatively safe from attack or capture, Baz shut off speed, slowing the revs down to a minimum. He allowed his aching shoulders to sag, put a hand to the back of his neck and leaned forward. He couldn't escape the awful images that flashed through his head, or the pounding in his heart, no matter how hard he gunned the motor or how fast he travelled.

Jesus. That was awful. The sight of that diving mask, shooting up out of the water. The thud of the boat as it had ploughed straight into . . .

And the explosion. Again and again the explosion replayed itself before him, ripping through the side of the salvage boat – arcs of burning fuel shooting out like flamethrowers across the water – the painted word *Cormorant* swirling away into darkness – and the last deep belch of the ocean as the boat was swallowed up.

Preacher John was dead. And Isaac was dead. The two divers . . . he couldn't tell. They might have survived, might be swimming for the mainland right now, or they might not. It didn't matter. What mattered was that the bomb had actually worked.

And now it was over. The Ecks were gone.

But what was he planning to do next? Go back to X Isle? How?

Baz tried to get his bearings, looking from the blue hills of the mainland to the empty horizon on either side. But from which way had they come? Over there? Yes, he thought it was from the right. So . . . if he kept the mainland behind him, and to his left . . .

Yet if he was wrong he could miss the island completely, and simply keep travelling for ever. Or until the fuel ran out.

Baz looked beneath the seat of the boat and dragged out the red plastic fuel can. It was reassuringly heavy. Probably it had been filled in preparation for today's trip. He guessed that the petrol tank was full too, and maybe he'd check in a minute. What was that, though? Baz could see something else beneath the seat. A bottle of water! The divers had obviously come prepared to use the boat. As he reached down to retrieve the water, he discovered yet another object – some orange-coloured thing.

It turned out to be an old fishing spool – orange nylon line wrapped around a squareish wooden frame, the whole thing wedged firmly in between the seat supports and the planking. And this had been stuck under there for years by the look of it. It might even have been to the bottom of the ocean and back. Baz unwound a metre or two of the line from the spool. There were several ancient and rusty hooks, vicious-looking things, and he had to watch his fingers. Then came a circular lead weight, tyre shaped, a series of raised hemispheres pimpling its surface. Baz examined the hooks again. Amazingly there was still a fragment of bait attached to one of them, a long dried-up strip of fish, perhaps. Well, it was no good to anyone now.

He put the fishing spool and the bottle of water beside his feet, and checked his direction again. Was he really going to do this? There were only two choices, when it came down to it. Either he returned to the mainland, with all its hardships and danger, or he risked trying to find his friends. Risked going back to X Isle. And maybe never reaching it . . .

His dad would be there on the mainland, ready to take him in, and look after him. But the divers could be there also, watching the shoreline. Waiting for him. What would they do if they ever caught him? And what might they do to his dad?

Baz took a deep breath and opened up the throttle. One last look behind him, and then he swung the tiller round, adjusting the angle of the boat so that he was guiding its prow towards the blank and endless horizon.

CHAPTER
TWENTY-SEVEN

The weather had changed. It was just a growing mistiness to the air, nothing unusual, but for Baz the effect was devastating. The line of the horizon had gradually become less distinct, until it had finally disappeared. There was no sign of the island. And the mainland – his only possible reference point – had long gone, vanished into the surrounding haze.

Visibility was down to maybe a couple of hundred metres, so that the dinghy seemed to be in the centre of a huge circular tank of sea water. And for all Baz knew, he was simply going round and round the tank.

He shut the engine down to tickover, and took another swig from the water bottle. It was already half empty. He'd have to start being a bit more careful.

The surface of the sea had calmed, no waves now, just an oily rhythmic swell. Rising . . . falling . . . rising . . . falling. A terrible feeling of eeriness descended upon Baz, creeping across his shoulders and up the back of his neck. He was so completely alone, and so lost. Hopelessly, hopelessly lost. What was the point of wasting petrol when he hadn't a clue where he was?

Maybe he should just sit here until the mist cleared. Wait it out.

That could take hours, though. Days, even. He could drift miles and miles out of his way in that time, and never see land again. No. Keep going. Baz opened the throttle, and the engine picked up speed, a sturdily confident note that kept the sea-ghosts at bay.

It didn't last. A couple of minutes later the motor faltered, spluttering out of time alarmingly. It fired again, just briefly, and then died away. A last hollow rattle, a final cough. Silence. Baz stared at the engine in horror, and it took him a long moment to realize the likely cause of its failure. It had run out of fuel. He reached under the seat and pulled out the red plastic container once more.

The heady smell of petrol was reassuring, rising from the tank like a genie to grant Baz the wish of power. But once this fuel was gone, he was done for. Up the creek without a paddle – for a paddle was one piece of equipment that the divers had not bothered to include.

It took a good few pulls before the motor came back to life. Baz sat down, relieved if slightly out of breath, and knocked the engine into gear. Something flashed across the bows of the dinghy. He had no time to even blink, let alone wonder what it might be. And then the exact same thing happened again. And again . . .

Fish! A school of bright mackerel, dozens of them, silvery blue against the smooth surface of the swell, were passing from right to left, shooting out of the water at amazing speed. Baz immediately swung the tiller hard round so that the boat altered course. There was no reason for him to try and follow the mackerel shoal, other than that it was such a miraculous thing to witness. When was the last time anyone had seen a real live fish? Baz opened the motor flat out and leaned forward in his seat, craning his neck for a better view. He was never going to keep up with that glorious dancing display, but he wanted to watch it for as long as he could. More fish appeared – to his left and to his right – overtaking the dinghy and all heading the same way. He could see every detail of them now, the black and blue stripy patterns across their backs, the sharp-cut fins, the faces open-mouthed and wide-eyed, each with its permanently startled expression. Maybe something was chasing them, trying to catch them.

It occurred to him that if he was to use the fishing spool, he might catch some himself. How amazing would that be – to turn up on X Isle with a string of fresh mackerel?

To turn up on X Isle . . .

What did he think he was doing, chasing fish around and wasting fuel? He was supposed to be trying to find the island. And now he was more lost than ever. Baz turned down the throttle.

The leaping fish were far ahead of him, nearly out of sight. But then the entire school suddenly veered to the right, heading off in a new direction entirely. It happened as if at a given signal, or as though the surrounding wall of mist truly was a barrier that they couldn't pass. Most likely some fresh danger had caused the mackerel to abruptly alter course, but as they finally disappeared into the swell, Baz felt once again that he was trapped, doomed to patrol a circular arena from which there was no escape.

He idly allowed the boat to cruise towards the spot where the mackerel had swerved away, but found nothing there to explain their behaviour. Whatever secrets lay beneath the filthy grey water would remain hidden from him. The boat chugged on a little further before Baz grasped the meaning of his own thoughts. The filthy water . . . water that was no longer clear . . .

He swung the boat round and retraced his course, keeping the engine speed low as he studied the surrounding waves. They had become blue-green again. Somewhere around this area the murk had given way to clearer water – although it was difficult to pinpoint where exactly. In fact the change was more noticeable when viewed from a distance. Baz found that if he focused his gaze to about a hundred metres away, he could see a vague line – a difference in both the colour and the surface of the sea. Choppier that side, where the water was grey and muddy. Smoother here, where it was clear. As though two currents were meeting, fighting against one another.

It was the same line of change that had been seen from the island.

So . . . if he were to follow it, guide his boat along that path, would he be led to the island? Or some-where near it?

Baz looked from left to right, thankful to have found a starting point, but daunted by the fact that he now had to choose which way to turn. He decided that he would continue to follow the direction the mackerel had taken: to the right. They would be his guiding stars, his good-luck charms. Baz hauled the tiller across and increased the engine speed.

The visibility got worse if anything, the circle of mist drawing inwards, but Baz could still see the vague line that divided the fresh water from the foul, and he pressed on. He had no sense of time, no idea of how long he'd been out here, and for all he knew he was sailing in the wrong direction completely. Night could be about to fall, and he could be fifty miles from any land.

It was a terrifying thought, and so the sight of the hammer-head crane looming through the mist came like a vision from heaven. Baz could have wept.

Instead, he found himself whispering, 'Thank you! Oh, thank you, thank you, thank you!' He wasn't sure whether he was thanking God, or the mackerel, or the sturdy little Seagull engine beside him, but he was truly grateful.

The crane was far over to his right, which meant that the line of clear water must have moved yet further across. Baz altered direction and approached the precarious archway of stone and twisted metal. There was plenty of room between the crane and the church tower for the dinghy to pass through, and Baz wasn't concentrating particularly hard. As he stared into the lapping waters, he saw that there was something down there, a shimmering silvery oval, monstrous yet familiar. He sat back in shock. It was the church clock, dancing beneath the waves, as massive and as pale as a harvest moon.

The boat slewed round alarmingly and Baz had to

act quickly in order to avoid colliding with the crane. A few weeks ago that clock would never have been visible . . .

When he got to the jetty, Baz was amazed to see that the waves that slapped against the stone and concrete were tipped with white foam. The filthy soup that he'd been used to had all moved away. It had happened then. The waters around the island had cleared. It looked as though Preacher John's prayers had finally been answered. Too late for him, though.

It wasn't until he had tied up the boat and clambered to the top of the jetty that Baz gave any thought to what he was actually going to do next. All his concentration had been on his own desperate fight for survival, from the moment that he'd left X Isle to the moment of his return. And by a miracle he had survived.

But what now?

CHAPTER
TWENTY-EIGHT

Baz stood uncertainly beside the altar and gazed towards the high windows of the school building. Would somebody be on the lookout? Should he be trying to make his presence known, or should he be keeping his head down? There was no way of telling. He began to walk cautiously along the jetty.

The glass doors of the main entrance were open. Baz paused just inside the building, listening. All was silent. But then, as he approached the sort room, he heard Steiner's voice.

'Right, then. All chuffin' day we've been running around, turning this place upside down, and now that's it. We're not gonna waste any more time. Last chance. Where are those girls?'

It sounded as though Steiner had recovered from his punch in the head.

One of the fire doors was wedged open with a piece of wood. Baz inched a little closer. He could see some of the boys now, standing with their backs to him, just beyond a couple of half-stacked pallets. And in between the gaps Baz caught a glimpse of Steiner . . . Hutchinson . . . somebody else . . .

'Arghhh! Arghhh . . .' A cry of pain. Baz flinched at the sound. What was going on in there? He put a hand against the door frame and stood on tiptoe, craning his neck for a better view.

Jubo. He could see Jubo's face screwed up in agony, the top half of his body rocking from side to side. Steiner and Hutchinson were standing close to Jubo . . . doing something to him . . .

'Arghhhh.' Another yell . . .

They had his hand in the bench vice! A couple of the boys shifted position and Baz's view became clearer. Jubo's face was battered – a big red graze across one of his cheekbones. He looked as though he'd already taken a hammering, but now he was being tortured, his right hand trapped in the heavy vice. Hutchinson was brandishing a length of wood – a pickaxe handle by the look of it – keeping the boys at bay.

'Get back!' Steiner roared. 'Or I'll break his bloody fingers! Back!' The group of boys had instinctively lurched forward, but at Steiner's threat they hesitated. Hutchinson moved belligerently towards the boys, the pickaxe handle raised to shoulder height like a baseball bat, and the boys retreated. It was clear that any rescue attempt would only make things worse for Jubo.

'Let him go! You friggin' . . .' Amit was hissing with fury.

'Yeah? You think this is bad? You think I'm just playing around here? Watch!' Steiner continued to face the angry boys, his front teeth biting down on his lower lip, shoulders jerking to one side as he tightened the vice.

'Gaaaaaahhhhh! Aaaahhh!' Jubo was screaming now, a terrible sound.

And then the back doors of the sort room gave a rattle, and Ray appeared. He stood against the light, his hands raised, waving . . .

'OK! OK! I know where they are! Stop! Stop!' He looked as though he were trying to flag down a train. 'I can find them! I know where they are! Stop!'

'Aha! *Now* they start showing themselves. *Now* we're getting somewhere!' Steiner turned towards the back door. He must have loosened the vice a little, because Jubo stopped screaming. His head fell forward, then rocked back again, eyes closed, mouth still open. Sweat and tears poured down his face, and his dark hair was drenched.

'Yeah, now we're getting somewhere,' said Steiner. 'Should have done this in the first place, shouldn't we? 'Stead of sodding around all day! Right, you little tart – go and get those girls back here.'

Ray didn't go out the way he'd come in. Instead he made his way across the room towards the fire doors, weaving quickly through the clutter of crates and boxes. All eyes followed him – and then widened in dis-belief. Baz had decided that there was no longer any point in attempting to hide. He stood just inside the doorway now, and stared back at the shocked faces of his friends.

'Baz? Oh my God . . . you're back . . .' Ray took another couple of steps forward, looking as though he might collapse. 'What . . . what . . . ?'

And then all the other boys were murmuring his name in wonder. *It's Baz . . . Baz . . . he's back! God, he made it . . .*

Steiner's loud voice rose over the boys' heads. 'Oi!

What's going on down there? Who's that? Is the boat back? Right. You better get going then, Cornflake. 'Cos if those girls aren't here in two minutes—'

'The boat isn't back,' said Baz. He was looking directly at Steiner, but his words were for his companions. 'And it isn't coming back, either. Preacher John's dead. Yeah. Along with all the rest of them.'

'What?' Steiner's mottled jaw was hanging open, in an expression of total incomprehension. But Baz didn't say any more for the moment. He looked at Ray, then the others. Saw their eyes as they took in the meaning of his words – disbelief at first, then hope, then the realization that he was telling the truth.

'What d'you mean, *dead*? How?' Steiner couldn't get it at all.

Baz let his eyes travel around the group, returning every stunned gaze with a slight nod of his head. *Yeah, it's true. Amit . . . Dyson. Gene, Robbie. It's true. It's true, Ray. We did it.*

He looked across the room at Jubo. The poor guy was obviously still in pain, and still held captive, but his eyes too were filled with amazement.

'It's true, Jubes,' Baz called out. 'We've done it.'

Steiner and Hutchinson exchanged a quick glance, their manner uncertain.

'What're you on about?'

'Yeah.' Amit was the first to turn towards the capos. 'Sort of makes a difference, doesn't it? It's just the two of you now. And us.'

'You better keep back, Amit.' Hutchinson lifted the pickaxe handle from his shoulder. 'Unless you want your brains spread all up the wall. I dunno what's going on here, but if something's happened to Preacher John, then we're taking over.'

'That's right.' Steiner seemed to be regaining some confidence. 'This kid's talking bollocks for all we know, but we're in charge either way, so don't forget it. Right, you – Cornflake. Go and fetch those girls. Let's get you all here where I can see you.'

Ray pushed past Baz, gripping his arm briefly and giving it a squeeze. As he disappeared into the corridor he muttered, 'Back in a bit.'

'Hey, Steiner.' Gene spoke up. 'Why don't you just let go of Jubo and we can talk about this? There's no point in anyone getting hurt. Not now.'

'Belt up.' Steiner wasn't prepared to negotiate. 'Nobody's letting anybody go, so get that straight. You.' He pointed at Baz. 'What's happened to Preacher John?'

'He's dead,' said Baz. 'The boat sank.' He thought about that for a moment. Should he say how? What difference did it make now? 'We sank it,' he said. 'We sank the *Cormorant*. All of us. We blew it up.'

'You sank it! Yeah, right.' Steiner's voice was a massive sneer. 'How could you do that? You were all here.'

'We built a bomb,' said Gene. 'Put it on the boat and wired it up to the winch motor. It wasn't that hard.'

'A *bomb*? You're lying.' Steiner was still aggressive, but he seemed less sure now.

Gene just shrugged. 'That's what we did. Makes no difference whether you believe it or not. Come on, Baz. Tell us what happened out there.'

'OK.' Baz took a deep breath. 'Well, we got over

443

Skelmersley way, and there was this petrol sign sticking up. BP. Looked like there could be a store there or something. So the divers went down. I . . . I was in the cabin . . .' His voice began to falter as he relived the moment. 'Preacher John was making me pray. And then Isaac came in. He had a shotgun. He was gonna kill Preacher John while the others weren't around – shoot him – like that's what he'd planned. So he could take over, I suppose. But Preacher John was ready for him. He'd already taken the cartridges out of the gun. Then Preacher John shot Isaac instead. Sacrificed him.'

The sort room had gone completely quiet. Everyone was hanging on his words now – even the capos.

'Yeah. And then there was this bell, like a signal from the divers to winch the salvage up? So Preacher John chucked me overboard, and he pulled at the starter handle. Tried to start the winch motor. I was . . . I just . . . tried to swim out of the way. And then Preacher John saw I was still alive, and that maybe he should have got rid of me properly. So he took a few shots at me too. But I think he ran out of bullets. Anyway, he went to have another go at starting the motor. I got round . . . swam round the back of the boat. And then . . . then it . . . blew up. Just like we imagined it, Gene. It was massive – fire everywhere – and a huge great hole in the side of the boat. It sank. I still can't . . . I still can't believe it happened.'

Gene shook his head and slowly let out his breath. 'God . . . so what did you *do*? How did you get back here?'

'Huh? Oh. I was in the tender. That's what they

444

called the dinghy. I got in the dinghy . . . tried to cut it loose. And then the rope snapped. *Cormorant* went down . . .' Baz couldn't say any more. He felt very sick and shaky all of a sudden.

'So you came back in the dinghy?'

Baz nodded.

Again there was a long breathing silence, the information, and what it meant, slowly sinking in.

Steiner turned to Hutchinson and muttered, 'Chuffin' hell. I think they mean it. They've bloody killed 'em all. Friggin' unbelievable . . .'

'Steiner . . . let me go, man. Please . . . my hand . . .' Jubo was swaying in agony, his face still wreathed in sweat.

'Shaddup.' Steiner flicked the backs of his fingers across Jubo's face. 'You've got whatever's coming to you, arsehole. And you've had it coming a long time. Yeah, and if there's no Preacher John to stop me, I can do what I like, can't I? Eh? Think about that!' He gave the vice a quick tweak, and Jubo yelled out again.

'Eh? Right? Right.' Steiner looked around at the group of boys. 'You know what this means, don't you? You know what this makes you? Murderers. I dunno how you've done it, but that's what you are – murderers, the lot of you! Well, you might have got rid of Preacher John, but now you've got us to deal with instead. Maybe you never thought of that. But from now on we take over. And you'll work for us.'

'How you gonna make us do that?' said Amit. 'There's seven of us. Only two of you.'

'How'm I gonna *make* you? Well, I could start by kicking the crap out of you. How would that be?'

445

'You gotta sleep sometime, Steiner. What're you gonna do – take it in shifts?'

Steiner looked as though he would have gone for Amit there and then, but that would have meant letting go of the vice. He pointed a shaking finger at Amit.

'Don't you worry about me sleeping, pal. You better worry about whether you'll ever wake up again.'

'Yeah, yeah. You're all gob.' Amit was deliberately taunting Steiner, trying to get him to make a move.

'Whoa – hang on. Don't fall for it.' Hutchinson put a hand on Steiner's arm. 'Just stay cool. Think about this for a minute.'

Steiner drew back. 'Yeah.' He looked at the crowd of faces. 'Yeah. You know what, though? He's right. We've only got to take an eye off them for a second and they'll do us like they did Preacher John. So there's only one choice, right? We gotta get rid of them first.'

'You reckon?'

'Well, think about it. What do we need them for? What good are they now? There's enough in t' store-room for you and me to be going on with. Maybe for years. No point in feeding this lot, is there? So let's get shot of 'em.'

Hutchinson stood facing the boys with his pickaxe handle raised. 'Yeah, you're right,' he said. But then he seemed to reconsider. 'What – you mean, now?'

Steiner said, 'No. Not like that. I got a better idea – but we're gonna need some guns. Couple o' guns.'

'You wanna shoot them?'

'Not unless they make us. We'll give them a sporting chance at any rate. Take 'em down t' jetty, is what I'm thinking, yeah? Get 'em to jump off and start swimming for it. Count to sixty and *then* start shooting. Make it more fun. Here . . . I've got the keys . . .' He reached into the pocket of his shorts. 'Go t' storeroom and unlock the armoury. Get us a couple of guns – whatever's in there.'

'And leave you here by yourself?' said Hutchinson. 'Don't think so.'

Steiner thought about that for a few moments. 'OK,' he said. 'Gimme a hammer, or a crowbar or something. Make it heavy.'

Hutchinson turned towards the workbench. He looked quickly from left to right, then grabbed a claw hammer from where it hung on the wall. 'Here.' He handed it to Steiner.

Steiner raised the hammer above Jubo's head, his other hand still gripping the vice. Jubo was bent over, cowering, trying to shield himself from the hammer. But there was nowhere for him to hide.

'Right – get over in t' corner, the lot of you! Over there, away from t' door! Go on – move!'

Baz looked to Gene for guidance – ready to rush the capos, if that was to be the decision. And for a moment it was touch and go, the boys beginning to inch forward, weighing up their chances. But Gene muttered beneath his breath, 'No. Don't try it. That's Jubo's head.'

'Move away!' Steiner yelled again, and the boys shuffled back towards the corner furthest from the door.

'Right! Here's what's gonna happen. Hutchinson's gonna be out of here for maybe a minute. Maybe less.

And if anyone tries anything, I'm gonna smack this guy so hard his friggin' eyeballs'll fall out! You think I wouldn't do it – you watch me! It'd be a chuffin' pleasure, and one less piece of crap to worry about. Ready, Hutch?' Steiner was sweating, his face glistening in the light.

'Yeah – hang on a minute. Which key is it?' Hutchinson had his pickaxe handle tucked beneath his arm now as he sorted through the heavy bunch.

'For Chrissake. It's the two padlock keys. Pair of— What the chuff's this?' Steiner was staring towards the doorway.

Baz turned to look. Ray was walking into the room, followed by Nadine and Steffie. The two girls were close behind him, each carrying something as though to conceal it. Jam jars? They looked like jam jars . . .

No pausing, no hesitating, no stopping to weigh up the situation, the three of them marched in single file towards the workbench. As they neared the astonished capos, Ray peeled off to the left. He reached beneath the far end of the bench and grabbed what looked like the end of a broomstick – but it was one of the torches that Gene had made for lighting the altar fires. Ray took a cigarette lighter from his pocket, held it to the oily rag . . . and flicked it . . .

'What the hell . . . ?' Hutchinson dropped his bunch of keys and fumbled for a grip on the pickaxe handle.

'Now!' said Ray.

Hutchinson staggered back against the workbench, soaked from head to foot in whatever Steffie had just thrown over him. At the same time Nadine hurled the contents of her jam jar at Steiner – a great slew of liquid that caught him straight in the face and splashed all down his clothing. His T-shirt and shorts were instantly dark-stained and dripping.

'You friggin' little bi—' Steiner reeled sideways, spluttering and choking, wiping his streaming eyes. He half recovered, got himself upright and swung his hammer into the air above Nadine's head. 'I'll bloody kill you for that!'

And then he saw the blazing torch . . .

Ray was coming at him, waving the firebrand from side to side, the flames making a dull roaring sound. Steiner immediately dropped the hammer and backed away, his eyes wide with horror.

'Jesus!' Gene was the first to grasp what was happening. 'They've covered 'em in petrol!' He leaped forward. 'Ray! Ray! Don't do it!'

But Ray had the two capos backed into a corner now. They tumbled over one another, crying out with terror as Ray danced in front of them, jabbing the flaming brand perilously close to their writhing bodies.

'Ray! Ray . . . Ray . . .' Baz tried to get in between Ray and the capos, moved towards him in a crouch, his arms extended. 'Don't! Just . . . just don't, OK?'

He didn't seem to be getting through. Ray's eyes were wild – fevered – as though he were in some kind of trance. Jabbing, poking, weaving from side to side, he brought the flames time and again to within centimetres of the terrified capos.

'No! No! I haven't said anything! I won't tell! Urrghhh—' Hutchinson's pleas and squeals were cut short as Steiner elbowed him in the face, the two of them each fighting to get behind the other for protection. On bare knees they crawled, scrabbling at the wall behind them, cornered like rats in a barn. Black oily smoke surrounded them, and the air was filled with the smell of raw spirit.

'Burn 'em, Ray! Jus' do it, man!' Jubo pushed himself into the circle, sucking at his injured hand and egging Ray on.

And then others joined in – urgent mutters through gritted teeth. *Go on, Ray, torch those toe-rags! Do it!*

'For Chrissake, Jubo!' Gene tried to make a grab at the waving brand of fire, but Ray simply switched hands and fended him off.

'Rrrr . . . rrrssss . . .' He was growling, hissing, teeth bared – a wild animal taunting his prey. Baz was frightened of getting too close, of physically intervening, knowing that if he tipped the balance the wrong way, the two capos would go straight up in flames. They'd be burned alive.

Someone wriggled past him, forcing him to one side. Steffie . . .

'Hey – Ray. Ray . . . come on, babe. It's OK. Come on – give it to me.'

Steffie put a hand on Ray's back, moved it up to his shoulder. Ray flinched, but didn't pull away.

'It's only me, Ray. Come on, that's enough. We've done it, yeah? We've done it.'

Steffie's arm was around Ray's shoulder now. She pulled him sideways towards her, holding him tight for a few seconds.

And Ray responded. He lowered the torch. There was no resistance as Gene reached towards him and gently took it.

'OK?' Steffie leaned forward and looked into Ray's face. 'OK, babe?'

'Yeah.' Ray's head hung down. 'Yeah.'

Steiner and Hutchinson untangled themselves and rolled over onto their knees, but Gene stopped them from going any further.

'Stay there,' he said. 'We haven't finished with you yet.'

'Say right.' Jubo was brandishing the claw hammer in his uninjured hand. 'Payback time.'

'Whoa, hang on, Jubes.' Gene held the torch upright and looked around at the circle of boys. The room was heavy with smoke, hanging in a pall below the high ceiling and giving everything a slightly blurred look.

'What are we gonna do with them?' said Gene. 'I mean, seriously.'

'How about seriously doing what they were gonna do with us?' Amit had retrieved the pickaxe handle, and he jabbed it at Steiner's shoulder. 'How about we get a couple of guns and then chuck these two off the jetty? Give 'em the same sporting chance that we were gonna get?'

'No,' said Gene. 'No guns. I'm not having that.'

'Well, they can't stay here. Not alive, anyhow.' Amit gave Steiner another prod. 'We either kill 'em or we make 'em swim.'

'Give 'em the dinghy.' Robbie made the first practical suggestion. 'Send 'em back to the mainland.'

'The *dinghy*?' Amit wasn't keen on this. 'That's our only way out of here. What do we wanna give 'em that for? Make the sods swim, that's what I say.'

'No, the dinghy's not a bad idea,' said Gene. 'We could maybe build a raft or something if we ever wanted to. Got plenty of wood and water butts and stuff. Come on. Let's get rid of them now, while we can. Then it's done. Yeah?'

'We do a vote,' said Jubo. 'I votin' we shove 'em on the altar and torch 'em. We take 'em to the jetty and talk about it on the way down.'

'I'm not setting light to anybody, Jubes. I'll tell you that now.' Gene was adamant.

'You won't need to, mate,' said Dyson. 'There's plenty of others here that'd do it. Me, for a kick-off. And it's not up to you in any case. So let's get 'em to the jetty and take a vote. We do it like we always do it, yeah? Everybody gets a vote.'

Gene looked at Dyson, and seemed ready to argue some more. But then he shrugged. 'OK, have it your way. We'll take a vote, and whatever it is I'll go along with it. Hold this, Baz.' He handed Baz the flaming torch, went over to the workbench and took down a roll of electric cabling that hung on a nail. Then he rummaged around the cluttered bench until he found a pair of pliers.

'This'll do.' Gene cut off a length of cabling. 'Right,' he said to the capos. 'I'm gonna tie this round your ankles. You try anything and you're gonna get whacked. Got it?'

Steiner and Hutchinson scowled up at him but said nothing.

Gene crouched down in front of the capos. He tied one end of the cabling to Hutchinson's left ankle and then began to tie the other to Steiner's right, leaving about a half-metre length between the two.

Robbie turned to Steffie and said, 'So where were you anyway – the library?'

'Yeah,' said Steffie. 'But then we went back down to the art room. Tell you about it later.'

'OK.' Gene got to his feet. 'They can walk, but they can't run. Now get up.'

It was a strangely silent procession that made its way down to the jetty. Gene was out in front, alone. Then came Steiner and Hutchinson, hobbled together and flanked on either side by Jubo and Dyson. Baz walked immediately behind them, still carrying the torch – although by this time it was merely smouldering, the oil-soaked material having turned to a fragile bundle of layered ashes.

And then came everybody else, a loose and ragged crowd. So much had happened, and there was so much to think about. Perhaps that was why so little was being said.

Baz held an image in his mind of Steffie putting her arm around Ray's shoulders. Calling him 'babe'. It hadn't merely been a gesture of persuasion or restraint. It had been one of comfort and affection – more than that even. Familiarity. The hug of a friend . . . a loving friend . . .

And Ray had listened to her, responded to Steffie's words. They knew each other, Baz was sure of it. He glanced behind him, and saw that Ray was walking with Nadine and Steffie now, a threesome, slightly apart from the others. It hurt him to see it. Here was he, back from the dead, having gone through an experience that was sure to give him nightmares for months, and Ray had barely spoken to him. Instead he was walking with Nadine. And Steffie . . .

They came to the beginning of the jetty, and the capos hung back, plainly terrified of going any further. Hutchinson began to bluster and then to blub.

'You can't do this! We . . . wouldn't really have hurt you. We were just . . . Gene! Don't let them. Don't let themmmm . . .'

Gene turned round to look at him. 'Too late for all that,' he said. 'And I can't save you in any case. We have to go with the vote, mate. Majority rules. Sorry.' He seemed to have given in – prepared now to burn these two on the altar, if that was what everyone decided.

Steiner's face had gone a weird grey colour beneath his mass of freckles. 'Listen, Jubo' – he was trying to sound reasonable, but his voice shook as he spoke – 'back there . . . you know . . . with the vice. I was just worried about the girls, right? I had to find them before the boat came back. Sure, it was a bit rough – but I was running out of time, yeah? I didn't have any choice. Look. We don't need to do this . . . we can talk . . .'

Jubo reached in his pocket as Steiner blabbered on.

'And we can all just stay here, can't we? Now that Preacher's gone? We could all—'

Jubo thrust a cigarette lighter into Steiner's face and clicked it. Steiner jumped back from the flame, barging into Hutchinson so that the two of them almost fell.

'Guess which way me gonna vote,' said Jubo. 'You wan' me give you a clue?' He waved the lighter a couple of times and put it away. 'Jus' keep walkin',' he said.

The altar was a horrible sight. The blackened remains of Old Bill still lay there, a charred and rain-sodden mess amongst the bits of unburned wood. Baz looked at it for a moment and turned away. No matter how much he had suffered at the hands of Steiner and Hutchinson, he knew that he could never condemn them to that – nor stand by and watch it happen. He wondered if he was going to be put in the crazy position of having to defend the pair.

'OK,' said Gene. 'We'll take a vote then.' He waved a hand towards the altar. 'Either we sling 'em on there and set light to them, or we kick them off the island. Which is it gonna be? Hands up those who want to watch them burn.'

Hutchinson collapsed. He fell to his knees, wailing like a child. 'No . . . nooo . . .'

'Hands up!' cried Gene.

But nobody raised a finger, not even Jubo. The boys shuffled uncomfortably, glancing at one another beneath lowered brows.

He was a clever guy, thought Baz, that Gene. He'd known all along that nobody in their right minds would have voted for such a terrible thing once they were faced with the reality of it.

'OK. So they can have the dinghy and take their chances. Come on.' Gene moved away from the altar and walked to the edge of the jetty. 'I'll get the engine started.' He began to clamber down the stony slope.

Steiner and Hutchinson were being roughly man-handled across the jetty. Maybe there was a general feeling that they'd got off lightly, or maybe some of the boys saw this as their last chance to get a bit of revenge in, but the capos were being helped on their way by numerous sly kicks and punches.

Baz didn't join in. It had already occurred to him that the capos weren't getting off lightly at all . . .

Then, amidst the hoots and jeers of the boys, came one of those sudden and unaccountable pauses – a chance moment when everybody must have been drawing breath at the same time. An empty space. And into that space, from somewhere behind him, Baz heard a voice, low and urgent.

'Well, we can't go on like this. You're gonna have to tell him sometime—' The speaker stopped, apparently aware of the silence. Baz turned round and saw Steffie's guilty face, a sideways glance towards him, her mouth still close to Ray's ear.

Baz could feel himself beginning to burn inside, a horrible sense that he was being betrayed in some way.

Then Dyson was grabbing his arm, pulling him towards the slope of the jetty. 'Come on, mate. You're missing it all.'

Baz knew that he was missing something, but he couldn't figure out what.

Drrm-dm-dumdum . . .

Gene had already got the motor started. He stood up in the stern of the boat and shouted, 'OK! Get 'em in here.' Steiner and Hutchinson were being hustled down the slope.

Baz looked at the dinghy, the little Seagull motor chugging away, and it was like looking at an old friend. He knew every bit of that thing now, a deep and personal contact. Yet it had only been today that he'd first sat in it. Only today. Already it seemed like a lifetime ago.

'Hey, Gene!' he shouted.

Gene looked up at the sound of his name, brushing his fingers back through his unruly curls. 'What?'

'There's a fishing line in there,' said Baz. 'I wanna keep it. Get it for me, willya?'

Gene looked around the boat and stooped down. 'What, this thing?' He held up the fishing spool.

'Yeah.'

'OK.'

Steiner and Hutchinson were in the boat. They sat side by side in the stern, two wretched figures, and Baz could see Gene leaning forward and giving instructions. Move the tiller this way, move it that way. Throttle open, throttle closed. Reverse gear, forward gear. Baz knew all about it.

Jubo and Amit had moved a little closer to the waterline. Baz saw Jubo stoop to pick up a stone, and then Dyson, off to his right, do the same.

Gene got out of the boat. He was pointing towards the crane and church tower, dark shapes in the mist. He might have been giving directions to a couple of tourists.

The boat began to pull away, bumping awkwardly along the concrete blocks of the jetty. Steiner was at the tiller. He swung it round the wrong way, and the dinghy hit the jetty again. Then he seemed to get the hang of it, and the boat nosed its way into clear water.

'Ow!' Hutchinson grabbed at his elbow – somebody had winged a stone at him. Jubo.

'Ey! That one from me, you rass!'

Another stone. And another. Gene ducked low as a growing hail of stones rained down towards the boat. Everyone had seen their chance, and now they were all at it, scrabbling around on the side of the jetty for likely lumps of stone and concrete.

'Yah! Get out of here, you friggin' weirdos!'

The engine nearly cut out – Steiner presumably having turned the throttle the wrong way – and Hutchinson's voice could be heard, shouting above the catcalls of the boys.

'You call *me* a weirdo?' He twisted round in his seat, his face snarling with pain and rage. 'Yeah, well, I know a few things you don't! Ask that one!'

He raised an arm and pointed to the top of the jetty, where Nadine and Ray and Steffie stood all in a row. 'Yeah – that little tart!'

CHAPTER
TWENTY-NINE

A couple of the boys turned round to look, just briefly, but most took no notice. They continued to hurl stones after the receding boat.

'Yah! Bloody good riddance!'

Baz stared at Hutchinson. It was the second time that the capo had hinted at some private piece of knowledge, some hidden information. What was it that he was carrying away with him?

Steiner had apparently learned how to work the throttle, and the dinghy was soon out of throwing range. Its outline became less distinct as it approached the fallen crane and tower, heavy mist enveloping it, flattening it to a vague grey shape. The engine note slowed. Baz could just see the dinghy edging its way through the arch of stone and metal, and then it was gone, disappearing into the mist.

They stood there motionless, the X Isle boys, and listened to the fading sound of the Seagull motor. For a long time it remained audible, a buzzing insect, shrinking as it flew. A bee . . . a fly . . . a gnat . . . a nothing. Gone.

And even when there was nothing left to see or hear,

each boy remained where he was, looking out at the blank white fog, a long moment of reflection.

Gene turned round and climbed the stony slope, and then others began to move as well. They became a group again, gathering together at the top of the jetty, drawing Ray and the two girls into their number.

Gene handed Baz the fishing spool. 'Reckon they'll make it?'

Baz looked down at the spool and shook his head. 'I wouldn't wanna try it. There's only about half a tank of petrol. And you can't see a thing out there.'

Another spell of silence as everybody thought about that.

'Tough, man.' Jubo wasn't sympathetic. 'Better they *don't* make it. People know the preacher gone an' they *all* be comin' over. We don't be here on our own too long then.'

'Here on our own . . .'

'Wow.'

'My God.' Amit looked around in wonder. 'We've *done* it! We've really actually *done* it . . .'

And at last it began to sink in. No Preacher John, no Isaac, no divers, no capos . . . the island was theirs. Amit drew back his arm and hurled the final stone far out into the sea. Bright droplets rose from the surface, sparkled briefly against the light and disappeared into a spreading ring of white foam. Clear water. Clear, clean water . . .

'Wow. Look at that.'

'But what are we gonna *do*?'

'Yeah, where do we start? Come on. No good just standing around here.'

'We gotta celebrate. Gotta celebrate . . .'

A wild energy was starting to build, a head of pressure that had to be released.

'First t'ing I gonna do is *eat*,' said Jubo. 'Me got the rumbles, man.'

'Yeah – a feast!'

'Feast! Feast!'

'Feast . . . feast . . . feast . . .'

The chant was taken up, and the boys exploded into life, leaping, jumping, punching the air, kicking at the gravel with their feet as they danced down the jetty.

'Hot chicken curry!'

'Tuna fish and rice!'

'Spaghetti and meatballs!'

'Yay! Come on, Baz! Come on, girls – feast! Woo-hooo!'

Away they went, a twirling, skipping crowd, leaving Baz to follow at his own pace. Maybe he'd seen too much today, knew too much of what it was like out there on that empty sea. He'd witnessed death and devastation, and had come horribly close to being lost for good. There would be nightmares, he knew, and they would surely haunt him for ever. He didn't feel up to joining in with the mad celebrations.

'Baz?' Nadine caught up with him, touching his arm, gently holding him back. And then Steffie and Ray were there as well. None of them were looking particularly jubilant, considering their brilliant success in dealing with the capos. In fact Ray looked scared if anything.

'What?' said Baz. He knew something was coming,

and he had the sinking feeling that he wasn't going to like it.

'Listen . . .' Nadine's beautiful eyes were troubled, serious. 'You need to talk to Ray. I mean, the two of you are friends . . . you have to . . .'

'Yeah, look, Baz,' said Steffie. 'Me and Nadine are gonna go on ahead. But you just stay here for a minute and talk to Ray, yeah?'

'OK.' Baz shrugged. He didn't know what it was he was supposed to talk about.

'And you . . .' Steffie turned towards Ray. 'Don't bottle it, OK? How do you think he's gonna feel if he hears it from someone else? Yeah? All right?'

Ray nodded. 'Yeah.'

'Right, then.' Steffie pushed her hair back behind one ear and smiled. 'Come on, Nad.'

The two of them walked away. They were scruffier now than when they'd first arrived, clothes a little grubbier, hair not quite so neat. But they still had an elegance about them, a way of moving that was quite different to the gaggle of boys now disappearing up the pathway to the school.

'So . . . what?' Baz turned to face Ray. 'What is it? You were great today, by the way. I didn't . . . I didn't get to say that yet. But you were just amazing, all three of you.'

All three of you . . .

'You know them, don't you?' he said. 'I mean, Nadine. And . . . and Steffie. You know them from before somewhere.'

Ray looked at him, big dark eyes so solemn and worried looking. He lifted a slim hand and tucked his hair behind one ear, shook it back. A graceful movement.

'Yeah,' he said. 'We were at school together. Here. At Tab Hill.'

'Here? You can't have been. This was a—'

And then Baz saw it. At last he realized. At last he understood. And it was a thing so shocking that the whole world seemed to tilt around him. The stones beneath his feet were soft as marshmallows, sinking at his heels so that he had to tip forward to keep his balance.

'Jesus . . . Jesus. I can't . . . can't believe it.' He stared back at Ray, and saw every feature as if for the first time. So plain and so obvious now. 'You're a bloody girl, aren't you? You're a bloody *girl*!'

Ray blinked, taken by surprise perhaps at not having to spell it out after all. 'That's right, Baz. I'm a bloody girl.' The tiniest trace of a smile, there and gone. 'I'm a bloody girl.'

'Oh my God . . .' Baz put a hand to his forehead, feeling as though his brain were about to leap out. 'Oh my God . . . you were . . . all along, you were . . .'

It began to make sense. The way Ray was always up first every morning, the first to use the jakes, the shower . . . always so private. How it was Ray who had instinctively understood the needs of the other girls when they arrived, sorted out their washroom stuff. The other girls . . .

'They didn't know I was here, though. Nad and Steffie. And I didn't expect them to be turning up. I told them not to say anything. Not to tell.'

Baz remembered the look of shock on Steffie's face

when she'd first seen Ray. Helping with the bags in the corridor.

'So they knew you as . . . like . . . somebody else. How did they get used to calling you Ray?'

'They've always called me that. It's spelled R-A-E, though. Rae. Short for Rachel.'

A fresh wave of shock and bewilderment washed over Baz. He was never going to be able to get this into his head. R-A-E. Rae.

'Baz? Listen, it's still OK, isn't it? We're still OK?'

Ray . . . Rachel . . . put a hand out as if to touch him, but Baz couldn't let that happen. He backed away, his own hands raised in defence.

'Whoa. Whoa. This is too weird. I can't just . . . I mean, I feel . . .'

Stupid, was what he felt. And angry. Everything had been turned around, tipped upside down and inside out. A trick. A joke.

He began to walk away, furious that he'd been so exposed, so taken in.

'Baz, please! Please don't . . .'

Ray caught up with him – this new Ray, this stranger. Rachel. She grabbed at his arm. *She* . . .

'I had to do it! I had to!'

'What d'you mean, had to? Had to make me look an idiot?'

'Me and Mum – we were desperate. Mum was sick for nearly a month. She couldn't . . . couldn't work. No food. We didn't have any way to live. I knew Mum'd be better off without me around. So we tried this. I made her let me. But they would only take boys, and so this was the only way I could get here – if I was a boy. So I

464

cut my hair short, scruffed myself up a bit. Mum reckoned I'd be found out straight away, but I said it had to be worth a go. The worst that could happen was I'd be sent back. We didn't know it'd be so dangerous here . . . Baz, please! Please stop a minute. I don't want to walk in there with the others around. You've got to let me try and say how it was.'

'I don't *care*, OK?' Baz came to a halt. 'I don't care why you had to come here, or pretend you were a boy . . . or whatever. But you could have told me. You didn't have to let me go on thinking' – Baz struggled with the words – 'go on thinking that . . .'

Go on thinking what? He didn't know. 'You should have told me, that's all.'

'I wanted to. I really wanted to. But how could I? I didn't know what you'd do, or what you'd say. If anyone found out – and they *would* have found out – what would've happened to me then?'

She was holding onto his arm, eyes filling with tears. Her hand was shaking.

A horrible thought came into Baz's head. 'Somebody did find out, didn't they? The capos. They knew, didn't they? What did you do last night, when Steiner caught you? What did you *do*?'

'Nothing! Nothing!' Rae was really crying now, tears streaming down her face. 'I just told them, that's all. They were gonna put me down the hole. So I told them. Told them I was a girl, told them everything. And they believed me. But then, when they did believe me, they said OK, they wouldn't put me down the hole, but I had to make them a promise. They made me say that next weekend . . . next Sunday, I'd prove

465

it to them. They said they'd keep it a secret, but that next Sunday I had to go and have a drink with them. Have some fun, they said. And so I promised . . .'

She looked so vulnerable, so unhappy, and Baz wanted to respond somehow. Wanted to reach out to her. Hold her hand. But he couldn't.

'Well . . . I'm sorry,' he mumbled. 'I'm really sorry. But this is just too weird for me. It's just too friggin' weird.'

They stood there awkwardly, Baz digging at the stones with the heel of his trainer, Rae wiping her eyes with her fingers.

'What do you want me to do?' she said. 'There's no point in keeping it a secret any longer. No need to. But maybe . . . maybe I shouldn't tell everyone right away. Maybe I'll say nothing for a bit. What do you think?'

Baz shrugged. What difference did it make? But then, perhaps she was right. He could just picture the looks on their faces – all the other boys – and the uproar it would cause. The digs, the teasing, the stupid remarks.

'Yeah,' he said. 'OK. Maybe say nothing. Look . . . Rae . . . just give me chance to get used to the idea, all right? I don't wanna walk in there now and for everyone to know, and then have to deal with all that. Not right now. Not after today. Maybe we could just leave it till tomorrow, yeah?'

'All right. I don't think I could handle it either.' Rae seemed relieved. 'And tonight . . . well, I'll just sleep upstairs with Stef and Nad. Nobody'll notice.'

'Yeah.'

They began to walk along the jetty.

'You still mad at me?'

Baz sighed. 'No, I'm not mad. I'm just wiped out. I've friggin' had it.'

And this was still too weird, he thought. Ray was a girl. A girl. And her name was Rachel . . .

No, he couldn't cope with that at all.

'Hey – where've you two been? Come on!'

The celebrations were already under way. Bottles and cans littered the seating area of the slob room, and everyone was sprawled around, eating and drinking and talking all at the same time.

'It worked. I just can't believe it really worked. I *never* thought it would . . .' Robbie, staring down at the tin of tuna fish in his hand, shaking his head.

'Yeah. But the sort room – that was the best bit! Ray coming in like that, and Nadine and Steffie. Hey, Ray' – Amit looked up – 'what happened? How did you plan that one?'

'Wasn't really me.' Ray – Rachel – sat down and grabbed a can of Coke from one of several multi-packs that lay around the floor. 'Christ,' she said. 'Where did you get this lot from? What did you do? Break into the store?'

She'd instantly assumed her disguise, become one of the lads again, her husky voice calm and steady, no more tears. Baz just stared at her in wonder. Were all girls such good actors?

'Yeah. We used Steiner's keys,' said Amit. 'Come on, though – tell us where you've been all day, and all about the jam-jar thing, and the petrol.'

'I'd got up to go to the jakes' – Rachel rubbed the

467

back of her hand across her nose and sniffed – 'really early this morning. And then Baz came in and we heard the divers talking outside the back window. They said they were going to take the little one with them. Tie her up. Tie her to the whatsit . . . the transom. So I . . . we . . . thought that meant Steffie. We thought they were taking Steffie out on the boat. She was gonna be on the boat! I couldn't believe it. So I ran upstairs to the art room, and got Steff and Nad, and then we all snuck down through the kitchen, up the back stairs and hid in the library.'

'They didn't mean what we thought they meant, though,' said Baz. 'Turns out they were talking about the *dinghy*. They were gonna tie the dinghy to the transom.'

'Yeah? Oh. Well, I didn't know that. The dinghy . . . right.' There was a pause as Rachel popped open the can – *pshtt* – and took a quick swig.

'Anyway, so then we tried to think about what to do if we were caught. Stef had this idea. She said there was a big bottle of stuff in the art room for cleaning the brushes. Stuff that'd burn. It wasn't petrol, though. Something else.'

'Turps,' said Steffie. 'White spirit. Dunno what made me think about it. I'd seen Preacher John that time, throwing stuff onto the altar to make the fire burn, and I dunno . . . I suppose that's where the idea came from. I said, OK, if they found us we could throw turps over them, and stand there with a box of matches or a lighter, then they wouldn't be able to touch us. Might give us another chance to run for it. We talked about it in the library. But it was only, like, an idea to protect ourselves. Then later, Ray said sh— he'd go down and have a look and see what was going on. He came running back and said that Baz'd made it, but we'd got to do something quick. Like now. And the turps was all we could think of, so we ran back down to the art room to get it. Then Ray had this better idea, with the torch thing and the jam jars. And we had a go.'

'We reckoned if we could get close enough it'd work,' said Nadine. 'They wouldn't know what was in the jars, and they wouldn't be expecting much trouble from a bunch of girls.' She glanced across at Rachel. 'I mean, you know . . . us and Ray.'

'Well, it was friggin' *brilliant*.' Robbie rocked back in his seat, hugging himself with glee. 'It was all just brilliant. The bomb and everything. Thinking it up in the first place, and then Fart Club, and building the thing . . . finding that pressure cooker . . . and then BOOF – up they all went . . .'

Yeah, you weren't there, thought Baz. It wasn't brilliant, it was horrible. And scary as hell. And trying to get back to the island, lost and all alone in that dinghy, that was horrible too . . .

Somebody passed him an open can of drink, and Baz took a sip. Beer. He pulled a face and passed it on. Didn't like it.

The chattering voices grew louder, more excited, just a hum of noise now. Baz caught little snippets here and there, but he wasn't really listening. He heard Robbie say something about seeds – planting seeds – and that caught his attention for a moment. Then Gene was going on about his ideas for rafts, and how they might be able to build a diving platform out in the sea. And Dyson was explaining to Rae how to catch a rabbit.

It was a warm atmosphere, full of hope and companionship. Baz knew that he was amongst friends, people who truly cared about him, and that was a good feeling. But the others were already beginning to make plans, beginning to think about what would happen next. And he wasn't ready for that. Tomorrow they might build boats and catch rabbits and grow cabbages and play football – but that was tomorrow. He was still thinking about today.

He looked across at Rachel, her head close to Dyson's, chin in her hand as she listened to his talk. Dyson was holding a can of beer, and was consequently very talkative indeed. Rachel must have noticed that Baz was looking at her, or maybe she was thinking about him in that same moment. At any rate, she glanced over and gave him a slightly wobbly smile, rolled her eyes briefly, an indication that Dyson was being a bore.

Such beautiful eyes. He'd always thought so. How could he not have seen? How could Dyson or any of the others not see, even now? All the feelings of friendship that he'd had for Ray, the other Ray, were still there. He couldn't change them. He couldn't just transfer them across to this new person. Ray he'd been used to, but not Rachel. No, he wasn't ready for Rachel. Not yet.

The nightmares that he'd been dreading never came. Baz slept with his fishing spool beneath his pillow –

such luxury to have a pillow – and he dreamed of the mackerel. He was swimming with the fishes, flying with the fishes, across a bright blue sea. They were his friends. They talked to him as they guided him on, and he recognized all their voices. Taps was there. And Enoch. Even Cookie.

CHAPTER THIRTY

Baz opened his eyes and looked across at Ray's empty bed. No matter how early he awoke, Ray was always up first. And then he remembered. Ray didn't sleep here any more. Ray didn't even exist.

But Rachel did. And Rachel had slipped away with Nadine and Steffie the night before, unnoticed by anyone, to go and sleep upstairs.

Nobody else was awake. As Baz sat up and looked around the slob room, he could see the bundled-up figures, all snug in the new duvets they'd taken from the store. It was tomorrow and everything was different, and everything would be different from now on.

He got up, went to the jakes, came back, pulled on his clothes. Still no movement. Baz took his fishing spool from under his pillow, picked his way through the wreckage of last night's feast and slipped quietly out of the slob-room door.

It was strange to be in the kitchen again, the scene of so many panicky moments. Poor Cookie, frantically trying to dish up a meal for the divers, bandage trailing from his injured hand. Baz shivered, and opened the door of the food cupboard.

He rummaged around, pushing the tins and bottles aside until he found what he was looking for. Sweetcorn.

The air outside smelled fresh, chilly even, and the light was different. Baz walked down the steep pathway that led to the jetty, stumbling once or twice as he gazed up at the sky. There were clouds, thin wavy lines of cloud, pink-tinged from early sunlight. He couldn't remember when he'd last seen clouds like that, or when he'd breathed in air that wasn't heavy and humid. He half wished that he'd put on more than just a T-shirt.

And the sea . . . the sea below him sparkled so brightly that it hurt his eyes. Low sunlight danced and shimmered on the water, turning the waves into a million mirrors, winking and flashing their cheerful signals at him. It was like being on holiday, like the first day of a summer holiday, with all the other amazing days yet to come.

Baz walked along the jetty, kicking up the stones and chippings that he himself had helped to lay. His palms still tingled at the memory, the agony of pushing those barrows up and down. No more. He could let go now. And the altar, when he came to it, was also something he could let go of. It seemed like a relic, a monument from another age, the blackened cross erected by some ancient tribe who were long gone. History.

At the end of the jetty Baz stood and gazed out across the sunlit water. Only yesterday that same water had threatened to swallow him up, to drag him into everlasting darkness, and yet today he felt that he could dive into its dazzling light and swim right to the horizon and back. Or he could simply wade out amongst the waves and bathe himself clean.

Clean on the outside, at least . . .

Through the brightness of the day came this darker thought, rolling in like a thundercloud. They were murderers. Every last one of them. Amit, Dyson, Jubo, Robbie, Gene and himself – all were guilty of the worst of crimes. Even Nadine and Steffie had played their part. And Rae of course. Rae had played perhaps the deadliest part of all, arming the bomb that had killed Preacher John.

X Isle was an island of convicts. Not a holiday camp but an open prison. And here the prisoners would serve out their sentence, perhaps for ever more.

What else could they have done, though? What *should* they have done? Killers or freedom fighters . . . which were they? Baz knew that he would return to the question again and again, working through the threads of all that had happened in search of an answer. But right now it was beyond him.

He knelt down and began to sort out the fishing spool, unwinding the line, disentangling the knots. The scrap of old bait was still attached to one of the hooks, and Baz picked at it until it was gone. He laid the trailing line of hooks out straight, four of them in a row. Now he was ready to begin.

This was going to be his job, he'd decided. Gene could build his rafts, and Dyson could catch his rabbits, and Robbie could plant his vegetables. But he was going to learn to fish. He would be Baz the fisherman. Later he'd have to go to the library and find out about it properly, but today he'd just have a go and see what happened.

Baz lifted the ring-pull on the tin of sweetcorn and peeled back the lid. Sweetcorn was good, his dad had once told him. Good for bait. Dad said he'd always used sweetcorn when he was a boy. Dad . . .

Dad . . .

Oh, I miss you, Dad. I miss you so much. Where are you? Why aren't you here to help me? A great wave of emotion came rolling in from nowhere, slamming against him, choking him, flooding his throat and nose and eyes . . . *Oh God . . . Oh God . . .*

The tears rolled down his cheeks, his shoulders shook. He just couldn't stop crying. For ages he knelt there. Waited and waited until at last his sobs began to die down. Finally he sat back on his heels and wiped his arm across his eyes. Oh God . . . Christ . . . where had all this come from? Jesus . . .

The shape of the cross fell across his blurry vision, and it occurred to Baz that maybe he should stop cursing God so much. Stop cursing and learn to start praying maybe. He sniffed and thought about that for a moment. No, that was Preacher John's altar, not his. He might learn to pray, but he would never pray to that. And he was OK – as OK as he could be. Safe for the moment, and amongst friends. And his dad would be OK too. They'd see each other again. X Isle might not be for ever after all. People on the mainland would find out what had happened here. They were bound to in the end. Someday they would come, and his dad would be there among them, on the boat, on the raft, on the plane. Walking up the jetty, his old raincoat folded over his arm, ready to protect him . . . to look after him . . .

And besides, Baz reasoned, he hadn't come here to pray. Or to curse, or cry, or decide right from wrong. He was here to fish.

Do it, then. Baz took a handful of the sweetcorn and popped it in his mouth. His breathing hadn't completely steadied yet, and it wasn't easy to swallow, but the corn tasted good. Still chewing, he picked out a single golden piece from the tin, studied it for a moment and pressed it down onto one of the hooks. Then did the same with the other three.

He stood up and swung the lead weight around a few times experimentally. It felt solid and heavy, and Baz was hopeful that it would travel some distance. But how far? As a second thought he unwound a lot more line from the spool, coiling it loosely at his feet, making sure that it wouldn't snag.

OK, give it a go. Baz positioned himself right at the edge of the jetty, adjusted his stance and began to swing the weight. As it picked up speed, he let out a little more line . . . round and round . . . a little more . . . faster and faster . . . *now* . . .

Baz let go of the line and watched the weight go hurtling away from him. Up it went, soaring in a high arc against the sun, the baited hooks trailing behind it . . . on and on . . . and then down into the sea, disappearing with a gloop. An amazing distance, much further than he could have hoped for. The most perfect throw.

Wow. Baz kept his eye on the spot where the weight had splashed into the water. That was great.

But what did he do now? How would he know whether he'd caught something or not? He supposed he'd just have to haul the line in every so often and have a look. Whenever he got bored, or whenever he just fancied having another throw. It also occurred to him that there were some things that he would definitely not want to find on the end of that line. A conger eel, for instance. Or a diving mask . . .

Or a mackerel. Baz decided that if he ever caught a mackerel he would throw it back. He would keep a flounder or a herring, or just about anything else he could get, but he would never harm a mackerel. Mackerel were his saviours and his friends.

His lucky fish.